Praise for *Must*

"A fresh, charming new voice."

— Tessa Dare, *New York Times* bestselling author

"Historical romance meets sci-fi time travel, and what a fun intersection of genres it is! ... It's a delicious twist on historical drama and romance, and let me assure you, there is plenty of romance and sex."

— *USA Today*

"Time travel and romance taste great together in Quarles's Must Love series launch.... Filled with historical tidbits and larger-than-life characters, the sweet story is a delight..."

— *Publisher's Weekly*

"... clever, original, and so good that you want more as soon as you put it down. It's a delicious mash up with something for time travel romance lovers, Jane Austen devotees, and those who simply enjoy a fresh take on historical romance. Her unique premise combines the best elements of contemporary and historical romance, while incorporating all of the fish-out-of-water elements a time travel romance."

— a *Night Owl Reviews* Top Pick

"Time travel is a tricky genre to play in and 'Must Love Breeches' broaches the subject well, delving into the past with ease, and returning to the story's present with deft ability."

— *InD'Tale Magazine*

"The moment I started reading this book I immediately thought of Outlander by Diana Gabaldon and Confessions of a Jane Austen Addict by Laurie Vierra Rigler. The concept of time travelling to one of my favourite time periods. I immediately fell in love with the concept and the plot! This book was amazing! A definite top ten contender and I can't wait to re-read it as I breathlessly read as fast as I could to learn what would happen next."

— *Kiltsandswords*

"Ms. Quarles has a tremendous talent for writing. This time travel historical romance makes for a captivating read. It left me wishing the book went on forever. The dialogue, all the charming wit, and amazing sex scenes make the story a page turner. Her name should be beside Karen Marie Moning and Diana Gabaldon."

— Miranda with *LovesHistorical*

ALSO BY ANGELA QUARLES

Beer and Groping in Las Vegas
Must Love Breeches
Steam Me Up, Rawley

MUST LOVE *Chainmail*

A TIME TRAVEL ROMANCE

MUST LOVE SERIES BOOK TWO

ANGELA QUARLES

Unsealed
ROOM PRESS
Mobile, Alabama

MUST LOVE CHAINMAIL
Copyright © 2015 Angela Trigg
Cover design by Kim Killion
Developmental editing by Jessa Slade
Line editing by Erynn Newman

Unsealed Room Press
Mobile, Alabama

ISBN: 0990540057
ISBN-13: 978-0-9905400-5-2

To anyone who's always fantasized about a hunky medieval warrior in chainmail. You know who you are :)

DISCARD

Chapter One

৩

And Kynon the son of Clydno asked Kai for that which Arthur had
promised them. "I too will have the good tale which he promised to
me," said Kai. "Nay," answered Kynon, "fairer will it be for thee to
fulfil Arthur's behest in the first place, and then we will tell thee the
best tale that we know."
The Mabinogion, an ancient Welsh romance

*I*F SHE WERE CAUGHT—caught doing what she'd promised to give
up—what would the cost be? Too high. Oh, but the *need*. The
need itched across her skin, jerked her fingers toward her phone.

Outside a stacked-stone Welsh church in Flintshire, Katy Tolson
snugged her pashmina scarf tighter against the pine-scented October
breeze whipping through their tour group and across the rocky terrain.
Ruining our bachelorette vacation, my butt.

Maybe just a quickie?

Katy slipped her phone from her coat pocket and clutched her
connection to the world—to her wedding preparations. Restricting
herself to five uses a day? Not possible. But if her bridesmaids caught
her with her phone for, okay, the umpteenth time, they might make
good on their threat of a penis piñata.

Katy had managed to make her bridesmaids behave during their
week-long trip, but only because she'd promised they could do the
traditional wild party on the last night. And that was tomorrow. The
trade-off was, for every illicit phone use on Katy's part, they got to
add something tacky or outrageous to the night's festivities.

The rest of the group stared down a stone well. Ha, her chance at
last. She slipped around the church's corner and pulled out her phone,
thumbs flying across the keyboard, the relief at being able to take
care of tiny details poignant. At the next corner, she pulled up short.

A dark-haired man, dressed in form-fitting coat and pants—as if

1

he were an extra in a Jane Austen movie—leaned against a headstone, his back to her. A tour guide? Grief hunched his shoulders, a spray of violets clutched in his gloved hand.

He turned slightly, revealing glasses perched on a handsome face. He pulled a small object from the inside of his coat and extracted a small card from it. He kissed the card and placed it on the headstone, his fingers tapping it several times.

His head jerked up. Had she made a noise? She flattened against the wall just before his bespectacled gaze swept by her. She cast her gaze skyward. Why the heck was she hiding from the guy?

She peeked around the corner. Air shimmered around his form, the autumn leaves and crumbling headstones in his vicinity wavy and ultra-saturated with color, as if she were looking into a water tank.

Uh, yeah. That wasn't normal. *What the hell?*

Pop.

The air compressed, and the minor concussive force pushed her back, her elbow scraping against the stone wall. Everything within a foot of the figure pinched to a small point and then flashed bright. An object, glinting silver in the afternoon sun, dropped from the flash point and landed with a bounce and a dull *clunk.*

The man was gone.

As in—Not. There. Anymore.

Her mind seized up at the impossibility even as she staggered down the slight incline and slid, leaves scrunching and scattering, her heart beating in what-the-heck spurts. He *had* to be there. Fallen behind a headstone, head bashed in and bleeding. Or something.

The murky sun glinted off a smallish metallic object nestled between two moss-covered rocks. But no Austen-dressed man.

She picked up the object, the metal warm against her skin, a tiny stream of energy surging into her body like an aftershock. Her pulse missed a beat and skittered onward with a reverberating *thunk-thunk.* Because the object she held—no bigger than her palm—looked like Isabelle's calling card case, the one that for some woo-woo-weird reason allowed her friend to time travel on nothing but a wish. Four months ago, Isabelle had made a careless wish to visit 1834 London on a case such as this. And had. And stayed. Damn her.

Katy turned the case around. It lacked the engraved monogram.

So, not the same case.

Katy did a quick pivot. Still no one near. She pinched the button on the side of the case and eased it open. Hand-engraved calling cards clustered inside with just one line:

Mr. Bartram Podbury, esq.

Podbury. Podbury. Definitely familiar. A connection to Isabelle, said a little niggle in her gut. Or was it only the eerie similarity of their cases and the dark-haired man disappearing? Disappearing in a flash of light. The hairs on the back of her neck rose as if to say, *pay attention.*

Katy rifled through the cards, but nothing else materialized.

She surveyed the headstone. A turtledove cocked its head, flicked its mottled brown feathers, and lifted into the air with a parting whistle-tweet. One of Mr. Podbury's cards fluttered to the ground in its wake.

"Katy!"

She whipped her head up. Traci waved from the church.

"You're missing the tour."

Drat. And she hadn't texted the florist. Katy tucked the case into her coat pocket and climbed up the hill.

"And I see your phone." Traci smiled, mischievousness lending it a sharp edge. "That's one for me tomorrow night."

"But I wasn't using my—" She looked down. Dang. It was there, in her hand still.

Traci rubbed her hands, plotting already, no doubt.

Great. The penis piñata.

Katy tucked her phone into her purse and shuffled behind the rest of the dozen-odd members of the tour group into the church, kinda stunned she wasn't babbling about the disappearing man. The cool air embraced her with its smell of dry stone and stillness.

She fell in with her bridesmaids in front of the elderly lady—their guide around St. Cefnogwr's Church. Dammit. The colorful local legends had enticed her, but now her need to focus on all the wedding details overshadowed the charm. She wasn't even going to *think* about Mr. Podbury right now. Could she sneak her phone out? No. Traci had magic eyes in the back of her head. Magic I-know-what-you're-planning, witchy eyes.

3

Katy followed the others down the central aisle, probably no longer than a tennis court. "Come on, come on, come on." Just one chance to sneak a text out.

The stretches in between uses felt like she was free floating...and not in a good way. Tethered. She needed to be tethered. Katy judged the distance to the side door—twenty some-odd steps—and the likelihood of escape. Yeah, none. She peeked at Traci, whose casual lean against a pew while twirling her dark hair, gaze locked on hers, didn't fool Katy; her friend was wise to her plan, damn her.

They reached the east side, and the weak sunlight through the multicolored glass bathed the dark recess in an otherworldly glow. Everyone stilled. Their shuffling feet stilled. Even the air stilled.

A chill skittered down Katy's spine. A church-going chick she was not, but it was moments like this when something unexplainable seeped in and tugged her.

The guide waved toward a white marble figure of a knight lying on a stone slab, the muted jewel tones from the stained glass windows shifting across the surface. "Here before you lies the memorial to St. Cefnogwr, though he is not buried here, of course."

At her words, an uncanny *knowing* flushed through Katy and, crazy-of-crazy, transfixed her.

"Why? Where is he?" Traci stepped forward, hand on her hip.

A you're-right-on-cue look crossed the guide's face. She pointed to the ceiling.

Traci scoffed. "I meant, where's the body?" Her American southern accent lent a strange contrast to her skepticism.

Again, the tour guide's arthritic finger pointed upward, and a smile tugged at her lips, the smokers' wrinkles on her upper lip smoothing out. "That's the miracle that made him a saint, you see. Throughout the twelve hundreds, the Welsh struggled to maintain our independence from the English. During Madog's Rebellion in 1294, St. Cefnogwr, a noble Norman-English knight, turned against his liege lord and sided with the Welsh—"

"Norman-English?" Katy frowned, her voice raspy in her dry throat. "Why would a Norman have a Welsh name and side with the Welsh?" She might be an American, but her years living in England had taught her that was unusual.

4

"The English nicknamed him. It means 'sympathizer' in Welsh. The knight was captured and, for his crime, sentenced to hang. As he swung, the rope creaking in the crowd's silence, an angel of mercy swooped down and—" She clapped her hands in one decisive smack, and everyone jumped. "The rope dangled empty, free of its burden. Proof, we say, of his noble cause. He's been venerated ever since as a Welsh hero."

Another chill danced over Katy's skin. A chill that flashed warm as the story seeped into her.

Familiar. Achingly familiar.

Unease followed—this existential stuff was so not her.

"His rescue by an angel was enough to make him a saint?" ever-practical Traci asked.

"Unofficially. The Welsh named him one, and eventually it became a fait accompli. Now, please follow me." The tour guide stepped toward a side door.

Katy let the others pass and approached the knight covered in chainmail and other medieval-looking doodads. Only his face peeked out from a tight-fitting, chainmail hoodie-thing. One hand gripped a shield, the other, a sword. She touched his straight nose, the marble a cool kiss against her finger.

So. This person had lived about seven hundred years ago. His angular features were starkly masculine. Probably had women admiring them in the flesh. Had he loved?

An odd...void bloomed within, tugging at her, as if it were the absence of a feeling seeking wholeness. Evidence of past lives frozen in time always made her feel...disconnected. Disconnected and disturbed. Unable to grasp some larger meaning. Especially since Isabelle was in the past now too, instead of here as her maid of honor.

She traced along the knight's torso, the bumps from the carved chainmail teasing her fingers.

"The tour group is getting on the bus. Hurry." Traci's voice came from the door.

"Coming." One last glance at her knight. Katy ran a finger down his strong nose again. "Bye," she whispered.

THAT NIGHT IN THE B&B, Katy sat on her bed, feet tucked under her, and caught herself staring. At the white lace curtain. Sure, it was a nice curtain, but...

She sighed. That damn knight still cluttered her thoughts. She'd been happily annotating her mini Erica Conklin date planner with notes about tomorrow, and then her memory flashed to the sight of her finger brushing down his nose, the cool feel of the stone. Thoughts strayed from there and...yeah, the curtain.

She straightened and pulled the stack of Isabelle's letters into her lap. In the privacy of her room, she'd already taken care of any texts she needed to send, and her day tomorrow was reviewed. Washi tape lay scattered in multicolored disarray around her. Now she had time to satisfy her curiosity about Mr. Podbury. Maybe that would take her mind off that stupid knight.

"Isabelle. Why did you go back? Why did you go back and *stay*?" Her whispered question was drowned by the night traffic and low hum of the Welsh town of Corwen seeping through her window.

It was the why—the *why*—that always eluded her. So much so, she had brought the letters with her, creased and crinkled and coffee-stained from constantly scouring them for a clue to her friend's... madness. And she scoured them again for mention of Mr. Podbury of the silver case, and bingo—he was the funny guy Isabelle had met in 1834 researching time travel at the Royal Society.

Katy couldn't help it, she shuffled to the last letter and bit her lip, sadness curling through her. She'd received it a month ago, along with ten others in one batch. One batch that represented the rest of her best friend's life, delivered without fanfare three months after Isabelle had abandoned Katy, abandoned her exciting career, abandoned her own time, and gone to live with this Lord Montagu.

Barclay's Bank had called, the attendant no longer surprised she had time-dated material from the nineteenth century left in trust for her in their vaults. As with the first batch, Isabelle had planned it well, bequeathing the contents of her safety deposit box to whomever lived at a particular address at a particular time—which just happened to be Katy's. A Time Capsule Experiment, it had been called in the papers, and she'd had to deal with some publicity, but when she'd revealed it was only letters, interest vanished. To the odd museum curator who inquired, she'd endured their blistering you're-a-heathen stares when she said she'd destroyed them.

She fingered the wooden object that had arrived with the packet of letters, its smooth surface, its carved lines calling to her.

She read the final letter. Again. The ending she almost had memorized:

> *...I found the item in the accompanying box at a little curiosity shop in Wales. Go ahead and open it. Okay. Isn't it just too cute? Phin wondered why I'd become so attached to "an old wooden bird," but the carving, while not artistically perfect, I thought captured the essence of a small bird in flight. For some reason, the bird reminded me of you, so now you have it. The shopkeeper claims it's from the Middle Ages, but I've found antiquity dealers notoriously unscrupulous.*
>
> *With this gift, I'm also saying goodbye. I realized that continuing to write letters to you about my happenings here and how things go on, wouldn't be fair to you. All at once you'd receive the whole of my life. I'd rather you keep thinking of me living my life here at the same time you're there.*
>
> *And I've never regretted going back in time. May you find happiness, my friend.*
>
> *Love,*
> *Belle*

The hand-carved bird *had* spoken to Katy, though. It was the main reason she'd picked Wales for her bachelorette trip. She lay back on the bed with a sigh and, unbidden, the warrior-saint from the church filled her thoughts.

7

Chapter Two

"Now of a truth, Kai, no man ever before confessed to an adventure
so much to his own discredit; and verily it seems strange to me, that
neither before nor since have I heard of any person, besides myself,
who knew of this adventure, and that the subject of it should exist
within King Arthur's dominions, without any other person lighting
upon it."

The Mabinogion, an ancient Welsh romance

*ATY RAN HER SHAKING FINGERS down the taut muscles of his abdo-
men, the soft, flickering glow from the nearby candle lending an
unearthly glow to his skin. The heat of his body nearly burned her fingers.
Such power coiled within, but also a soul-deep yearning suffused her that
no touching of skin could satisfy. She glanced up to his face—*

"Earth to Katy."

A soft, dry—something—slapped Katy's cheek. The end of a
croissant.

"What?" She collected the crumbs and brushed them onto her
bread plate.

She and her bridesmaids were tucked around a bistro table in the
back corner of their B&B's dining room. Her soon-to-be sister-in-
law, Catherine, who barely knew her, displayed only a pleasantly curious expression. But the others? Not so much. Lizbeth and Sandra
bore matching who-are-you-and-what-did-you-do-with-Katy expressions, and Traci's was crossbred with a healthy smidgeon of concern.

"You've been zoned out ever since you woke up this morning.
What's up with you?" Traci cocked her head, her hair collected into a
careless, but somehow fashionable, bun. Whenever Katy tried that, it
looked, well, *messy*. "It's a new look for you, and frankly, it's unnerving."

"Missing Preston?" Catherine's voice was tinged with the eager-

8

ness of an outsider hoping she was group bonding.

A weird feeling of disconnect permeated Katy, because, no, the hogger of her attention was *not* her fiancé.

Instead of dreaming about Preston, she lusted after a medieval warrior-saint. A lot. As in all last night he'd so crowded her dreams, she'd awakened feeling as if she knew him. As-if-he-were-her-lover knew him. And missed him. How could she miss someone she didn't know?

But she was immersed in him, in the dream, like water, and seeing the world through its saturated lens. She couldn't shake it. And wasn't that effed up? *Sorry, Preston, can't marry you because I'm lusting after some dead guy in chainmail.*

This was so unnerving, so unlike her. Practical and organized, that was her. Not someone carried away by this ephemeral stuff.

But she did the I'm-fine nod and pasted on the I'm-feeling-even-better smile and sought to latch onto a detail, any detail to give her focus and control. "What do we have planned today?" She pulled out her mini-planner.

"You're kidding, right?" Traci motioned to the folders under Katy's hand. "You tell us."

Katy took in the neatly stacked folders she'd prepared before leaving her apartment in Stratford East London, each with their name and today's date meticulously printed from her favorite label maker.

"Oh. Right." She passed them out. The focus on details helped center her. She was in control, dammit.

"After breakfast, we have a forty-minute drive to Castell y Bere for a self-guided tour. Then lunch at a cafe in the nearby village of Abergynolwyn, followed by some shopping in Tywyn. Tonight, we'll—"

The chirrup from her phone interrupted her recitation. A text from Preston:

Need advice on the groomswear!

Frustration lanced through her as her friends glared. "It's from Preston."

Traci held out her palm and beckoned. "Come on. Pay up. I know you want to call him."

Katy sighed, rummaged in her purse—the back of an earring stabbing under a nail—and plopped one of five red poker chips into her friend's waiting hand. She gave a quick suck on her wounded finger.

Every day, they returned the confiscated chips to reuse. Phone addict that she was, this was what they'd hit upon to attempt to cure her. She didn't want to think about how many times she'd had to use it past the five. Tonight at the hen party, she'd pay for that. Yesterday had been a disaster—she'd surrendered all five before noon, which was why she'd had to sneak outside the church. Today, she'd do better.

She excused herself, stepped away, and called her fiancé.

"Hiya, sweetheart. Sorry to interrupt your hen party, but I need your advice."

His voice. She let the cultured Oxford, but not too snooty, accent roll over her as she scanned the village street of Corwen and tried to anchor herself with him, instead of this strange dream-memory.

"Sweetheart?"

"Yes. What's up?"

"I wanted to get your thoughts on the dinner jackets for the groomsmen and myself. What should I tell the tailor?"

"What do you mean? I thought you said you'd already made arrangements." She worked to keep her voice calm, in control. She would *not* bite his head off.

"About that. I hadn't. But I'm at the rental place now, and I wanted to run it past you."

"Wait. You lied about having taken care of this? Preston, the wedding is a month and a half away. And we already agreed on what kind to get."

"Well, I had planned to take care of it. And I'm here now. I know we decided on the modern, but he's asking about a slim fit kind. Should I get that?"

She straightened her spine, some of her old cares, her old self, trickling into her. He rattled off more choices. Normally, she gorged on details—how else to ensure her life and their relationship went smoothly? But all the details of the wedding were burying her. Couldn't he figure this out on his own? Couldn't his *mates* help him?

But she tamped down her instinct to pitch a hissy fit, because losing control of her emotions never ended well.

Be calm. Be calm. Usher him through this hurdle, and everything would be okay. They'd be married soon, and everything would be okay. It *would* be. Preston depended on her organizing ability, her talent for making sure all ran smoothly, and she'd make sure this went smoothly too. She *had* to.

"Put the fitter on the phone." She sighed and answered the questions he peppered her with. Soon Preston was back. Since she'd already allocated a phone-time chip, she took advantage of the opportunity. "Everything else okay?"

"Yes. Try to relax, sweetheart. It *is* your holiday. I have your instructions, in triplicate. I even put a copy in my car visor's flap."

He knew her so well. Yes. This. His easy acceptance of her need—her obsessive need for feeling connected—threaded another hook back into her reality. This was Preston. Solid, dependable Preston, who'd never leave her. Unlike Isabelle. Unlike her father.

But his voice didn't calm, and that sent another ripple of doubt through her. And why was she even grasping at his voice's threads as if she were the one being abandoned, being left behind? Being drowned by a dream?

Really, Preston was great. The ideal husband. Sizzling passion and sappy soul connections were for romantics and romance novels. Their relationship was a partnership. Their relationship made sense. Their relationship kept her strong.

But her pep talk did nothing to shove aside this sense of unease that constricted her chest. Or the haunting images of the man from last night's dream.

ᘓᕽ

VERDANT GREEN AND BURNT UMBER hills dominated both sides of the road as their rental car tooled down the lonely road that meandered through the Dysanni Valley to Castell y Bere. Katy put down her window, the fresh air buffeting her skin, her hair, her thoughts.

Catherine snagged the guidebook. On their trip, they had settled into a routine—she read the blurb of the upcoming tourist site. She opened the book to the next numbered tag Katy had placed within.

"All right, ladies, what we have here is..." Catherine wiggled in her seat and straightened, donning her Official Tour Guide voice and demeanor. Like her brother Preston, she had strawberry blonde hair with a cowlick above her forehead, though she tried to disguise it with a loose perm. " 'The Welsh prince Llywelyn Fawr, or Llywelyn the Great, commissioned Castell y Bere in 1221 to secure his dominion in Merionnydd.'" She plopped the book into her lap. "Seriously. These Welsh words are bloody murder on the tongue."

Traci elbowed her. "We don't know the difference. Keep going."

"Quite." Catherine giggled. "All right, it says it was 'the last Welsh castle to fall to the English during King Edward's final conquest of Wales in 1283. The D-shaped towers are typical of Welsh strongholds. Today, the once proud castle lies in ruins, burnt and abandoned after a Welsh siege during Madog's Rebellion in 1294.'"

Katy let the stark scenery of the valley scroll by, undulating in greens and ochre and bursts of trees and the occasional cute puff of a sheep. A harsh landscape to make a living on but eerily beautiful.

Catherine's voice continued, weaving into the landscape. "The write-up prattles on about the type of stone used, blah, blah, blah." A page turned. "Oh, listen to this. This couldn't have made the Welsh happy. Says here the Marcher Lords who ruled the Welsh border pretty much had free rein to quell the rebellious Welsh."

They pulled into an empty parking lot below Castell y Bere, gravel crunching under their tires. Katy leaned across Catherine's lap to peek at the castle, but all she could see was scraggly brush and rock and sheep.

Katy jumped out of the rental. Higher up, the valley's view had to be even more incredible. Maybe soaking in the beautiful scenery could burn off this dream that had settled over her like a second skin.

Traci creaked open the metal gate in the chicken-wire fence enclosing the base of the castle's ruins. Presumably. All she could see was that they were at the base of a green hill covered in trees. Once past the hill, the view opened up. Before her was a rocky promontory, still covered mostly in trees, but she could see the crumbling stone ruins embedded in the outcroppings, like it had been made to fit the terrain.

They trudged up the path that disappeared around a bend.

"God, I still can't believe how clueless Preston was in that phone call earlier." Lizbeth winced at Catherine. "Sorry, I know he's your brother, but..."

"You'll get no argument from me." Catherine grinned at Katy. "I think you handled it well. I would have laid into him myself."

Katy nodded but saw Traci's concerned gaze. Katy looked away and trailed behind her friends, who laughed and pointed at the sheep or exclaimed in excited voices as parts of the crumbling ruins were revealed. But her? Preston's call bothered her on some cell-deep level, and she didn't want to talk about it with them. Exploring how off-balance it left her would shatter the thin veneer of control over her life, the veneer she tacked over her as a shelter, relentlessly patrolling its perimeter to make sure it fit snug at each corner, its lines crisp and sharp.

And it didn't help that the dream permeated everything. Still. Despite the awe-inspiring landscape. Despite her friends' animated banter.

Shake it off. Shake it off. Before her well-meaning friends questioned her too closely. Especially Preston's sister, Catherine.

The hike up the scraggly outcrop shortened everyone's breath, and conversation stalled. Finally, they reached the southwest entrance. Sun-bleached wooden stairs arched over a rock-and-bramble-strewn ravine and led into the castle proper. Or what was left of it.

"Hey, guys, you go on up. I'm going to walk around."

Traci stepped forward. "Are you sure? Are you okay?"

"I'm fine. Just need to clear my head. Got a little car sick."

Traci's pretty features scrunched up. Katy made a shooing motion, but her friend shook her head.

"You're not fooling me." Traci side-hugged Katy, the scent of her coconut and citrus shampoo dousing Katy, and steered her to a wooden bench along the path. "You've been distracted this whole trip, but especially since yesterday. What gives? You're getting hitched in a little over six weeks. Talk to me."

Traci's words batted at that veneer, and in recognition, Katy's stomach shied away and shriveled up. But that was ridiculous. Everything was okay. She just needed air. And personal space. And time to think.

She deflected Traci with a laugh, but even she heard its I'm-faking-it tones. "There's nothing to talk about. Preston's a wonderful guy. I'm really lucky. He loves me to pieces. What girl wouldn't want that?"

Yeah, what was wrong with her? In six weeks, she'd be happy. In six weeks, she'd have secured her future. In six weeks, she'd have accomplished another long-term goal—marriage before thirty. She was rapidly and efficiently crossing off her cherished goals. Career as a French translator for an NGO established? Check. Retirement fund established? Check. Next up, kids after five years of marriage.

They settled onto the bench, the cold of the planks seeping through her jeans. She scooched forward so only her coat-covered butt rested on the bench.

Traci grabbed her hand, the warmth—physical and emotional—welcome. "You may be all smiles, but the cheer isn't reaching your eyes. Your all-put-together act? It isn't fooling me. Something's off."

Katy snatched her hand away and stood. No way could she face her friend if she were that perceptive. Besides, Katy had no clue what to think herself. What *was* wrong with her?

She waved in Traci's general direction. "I love him. I do. He's nice. He's responsible. He has a steady career. Besides, I can't back out now. My mom's spent loads of money. The cost of the family's plane tickets from the States alone..." Except for her dad. Just a Happy Engagement card from him. "Everyone's looking forward to it. Preston..."

"Katy. You can't seriously be telling me you're marrying him because you don't want to disappoint anyone, disappoint Preston? That doesn't sound like you."

A panicky, fluttery rush of blood heated her skin, like a naughty kid caught in a lie and forced to face reality.

"Don't be ridiculous. No. This is what I want." She took a deep breath. "It is. This is just normal pre-wedding jitters."

Yes. Pre-wedding jitters. Her unease had nothing to do with the future stretched out before her, having to be constantly "on" with Preston, having to lead and direct every aspect of their lives, having to make sure she presented a put-together front. Their increased time together leading up to the wedding was already exhausting.

Traci stood and crossed her arms, her assessing gaze a threat to any potential bullshit dispensing. "I don't know. You need to use this trip to sort your feelings. This is the rest of your life we're talking about. Are you doing this because you love him, or because getting married is part of your ten-year plan?"

"Ouch." Katy eyed her friend. Purposeful organization and planning wasn't a fault. At least not as far as she was concerned. *How else do you keep chaos at bay?*

"I call it like I see it, sister." Traci fisted her hands on her hips. "I've seen you two together, and I tell myself I can't know the full dynamic, but honestly? Katy. The relationship, at least from the outside, looks...uneven. Promise you'll think about what I said?"

Uneven? What the heck did that mean? "Yes," the word drawn out as if pulled from her struggling and screaming. "But don't say anything to Catherine."

"I'm not an idiot. Take time to compose yourself." With that, Traci pivoted and headed back up to the castle ruins, the *scrunch-scrunch* of her hiking boots cutting through the background of rustling leaves and bleating sheep.

Compose herself? More like find herself. Katy dragged in a shuddering breath and hiked up the rocky hill after Traci.

Ten-Year Plan.

So she had goals. It kept her focused. It kept her on task. It kept her safe. Oh, how she envied Traci's ability to live spontaneously. Traci could just...just...*wing* it, which both terrified and fascinated Katy, as if she craved orbiting such a personality, basked in it, but was simultaneously afraid it'd be catching.

Wind whipped around her, a slight bite on the October air. She hunched into the wind and shoved her hands into her coat pockets. Her fingers grazed the cool metal of the calling card case she'd found yesterday. Her thoughts darted to Isabelle. Isabelle who was happily married back in 1834 of all freaky "places."

Gah. Those letters. A month since that last batch, and still the loss of her best friend burned. Missed her, yes. Loved her dearly, yes. Tried not to feel like Isabelle had abandoned her too, yes. But understood her? No. How could Isabelle abandon the modern world for love, of all things? Isabelle had been a smart, career-driven woman.

Baffling. The whole thing, baffling.

"What should I do, Isabelle?" Katy whispered, her fingers rubbing the case. "I wish I knew why I'm not as happy as I should be." Because Traci was right, dammit, something was off, she'd just been too busy to really see or admit it to herself, too busy checking off items on her must-do-before-thirty list, too busy to friggin' question any of it because it was easier not to.

She clasped her stomach—whoa. It felt as if she actually *were* car sick, her belly's contents not at all having a fun time as it swirled and churned. A particularly strong gust of wind pushed against her back. She stumbled and slid down the rocky incline, the scenery whirling more than it should for a small slip. She flung out her arms for balance, teetered, and...

Oof. The bottom of the rocky ravine jarred her tailbone. She closed her eyes and inhaled deeply. Settle down there, stomach. And, world? Please stop spinning. She slitted her eyes open for a quick peek, and the ground was blessedly still. A purple iridescent beetle worked its way around a few blades of mottled-green grass.

Katy stood on wobbling legs and dusted off her butt. She shifted to look back up the ravine's slope, to call out to her friends that she was okay if they'd seen her fall.

And plopped back onto said butt—panic, disbelief, and this-can't-be-happening a pulsating and tangy taste on her tongue.

The formerly ravaged side of the castle's wall? Now solid. And the stone freakishly fresh.

Chapter Three

And the rider wore a coat of yellow satin sewn with green silk, and
on his thigh was a gold-hilted sword, with a scabbard of new leather
of Cordova, belted with the skin of the deer, and clasped with gold.
And over this was a scarf of yellow satin wrought with green silk,
the borders whereof were likewise green. And the green of the ca-
parison of the horse, and of his rider, was as green as the leaves of
the fir tree, and the yellow was as yellow as the blossom of the
broom. So fierce was the aspect of the knight, that fear seized upon
them, and they began to flee. And the knight pursued them.

The Mabinogion, an ancient Welsh romance

KATY SLOWLY CLOSED HER EYES, let the cool ground soak into her
hands and butt, let the uncomfortable pebbles make themselves known. She counted to three and opened her eyes.

Intact castle wall? Still there.

A frantic fluttering whipped through her chest and choked her
throat. "No, no, no!"

Her whole body shaking, she pushed up on a nearby rock and
stood. She tugged on her coat's zipper and yanked it up to her neck.
She gazed at the castle.

No freaking way. Intact castle walls soared skyward, not stumpy,
crumbling stone courses pockmarked with bird's nests and tufts of
grass. She whipped around. No deck steps arching over the once-
ruined entrance.

She shoved her hand into her coat pocket.

Dread curdled in her stomach.

Shit. No case.

Oh God. The case worked. The case transported her back in
time. Just like it had with Isabelle. Sweat bloomed on her skin in the
chilly air, overheating her in her winter coat.

But she hadn't made a wish. Had she? Then her whispered words of a moment ago came back to her: *What should I do, Isabelle? I wish I knew why I'm not as happy as I should be.*

Shit. Shit. Shit. She spun around and raked her gaze along the hillside. This crazy-ass, zapped-back-in-time thing could all be fixed with a quick wish.

But...she dared not move. Getting turned around and missing it because she was searching in the wrong spot would suck. Big time.

She scrutinized the ravine, keeping her breathing steady. If she didn't panic, everything would be okay. Just a little blip she could laugh about—to herself—later, and get a spike of adrenaline thinking of her narrow escape. Yep. Mm-hmm. The guy line securing the thin veneer of her control strained and creaked.

Okay. She'd come along that path, and had, oh God, made that wish on the stupid case. Smooth, Katy. Then the queasiness. And a gust of wind. She'd started sliding down the incline and...flung out her stupid-ass hands. With the case probably sailing away.

So, with the right hand doing the flinging... She charged up the hill and inched along its edge, on the lookout for a shiny glint of silver.

An odd, pounding noise sounded behind her, and the ground vibrated slightly. What could...? Oh God, no. She wheeled around, her pulse beating frantically, and yep, the hugest, scariest war horse she'd ever seen galloped straight for her. She assumed it was a war horse, well, because it was so...large, and it had...Jiminy Cricket, it had *chainmail* on it. And, of course, some guy on its back, with chainmail and some kind of tunic, as well as a clothes-iron-shaped shield and friggin' sword.

Her muscles tightened, shivered, and she almost—swear to God—peed herself.

She scrambled down the ravine. *Find the case. Find the case.* And the scary man on horse would be gone. She slipped and landed on her ass, sliding the rest of the way, her hands scraping and stinging on the rocks.

The horse stopped above her, snorting loudly. She scowled over her shoulder—was she about to get skewered? Cuz she'd want to know. Not that she could do much against a muscle-bound, medieval guy bent on running her through with a sword. Or worse. Except find that case. She had maybe twelve feet of distance on him.

He lifted his helmet free with two mail-clad hands, the clang of metal against metal loud, and let it fall to suspend from a chain at his belt. Helmet removal was a good sign, wasn't it? At least it wasn't sword removal. The early afternoon sun shone from behind him. She couldn't see his face.

Gibberish popped from the dark shape. Coupled with his arm pointing away from the castle.

Er, what the hell kind of language was that?

Fear and a bit of oh-shit-what's-happening slithering through her, she rose and faced him. "What?" Peering right and left with only her eyes, she searched for the stupid case. Her only salvation.

He cocked his head and spouted more nonsense. Slower, sure, but still nonsense. She edged back and continued to search the ground, pebbles clicking against rock as her shoes scattered them downhill.

More gibberish, but it grew closer. She looked up. He'd dismounted and was stomping down the hill.

Oh, hell no.

She sprinted along the ravine, praying she'd see her case but knowing she probably wouldn't. Blood pounded in her ears, as jarring as her frantic footfalls along the hard ground. She sucked in short gasps of air as his steps drew closer. C'mon, all those gym sessions had to count for something.

A strong arm clamped around her waist, yanked her back against a solid wall of chainmail-covered man, and lifted. She slid down his body until his forearm nudged the underside of her breasts. She instantly stilled, breathing still panicked, because she'd read enough romance novels, and damned if she'd be one of those annoying heroines who got all feisty unprovoked. Pissing off someone who hadn't yet hurt her would be epically stupid.

He inhaled sharply. Melodic, darkly-rich words vibrated from his chest to fill her ear, his warm breath sending chills across her skin. She could hear the question in them, but not knowing what he so softly demanded, she remained frozen.

She'd need any ally she could get, because yeah, she'd gone and wished herself back in time. All because she'd second-guessed her plans.

He grunted and marched up the hill, easily carrying her against him. At the top, he whistled and...his horse came to him. Of course. Then he draped her in front of a saddle like none she'd ever seen, jumped on, and galloped across the rocky terrain. But not before she saw her case, winking in the sun as they passed.

"Hey— Wait! Shit."

Oh, crap, this was *not* comfortable. She clamped her jaw tight, afraid she'd bite her tongue with all the jouncing. Brief flashes of scenery and activity stuttered by. Flash—a white flower between two rocks. Flash—a cluster of colorfully clothed people. Flash—a woman with two children, one on her hip. Flash—a man driving a donkey laden with baskets. And all, all of them, hurrying. Hurrying in the same direction, into the castle. Behind its walls.

That couldn't be good.

❧

SIR ROBERT BEUCOL KEPT A STEADY hand on the lady's back and steered his destrier up the outer bailey steps, his horse's iron shoes ringing against the stone. He nodded gruffly to a sentry and clattered across the drawbridge over the natural ravine, through the gate, and into the bailey, the lady thankfully quiet. For lady she was, despite wearing strange hose and an oddly shaped cloak. In truth, he'd mistaken her for a young lad bent on play, when all sensible townsfolk were heading for safety.

The Welsh were uprising again.

His task had been to ensure all were within the inner curtain wall, and this benighted fool had defied good sense. Robert had tried instilling some into the lad, but the one word he'd uttered had confused Robert further. English, mayhap, but the peasant tongue was an unfamiliar one. No doubt one of Good King Edward's new colonists. All the more reason to herd him to safety.

Patience spent with the lad's antics, he'd wrapped his arms around the boy. And was hit with an armful of soft curves and feminine scent. Not a lad, then.

God keep him, remembering the feel of those soft curves pushed against him shot lusty thoughts through his body and stiffened his privy counselor. Heavenly, she'd smelled, like the lushest fruit. Obviously one of the wealthier colonists. He halted any further conjecture and allowed cool determination to cleanse away any flicker of desire. He could ill afford such a dalliance.

He led his mount at a trot to the keep's stables, eliciting a drawn-out moan from the lass.

"Guy." He motioned to one of the stable lads, his voice curt, cold. "See to Perceval," his Anglo-Norman French crisp in the October air. Once dismounted, he removed the lady from her perch.

Once on the ground, she wavered and stumbled into him. He put a hand to her shoulder to steady her but pulled it away and stepped back the same moment she flinched, chin raised. The space between them coiled with sharp *knowing*. He stilled, mouth dry. Now able to behold her clearly, he noted she possessed clear skin, shining, hazel-colored eyes wide from fear. Raven black hair, shorn halfway to her shoulders, exposed a long, graceful neck. A higher-than-normal forehead jarred, but as he stared, he realized her features complemented each other to make a pleasing whole.

Though the short hair hinted at a criminal past, no rough hand had created that straight, pleasing line. Strange.

At his unusual licentious reaction, he swallowed and stepped away, fists clenched. God's balls, he needed not the distraction of a comely wench. "You are safe now." He was pleased to hear his usual clipped, no-nonsense delivery. "Locate your kin, and aid in the castle's defense."

Her eyes widened anew, and she began speaking, but its meaning he could not fathom. Yes, the coarse Saxon tongue, for certes, though in cadence oddly flat. One thing was clear: her voice, while pitched low and seemingly calm, held a note of panic and urgency.

"Guy, do you speak English?"

"A little, sir, but the devil only knows what he's blathering about."

The lady kept talking, hands twisting before her, but he had no more moments to spare, pleasing face or no. Sir Robert Staundon awaited his scouting report. Assignment to this backwater of a royal castle had not been part of his plan. Matters were moving too *slow*. How could this possibly bring him to the attention of his king? Attention he desperately needed if he were to restore his family's land.

Enough.

"I must go." He bowed and strode to the middle tower, ignoring the trickle of guilt at abandoning her. What in all of Christendom gave him cause for guilt? She was safe inside the castle walls, was she not?

Inexplicably, the weight of her stare prickled along his back, and it took all of his control not to turn around and behold her once more.

He shrugged off the guilt. She must be new to the frontier and frightened by the rush to defense. The quicker she learned that life in the English settlements was never secure, the better.

⌘

KATY STOOD WITH HER MOUTH OPEN, fighting the numbness that froze her muscles, and watched her abductor walk away. Okay, so he wasn't her abductor.

The numbness, the fluttering panic that agitated through her was nauseatingly similar to only one other time in her life. The time when shame had been a hot, confusing, constricting emotion as she played with her Barbies on her bedroom floor in their North Carolina beach house. Tears made dark patches on her dolls' clothes. Shame that she'd thrown a temper tantrum. At her own birthday party.

Her family was already teetering, threatening to fall apart—her eight-year-old self had discerned that much. And she'd gone and pushed them over the edge with her selfish indulgence of emotions. If she'd kept better control, maybe her family wouldn't have self-destructed. But no.

And a temper tantrum over what? She had no clue now. All she could remember was the shame, the Barbies, and the knock on her door.

Her mom had entered and said Dad had left and would never return. The Barbies in Katy's hands dropped to the floor. She stared while inside this panic raged, even more forceful. Her parents had been arguing for a while, threatening divorce. But she hadn't thought them serious. Until that day. The day she'd indulged in a temper tantrum during her birthday party and her father walked out of her life. Ever since, she'd made damn sure to keep her emotions, and every other aspect of her life, under control. Ever since, she'd prided herself on keeping everything just *so*—she'd ensured that she gave no one cause to leave her again.

And now, with this knight's departure, that same panic enveloped her—that same feeling of abandonment, of loss. Which made no sense.

The kid near the stable—Guy?—stared at her, especially at her shoes and jeans, his baby-cheeked face and round eyes the archetype across time of gawking teenagers.

Oh God. She needed to find period clothes, and quickly, before anyone else noticed her. That the scary dude hadn't looked closer had been pure luck.

She held her hands palms out and eased back. She wouldn't notice her shaking hands, oh, no. Over her shoulder, an alley lay between two stone buildings. She sidled along the stable wall, keeping her eye on Guy until he shrugged and ran into the stables. At the alley, she dashed to the dead end, whipped around, and slid to the cold ground, legs shaking.

Being temporarily stranded in the medieval era wasn't the scariest part.

No. The scariest part?

When Sir Chainmail set her down and locked his gaze with hers, that dream-skin she'd worn all day shifted, merged, snapped into place with a resounding *click.*

Chapter Four

❧

"By the hand of my friend," said Kai, "often dost thou utter that with thy tongue, which thou wouldest not make good with thy deeds."
The Mabinogion, an ancient Welsh romance

I'VE GONE BACK IN TIME.
Think, Katy. And, uh, calm down. She pressed back against the castle's cold stone wall. The short, cobble-lined alley opened onto an astonishing slice of her new world.

Her heart did the oh-shit dance, popping panicked dots of sweat across her skin. She lifted a hand. It shook. Eyes screwed shut, she thunked her head several times against the stone.

Breathe. Breathing should help.

In. And out.

Sir Medieval Warrior had yanked her from a chance to return to her time. Under the bristling battle armor, was there any hint he might understand, might help?

His face appeared in her mind—the face she finally and clearly saw by the stables. A tight-fitting, quilted hoodie covered his head, a lock of black hair curling along his brow. Oh, and what else...

The black horizontal slashes of eyebrows, which shouldn't have looked right on his face, but did. The honey-brown eyes, sharp cheekbones, Roman-straight nose, and the hint of a strong jaw under the skin-tight, wrap-around cloth hoodie.

The strength and power and do-me-now virility radiating from those eyes, nose, chin, oh, hell...from everything—yes, she'd felt that zing between them. Her shoulders where he'd touched her still tingled. Crap.

But he had one flaw, thank God—a mustache and what looked

like a beard tucked into the tight hoodie. For her, bearded men had never put the bounce in her flounce.

Then the sunlight had caught the thick scattering of reddish-brown freckles across his forehead, oddly making him look vulnerable, and almost she'd told him to go ahead and knock her over the head and have his wicked way.

Except for one thing. Well, besides being wildly out of character and inappropriate.

His eyes. Flat, emotionless, cold, those brown eyes radiated a soul-deep disillusionment and clashed with the immediate warmth she'd initially felt. It was jarring—so like her dream knight, but...not.

No. No help there. She shoved Sir Chainmail from her mind and let the nearby sounds settle over her—the odors she couldn't avoid. Frantic shouts in an unknown language pierced the air. Animals bleated, what sounded like a flute piped, and dominating all, a noxious brew of rotting straw, horse manure, and the cooking smells of medieval-y foods.

Okay. Okay. Okay. Oh. God. She opened her eyes. Time to evaluate. Obviously, she was in medieval Wales, as this was the same castle, only spiffier. But what was the language?

In high school, she'd had to memorize the opening of *Canterbury Tales*, and while not modern English, the words had been somewhat understandable. The first two lines she could still remember:

Whan that Aprill, with his shoures soote
The droghte of March hath perced to the roote

She mentally patted herself on the back. All right, but what came out of Sir Chainmail's mouth didn't sound Chauceresque, or like any version of Welsh she'd heard on her vacation.

If only she'd paid more attention in history classes. One date stuck: 1066, the Norman invasion. If this were after, could he be speaking a dialect of French?

Oh, that'd be sweet. Finally her French translator job would have an application outside work. Perhaps his was a Norman dialect of medieval French, which presumably differed from modern French as much as modern English did from Middle English.

Latin. Didn't they still speak Latin?

Her stomach growled. Enough about language. Top priority:

blend in, and these clothes shouted not-from-around-here. But stealing made her cringe.

No. No time for scruples—this was friggin' survival. It didn't take a PhD in Medieval history to know being different spelled trouble. Being found with modern, unexplainable items was too risky. What was their punishment if she got caught stealing? Probably better than being suspected a witch.

Spying several wooden, waist-high barrels stacked against the wall, she scooted behind them, shielding her from the alley's entrance. She dumped the contents of her humongous purse on the ground. Fear crawled over her scalp, tightened her neck and shoulders—too many things outside her control.

No. Concentrate on small tasks.

Fingers shaking, she sorted the contents into useful and not-useful/dangerous-to-be-caught-with piles. Her phone went into the latter, along with anything modern. Including, sniff, her mini-planner. The red poker chips...

The useful pile was pitifully small: a pair of nail clippers. Everything else—money, ID, everything she depended on in her own world to survive—was useless.

Her engagement ring. She twirled the golden band around once, twice, the cool slide against skin, one side slightly heavier with the stone, familiar, comforting, encompassing all her dreams. How many times had she spun the stone around with her thumb in moments of anxiety, moments when she'd fought for control of her emotions?

No. Her ring must also be hidden.

Sorry, Preston. Swallowing hard, she slipped the flashy ring past her knuckles and zipped it inside a purse pocket.

She shed her coat and snipped off the manufacturer tags with the nail clippers. Dare she do more? She darted a glance around the barrels—few people passed by and none looked her way.

Screw it, she'd risk taking off her clothes.

She whipped off her sweater, bracing herself against the chill wind swishing down the alley and over her bare skin. She clipped off its tag, took off her bra, and scrambled back into her sweater. Later, she'd do the same with her jeans and underwear. *Please no one find me before then.* She threw the incriminating tags into her purse, along with the items in her useless pile, until she reached her phone. She lit the screen. Comforting, colorful icons mockingly glared. So much of her life was contained in this thing. She glanced up to the battlements and bit her lip. And now completely useless. Completely useless in making her feel connected and in control.

With a resigned sigh, she turned off the phone and snuggled it securely inside her purse. The same with the mini-planner.

Next, her sneakers. Too risky. And Preston had found humongous purses pointless? Ha! She stuffed her sneakers inside, a French-manicured nail catching on a clasp. Too conspicuous. *Snip, snip*, she cut them short and stashed the clippers in her purse.

Now, where to hide her purse? Isabelle had needed to prove her time-traveling story, and so Katy wouldn't throw away that opportunity. Besides, she wasn't checking into their Extended Stay Suite—as soon as she found her case, she'd get her purse and skedaddle from the past to the present. Easy, peasy.

But first, a hiding place. Above, the sloping thatched roof hung low. She peeked down the alley, rose, donned her coat, and clambered onto the barrels and then the roof. She lay flat, heart pounding. The only risk of being seen was from the castle walls.

She crawled across the roof and shoved the purse into the crevice between the roof and wall. The earlier shouts grew urgent, and the flute stopped, which acted like a record screech on her heart. What the heck? She edged forward to the roof peak, and surveyed the main area.

Along the walls, knights and crossbowmen—crossbowmen!—patrolled its length. By the well, a bucket brigade distributed full buckets at random spots. No, not random. At each thatched roof.

A couple knights in chainmail hustled to the walls. She craned her neck—the drawbridge was up.

Dread coated her mind and slithered through her blood to pool in her belly. Oh God, they expected an attack? Whoa, scary knight guy had been rescuing her. And the villagers were refugees.

Great. What luck. She wouldn't be looking for her case any time soon. And if it rained? Or one of the attackers found it? Panic again tumbled in her stomach. She tamped it down. She would *not* get discouraged. Not yet.

But chaos could be helpful—something, as a chaos-avoider, Katy never thought she'd say. But in this case? Yeah. It might provide the cover she needed while she assembled a passable outfit. She rubbed the back of her neck. And posing as a man would be safer.

A cluster of villagers waited to be blessed by two black-robed monks. *That* could be the perfect camouflage—body shape disguising, the excuse for being a stranger, the means to—one of the monks' hoods fell back—uh, shave the top of her head? Yikes, no.

She dropped her forehead to the straw, a stray piece poking her chin and nose. *Buck up, kiddo,* Dad would say, the only phrase of wisdom that ever sputtered past his I-can't-stick-around-in-your-life lips. She breathed in and forced a calm exhale. There *had* to be a way to use this chaos.

જ

ROBERT STRODE THROUGH THE MIDDLE TOWER, across the bridge over the ravine, and into the south tower, the memory of the mysterious wench still an irritating itch along his back. He sought Staundon, the royal castle's constable since the departure of Baron Fitzwalter a year hence. Robert nodded to several crossbowmen hunched over their weapons, lubricating the gears and joints, their voices low, subdued. A fellow knight ceased contemplating a flagon of ale at the hearth and angled his head to a screen cutting off the far corner, obviously aware of Robert's mission.

He followed the knight's direction and found Staundon with two other castle knights engaged in a heated debate, ranged around a trestle table. Staundon's mangy greyhound gnawed on a bone beneath the table. Robert caught the gaze of the acting commander, who held up his hand to the others. All talk ceased.

Staundon motioned Robert forward, the sweaty disarray of his commander's dark hair attesting to the recent removal of his helm and arming cap. "Tell me, what did you discover on your scouting mission?" His voice held the tired resignation of the little-thanked official constantly wielding the responsibility of the long-absent superior.

Robert braced his legs apart. "The Welsh, under Madog ap Llywelyn, are indeed rebelling. Already have they razed the new royal settlements nearby and now march on ours. I ushered the town folk to safety within the walls. However, rumors abound the rebels sacked Caernarfon, but I have been unable to confirm. Could merely be Welsh boasts."

Although his fellow knights had listened in silence, the air thickened with anger and aggression as Robert's final words fell into the space between them. One of the king's most prized castles, Caernarfon was a vital linchpin in Edward's plan to subdue the Welsh.

"If Caernarfon could fall..." Staundon raked his hands through his dark hair, frustration evident in his tired gaze.

A knight banged his fist against the wall, startling the greyhound. "Those Welsh savages. The Devil only knows what's on their pagan minds. We subdue them in one area, and they spring up elsewhere. Don't know how to stay civilized."

Robert stiffened but kept his features neutral. Long ago, had he learned to keep his face free of telltale emotions. Only Staundon noticed his change in posture and shot a look laced with warning. Soon enough would the rest learn. No sense in exposing his origins in an atmosphere so charged. So new was his posting at Castell y Bere, he'd yet to fully befriend the other men.

Robert gripped his wrist behind his back and widened his stance. "The approaching number is at least two hundred strong, with one quarter mounted. An equal number of siege ladders, but no other siege weapons I could discern, though some of the men-at-arms could be sappers. Their forces are most likely a mixture of northern and southern Welshmen, for they had both spear and longbow." He threw his parchment tallying the forces onto the table. He did not relish what he had to say next. "I estimate they will reach our valley by night fall, with a likely attack on the morrow."

"We've begun siege preparations." Staundon leaned into the table, arms spread wide, palms flat, head dipped. "The villagers. Did they come willingly?"

"Yes, though some of the leading merchants were loath to leave their new homes undefended." He omitted mentioning the wench dressed as a lad. He'd gotten her inside the wall, had he not?

"How many are able-bodied men?"

"I daresay no more than sixteen, mostly English, and that's stretching it."

Staundon dipped down, elbows bent, then pushed away from the table. "Christ on a cross are we outnumbered and ill-prepared for a siege. Fitzwalter, damn his hide, left this castle in a shambles. With the villagers here, we have grain for a week at the most. One milk cow, a half dozen sheep, and two pigs." Staundon cursed and poured a flagon of wine. He took a healthy swallow and wiped his mouth with the back of his hand, a garnet-red droplet clinging to his mustache.

Another knight leaned forward, fists on the table. "We must alert Fitzwalter of our plight. He may not have left for Gascony. With your permission, I will depart through the sally port and ride for Harlech Castle."

"Is this wise, Commander?" Robert asked. "That will leave us with only four knights."

"You haven't heard. Make that six. Whilst you were without, your former liege lord arrived with one of his knights and four crossbowmen. Combined with ours, that makes an even dozen."

"A slim force, nevertheless, you must agree," Robert said. Though Sir Hugh de Lacy's arrival was welcome news indeed.

" 'Tis, but mayhap Fitzwalter can send reinforcements. After all, this is a royal castle, ill-provisioned though it is." He placed a hand on the volunteering knight's shoulder and gently squeezed. "Go now and God speed."

The knight nodded and marched out of the hall.

"Locate Sir Hugh in the round tower," Staundon said to Robert, "and assist with the defense. He coordinates the village's refugees, and you will be familiar to them." He glanced over Robert's shoulder and beckoned. "And here's Sir Hugh's vassal knight. Perchance you are acquainted?"

Robert locked down all emotion. One knight served under Sir Hugh whom he'd gladly beggar his soul to never see again. However, he knew with a sense of inevitability whom he'd behold—Sir Ralph de Buche. His childhood friend. His childhood confidant. His childhood nemesis.

The passing years had added bulk to de Buche's lanky frame and a hardness to his angular features. Robert returned his attention to Staundon. "Commander." The greyhound's ears lay flat, hair raised along his spine, wary eyes fixed on de Buche.

Robert bowed and strode by de Buche, sparing only a curt nod. The sooner Robert checked in with Sir Hugh, the sooner could he see to the castle's defenses.

"Naught to say for yourself, Beucol?" came de Buche's familiar, reedy voice.

Robert faced the blackguard straight on. "I was unaware aught was needed." He kept his gaze locked with de Buche's until the latter's jaws bunched. Robert stepped forward, and de Buche straightened, but backed away not. "Oh, I'm sorry. Welcome to Castell y Bere." Robert gave a mock bow, complete with hand flourish.

"You'll never win your suit."

Robert clenched his fists, a desperate need coursing through him to smash that blade-thin nose, just as he'd once done gleefully as a youth. Not a noble sentiment, but then again, Robert had no illusions he possessed a noble soul. What honor had been left to him? None, thanks to his treasonous father. Impotent anger surged through the familiar hollowness within, a sentiment that arose whenever thoughts turned to his father's selfish actions.

Not breaking eye contact with de Buche, Robert replied, voice cold, measured. "I shall prevail. The honor of Llangollen has been in my family since we Normans first settled the Marches, indeed before William the Bastard ever set foot on these shores. The title and castle will be mine. The king shall settle the matter thusly, of that I have no doubt." Prevailing in this was all that was left for him. All that was missing to make him feel whole. Feel honorable. Feel like he had a purpose. Attaining it *was* his purpose.

"I wouldn't be so certain, old friend. My father has the ear of Lancaster." He glanced at the assembled knights, his features smug. "Have you informed them of your family's stain? Or do you still befriend others under false pretenses?"

Shame, hot and sharp, punched Robert with the power only reminders of childhood hurts could inflict. But he let it curdle and drew strength from the hardened shell, like he'd learned to do so long ago. "Bitter, de Buche? My affairs are mine own. In case you've forgotten, this castle will soon be under siege. You may wish to look to your own affairs." With that, Robert pivoted and strode from the hall, de Buche no doubt glaring at his retreating back.

No matter how hardened Robert had become, no matter how accustomed to the opinion of his peers, no matter how much he averred that he cared not, de Buche had the unerring ability to burrow under his guard and rile him like some untried squire. Ridiculous.

He unclenched his fists. He would *not* allow that scoundrel to unnerve him. The stain on his family's honor, Robert could not avoid. It would come out eventually, his father's treason. But on one point, de Buche was wrong. Robert *would* regain his family's land and title. Nothing else mattered. Nothing.

☙

POINTY BITS OF STRAW DUG into Katy's stomach. She had to admit a thatched roof wasn't her first choice for a perch. And she'd ignore the spot by her thigh where things *moved*.

Below, a makeshift washing area had been rigged, with an array of colorful clothes—in earth-tone shades from dark green to a muted red—stretched to dry across poles. She gripped a stick she'd found in the alley in her sweaty palm and eyed the tunics and cloaks worn by the village men. If she had time, she'd snag the colorful hose they wore as well.

As far as she could tell, the dead-end corner received little traffic. Even so, no way would she risk jumping down, since she'd have no easy access back to the roof.

She shifted to the opposite side. Anyone returning? Villagers and soldiers alike seemed focused on the gatehouse and the well. This was her chance.

Having mentally worked out the best angle to grab the clothes, she crawled back and slipped the forked stick under the cloak, the highest priority, and lifted. When close enough, she grabbed the cloak and flipped it onto the roof.

She paused. No approaching footsteps. Maneuvering the stick, she pulled the other cloaks across the pole and eliminated the incriminating gap.

Now, the tunic.

Feminine voices floated up from around the corner—they were

coming back. Katy thrust back from the edge, dragging with her the tunic, plus straw dust. She sneezed. At the wall, heart pounding, hands shaking, mind screaming *this-is-so-so-so-crazy*, she spread the clothes on the sunniest part of the roof. The women had wrung them out, but they were still damp.

What time was it? Instinctively, she reached for her phone. Hand poised in the air, she let it drop. Talk about quitting cold turkey.

Overhead, the sun peeked from the scattered clouds dotting the slate-gray sky. Late afternoon sometime then? Shit. She had to get outside the castle walls before the sun set. But how soon were they expecting an attack? Not knowing all the details caused a flutter in her chest, fueling her sense of helplessness, her sense of loss of control.

And her phone and mini-planner were no shield against that chaos here.

No. She had to risk it and find that silver case, period. Before someone else found it.

She held the woolen cloak to the wind, while below, the women chattered, the rhythm and pattern familiar, but the meaning still not gelling. Maybe Middle English?

Oh God. Could she do this? Dread coiled in her stomach, but she curled a hand against her belly and pulled in a strained breath.

She had no choice.

Her arm ached from holding up the cloak. Too risky to wait longer. Lying prone on the roof, she stripped down to her My Lover's Secret panties, threw on the rectangle-shaped, knee-length green tunic, and topped her outfit with the dark brown cloak. Probably needed some type of shirt under the tunic, but she hoped no one would notice. The bare legs could be a problem, but screw it—the jeans would stick out more.

She stuffed her clothes into the crevice next to her purse.

What next? Her socks. Barefoot would be safest.

Just...ignore what you step in.

She sighed and pulled off her socks, tucking them into the crevice. She crawled over the roof, the straw scratching her skin and its dust irritating her nose.

Drat. The gate? Still closed.

She repeated the Latin she'd dredged up earlier: *ego externus.* Not

33

a complete sentence, but who cared, if it got the point across. If that failed? She'd try modern French in case it was after 1066: *Je veux aller à l'extérieur.* I want to go outside.

Okay. This was it. Time to skedaddle. Not that they'd likely let her outside, but she shoved that possible outcome away. She *had* to get outside. She had to find her case. She had to return home. Home where she had a planned role. Home where she wasn't subject to the whims of medieval life like rape, pillaging, famine, antiquated diseases, arrows to the knee. Home where women had agency.

Hands shaking, Katy gripped tufts of straw, pressed herself flat, and eased one leg, two, over the roof's edge. With her pointed toe, the rough straw rasping against her stomach, breaths straining through her nose, she felt around until she touched the barrel and lowered herself into the alley. Hood over her head, she brushed off bits of straw, exited by the stables, and walked on jelly legs toward the gate, feeling as if a big-ass sign was taped to her back saying, "Chick from the future—nab her!" Or maybe, "Ye olde maiden from the future—to the dungeons with her!"

In the blue-gray shadows of the walls, the cold of the stone cobbles seeped into her bare feet. Head lowered, she sidestepped puddles and questionable substances, blood pounding in her ears, and skirted between the well and the steps leading up to a round tower.

This had to work. Get out, find case, back in for her purse, then *poof.* No proof she'd ever been here. No evidence to mess up the timeline.

Yes, leave. If she wanted. Or take a moment to sightsee. But the lack of choice shook her. She *needed* that case, needed the security of being able to leave whenever *she* wanted. That inability rattled so much, she couldn't even begin to take in the surrounding sights. Step One: the case. Step Two: assess.

As long as she didn't run into that knight again. With each passing moment, the energy of the place seemed to vibrate more and more at her frequency, with the center being Sir Chainmail. She rubbed her arms. If she stayed too long—she could just *feel* that his presence, his eerie similarity to her dream knight, was a threat to her well-laid plans.

At the gate, Katy took a fortifying breath and—oh man, bad idea.

The stench. She coughed, eyes watering, and stepped up to one of the guards, a beast of a man. His chainmail glittered in the sun, his lethalness written in the bulky muscles, wicked battle axe, fierce expression.

She bowed. Was that normal? Oh well—her clothes wouldn't rank her high, and politeness never hurt.

She pointed at herself and to the gate, deepening her voice as much as she could muster. "Ego externus?"

The guard's eyebrows arrowed down.

"Je veux aller à l'extérieur?" Again, she made hand motions indicating her wish.

He widened his stance, crossed his arms, and said something unintelligible. But the head shake? Pretty clear.

She swallowed the panic and frustration threatening to burst up her throat. This *had* to work. In case the denial meant he didn't understand, she asked in English, "Can I go outside?"

The guard stepped back.

What the—?

Then, from over her shoulder, a forceful voice she recognized, but didn't understand, washed over her—a threat, a promise, a mystery.

Chapter Five

So the maiden stopped, and she threw back that part of her head
dress which covered her face. And she fixed her eyes upon him, and
began to talk with him.
The Mabinogion, an ancient Welsh romance

W HAT IS THE TROUBLE, GUARD?" Robert asked. A hooded villein
was obviously causing trouble, and trouble from a peasant
was not what they needed at this moment. Especially, one dressed so
oddly with a short tunic and no hose.

At his query, the peasant stiffened. Well he *should* fear the consequences. A siege was imminent, and no time had they to waste. Everyone, every *one*, must pitch in.

The guard maintained his proper mien, but relief flashed across
his eyes. "He's not making any sense."

Robert snapped a finger at a squire running past, carrying a barrel
loaded with crossbow bolts. Tips freshly minted from the blacksmith, no doubt. "After you deliver those, locate Sir Hugh in the
round tower. Tell him I shall be there momentarily."

The squire nodded and took off, bolts rattling with his steps.
Robert returned his attention to the guard and the troublesome
peasant. "What's he saying?"

"That's just it. He's speaking in a tongue that's beyond my ken.
One sounded like Latin, but I know it not."

Latin? How would a peasant know Latin? He faced the cur, dis-
pleasure and impatience coloring his tone. "*Quid vis?*"

The peasant shifted toward him, his head low. "Ego externus."

He frowned. So, not fluent. He opened his mouth to question
what he meant, because of course the poor devil *was* outside. The
peasant's hand lifted and pointed toward the gate.

Oh. So he had a death wish. Mayhap he was simple. Again, Robert took a breath to answer when the peasant spoke further words, which were not Latin, but were indeed unfamiliar tongues—a pause and a different cadence, signaling a different tongue.

What in all the saints? He stepped forward to pull off the hood, for no peasant should know aught beyond his native tongue, much less a halting Latin. His fingers, tense with suspicion, closed on the rough wool of the oddly damp cloak and pulled. Too late, the rogue realized Robert's intentions and jumped back, hand batting against Robert's arm.

He growled. "You!" For it was the wench he'd rescued, then in some foreign garb, now in peasants.

His narrowed gaze swept down her form, which she now tried to hide by wrapping her cloak around those womanly curves that had been pressed against his body scant hours earlier. At the memory, his cock stirred, and he told it to bugger off. A quick tumble in the dark of night was the only use he had for such lush, feminine curves, but something about her mien told him she would not entertain such a fleeting encounter. Besides, no room had he in his life, in his schemes, for aught else. No room? Ha, he had not the means.

Bare toes peeked from underneath her cloak, and he leaned over to peer closer. Her toes... She'd lacquered them in some permanent manner, a deep pink. He cocked his head and looked back up at her. Never had he heard of any foreign cultures that engaged in such a ritual. A deep blush crept up her neck and face. Interesting.

Who was this woman? Definitely not the English settler he'd assumed. Nor was she Welsh, as he was familiar with their customs and speech. How had she fetched up here on the edge of civilization? He peered closer at her face. Clear skin, bright eyes. Healthy. He grasped her hand, ignoring the tension sizzling between them, and she tugged. Oh, but he would have his answers, so he held firm. He turned her hand, palm up, and pried open her fingers, skimming up the insides of her knuckles and over the pads. She shivered.

Not calloused. Highborn, whomever she was. Without protection.

A shout sounded from behind, and he glanced back. Sir Hugh beckoned.

Reluctantly, he dropped her hand and arranged his visage in the harsh, impartial lines he'd learned cut an easier path through life. He yanked her hood back up and spoke in a commanding tone, slowly, in halting English, "Come with me."

One of her phrases sounded like a badly accented version of English, so mayhap she'd learned a smattering in her land.

Her eyes widened, and another string of English-sounding babble emerged from her lush lips, but his English, while halting and spotty, was nothing like this. No time now to puzzle out her actions, but he could not allow her to wander.

He grabbed her wrist and pulled her forward. She yanked, but didn't break his grip. She kept pulling. Ha. She thought him a weakling? He leveled her with a stare, and she stilled. Better. He marched toward the round tower, her steps stumbling behind him.

"What cause for delay?" Sir Hugh asked. "Who is this?" The past ten years had added lines to his former lord's face, but he still looked as formidable as ever, despite his shorter stature. Many a young squire had underestimated this man's strength as well as his strength of will and was the sorer for it. By Gad, it was good to see him.

"My new squire," he answered, surprised as soon as the words left his lips. He nevertheless, retracted them not. Why, he had no idea, but his instincts had always kept him alive. Mayhap she'd serve some useful purpose.

"You found a noble family willing to foster their son with you?"

He stiffened at the disbelief. Besides Staundon and de Buche, Hugh was the only other knight present who knew of his dishonorable background.

"No offense meant. I hear you are now Lord Chirkland's most able household knight. Your reputation in the lists is becoming legendary. Mayhap that was enough."

Robert bowed his head. "What task have you for me? How goes the preparation?"

"Oversee the villagers to fill bowls with water, distribute them around the walls, and assign someone of nimble foot to watch those bowls as soon as the besiegers arrive. No catching us unawares with tunnels."

"Understood. Anything else?"

"Afterward, take your turn manning the walls. How far out are they, do you think?"

"They'll be here by Vespers."

Sir Hugh located the sun's position in the cloudy sky. "Not much time." His lips thinned. "And, Robert? Distinguish yourself in this fight, gain the notice of our king, and your future will be yours to dictate. The king might see fit to grant your suit."

So Hugh had heard. "That is my hope as well."

He gripped Robert's upper arm and squeezed. " 'Tis glad I am to see you. You've fared well. I've heard your fighting skills have only increased. But beware of de Buche. Sacrifice not your personal honor, no matter how he provokes you. It's his aim to portray you as uncouth, as no different than the rebellious Welsh. Brawling with him will not forward your suit with our king. Keep calm, and you shall prevail. I'm certain of it."

"Meeting him across lances in a tourney is too tame. My fists ache for a more blunt and brutish encounter. What do I care for personal honor?" Given a choice between personal honor and attaining his goal, personal honor could go beggaring. Regaining his *family's* honor, and that of his king, was all that mattered.

"You used to care."

Bitterness coated his tongue. "When but a misguided lad, drunk on milksop Arthurian tales. Such scruples have no place in this modern, changing world. All the honor I desire is what I can regain for my family's sake." Mayhap then, this aching hollowness that seemed to define him would be filled, the bitterness blunted.

Sir Hugh's green eyes held his, grim and determined. "In all your boyhood encounters, he never bested you on his own. Your father could best any man in the Montfortian or Edwardian army, and you could best your father. But I knew what kind of man de Buche was from his father's boasts. Bragged he did about how his only son killed his mother in his determination to arrive thrashing into this world. Told that story to anyone who would listen, whether his son was present or not—that his son was a killer, and damn proud he was of it too."

For the second time, shame burned his gut at the mention of his own father, for it brought to mind the stain he could not shed. The stain on his family's honor. But he stifled the useless emotion before it could gain a foothold, for none of that mattered if he was successful in his plan. Once he gained back his land and titles, all would be well.

Sir Hugh gripped Robert's shoulder. "Just be vigilant, lad."

∽

KATY SHUFFLED BEHIND THE KNIGHT, while her stomach alternated in a panicky dance between feeling leaden and threatening to choke up her throat in a scream.

Breathe. Breathe. Long and deep. She clutched her stomach, nails digging into the rough woolen cloth. *Remain calm unless he threatens me.* Like a spider's victim, she was well and truly caught in a web. If she struggled, she'd draw unwanted, and deadly, attention.

Survive. Lay low and observe. And then break for outside.

Near the wooden water trough by the stables, he scooped up some mud. With a shushing motion and a scowl on his brutally handsome features, he squatted, chainmail links clinking against chainmail. His blunt fingers, hesitant at first, smeared cool mud over her toes. She swayed, stunned by the incongruent gentleness, but also for his foresight and understanding. Somehow, he'd not only known she was a stranger, but also her need to keep that fact a secret.

His flat, honey-brown eyes locked with hers while he crouched at her feet, and again heat rushed up her neck and face, remembering his stare earlier when he'd noticed her painted toes. Stupid, stupid, stupid. Why hadn't she found a way—like this—of hiding her otherness?

Her toenails disguised, he stood, not breaking eye contact, and signaled to follow, his head cocked in question. *Will you obey?*

She nodded, and he marched to a section of the large enclosure she'd not seen. Cluttering the surface was a makeshift tent city. Colorfully garbed people swarmed the area, erecting lean-tos against carts, bundling straw, and basically making themselves comfortable.

A commanding shout came from the walls, and the interior gate swung open. She edged away from Robert and eyed the gate. A group of five haggard villagers staggered in through the widening gap.

Her case was through that gap. Adrenaline pumped through her, whispering, *Run, run, run!* A quick glance confirmed her knight was deep in conversation with a villager.

She broke into a sprint, arms and legs pumping. In five minutes this nightmare would be over. Bare feet splashed through God knew what. Who cared when a nice hot shower and a cocktail with friends beckoned?

The doors began to swing slowly shut.

No.

She pushed harder, lungs straining. *Come on, legs, need more strength, more speed.* Then a strong arm clamped around her waist, and she was momentarily in the air before being hauled up hard against an unyielding body.

She panted in stuttering gasps as her captor's breath fluttered near her ear. She glanced up, the back of her head sliding across his tunic. Her scary knight dude's face—what she could see anyway— was drawn in tight lines of fury. Fury and suspicion.

He set her down, spun her around, and gripped her arms. A torrent of harsh words followed, none of which she understood, but she could guess the meaning. He was a bit peeved. Eyes flat, his gaze bored into hers. Did that face ever smile?

She shifted her feet and stared back, uncomprehending. Finally, he looked away and barked more harsh words. She'd bet her favorite organizational stickers he'd just sworn. She peeked over her shoulder and watched with dread as the doors clunked shut.

Oh God. He was her only ally, and she'd just pissed him off. She dropped her head in submission, while it surprised her that despite his harsh words, and hard features, she felt no fear. No fear, at least, that he would harm her.

He crossed his arms, his biceps under the chainmail bunching impossibly further, and when she looked back up, his fierce eyes pinned her in place. She swallowed around a hard lump and tapped his shoulder. He arched a brow.

She pointed to herself. "Katy." And then pointed at him. Shit. She might have given her gender away with her name, if he hadn't already guessed. Who was she kidding—he knew.

Tension crackling between them, he nodded and jabbed his

thumb against his tunic-clad chest. "Robert," but pronounced with a French accent.

She stifled a giggle. Such a normal-sounding name amongst so much that was just...you know...not normal.

He tilted his head, indicating for her to follow, and she relaxed at not having his full attention. He stopped at one of the wealthier-looking refugees, whose sprawling family made themselves comfortable between two carts. The wife had a small fire going. Robert talked to the husband, who shook his head, but pointed to another family several lean-tos down. At that lean-to, Robert handed a couple of coins from a belt pouch to the man, who studied her feet, rummaged through several trunks, and returned with a pair of shoes.

Oh, sweet. "Thank you. *Merci.*"

Robert cocked his head and narrowed his eyes, a slight interest stirring in the flat depths. Did he speak French?

She shoved her feet inside the supple, brown leather shoes and secured the flap by her ankles with a button. The shoes narrowed to an extreme point at the toe, adding a strange clunkiness to her sense of balance, but, hey, better than nothing.

Robert returned to the first man and spoke to him at length. The more she listened, the more the cadence sounded like a French dialect. The man faced the rest of the refugees and clapped his hands together for attention. Robert put his fingers to his lips and let out a shrill whistle.

Her knees shook. Surely he wasn't calling her to their attention. What the heck was going on? But no, he spoke to them, gesturing to different parts of the castle, never once referring to her. When he was done, all the able-bodied people strode with purpose to whatever task he'd assigned—at least that's what it looked like.

An auburn-haired, lanky boy of around ten stood by Robert's side. He spoke to the kid, who gaped at her with big eyes. Robert appeared to urge the boy on. Finally, the boy stepped forward and said something to her. Robert barked out a word, which must have been the word "slower" because the boy nodded and said what sounded vaguely like, "My name is Alfred. He said you are called Kay and are his new squire?"

It took her a moment—initially the sentences hit her as some form of Swedish with their lilting cadence—but then the sounds coalesced into *words*, and a fraction of her tension eased. Robert had found someone who spoke a form of English. For the first time, she could grab on and make some sense of the world, like a key had been handed to her, a key that could grant a measure of control.

Squire? Wasn't one of Arthur's knights named Kay? She lowered her voice. "Hello."

Alfred frowned and exchanged a few words with Robert. Hopefully saying she spoke weird English, and not that she didn't seem like a guy. If she could make out a fraction of what Alfred said, it was better than nothing.

She looked to Robert. "Merci."

He replied with more French-sounding phrases and waved them toward the round tower. On the way, he stopped by the blacksmith's, and after some bargaining, shoved a wooden staff with a wicked metal barb on the end into her hands. He spoke to Alfred, who related something like, it was for her, a weapon.

As they walked, no one paid them much attention. Except for one knight who stood by the well, his sword stuck in the ground, his arms resting on the crossguards. His helmet, dangling from its chain at his waist, had a ring of peacock feathers around the crest. He wasn't as tall as Robert, but he was built along football-player lines. And the hate that poured from his eyes as he watched Robert pass raised the hairs on her arm. Then his gaze swung to hers, and she hastily turned away.

"Alfred, can you keep talking?"

It took him a while to understand what she wanted, but soon he was narrating what was happening. "I'm walking behind Sir Robert—I'm waving to Mistress Maude," and the like, and she studied him closely and listened to his sing-song version of English, in which some words sounded Germanic, and others French. What a hodge-podgey-sounding language.

At the round tower, Alfred switched to relate what Robert was doing. She didn't catch half of it, and reminded him to speak slower. After a few minutes, one thing was clear—what she'd feared was true: they expected an attack.

And it was soon. As soon as the morning.

Shit. Shit. Shit.

Her chances of getting outside, finding her case, and getting the hell out of here had just narrowed to—oh, let's make it zip. Oh God, she was stuck here.

The attackers might find it.

The attackers would churn up the ground.

The attackers could obscure the landmarks she'd need.

The attackers could...

Her gaze swung to her weapon, and her stomach dropped down to her feet—

The attackers could, well...*attack* her.

And she might be expected to fight? Fight for her life? Oh God.

Chapter Six

"Lady," said Gwydion, "there is none other counsel than to close the
castle upon us, and to defend it as best we may." "Truly," said she,
"may Heaven reward you. And do you defend it. And here you may
have plenty of arms."
The Mabinogion, an ancient Welsh romance

THAT EVENING, ROBERT STRODE into the south tower they used
as a keep. As predicted, the Welsh had arrived at Vespers
and set up camp. They would not attack at night, but just the same,
he and his fellow *chevaliers* stayed alert with a contingent of men-at-
arms and crossbowmen. Sir Hugh wanted them fresh for the morning, so he rotated the watch in three-hour shifts, and Robert's had
just ended. Kaytee followed silently behind, her presence a physical
weight, a presence that queried—what now?

Damned if he knew. He beckoned to a castle servant. "Fetch
more hay. My squire requires a pallet."

Robert had claimed a bench in the corner, and he strode there now
and opened his trunk. He pulled out four wool blankets and handed
her two. He looked at the bench—latent instincts screamed he forfeit
the bench to her, but if she were to maintain her ruse as male and
squire, giving her the superior spot would raise unwanted attention.

The servant returned with the straw, and Robert arranged the
bundles beside his bench. A new...*feeling*...flickered within him, indeed was like an incessant moth fluttering within. Annoying. He
must pinpoint and root the feeling out. His fingers reached for his
sword belt, but he glanced toward Kaytee. Eyes wide, she stared
around the great hall.

The hearth's fire played across her face's lovely shape, partly dis-
pelling the shadows cast by her hood. Had she ever experienced
hardship? Her hands and demeanor could be evidence enough that

she had not, but it was her eyes which definitively told him no. Too innocent, those eyes—they'd not gazed on death or experienced real fear. A simpleton's wouldn't either, but she was no simpleton. Besides the fact she knew fragments of Latin and other languages, intelligence glittered in those eyes. From where did she hail? And why had she come here of all places in Christendom?

As soon as they could converse, he would find out, for certes.

And then the source of the unexplained feeling hit him, as he gazed upon her profile, the soft hairs by her temple. He felt a surge of protectiveness. Of blasted chivalry.

God's left testicle.

What had befallen him? They were on the eve of battle. His life was a harsh one. He had no room—*none*—for the softer, weaker emotions. Ruthlessness was required in his machinations against de Buche. He must react swiftly to circumstances, turn them to his advantage. Surely this *feeling* wasn't responsible for his impulse to make her his squire?

Chivalry existed only in the tales of bards, not on the Marches of Wales.

No. He shook his head and gripped the curves of his sword's quillon, the dull points of the crossguard biting into the flesh of his palm. She possessed secrets. That, he knew. And secrets had value. The highborn had value.

Yes. Of course. He'd recognized her potential for achieving his aim. A reward, in gold, from her kinsmen would be a welcome addition to his coffers. Gold he'd need to fatten officials who lay between him and his king. Gold he'd need to win back his family's land from the de Buche family.

A source of advancement was all she represented. And *that* he'd do well to remember.

Meanwhile, appearances must be maintained.

Though English was not his native tongue, he knew enough to command the men at arms. He assayed it now. "Attend me." His voice low, commanding.

She startled and turned huge eyes to him, eyes that said she understood him not. Well, they would simply have to make do, would they not?

He removed his sword and belt and held them out, his gaze catching hers. *Pretend to be my squire,* he tried to impart.

She frowned, head tilted slightly, eyes probing his for meaning. Her curiously cut hair curved under her jaw and slid forward, calling attention to her graceful neck. He cleared his throat, cast his glance exaggeratedly around the crowded hall, and returned his gaze to hers, attempting to impart the need for the ruse. She looked around as well, the central hearth fire highlighting half her form. Unease wormed through him. She must understand. Why had he not thought to ask Alfred to explain her duties?

Finally, her face cleared, and the tension in his gut unknotted. She took the sword and belt, and he nodded to the bench. He removed his green surcoat, and when she returned, he handed it over, the satisfaction of their mutual understanding like an oil which made their movements efficient, dare he say, companionable. Curiously, she bowed, folded the surcoat into a neat square, and placed it on the bench.

Though used to removing his own hauberk, he motioned her forward and bent over at the waist. He tugged the bottom edge and caught her eye. She nodded and stepped closer, pearly teeth denting her bottom lip. Her scent—like some fruit plucked only for the king's table and mixed with her unique womanly scent—washed over him. His gut tightened, and his heart sped faster. Her heat, her presence thickened the air between them. Limned by the firelight, her forearm slid free of the mantle. She gripped the edge and pulled the heavy mail over his head. She stumbled not under the weight, though surprise softened her features.

Slowly, he straightened, his body reacting to her closeness in a manner no squire would have caused. Swallowing hard, counting his breaths, and ignoring her *closeness,* he unfastened the leather poleyns protecting his knees, removed his quilted gambeson and cap, chausses, and hose. He glanced up, clad only in his braies, and caught Kaytee's flushed regard.

Her wide-eyed perusal knifed arousal straight through his body. Christ, he couldn't strip while stiff as a lance. He overruled his errant cock by picturing all the steps to polishing and maintaining his mail, leather, and weapons. Her eyes snagged his, and she reddened further.

Thankfully for his peace of mind, she whipped around. So, she had an over-developed sense of modesty.

He carefully stowed away his weapons and armor, placing each with purpose and deliberation. Thoughts and body now firmly under control, he stripped and settled on his pallet on the bench, his blanket pulled up against the chill. The knowledge of her presence sent prickling heat along his back as she settled onto her pallet. It would look peculiar for her to retire fully clothed, but she had to, did she not? Better that than reveal her true sex. He tried not to think about what curves lay beneath her peasant's garb. That way led to madness. Led to a thwarting of his plans.

ↄ

THE RUSTLING BEHIND HER indicated Robert had settled into bed, but her heart, oh no, her heart had not settled. Before, seeing the oval section of his face revealed by his chainmail outfit made him seem anonymous. Formidable, with handsome features, sure. But now?

After helping peel off his layers to expose the man within, the shock of seeing him almost naked still had her all quivery. His gloriously muscled chest in the flickering light, the crisscrossing scars, and the strength and power coiled within, were disconcerting, like she was meeting a whole 'nother stranger, not *her* stranger. Actually, like she wasn't seeing a stranger at all.

And when he caught her staring, his hot gaze...

Katy let her knees give out and plopped on her straw bed on the floor and folded her legs up to her chin. A spark definitely snapped between them every time they drew close. What the hell was she going to do? Everything—*everything*—was alien. In the smoky, fitful torchlight, the men had no qualms stripping until buck naked and sleeping in the same room as everyone else.

Dogs and cats roamed and fought over scraps of food. Someone on her left let rip a loud fart, and from her right came a moan and a slick slapping sound. A man hunched on a bench, his hand moving—*oh, you've got to be kidding me.*

She whipped around and scooted under her rough, wool blanket, yanking it over her head. Didn't these people think masturbating was a sin in this time? Clearly, they flagrantly ignored the Church.

Again, her hand reached for her absent phone, and she tightened it into a fist. Maybe if she went to sleep, she'd wake up and find this was all a nightmare. One could hope, right? At the moment, she'd settle for being able to close her eyes and obliterate the strange sounds and sights. And smells.

One breath. Two. She'd control the panic that surged through her, threatening to erupt into either a hysterical laugh or a bout of tears. She locked those emotions down. She wouldn't lose it. She wouldn't. Her situation always got worse when she lost control and let her emotions take over.

Her measured breaths were largely working, but then, oh God, that chest, gleaming in the torchlight, painted across her eyelids. She groaned in frustration.

∽

KATY STEPPED THROUGH THE RUSHES strewn across the floor, her hand gripping the cloak tight by her neck. In the shadows around her loomed overlarge depictions of medieval knights with their hacking swords and rearing horses. A cleaved head here. A bloody sword there.

"They're just drawings," she whispered.

Still, with the flickering light, the battle scenes painted in stark red and black seemed larger, more menacing. She shivered and stepped around another snoring figure.

She'd woken up in the middle of the night needing to pee. Badly. But where to go? Did they have some kind of bathroom? Did she dare explore?

She reached the far wall, and the general smell of the hall—stale sweat, stale food—sharpened to a more specific smell—eau de latrine. She saw a naked man leave from an alcove in the wall further ahead.

Over her shoulder, a horse's hooves thrashed in its frozen tableau. Breath held, she did her business, but, oh God, she needed to get the hell out of Ye Olde Middle Ages.

∽

SHIVERING AGAINST THE DANK MORNING CHILL of the castle, Katy retreated into a dark corner. Servants rushed about rousing everyone, and men crowded near smoky fires eating. In the dim morning light filtering through the small windows, the details popped more than they had in last night's gloom. Richly carved stone arched over the windows and doors. She craned her neck and—stone-carved human heads?—supported the vaulted roof. And the fighting knights and horses painted on the walls returned to being flat representations.

Alfred tugged on her sleeve. "We must grab what fare we can." He motioned toward one of the hearth fires. He'd arrived earlier and said her knight was to return shortly. Oddly, without him she grew more fearful, like her lack of knowledge of her surroundings made her more exposed, more vulnerable, without him as a shield. Yep, she'd stick to him like the small dagger at his side until she got her case back, if that was possible with the siege. But in one thing she was determined—if there was any way to get outside safely, she would.

She grabbed a hunk of bread and cheese and, gaze darting around, sniffed both. She bit into the crusty loaf, the taste like a rich, wholegrain bread, with a subtle dash of some spice. The hard cheese was not unlike the farmer's cheese they'd had on one of their stops through South Wales, only a tad saltier. She scarfed down both. Thank God for all the newcomers inside the castle walls—no one questioned her presence. Though, what was Robert speculating? His stare had bored into her at various times yesterday, and she knew that once they could communicate, he'd have some questions. Questions she couldn't answer. So she needed to find her case before he got the chance to ask.

As if her thoughts conjured him, Robert strode through the large hall doors, his body moving with power and grace and ease across the rush-strewn floor. He seemed unaware that the other knights and men subtly signaled with their postures that they found him superior in strength.

She stilled. Part of her was relieved to see him, though another part, the stronger, practical part, not so much. Each time he drew near, another hook to this time slipped into her, holding her here.

She straightened. This was *not* her life. She *would* resist.

The light behind and above him highlighted the dark green tunic draped over his chainmail shirt and leggings. Lord knew what they were called. The chainmail hood bunched loose around his neck and back. Unlike yesterday, his head wasn't encased in the quilted hood, leaving his wavy dark—almost black—hair to curl just past his ears. One errant piece fell across his forehead as he strode toward her, his expressionless eyes locked on hers. Though not quite expressionless. She'd swear frustration lurked there. Combined with his controlled, almost conscious movements as he drew nearer, it seemed he was just as bothered by this...this attraction that pulled.

His trim mustache and beard hugged his upper lip, chin, and jaw, and all she could think, as he stalked toward her, was—Good God, how manly. Sign her up as a beard fan now, please.

Shit. Knowing this was the same man from last night now clad again in his hunky knightly armor was a strange aphrodisiac. Yeah, a hot look, no denying. And this wasn't some reenactor posing in his gear. This was the real freaking deal—a knight who knew how to fight and had scars as proof.

Robert stopped at his trunk in the corner, raked a glance down her body that left her feeling exposed, and retrieved his helmet, a fancy number that sloped into an almost-point, topped with a crest, and a green cloth knotted and tied to fall down the back. The face guard had two horizontal slits for eyes, and breathing holes below. He motioned her forward, handed over his helmet, and pointed to her and to his eyes.

Watch what I do, he seemed to say.

He pulled the beige quilted cap over his head, stuffing his hair inside, and tied it by a string at his chin. She knew why he wanted her to watch him—to train her as his squire—but that meant she noticed small details, like how strong, and well-formed his fingers were.

Stupid fingers.

He tugged his chain hood-thing over his head and drew the longer piece near his right ear around his neck and chin, fastening it closed by his other ear. Another string, woven through the chain links around his forehead, he pulled tight and knotted.

Next, flaps by his wrists encased his fingers, like mittens with a leather palm. Alfred had now scampered over, bread crumbs on his chin, and named each piece, but the strange names didn't stick.

Robert stood motionless and watched her in anticipation. Oh, the helmet. She stepped close, steeling herself to his commanding, hypnotic presence, and handed it to him, his he-man scent trying to steal past her defenses. He nodded and placed the helmet atop his head.

A warm heat flushed her skin. She inhaled deeply and darted back. Every single inch was defensively covered, mainly with mail. Even his feet were covered by his leggings—no separate shoes, only spurs attached to his heels. Like chainmail footie pajamas, but, yeah, *not*. Surely they were lined with something and he wasn't walking on chainmail alone.

Over the mail was a long green tunic thing with a coat of arms in white, gold, and red on his chest—a *surcoat* Alfred told her. At the waist, a loose leather belt.

The whole effect? Warrior. With a big, hard, sharp-edged, capital W.

Next to the sword at his waist, he hung a wicked-looking battle axe like it was nothing. He motioned her over, handed her a knife, and pointed to her belt. She gulped.

He retrieved another knife from his trunk and strapped it in place.

How many weapons did he need? He pointed to the staff that he'd bought for her yesterday and jerked his head toward the battlements. She clamped her fingers around the staff in a sweaty grip. Oh, shit. She...she couldn't. No way. She stared at the deadly barbs at the end. Blood pounded hotly through her, cold sweat an acrid coating of fear on her skin. No way could she...could she *push* this into another human being.

Another knife went to Alfred, who, unlike her, looked extremely tickled by the loan.

All set, her heart pounding faster than their footsteps, they went through the main door, flanked by stone-carved figures of lance-wielding soldiers. In the early morning sunlight, a mist hugged the ground. Her breath rose in white-gray puffs in the chilly mountain air.

A stout wooden bridge stretched between the hall where they'd slept and the rectangular tower ahead, extending over a rock-strewn ditch. Another defensive measure? Presumably, defenders could destroy the bridge and hole up behind her in the hall. Once through the other tower and down the steps, they were back in the familiar courtyard where she'd been most of the day yesterday.

All around was frenetic activity. The insistent *ta-ting, ta-ting* of the blacksmith, the bleating from sheep that must've been herded within, folks jostling by on various errands. Robert made his way to the round tower that was obviously the command center for his captain, or whatever he was called. He found the man without much trouble and exchanged a few quick words. Like the other knights, only his face was visible, this one of a battle-hardened man in his early fifties.

She tugged Alfred's sleeve. "What's going on?"

Her translator jumped. This must be new for him too, though his rapt expression said he found it exciting, while she...yeah, not.

"We're to head back to the middle tower. No movement as yet from the Welsh."

"The Welsh? They're the ones attacking?"

Alfred frowned, his expression bordering on questioning her wits. "Aye."

What had the various Welsh tour guides said? Some turbulent years where the Normans fought the Welsh, so she must be during that time—eleven or twelve hundreds?

"Alfred, what year is it?"

"What year?"

"Yes."

He scratched his chin. "I believe it to be the twentieth year of good King Edward's reign."

Okay. That didn't help—she barely knew the names and order of the English monarchy, much less when each reigned. "Yes, but what year?"

He frowned again, head cocked.

Wait, didn't they go by A.D.? "Anno Domini?"

He puffed up his chest. "It is twelve hundred and ninety-three, no, ninety-four years since the birth of Our Lord Jesus Christ."

1294? Oh God. She continued walking, legs feeling like half-baked biscotti, racking her brain for scraps of history from that time.

And drew a blank.

Then she sucked in a deep breath and stumbled. When was the Great Plague? *Think.*

No, wait, she had a few years to go. She couldn't remember exactly when, but sometime in the thirteen hundreds, because for school tests she'd associated it with unlucky thirteen.

Still. 1294? Yikes.

Right now, she'd chew off her right arm to be curled up on her sofa in the safety of her Stratford East London apartment, chenille throw wrapped tight around her knees, favorite book in hand.

"And it's early October?"

"Aye."

At the tower, Robert spoke with Alfred, who looked like he was pleading. Robert shook his head and pointed back toward the villagers' camp.

Alfred turned to her, his lower lip sticking out. "I must leave you now. Sir Robert wishes me to return to my family. For my *safety*," the last said with all the disdain of a pre-teen. "Since you are his squire, you may remain with him."

Oh, joy. "Thank you for helping me. I hope to see you again soon."

"On the walls above are shallow bowls filled with water. He wants you to watch them for vibrations and alert him if you espy such."

"Why? What does that mean?"

"That someone might be tunneling under the walls."

Tunneling under the—her gaze snapped to said walls. Oh, man, she was so in over her head. People's *lives* were going to depend on her?

With that, she shuffled after Robert as he mounted the stone steps, which switched back on themselves. His chainmail-clad feet dinged against the stone surface as he climbed. At the top, he ducked through an archway onto the inner wall that extended to the round tower. But Robert entered a covered hallway to the left that ran along the outside of the middle tower and formed part of the wall overlooking the space between the two gates—what had that tour guide at Caernarfon called it? The outer bailey?

Their steps echoed in the cool, dark, stone interior. At the door

on the far side, he held up a hand—*wait*—and stepped into the sunlight. She hovered by the stone-framed doorway, while he consulted with the guard on duty. The other man left his station and marched by her, silent.

Robert patrolled the wall without a single glance at her. She was alone.

She eased onto the parapet. In front of her, the wall overlooked the ditch between the middle tower and the keep, with a steep, rocky drop on the other side. To the right, a wall stretched in graduated steps down to the outer gate. She stepped up to the vee where these two walls met, dizzy at the height, and peeked between the stone gaps. Below—her heart sped up, thumping a you're-so-near beat— was the ravine where she'd stumbled. If she could find a way down— and find her case—she could be with her bridesmaids having a cocktail. Hey, it was five o'clock somewhere. She stuck her head out farther and slumped back. Shit. Too high to jump. She peered back out. So close... She scoured the area for a glint of silver but saw nothing.

Trumpets blared all along the walls, startling her. And not a nice, I've-got-an-announcement-to-make kind of tooting. This was definitely a we've-got-incoming alarm. Her skin prickled at the menace, warning, and intent all packed into that shrill, blasting sound.

Chapter Seven

ↄ

*...and when they came to the palace, the lady had arisen, and was
about to wash before meat. Peredur went forward, and she saluted
him joyfully, and placed him by her side. And they took their repast.
And whatsoever Peredur said unto her, she laughed loudly, so that
all in the palace could hear.*
The Mabinogion, an ancient Welsh romance

ATY SQUINTED AND, YEP, at the dark edge of the woods, roughly two hundred men formed a ragged line. Robert barked orders, and the crossbowmen let loose a volley of bolts. Unfortunately, they *thunk-thunk-thunked* into the ground, short of their mark by at least fifty yards. A clacking sound bounced along the wall as the crossbowmen cranked back their bolts for the next round.

At a notch where the two defensive walls met, she crouched, armpits slick with fear sweat. Shields in front, the attackers advanced until just shy of where the crossbow bolts had landed. Again, Robert shouted an order, and another flight of bolts twanged from the walls, flying straighter and farther to land several rows deep. From the pained cries, some had found their targets.

The Welsh gave a rousing shout and charged forward, oblivious to the bolts flying from the walls. One attacker fell to the ground, writhing. Another dropped, still in death, but a great many continued their charge. Were they crazy? Some carried ladders, while others hung back and let fly a cloud of arrows, which whizzed over the walls. A flaming arrow streaked past and clattered into the courtyard, the flame extinguishing from lack of fuel. But more flaming arrows sizzle-whined overhead. Soon, the reason for the water buckets became clear as an arrow landed on the stable's thatched roof, and the villagers doused it with a waiting bucket.

Shit. Where was Robert? There. His dark green surcoat stark

against the pale stone walls. A figure leaped over the wall behind him, and she screamed Robert's name, her warning shout drowned in all the noise. His own senses must have alerted him, for he pivoted and plunged his sword into the guy's belly. He yanked it out, and the Welshman clasped his stomach, his face a rictus of pain and shock, and tumbled into the outer bailey.

Katy gagged and slumped against the stone. She pulled in panicked gasps, trying to calm her roiling stomach. Oh shit. She stumbled to the courtyard entrance and puked over the side. She spit and breathed through her mouth.

Oh God. Oh God. Oh God. Not good. So not good.

Nausea receding, she fell back against the wall, a shaking, clammy hand on her forehead, the other gripping her stomach. What the hell was she going to do? All around, chaos roared.

She gathered all her resolve, all her strength. She hadn't asked to be a part of this battle, but here she was. And she'd be damned if she got herself killed because she was busy puking up her guts. She *had* to help with the defense. If the attackers gained the wall, it didn't matter where she hid.

Legs shaking, she stumbled back through the tower hallway. Outside the door, a knight and a wounded crossbowman pushed against a ladder top. Okay, she could do this. She sprinted up and, catching her staff's hook against the top rung of the ladder, helped push it far enough out to topple.

She darted with the others to the next one and pushed, this one harder since it carried someone. Finally they gained momentum and toppled it. And then a third. By this time, they'd reached Robert, who shouted at her, pointing back to the tower hallway.

She nodded and raced back to the hallway where a wounded crossbowman had an arrow in the meat of his left arm. His hand gripped the arrow shaft and, with a shout, he snapped it off. He was losing blood, and his head lolled back from the shock. Katy dashed to his side, pulled out her knife, and ripped a strip of cloth from her ankle-length mantle, tying a quick tourniquet just above his wound. She doubted he'd let her remove his leather armor to properly treat the wound, but he had to be overheated. She pulled off his helmet. He needed cool water. She sprinted down the steps and fetched a bucket. On her return, the crossbowman lifted his head and looked around, frowning. He stared at his helmet.

She bent next to him, dipped another strip from her mantle in the cool water, and swathed his face. He closed his eyes but soon lurched to his feet, donned his helmet, grabbed his crossbow, and ran back through the door onto the walls.

Remembering Robert's earlier request, she checked the shallow bowl Alfred had mentioned. Not jiggling. Good. Shouts and screams echoed nearby as the fighting continued.

She stayed out of the fighting and pulled the wounded aside. Thankfully, there weren't many. During lulls, she crouched in the gloomy hallway, listened to the battle waging along the wall, and watched the shallow bowl for indications of tunneling.

A string of nasal-toned words bled into the air to her right. She whipped around in a crouch, and there, feet away, was that knight who'd stared at Robert with such hatred. He had his helmet on, but she recognized him by his bulky frame, the red and gold colors on his surcoat, and the ring of peacock feathers on his helmet. She couldn't understand him, but she could hear the taunting tone in them. At his feet was a Welshman gripping his stomach, desperately attempting to keep his innards inside.

The nasty knight swiped his sword across both cheeks of his victim, all the while keeping up his nasally monologue. With a chilling and calm indifference, the horrible man continued to take casual swipes at his enemy, slicing an ear, and then his lip, clearly relishing the moment as the battle raged around them. The Welshman lay immobile. Then his hand lifted, and he blocked one of the knight's thrusts, turning it into a feeble *thump* against the knight's head.

Nasty Knight shrieked in outrage, all out of proportion to the harm inflicted. He didn't like his enemies fighting back, however little—that was clear. He took a mighty swing and lopped off the Welshman's head.

Katy's stomach heaved again, and she scrambled back inside the shelter of the hallway. No way did she want to see anything more or get in that guy's way. Holy crap. Holy crap. Hol-yyyy craaaap. Her whole body shook, and her breaths came in short gasps.

God, God, God, she needed to get back to her time.

Slowly, her body ceased shivering, though her skin was chilled, and a thin sheen of clammy sweat coated her.

Soon though, a shift in the tenor and atmosphere outside signaled a change. Curious, she flattened against the wall and peeked around the doorway. Several knights and twice that in crossbowmen lined the wall, breathing heavy, but not fighting. Some of the crossbowmen were still shooting.

Green, green. Katy's gaze frantically skipped along the rows of colorful surcoats until she found the right one. Relief flooded her limbs, and she sank against the door frame. Robert leaned against the back of the wall, catching his breath and shouting to those nearby.

She couldn't see a thing from her wall, just the outer bailey, so she dashed across the door opening, flattened herself, and peered over the outer wall.

The Welsh were in retreat!

"Kay!"

Robert. Seeing him striding toward her unharmed did something funny to her insides. She rushed forward, but slowed as she neared. Running up, throwing her arms around him, and squeezing hard was a need that coursed through her, urging her to step faster, but she resisted. She was supposed to be a man. He and Alfred were her only tenuous tethers to navigate and survive in this world; she couldn't lose one, much less the most important one.

☙

"ROBERT TOLD ME TO GIVE YOU THESE." Alfred thrust a bundle of colored fabrics into Katy's hands. Proper squire clothes, no doubt. It was now dusk, but the day's violent events still fired her nerves, made her jumpy. She'd hoped being inside the main hall around a hearth fire would help calm her, but she was still...raw, exposed to the chaos without a defense.

Katy placed a hand on top, brushing a palm along the rough, woolen material. "I will meet you back inside. I'm going to clean up and change."

Alfred darted off, and she grabbed a bucket and boiled some water. Clean. She literally itched to be clean. Water ready, sliver of soap she'd found in hand, she headed to her hidden alley. She dragged the barrels to screen off the back end and cleaned herself as best she could, using her discarded peasant's mantle as her washcloth and towel.

Okay, so, how was each item to be worn? The loose, white shorts were probably her underwear. Honestly, they looked like the underwear shown on depictions of Jesus on the cross. She eyed her boobs—thank God for being small breasted. With these less-baggy clothes, though, she should play it safe. She tore a strip from her old tunic and wrapped it around her chest, tying it tight under her arm. Squished flat, maybe her breasts would just look like she had a nice set of pecs.

She struggled with the folds of the underwear-thing—how to secure it around her waist was a complete mystery. She searched in the pile and found two belt-like things, but there were no belt loops in the underwear. Out of desperation, she donned the belt around her bare waist, tucked the top of the underwear up under it, folded the edge around the belt, and rolled the combo down several times.

She let go and wiggled her hips. Huh. Looked like they'd stay. Smiling, she slipped into the white shirt and ankle-length, earthy-red tunic. Next, her hose, shoes, and belt. She finished by tucking her knife into the belt. She stood a moment, eyes closed, reveling in the feeling of being clean, in clean, period-approved clothes, even if rough against her skin. Odd that basically a shapeless, ankle-length tunic "dress" identified her as male. She climbed to the roof. Whew, no fire had ravaged up here. She stuffed her panties with the rest of her clothes next to her purse.

Back on the ground, she gathered up the other clothes and supplies and headed back to the main hall—the south tower, she'd heard it called. She fingered her wet hair and shivered in the chilly air. Oh, for a hair dryer. She tugged the hood over her head.

In the main courtyard, she joined the flow of people threading through the middle tower, across the bridge, and into the hall. Their spirits seemed high, and several smiled and spoke gibberish to her. She nodded politely, smiled, and hoped like hell that was the right response.

Because surely the response she wanted to make—the response urged on and fueled by the adrenaline pumping through her—

jumping up and down, flapping her hands, and shouting, "What the hell have I gotten myself into?" wasn't the thing. Neither was stopping someone and saying, "Do you know how weird this is for me?"

Maybe not even a calm, "Am I fooling you?"

Alfred charged up, jabbering away.

"Slow down, Alfred."

A blush suffused his fair skin. He took a deep breath, the slow rise and fall of his chest like he was reminding himself of the weight of his responsibility, and spoke each word carefully. "We are to eat what rations we can inside. No serving milord as squires."

She followed Alfred into the main room, where they found Robert. She expected him, but still, her heart gave a little kick at the sight of him. An ankle-length forest-green tunic graced his tall, muscular frame, cut similar to hers, but embroidered in silver along its edges. No chainmail. It was the first time she'd seen him without his armor. Well, except for last night when he was almost naked. Her traitorous body flushed hot at the memory. At his throat, a bright red stone held the tunic together.

He caught her eye and slowly nodded, like an adversary facing off. Did he ever smile? Breaking eye contact, he motioned to the bench beside him, about midway up the side of the hall. All around were men, including the servants. Hesitating slightly, she settled next to him, and the warmth of his presence enveloped her. She peeked up. Only the tips of his curls were completely dry. So he'd bathed too. Alfred plopped down on her other side.

A servant placed a flat piece of bread in front of her and Alfred. Starving, she reached to tear off a piece, but Alfred shook his head and mouthed, "No."

Katy stilled, neck flushing hot with embarrassment. Nothing was as simple as it seemed. *Observe, or you'll give yourself away.*

Robert dunked his hands in a bowl of water, droplets trickling from his strong, blunt fingers. He wiped them on a cloth and passed the bowl to her. She wet her hands and rubbed them briskly. Alfred did the same and took clumps of food from the table's center, piling them on their flat piece of bread. So, it was a plate.

Stalling with an extra hand rubbing, Katy observed Robert's and Alfred's movements. No silverware to be found. Did they eat with their fingers like some medieval stereotype? Alfred pulled a knife from his belt and, combined with his fingers, ate with neat, deft movements. So did Robert and the others. Tentatively, she pulled her knife from her waist, wiped it under the table with the cloth, speared what she could, and nibbled from it, careful of the sharp edge. Mostly meats were on her "plate," along with spicy and sugared fruits, but no vegetables. Oddly, servants passed with platters containing nothing but vegetables, destined for the lower end of the hall—the poorer classes? She signaled to one of the servants, who, while obeying her wish, looked extremely shocked.

Robert shot her a funny look, and Alfred, like any kid she knew, shunned them, so she put them on her end of their communal plate. For drink, they had watered down wine. Unlike her picture of the Middle Ages, they were quite neat—no gnawing on huge turkey legs, picking teeth, spitting, burping. They were presumably more subdued than normal, due to the unusual circumstances, but still. Everyone ate with efficiency and left when done, no lingering, no carousing.

Nasty Knight glared their way several times though. Katy nudged Alfred. "Who is that knight?" she whispered.

"That is Sir Ralph de Buche, newly arrived with Sir Hugh."

She shivered. She'd steer clear of that guy. *De Buche...de douche. Yeah, that fits.*

Robert's voice rumbled near her ear, and she started. *"Fromage?"* He offered a hard chunk of cheese, eyebrow lifted in the universal signal of a query.

Though his accent was strange, a thrill shot through her. Finally a word in French she could pick out from his speech. She took the cheese, and his hand brushed hers. Her awareness of him bloomed as the world narrowed to the surrounding few feet, and his every movement filled with significance.

She shook her head. Shit. He only offered food, for Pete's sake. But she couldn't shed the feeling.

He peered down at her under his lashes. The nearby torchlight added a touch of mystery to his otherwise flat, tawny eyes. The mystery seemed to seep from that look and coil between them, into her, igniting some latent need within.

She took a deep breath. Crap. She couldn't get involved with him—with anyone—here. But her lady parts weren't listening, and a warm flush of desire spread over her. Crap, crap, crap.

A flush of guilt followed—her first reason for remaining uninvolved was because of the traveling back in time thing, not because of her engagement.

Preston.

A jolt tightened her muscles—this was the first time he'd popped into her brain since she'd hurdled back to the friggin' Middle Ages, and what did that say about her? About them?

She was stressed and freaked out. That was all. Once she returned home, everything would be fine.

Chapter Eight

And when he came there, he saw a great fire kindled, and two
youths with beautiful curling auburn hair, were leading the maiden
to cast her into the fire. And Owain asked them what charge they
had against her.

The Mabinogion, an ancient Welsh romance

ROBERT'S HURRIED SUPPER now weighing his gut, he sought
Staundon. He wished to discuss his assessment of the
siege and their chances of a successful defense. Christ, what had possessed him at supper? First, wearing his best tunic and then allowing
his touch to linger on her skin. A futile test that had been. Yes, he'd
verified a certain *attraction* existed between them, but what did that
serve? Naught.

Robert found Staundon in deep conference, standing around a
table with Sir Hugh, de Buche, and several other knights. Hugh
waved him into their circle.

Robert nodded to each, and Hugh said, "I was recounting how
we fared. Whilst this castle is nigh on impregnable, we're vulnerable
to fire and to starvation if relief does not arrive soon."

"I agree." Robert set his feet further apart and clasped his wrist
behind his back. "And we cannot send out foraging parties. Every
able-bodied fighter must be on those walls come the morrow."

"Injured?" Staundon asked Hugh, his mouth set in a hard line.

"Two villagers dead from stray arrows. Two crossbowmen injured,
but they assure me they can still set their weapons and fire. One
knight injured but able to fight."

"What of your new squire, Beucol?" de Buche asked with a sneer,
leaning into the circle. Behind Staundon, his greyhound cracked a
bone and licked his chops. "I realize you could hope for no more
than a bare-legged peasant for a squire, but surely he can fight."

Robert straightened. Why had he so hastily given her that role? "Too raw, untrained. Besides, he has no armor." He wouldn't force her to fight. Though her steadfastness in tending the wounded was admirable and invaluable.

"A fresh-faced youth, for certes, and rather old to begin training as a squire," Staundon added.

"Must needs and all that," was Robert's weak rejoinder. "I took the opportunity presented by an able-bodied villager without connections."

"Mayhap," said Sir Hugh. "Though none would be preferable over an untried youth. It won't reflect well on your image." He nodded subtly toward de Buche.

"The devil take my image." Robert's words surprised even himself. "The lad was willing, and we are at war, and my need was great."

Sir Hugh had the right of it, though, as his actions reinforced de Buche's aim to portray Robert as uncouth. Image was paramount in the noble spheres Robert wished to tread. Once she was safe, he'd rid himself of her.

Wait. Safe? No. He shook his head. Once he located her kin and claimed his reward, he'd rid himself of her. Protecting her, keeping her *safe*, had naught to do with it. *Naught*. Indeed, nothing and no one took precedence over his goal.

A red-haired knight swigged from his ale cup. "Yes, damn these Welsh." He slammed the pewter onto the table, causing an oil lamp to sputter. "Every ten years, they stir up trouble, me seems."

Robert tightened his hand around his wrist. "From what I understand, they objected to fighting in Gascony as well as the taxes to pay for it."

"Are you defending them, good sir?" Staundon queried as tension snapped around the gathered men, full Normans all, save him.

"Merely stating the circumstances," he replied through gritted teeth.

Staundon waved a hand. "Whatever the cause, we face them on the morrow. I want all resources in full force to prevent a fire from spreading. Pile all available cloth near the well for soaking and spreading over the roofs. Buckets—anything—filled with water. Even our piss pots. Get them stationed around the inner bailey."

Robert bowed. "I will see to this, my lord. I oversaw the villagers today. They are familiar with me."

De Buche cleared his throat. "Villagers unable to fight should be sent outside the walls, spare our rations."

"And leave good English stock to the cursed Welsh? Lose the king's income in taxes?" Staundon asked, the rebuke in his tone clear. "No. We will hold out."

"We cannot hold for long," argued Sir Hugh. "Though I don't condone sending the weak outside." He directed a quelling glance at his vassal, de Buche. "However, we must agree we find ourselves in a rather weak bargaining position, which does not bode well for us if the castle should fall."

Robert kept his counsel, though he agreed with Sir Hugh. Only a strong position could garner fair terms from a besieging party. Their only choice was to resist and pray the relief party from Harlech arrived in time.

"By Christ's death," swore Staundon. "How are we to withstand a determined siege? Today's assault was nothing."

"We could use the sally port," another knight offered. A time-honored tactic of besieged forces—using the hidden gate in the back to sneak out a contingent of knights to reduce the enemy's forces.

Staundon stroked his beard. "No. Too risky. We have not the men to both flank them and hold the castle for the king."

"I beg your leave, my lord. I shall see to the fire prevention." Robert bowed and backed away.

To be sure, he'd like nothing more than to sit down with the pretty "squire" and discover exactly from where she hailed, but the castle's defenses ranked higher in priority. He found her and Alfred huddled around a game of merrills by the hearth and apprised them of their new task. After Alfred interpreted, they made for the inner bailey and once again, he gathered the villagers together.

This time, it was not so easy to keep them focused.

"When may we leave to bury Ralph the Tailor and Fulk the Fat?" asked the same merchant he'd conversed with this morn. His wife stood by his side, arms akimbo, two children clinging to her skirts.

"You will need to bury them here, I am afraid."

They grumbled at that, and the merchant crossed his arms.

"They need to be in consecrated ground."

"I shall speak to one of the Augustinian canons, see if they can find a spot within the walls. 'Tis the best I can do. I know not how long we'll need to remain inside."

"By every holy saint, I wish I'd never agreed to settle here. Cursed idea," muttered a man to his left.

Robert crossed his arms and injected his voice with finality. "You knew the risks. You all did. These settlements are vital in promoting the king's peace in these parts."

Robert said what was required as the king's representative. More and more, though, he questioned King Edward's policies—harass and settle, push, harass and settle, until all of Wales was under the King's law.

But his private thoughts and opinions mattered not.

"Listen," Robert continued. "We shall resist as long as we are able—"

"Surely, Staundon will not surrender to them," a youth yelled, face red with frustration and fear.

"Men-at-arms and supplies are forthcoming. As it was today, our biggest threat on the morrow is fire. All of you must pitch in to prevent such." He repeated Staundon's directions regarding fire prevention.

All the faces now looked appropriately grim but determined. Good. "If any lack for food tonight, see the castle steward."

※

DARKNESS BLOTTED KATY'S SURROUNDINGS, muffling the visual evidence of her new, crazy, time-traveling reality enough to ease the pressure that had settled on her chest since her arrival. Somewhat. The darkness—whole, deep, punctuated by smoking torches—had enough of an "other" quality to keep an uneasy thrum inside herself. An uneasy thrum which she worked hard to quell. *Not* the time or place to freak out. But it was getting harder and harder to maintain that veneer of control.

Katy and Alfred set down their empty buckets and waited their turn at the well.

Wind whipped around them, scattering straw and leaves. An eerie moan rose from the well—just the wind tunneling though the crevices. Still, with the torchlights flickering in the darkness around them, it gave her the damn goose bumps.

"Jesus wept," whispered Alfred. "I didn't believe the guard, but now..."

"What?"

"Ghosts in that well, he said. Moans from the Welsh dead the Normans threw in there when they captured this castle about ten years past." His voice was tinged with fear and glee. Fear because the supernatural scared the kid. Glee because the fear thrilled him.

"It's just the wind, Alfred."

"How do you know?"

Katy contemplated the castle grounds. "You said the Normans took over this castle then?"

He frowned. "Yes."

"Then would they pollute their own drinking water with dead bodies?"

His rangy body stood straighter, chest out. "I had not thought of that." He nodded. "No ghosts."

"No ghosts," she agreed.

Still, she shivered looking over the short walls of the well. Not the round stone structures—with a quaint wooden roof—of her imagination, but rectangular, easily six by ten feet. Unfortunately, only two buckets on a pulley accessed the water below. Hence the wait.

Finally at the pulley, they quickly filled their buckets and placed them near the stables, the most vulnerable and largest thatched roof in the area.

Another hour passed scrounging for buckets and green-glazed jugs from the kitchen and storage areas—and filling and distributing them. The activity kept Katy's mind off her new reality—helping others, Good God, defend against an attack from hundreds and hundreds of years ago!

The folk tale she'd heard when they'd first arrived in this remote part of Wales came to mind: anyone who spent the night on Cadair Idris Mountain would wake up either a poet or a madman. And she was on a spur of said mountain.

She rubbed her arms. Well, she knew she hadn't turned into a damned poet.

♋

MID-MORNING SUN, which would have been a welcome splash of warmth on a chilly October day, instead acted as one more heat source pulsing against her, Alfred, and the others as they labored to fight the fires raging through the courtyard.

It was bad.

So much for thinking the Welsh's flaming-arrow assault yesterday was the extent of their abilities. Obviously realizing storming the walls was not going to work, they launched, one after another, volleys of flame-tipped arrows.

She and Alfred dodged through the chaos to refill buckets. "Why are they out of range of our crossbowmen?"

"Those are the dreaded Welsh longbowmen, and their range is farther."

Great. Just great.

One structure, of no strategic importance and isolated enough that its sparks posed no danger to other buildings, Robert had ordered them to let burn. He and most of the knights pitched in right along with them fighting the rest of the fires. The crossbowmen lined the outer walls.

Frantic shouts behind spun her around. The cluster of buildings that hid her purse and clothes were aflame. *Shit.* She sprinted with her full buckets, clambered onto the barrels stacked near the wall, and threw water from one bucket and then another over the flames.

"Here!" Alfred handed her another bucket, and she splashed the last of the flames. Legs shaking, she settled for a moment on a barrel and wiped her forehead. Soot and fear sweat streaked across the back of her hand. Her muscles ached as if they'd been pounded flat. The idea of even lifting them again?

She held out the buckets with arms that weighed like stone. "Go fill these. I'll be right behind you."

Okay. Get up. Stopping had made her body feel worse. She climbed onto the roof, grabbed a piece of wet cloth covering a portion, and

69

crab-walked to her purse. Whew. Still there. She plopped it in the center of the cloth and tied it, hobo-style. Her bundle of clothes she left to burn, if the worst came to pass.

All done, she slid back to the ground when Alfred returned, panting. They doused the roof again.

"What is that?" He pointed to her bag.

"My things. I had them stashed nearby and was afraid they'd catch fire."

"You should put them in the keep."

Could she spare the time, the energy? Another roof was on fire, but the villagers and Robert had it covered. The well was packed with others refilling. "Meet you back at the well."

He nodded, young face scared but determined, and dashed off. She bolted for the middle tower, across the bridge, and into the keep, legs and lungs protesting the whole way, and dropped her bag by Robert's trunk. Back in the courtyard, she flinched as another wave of flaming arrows whizzed over the wall with a weird sizzling, whining sound that she'd never, ever forget. Most clattered harmlessly onto the stone courtyard, but enough landed on roofs. Adrenaline, now such a familiar drug running through her system, eroded more and more of her energy, like a relentless ocean tide. At the well, she forced her body to bend one more time to the task—*yank, yank on the pulley rope, bend her aching back, lift the bucket*—

A trumpet blew on the walls, urgent. Now what? The knights, including Robert, drew their swords and dashed for the outer bailey. Another wave of arrows hissed overhead and slammed—*thunk, thunk, thunk*—into flammable targets.

Shit. Shit. Shit. One foot in front of the other, that was all she could do, all any of them could do against the relentless attack. Could they ever get any of it under control? *Don't think about that. Act.*

It was like the universe was testing her, seeing how much it could throw at her to break her of her vow to never lose control again, to never allow her emotions to bubble up and spill out in all their hideous glory.

She stumbled to the nearest spot vacated by one of the knights and helped extinguish the flames. Grimly, she worked, pushing herself past exhaustion.

Shouts erupted along the front wall, followed by the clash of steel and cries of battle and pain. The clash and cries echoed through her aching limbs. They were at the walls? Oh God, was she scared. *Fill this bucket. Douse that fire.*

Close my stiff fingers around this handle. Walk, put one foot in—No clash of steel. No cries of pain.

Arrows flew into the courtyard as thick as ever, though. What the—

She darted a glance to the gate—the knights rushed along the walls and spilled into the courtyard.

She picked out Robert's dark green surcoat as he hustled to his commander. Angry shouts and hand waving followed.

What was going on?

Chapter Nine

"Lord," said the nobles unto Matholwch, "there is no other counsel than to retreat over the Linon, and to keep the river between thee and him, and to break down the bridge that is across the river, for there is a load-stone at the bottom of the river that neither ship nor vessel can pass over." So they retreated across the river, and broke down the bridge.

The Mabinogion, an ancient Welsh romance

"WE MUST WITHDRAW NOW, STAUNDON," shouted de Buche, blood and soot streaking his face. "We cannot hold the outer wall for much longer."

"I agree." Sir Hugh's lungs labored as he fought to regain his breath. "We barely fought off that last assault. They'll overrun us on the next, for certes."

"Seek a conditional surrender," countered Robert. Muscles unfamiliar with the stretch and pull of slinging water buckets ached with strain, on top of the normal pangs of battle. None of them were injured, thank the Blessed Virgin, but they were no longer fresh. "Ask for two fortnights and, if help arrives not by then, we surrender."

"God's balls, no," cursed another knight, his red surcoat torn across his chest. "Already they know how weak we are, we cannot possibly achieve favorable terms. The Welsh aren't fools—they can easily take this castle. They know that now. The longer we resist, the worse it will be for the villagers and men-at-arms."

De Buche spit. "I agree. They are ruthless savages. They'll have no qualms putting everyone to the sword. Plus, some in these parts have grievances with me."

Fury choked Robert's throat, and he could hold back no longer. "You might have made enemies, of that I have no doubt, but the Welsh are not the savages you portray. This is one of the king's castles.

Are we to abandon it to them without negotiating first?"

"Yes," cut in Staundon. "De Buche, instruct the crossbowmen to hold the Welsh off on the outer wall as long as possible, then fall back to the second wall. We'll use that time to get everyone out. We withdraw to Harlech Castle, now."

"What about pursuit?" Robert asked. "Won't they know of the sally port?"

"The villagers will slow us down," de Buche added.

"Lookouts report the Welsh are concentrated at the outer gate." Staundon's breaths came sharp and fast. "It's a gamble, I grant you, but we can gain some distance before they fully occupy the castle, and I have hopes they're eager enough to gain a stronghold that they'd forgo pursuit." He slapped his thigh. "Let's away. Now."

%

EMPTY BUCKETS CLUTCHED in her aching fingers, Katy stumbled back to the well near the conferring knights. She caught Robert's eye, and his jaw clenched. He stalked over and issued unintelligible instructions.

Alfred dashed up, soot streaking his boyish cheeks. "He said the commander has ordered a retreat."

"Into the keep?"

"No, we're abandoning the castle. Grab your possessions. I'll come with you as I have nothing to save, and I can show you the way."

Word had spread. The villagers had scattered to their encampment, and the knights and squires were letting the horses, skittish from the smoke, out of the stables.

A bitter pang ran through her, as well as an upswell of panic—her case, if even there and not stolen or trampled into the ground, was exactly in the middle of the teeming Welsh. But what could she do? Nothing.

She took a deep, shuddering breath, letting what she could not control wash through her. Yes, the universe was testing her. "Come on, let's go then." With one last look at Robert, as well as the gate, she bolted for the keep.

Once inside, she dodged overturned benches, barking dogs, and servants dashing about and fetched her sack.

"I'll take my lord's trunk," Alfred said.

He staggered under the weight, clutched with determination and pride in his small hands. His cheeks turned red from the strain, though the trunk wasn't much bigger than her idea of a pirate's chest.

"Hold one side," she shouted, flinging her bag over her shoulder and grabbing a handle of the trunk.

Together, they rushed back across the bridge, through the middle tower, and into the courtyard. Alfred pointed to the far end, hand shaking, to the steps leading up to the north tower—No. To a gap in the wall to the left. A scraggly line of villagers headed for it, and the knights arrayed themselves in a defensive formation in the courtyard, their mounts stamping beside them, nostrils and eyes wide with fear. More roofs were aflame, and dark, oily smoke billowed greedily skyward, no longer kept in check by the defenders. She glanced over her shoulder. The crossbowmen had retreated to the wall at the second gate.

Arrows continued to fly over the walls. One landed in front of a stoop-shouldered woman, who staggered back, dropping her trunk. The contents spilled out, and the lady dropped to her knees and shoved her possessions back inside, heedless of the surrounding danger. Sunlight glinted off metal.

Her case!

"Hey—" Sharp pain seared her arm. She gasped and looked down. Her sack hit the hard ground with a *thud*.

She had a friggin' *arrow* in her arm.

✲

"THAT'S THE LAST VILLAGER," shouted one of the knights. "The Welsh are storming the outer wall."

Robert gritted his teeth and hurried Perceval and the rouncey he used as a pack horse to follow the villagers and castle servants through the sally port.

Above the cries and shouts, a familiar voice jolted him. Kaytee. She slumped to her knees, fingers clutched around her arm, from which protruded a cursed arrow. His heart thudded to a stop. She locked her gaze with his, and disbelief crossed her face.

Alfred was shouting to him and jumping around her. Robert's trunk lay beside them, and he was momentarily stupefied by their thinking of him and retrieving it.

He sprinted to them, pulling along his horses.

She grabbed a hemp sack and slumped sideways, hand to the ground for balance. As he approached, she got a foot under herself and began to stand, but the blood drained from her face, and she crumpled to the ground in a faint.

He landed on his knees beside her, his poleyns cushioning the jolt. "Jesus wept." He snapped off the end of the arrow, tore a strip from his surcoat, and tied it tight around the wound, leaving the point embedded for now.

"Up you go." He grabbed Alfred around the waist and hoisted him into the saddle. "Keep low and hold onto her—him."

He gathered up Kaytee's limp body and gingerly placed her over Alfred's lap.

He stared at his trunk and then at Alfred. "Thank you."

Bless them—that paltry trunk represented all his hopes and dreams, and to lose it now was not something he wished to contemplate.

He lashed his trunk and Kaytee's sack on his pack horse, attached him to Perceval by a lead and, with a last glance at the burning courtyard, followed the others through the sally port, picking his way down the sharp incline. He risked a peek at Kaytee. While the bleeding had stopped, her color wasn't good, and her wound needed tending.

Once they gained the valley floor, he threaded past the others in the retreating column until he reached the castle's chirurgeon.

"Attend to my squire, if you please."

The healer's gaze jerked to his, eyes wide. "Now, sir? But the savages could be on us any minute."

"Be that as it may, my squire requires attention."

"Begging your pardon, sir, but I'm responsible for all. I cannot separate from them to attend to one."

"The chirurgeon is right, half breed," sneered de Buche. "Mayhap you could petition your kin for succor. They should be on us soon."

Robert stared into the mean gray eyes of his boyhood nemesis and fought for control.

De Buche leaned down from his saddle to bring his face closer to Robert's. "After all, your family has a history of being traitors, no?"

Enough. Kaytee needed him. Robert turned his back to him and said in short, clipped tones to the healer, "Provide me with some ointment. I will see to my squire myself."

The healer grumbled, dug into his bag, and pulled out an earthenware jar and a clean rag. He smeared a generous dollop onto the cloth and handed it to Robert, along with a spare bandage, and a small earthenware jar. "Elder oil for you to boil and pour over the wound and a salve. Godspeed, sir."

Robert tied it closed and continued with the column as they hurried along. He kept a lookout for Sir Hugh.

At last, his former lord's surcoat bobbed into view, and Robert approached. "I must see to my squire. Do you know where we are headed?"

"What do you mean to do?" Sir Hugh's vigilant gaze roamed the valley behind.

"My squire was wounded during the retreat. I must attend to him."

His gaze snapped back to Robert's. "By God's spleen, you cannot mean to halt now. The Welsh will overrun the castle soon enough and could send out a party in pursuit."

"Regardless, his wound requires attention. Should be but the work of a moment."

"I like this not, Robert."

"You need not, but distract Staundon with regards to me. I should be able to join you ere he notices, but in the event I'm delayed, do you know where he plans to break for the night?"

Staundon's greyhound loped by, and Sir Hugh's horse sidestepped, head jerking in annoyance. "He mentioned making for Cymer Abbey by taking the eastern path around the mountains and camping along the Afon Mawddach River."

"Cymer? That's over twelve miles."

"Aye, he means to press through the evening." Sir Hugh looked from side to side. "There's not much shelter, Robert. Be careful, and be quick."

"I will. I mean only to make for yonder stream, clean the wound, put on what is surely a foul-smelling salve the chirurgeon gifted me, bind the injury, and return."

He turned to Alfred, still perched on Perceval. "I need you to continue on with them, lad. I'll be able to catch up on my horse better with only one other passenger."

"I could ride atop your packhorse," he squeaked.

"Nay. Your family will want you with them. I'll see you anon, lad."

Alfred gave a slow nod and slid down Perceval's side, careful to keep Kaytee across the saddle. Robert ruffled the boy's blond locks and nudged his back to send him on his way. With a final nod to Sir Hugh and Perceval's lead in his mailed fist, Robert turned away, only to be brought up short by a hand on his arm.

Sir Hugh bent down from his saddle, his gaze locked with Robert's. "Be careful, my friend. Tarry not. It will not aid your cause with the king if you anger Staundon." He finished with a glare at de Buche's back.

"Aye." Robert clapped his former lord's shoulder and pulled on Perceval's lead, pushing through the bilberry and Welsh poppies to reach the sloping bank of Afon Cadair. Quiet descended as the last of the column threaded out of sight. He searched along the river's length as long as he dared until he found a rocky outcropping that sheltered them from view. A moment to attend to this task, and he'd be on his way, likely not far behind the last of the stragglers. He'd be caught up with them in a half hour, at most. In the chaos, Staundon wouldn't notice his absence as long as Robert returned to the retreating line. If worst came to worst, he'd catch up with them tonight.

He eased Kaytee off the horse and settled her down on the mossy bank. Curse it, but she was still unconscious. He peeled back his mail mittens and tied them at his wrist to give his fingers free range and pushed her sleeve up over the broken shaft of the arrow. Careful not to disturb her, he unwrapped his crude bandage.

At the sight of the long, narrow arrowhead, he breathed easier. The barb had not penetrated but instead had lodged in the fleshy area of her upper arm and should heal clean. Frankly, he was surprised it hadn't fallen out on its own.

He tore the healer's extra bandage into strips and wet a piece in the river. He skimmed his hand up the smooth skin of her arm and held it in place. Gently, he withdrew the arrow, and her lips pursed, her head and arm jerking. He placed a hand on her shoulder, hating that he'd had to hurt her.

"Shh. Shh... I seek only to remove the arrow. All will be fine." She couldn't understand him, he knew, but he fervently prayed his tone communicated his meaning. Cries of panic he could not risk, nor any delay she might cause from it. The Welsh were too close. The longer he lingered, the more exposed he felt.

He pressed the wet cloth to her arm and cleaned the wound. He looked anxiously at her face. Christ on the cross, it was a little paler than before. Fresh blood welled from the wound, and whilst he applied pressure, he ran through different options should the Welsh pursue.

He dared not tarry further. He opened the bundle containing the healer's ointment and brought it to his nose. A pungent, noxious odor seared his nostrils.

He jerked his head away. Vile. What was in this stuff?

Actually, he'd rather not know.

He scooped a portion and smeared the greasy concoction over her wound, using gentle strokes, careful not to cause her additional pain. Taking the last strip of cloth, he wound it securely around her arm and knotted it.

She mumbled, and her eyes fluttered open. When her hazel eyes snagged his through the horizontal slits in his helm, they widened. She moved her arms as if to rise, winced, and slumped back. Low, questioning tones in her strange tongue fell from her shapely lips.

He swallowed to moisten his dry throat and motioned to her arm. In his own tongue, he said slowly, "You were wounded."

Her eyes searched frantically around, her unwounded arm clutching at the clothes covering her chest. She visibly relaxed. Upon seeing they were alone, he expected her to shrink from him, but she surprised him by regarding him with eyes bold, not in invitation, but absent of fear, and it puzzled him.

His fingers itched to have an excuse to run down the soft—*so soft*—skin of her arm. She'd flattened her chest in some manner, but he knew what lush flesh lay beneath. He could lean over and test how her lips tasted, see if they were as soft and sweet as he imagined. A keen yearning suffused and thickened the air between them. Her eyes darkened, and her breaths grew short, like his.

God's balls, he couldn't afford to be distracted by her. He slammed his control into place and lurched to his feet. He yanked off his helm and let it dangle from its chain at his belt. Water. They needed water. He stomped to his rouncey and rummaged for his traveling pouch, which he always had filled with provisions for such times as these. He removed a leather flask and picked his way through the brush to the swiftly flowing river and filled it.

At her side again, he eased his arm behind her shoulder, ignoring her warmth and scent, now absent that exotic fruit smell, but enticing nevertheless. He clenched his jaw and tapped the edge of the flask to her lips. Her eyes expressed her thanks, and he watched as her throat moved with her swallows. When she drew away from the flask and nodded, he settled her against the ground. He broke off a hunk of manchet bread and handed it to her. *Eat*, he urged with his eyes. Whilst she gratifyingly obeyed, he refilled and stoppered the flask.

He hated to ask this of her, but safe they were not. By now, the Welsh would have secured the castle. "We must go." He pointed to them both and to his horses.

She pulled in a ragged breath and nodded, saying something like "*Je comprends*," similar enough to "I understand." So, he'd not been mistaken that she spoke a strange dialect of French.

When she finished her bread, he held out his hand. Her warm fingers slipped into his, and he tugged her upright, admiring her grace. He returned his flask to his travel pouch, donned his helm, and reattached his mittens. Fabric stirred behind him, and her foot slipped into the stirrup. She bounced on her toes several times, but with only one functioning arm, it was clear she couldn't mount unassisted. Besides, he needed to mount first.

Locking down all feeling, he stepped behind her and stilled her. He swung up, reached down, and pulled her onto his lap, since there wasn't room enough for them both in a saddle meant to fit him snugly in both front and back. With her tempting thighs atop his, he urged Perceval up the rough path to the broad valley, her back brushing against his chest. But as he cleared the last stand of brush and trees, the open terrain filled him with unease. He noted the sun's position.

By all the saints' holy testicles, he'd spent more time than he'd planned tending her wound. And though 'twould be faster to use this open trail, it was too risky—they were too visible from all vantage points.

Move faster and reach the others at a canter in an hour at most— and risk being seen without the defensive benefit of numbers? Or head back to the river and take advantage of the cover it provided, and pick their way on that rocky and rough terrain at a much slower pace?

He canted his head to the side and examined Kaytee's pale face, soft in the filtered light from the cloud-covered sun.

Curse it.

Chapter Ten

And there arose a storm of wind and rain, so that it was hardly possible to go forth with safety. And being weary with their journey,
they laid themselves down and sought to sleep.
The Mabinogion, an ancient Welsh romance

BEGRUDGING THE LOST TIME, Robert swung Perceval about and
headed back to the river and its safer path, his rouncey
easily navigating behind to follow. A walk short of a full trot should
bring them into camp shortly after they bedded down for the night.
Mayhap in the chaos of setting up their camp, his absence wouldn't
be noted. For Sir Hugh was right, 'twould not reflect well on his petition to the king if he were thought to have abandoned his duties.

In front of him, Kaytee held herself rigid. It couldn't be comfortable sitting astride the high pommel. One arm he kept loosely around
her waist to hold her steady, though he longed to pull her against him,
to feel her back along his front, mayhap to ease one hand up her
waist to the lush curve of... He stiffened. By Saint John's sacred jaw
bone, 'twas good they were not entwined so.

After a moment, in her curious voice, she pointed to an oak and
said something close to *tree*. He nodded and repeated with his own
pronunciation, and she continued on in that manner with several
other objects, an activity they maintained for the space of the sun to
travel lower toward the horizon.

Her French puzzled him. In some respects, it resembled the
French of the king's court on the Ile de France, more polished than
the Norman dialect spoken in England. At other times, it differed
completely from it and his own. Some consonants she pronounced
with a harder sound, and once he understood which, he could antici-
pate the differences.

He grew hopeful they could soon converse, but erelong he had other concerns, for dark clouds amassed overhead, and a biting wind whipped through their valley, whistling through the trees and fluttering and snapping the folds of his surcoat behind.

Still no sign of his party ahead. Backward glance—no sign of pursuit. Or sound.

At the ford over a tributary of the Afon Cadair, he stopped. The bank on his side showed the retreating party had turned east as planned, following the branch to Lake Tal-y-llyn. To the north, however, was the western spur of the mountain. They could ford the river and take the Rhin Gwredydd pass over the mountain.

Dare he risk it? In the mountain slopes above, the Welsh could be found, for all knew they inhabited the upper regions and left the valleys for the foreigners, for the Normans and English. He could eliminate at least five miles from their journey in this manner—he might then meet their party as they swung to the north of the mountain range.

He forded the river. After they crossed three small streams, rain drops landed on Kaytee's increasingly pale face, and he urged Perceval into a trot, cursing that the terrain prevented a faster pace. If only they could reach the camp before it rained in earnest. But when sheets of rain began to pelt them, turning the earth to slippery and slick mud along the stones, Kaytee quieted and began to shiver, and he knew they could not continue. They must find shelter, and fast.

He reined in Perceval and listened to the forest, but only the hard hammering rain and the gushing river filled his senses. Crossing quickly through the pass was one thing, but seeking shelter on the slopes was another matter altogether.

Kaytee's chattering teeth decided him. He clucked to his mount and guided him across the river and upslope to the west, praying he'd find a hafod, one of the many summer huts used by Welsh herdsmen. Unbidden, a memory of tending a herd with Pedr, his mother's uncle, the summer of Robert's sixth year flooded him with pleasant warmth. He'd felt like such a man, helping his uncle, sheltering overnight, just the two of them, in a hafod.

The sun dipped lower as he scoured the mountain slope, working steadily upslope, but he finally found a round animal hide and bark structure, large enough to sleep four. He quickly dismounted and turned in time to catch Kaytee from slumping off the side. He grasped her tightly around the waist and lifted her free of the saddle, cradling her trembling form against his chest like a babe. He hustled them into the shelter.

"Thank the Virgin Mary," he whispered as water dripped from his face guard. The previous occupant had left a short stack of hides, clean straw, and several bundles of chopped wood and dry kindling. In the center of the ceiling, there was a smoke vent.

He eased her onto a bed of straw, and she softly moaned. He must get her dry and warm. Cursing, he whipped off his helm and built up a fire using the flint from his travel pouch and dry kindling, risking notice but praying the Welsh would assume only another of their kind would dare be up this high in the mountains. When the fire's first warm tendrils curled and crackled into their space, he looked at Kaytee's shivering, wet form.

No choice. "Begging your pardon, I must undress you. You must needs get warm and dry." She responded not, and a slight wedge of fear entered his heart.

Christ, had she lost consciousness? He peeled back his mittens and, with efficient fingers, stripped off her wet garments. There was nothing sensual about his actions. It was a matter of survival, and he focused on each step he must accomplish.

He paused, fingers poised at the knot under her arm holding the bindings around her breasts, a testament to her desire to pass for a man. But they were soaked.

Her health. Her health was paramount.

He closed his eyes and drew in a calming breath, willing a cool indifference. Ready, his own fingers stiff with cold and shaking, he loosened the knot—*ignore her lush curves*—until she lay before him, naked down to her braies and shivering. He snatched a hide and rubbed it vigorously in her hair and over her back, arms, torso and legs, which...were oddly smooth, as bare as a baby's bottom. He frowned. Yes, much about her was strange.

He shook his head to redirect his attention. He needed to get her not only dry, but warm. He wrapped a dry hide about her shoulders and spread another on her legs.

Not enough. He shoved two of the straw mats over to the fire and stretched another hide across it, fur side up. He transferred her to the makeshift pallet, tucked the hides over her, and waited.

Only then did he notice the wet, cold clothes wicking into his quilted gambeson. Blast it. His mail would rust if he did not have a care. But first, Perceval and his rouncey.

He coaxed his horses into the hafod, in the manner of peasants, but they needed tending, and their warmth would aid Kaytee. He divested Perceval of his accoutrements and rubbed him down, settling him against a wall once finished. He removed his rouncey's burdens and tended to her as well.

Grateful for his well-trained horses, he stripped down to his braies and laid their clothes on a straw mat. Not good enough; their clothes needed to dry faster. Outside the hafod, he searched until he found what he sought: two forked sticks and another long, straight one.

Inside, he whittled the ends of the forked sticks into crude points and worked them into the ground. He dried the pole as best he could, stretched it between the sticks, and laid out their clothes. His fingers hesitated at the belt holding up his braies. They were soaked now too, and he dared not risk it. While hers had been too, he couldn't bring himself to strip her that far. With quick movements, he dispensed with them and hung them over his makeshift drying rack.

He extracted the wool blankets from his trunk, piled them over Kaytee's still form, and crawled under them so he lay behind, but not touching her. Even at this distance, his warmth should help. The rain continued to beat against their roof, ever harder. Thank the saints they'd found this shelter in time.

But what cost this delay? Anything he could do to distinguish himself in this fight against the Welsh would increase the chances of his suit to regain his family's demesne. Better to fight here than in cursed France, and he'd not waste this opportunity. What better proof of his loyalty to the crown than to fight the Welsh, his mother's people? Never again would anyone call his family traitors.

His shivers subsided, but hers had not.

"Christ on the cross," he muttered. "Forgive me." He shifted closer and pulled her back against him, one arm wrapped around her shoulders, cradling her head, and the other wrapped around her stomach, her flesh cold and clammy. The knowledge that he held her form so firmly against his naked one was a thick, tempting coil wrapping around him, spreading betraying heat through his groin. He clenched his teeth, stared at the popping and flickering fire, and recited every saint's feast day he could remember. He resisted the call of her flesh. He willed it. However, her chilled skin and loss of consciousness worried him greatly, coupled with her wound.

He also willed himself to remain awake, mindful of the danger of the open fire near so much straw, and his need to leave as soon as the rain stopped and she ceased shivering.

✑

ROBERT AWOKE WITH A START. A warm female body was delectably draped over his. He smiled and tightened his arms around the lush, sleeping form, the intoxicating feminine scent of her filling his senses. But memory assailed him, and he stiffened and looked about.

Jesus wept. How could he have fallen asleep? Granted his chances for slumber had been few these last days, but he could ill afford the luxury. And by the hairs on God's big toes, how had she become turned around and snuggled up so deliciously against him?

Heart pounding, he held himself still, tension stiffening his muscles. He should...he should carefully place his hands on her delicately rounded shoulders and ease her off—*gulp*—off his now-aroused, naked body so she would not take fright upon awakening, and so, oh by all the saints' wrinkly knuckles, so he would not be *tempted*.

He screwed his eyes shut, willed himself to relax, and gently turned his head to check the fire. Now down to glowing embers, it barely put off heat, but their body heat kept them warm enough under the blankets. Judging by the early evening light filtering in, he'd lost another hour from his ill-advised and ill-timed slumber.

No sound of rain either. His heart sped up, sluicing energy through him. Surely the lass was warm and dry enough to continue their journey. For continue they must. They'd not reach the others before they stopped for the night, but the situation was still salvageable. If they left now. The short cut should still benefit him.

But as he shifted to wake her, she shivered, and worry cut through him, for her skin had become moist.

No, not a fever. She could not come down with a fever.

He eased her from his body and rose onto his elbow. In the dying light of the early evening, he sought her face. Her coloring had turned ashen, and sweat glistened across her brow.

Fingers tentative, he pushed her dampened hair back from her forehead. Christ, she was burning up.

He scrambled from the sheltering blankets and yanked them off her. He placed two hides side by side so it was long enough, draped one of his wool blankets over them, shifted her on top, and crossed her arms across her chest, sternly ignoring her pleasing form. He rolled her up, like a swaddled babe, and moved her as close as he dared to the dying fire. He built it back up and laid the rest of the blankets atop her, minus one, which he wrapped around himself.

They would not be leaving any time soon. Any hopes he'd entertained of reaching Staundon by nightfall vanished.

And then he caught himself. Who the devil was she to him? Why was his first impulse to include her in his plans?

He straightened and contemplated the darkened shadows in the space above. He could leave now, be with the men and, saints willing, not have been missed. She was warm, he could leave what food and water he had, and when she awoke, if she recovered, she could fend for herself. Mayhap he could contrive to lash his trunk to Perceval and leave her his rouncey. A costly proposition, but it eased his guilt.

That would be the prudent course. The wise course. Otherwise, de Buche would make the most of Robert's absence, spin it for his own ends. For de Buche was as determined to deny Robert his rights as Robert was to win them back. After all, the honors and property had been granted to de Buche's father after they'd been stripped from Robert's, and that knowledge rankled.

Yes. Leave her. That would be the smart course. His muscles tightened in preparation for waking Perceval, to move, to act.

But as he looked upon her wan face and felt that tug he couldn't explain, he found there was one course he couldn't take in the name of recovering his family's honor. He could not abandon her.

And he should be pissed. Pissed at this wisp of a woman upsetting his careful plans. But...he wasn't.

Perceval softly nickered, and the lass mumbled, rocking to and fro, but his tight bundling kept her from thrashing.

He hastened to her side. "Shhh. Shhh..." He knelt by her side, his blanket pulled tight around him, and watched her with a growing sense of helplessness. If her wound festered or her fever persisted, he knew no healing lore. He had enough food for only a day, but that did not worry him, for he had knife and wits to remedy that. However, his knife and sword, his skill at killing, counted for naught when it came to healing.

He reckoned it was shortly after sunset when her delirium set in.

Chapter Eleven

And Kai was brought to Arthur's tent, and Arthur caused skilful
physicians to come to him. And Arthur was grieved that Kai had
met with this reverse, for he loved him greatly.
The Mabinogion, an ancient Welsh romance

*S*HE WAS A RABBIT—*smelling rabbit things, eating rabbit things and
feeling good. But something was wrong. So cold. So hot.*

No. If only she could get to that stand of green shoots.

Her fur itched. Why couldn't she scratch it?

Ego externus.

Yes. She had to get outside. Not the grass shoots.

A hand on her forehead? A soothing voice murmuring in French?

But she was a rabbit...

*She needed to get outside for the grass shoots. It was important. Very
important.*

cx

SO HEAVY. SO DROWSY. KATY BLINKED open crusty eyelids, and her heart
seized up like an intern on his first high-stakes live translation job.
Where was she? It was stiflingly black, save for a faint, unsteady glow
to the right. She forced her head to move, rough fur brushing her
cheek. A banked fire. What the—

C'mon, what was my last memory? Visiting Castell y Bere with her
bridesmaids, climbing its rugged slope.

No. Wait. She squeezed her eyes shut. Surely she'd dreamed...she
hadn't gone back in time. No way, she told herself, even as a thread
of certainty grew and tugged.

The memories too detailed, too graphic. The siege. The flaming

88

arrows and constant fires. Robert. Her arm.

Holy-holy-holy crap. She'd been shot with a frickety-frick arrow.

The tidal wave of memory slammed into her, and she bowed up on a gasp, but scratchy blankets weighed her, wrapped her up tight, pinned her arms to her sides.

"Should've done more crunches," she muttered as she heaved upward an inch and plopped back, over and over, until dizziness fuzzed her brain and short-circuited her muscles. She slumped against whatever the heck kind of bed she was on.

Where the hell was she, and what had happened? And why was she as weak as a minute-old kitten?

A rustling near her feet had her looking down her nose. A dark figure ducked through an opening that parted as if made of some thick fabric. Adrenaline spiked, sending her heart beating fast, her spine locking in fear.

The man-sized shape stooped, and an armful of kindling tumbled to the ground. He methodically placed one stick after another into the fire. As the glow increased, its circle of light gradually grew to illuminate the figure's face. Robert!

In her relief, she must have made a sound, for his attention snapped to her.

"Kaytee." His voice was rough, laced with concern, and just hearing that small smattering of emotion—from a voice normally flat—pierced her with a strange longing.

She struggled against the constricting covers, not because he scared her, but because she'd never felt so confined, and it was unfriggin-nerving.

His large body loomed above, and she stilled, breath held, the shelter's interior suddenly smaller. He loosened whatever the hell she was wrapped in, and darted back to the fire. Why did—?

Oh. She was nearly buck naked. She narrowed her eyes at him, but he didn't look away. Shit. Would he take sexual advantage? Had he already? She mentally checked her body—no soreness, but her arm hurt like a mofo.

All other worries fled. *Shit, please don't be infected.*

She tucked a hide around her and shifted closer to the fire, her arms and legs weak, as if delayed by a half second. She angled her arm into the firelight and inhaled sharply. A dark cloth was knotted around, caked in blood. She tugged at the knot, but failed with only one hand available.

She checked the blanket—important bits covered? Yes—and held out her arm. "Robert, *m'aiderez-vous?*" His French was strange, and she knew he couldn't understand her, but she asked anyway.

He moved near, clad in only a loose-flowing robe, the space between them growing thicker with awareness, the sparks in the fire snapping and popping. His blunt, shapely fingers touched the cloth, and his gaze locked with hers. *Ready?*

Her heart fell over itself—for his once flat, emotionless eyes now stirred with unspoken thoughts and, dare she say, softness? This was her fierce, unsmiling knight? Memories surfaced of gentle, caring hands and soft tones cradling her as she slept off her fever. That...that had been Robert?

Stop. Speculation was useless. Useless and distracting. She nodded at his unspoken question. He tugged the knot free, but the bandage remained stuck.

A growing, roiling queasiness churned in her stomach, but she must remove the bandage. Earlier on horseback, they'd practiced each other's French. Had they made headway?

"Water?" she said in French, pointing to a nearby earthenware bowl. He nodded, left, and returned five minutes later with water in the bowl. She nestled it against the fire and examined their...what was it? Hut? Glorified teepee?

In the far corner, clothes hung on a propped up stick. "Clothes?" She motioned for him to bring them.

Where was Alfred? Despite the difficulty, they understood enough to get by, and at least the language had been her own. Sure, she spoke fluent French, and regularly dealt in dialects at her job, an NGO specializing in promoting peace, but she was—dammit—tired.

He brought her linen shirt, and she tore off a strip, waited for the water to boil, and struggled with the inability to pepper him with questions.

Robert settled nearby but made no attempt at conversation, because, yeah, that'd be kind of hard. Maybe if he could talk some, she could listen, learn more, remember more, and hear how his dialect

differed. Besides, she always understood a new foreign language better than she could speak it. Bonus points—talking might puncture
the awareness she had of his every move.

"Can you talk to me?" she asked in French.

Confusion showed in his scrunched brows, the firelight casting
shadows on his starkly handsome face. She indicated her mouth,
opened and closed her hand like a talking mouth, and pointed to
him. She cupped her ear and looked expectant. *Talk so I can listen.*

Understanding lit his face, and he nodded. He searched their
small space, as if for inspiration, and hesitantly began speaking his
strange version of French.

Yes, that was the voice which had spoken during her fever. The
voice which now shrank the surrounding space, the voice which
worked into her soul and joined with the gentle, caring voice of her
fevered memories. She understood maybe one word out of seven, but
then he got rolling and spoke at his normal speed. She held up a
hand and said in French, "Slow."

His mouth closed with a snap. Frustration and determination
marked his features—clearly he wanted to communicate just as badly
as she. He spoke slower, his words flowing over her, and she tried not
to grasp at everything and so catch nothing. Hopefully, listening to
the whole, the words would seep in and eventually become *meaning*.

The water began to bubble, and she dunked the strips of cloth in
it. Robert's rich, melodic cadence danced across her nerve endings,
twining inside her. *No. Listen to the meaning. Don't allow him to tie
you here. He's not for you.*

She nudged the bowl away from the fire, let it cool slightly, and
washed her hands as best she could in the hot water. She gently laid a
strip against her wound, soaking the clotted bandage with the warm
wet cloth. Eventually, she'd loosened it enough to pull away the bandage without ripping off her arm.

Was it her imagination that he was describing her actions?

Fresh blood trickled out, and she leaned closer to the firelight.
Angry red skin bordered the wound, glistening with some kind of
paste, but the skin wasn't hot. She cleaned the gash. Thank God, it
wasn't deep, only a smallish hole in her upper arm. Must make sure
nothing hinky was in there. She squeezed the water from another

bandage, the drops tinkling back into the bowl, and settled onto her back, her arm along her side.

"Robert," she said, interrupting his monologue. She pointed to the bowl and her arm. *Pour this over my wound,* she pleaded with her eyes.

He frowned, settled close, his body heat welcome, and carefully poured.

Damn, that hurt. She hissed and pressed her cheek against the furs, teeth clamped tight. When he finished, she lifted her arm and wrapped the bandage around, but knotting it closed proved impossible.

Robert's warm hand gripped her arm, and her belly did a slow, heavy flip-flop. He took her bandage, and she caught what sounded like the French words for "help" and "this."

She nodded, and he wrapped it tightly around her arm, his concerned gaze occasionally darting to hers as he tied it closed. She plopped her head back to the floor. Okay. She'd be okay.

She just had to figure out what the heck was going on, where she was, and how to find that villager with the case so she could return home and end this nightmare.

And so she could be far from this knight who threatened her carefully planned life with his mere presence.

Pretty please with sprinkles on top?

♥

BELOW, MIST CLUNG TO THE RIVER cutting through the valley to the east. Already the bright morning sun promised to burn it away, along with much of the dampness from the intermittent rain. Two and a half days of it.

Last night, Kaytee's fever had finally broken, thank Christ, and she'd redressed her wound. He'd already used up the healer's elder oil during her illness and was relieved to see it had worked wonders. He bit into a hunk of dried coney meat and washed it down with a swig of river water. He set aside the rest for Kaytee. He'd laid traps, for he'd quickly consumed his rations, but his haul had been meager—only enough to keep him fed while he waited out her illness. He must hunt for larger game. Tonight.

Though her French was passing strange, he found glimmers of

recognition in her speech and had hopes they'd understand each other soon enough to communicate with more than gestures.

But that mattered for naught compared with the need to break camp and head for the royal castle of Harlech, roughly twenty-five miles north through rugged Welsh terrain. Enemy terrain. How he would explain his absence, he knew not, but had hopes the answer would surface ere they arrived.

He checked the buckles and straps on his saddle, the lead attaching his rouncey to Perceval, impatient to set out. He glanced toward the hafod to check for the twentieth time whether the lass had bestirred.

Sleeping beside her last night had not been easy. During her illness, he had naught but worry for her, with no room for lustful thoughts. But once her fever had broken, and she'd looked upon him with clear eyes, trusting eyes, his thoughts... Well, he was a man after all, one too long from the comfort of a woman's thighs.

He smiled as he cleaned his nails with a pair of tweezers—she'd had no qualms ordering him about as she'd dressed her wound. Further evidence that a low-born lass she was not.

Well, high-born or no, she needed to arise.

He took two steps toward the hafod and stopped as she ducked outside. He caught his breath. Fuzzy from sleep, the morning light falling against her creamy, unblemished skin, she appeared vulnerable.

Only too aware of how exposed they were alone in Welsh country, and he her sole protector, he gritted his teeth.

She approached and uttered a garbled phrase. He caught the word "bathe" and, accompanied by her hand motions, understood her intentions.

"I shall accompany you to the river." He swept his arm downslope.

Her eyes widened, and her mouth opened, but he forestalled her. "It's not safe for you to be alone." He crossed his arms, widened his stance, and tried to impart with his glare, *In this, I will not be swayed.*

She closed her mouth, her serious, hazel-colored eyes taking in his stance. An irrational part of him wished that intent gaze studied his body for other reasons. He forebore from shifting his feet. Finally, she sighed, nodded, and headed down the slope.

Hand on his sword hilt, he grimly followed her lithe form, alert to any sight or sound that bespoke danger.

At the bank, he nodded and, cognizant of her sensibilities, turned his back, keeping close watch up and down the river. When he heard her slip into the water, he turned back so as to keep watch all around her.

He grinned: he'd turned in time to witness her delicate white shoulders dip below the water's surface.

Thankfully, she quickly completed her morning's ablutions and made a shooing motion with her hands. Back turned again, he waited for her to dress, all the while telling his privy counselor to cease its repeated suggestions.

Vegetation whispered behind him as she approached. Her warm presence drew alongside his, her fragile hands twisting the water from her short hair.

"We leave now." His voice had emerged rougher than intended, but damn it, how much could a man take? Seeking distraction, he said, "We're too long delayed to catch up to the others, so we shall head for their destination—Harlech Castle." He thought her suggestion from last night a wise one: the more they talked, the sooner they'd understand each other's dialect.

At their camp, he retrieved the rest of their belongings and confiscated two hides—they'd need them.

While he'd waited out her fever, in between his awkward ministrations and checking traps, he'd collected green branches, extracted their supple fibers, and braided several lengths of rope. He used these now to lash his trunk more securely to the back of his rouncey. Her woolen sack, he attached again to his baggage.

Curse it. He'd been so focused on ensuring her health, and their safety, he'd left inspecting its contents until last eve.

The hardened campaigner within had argued it was within his rights, for his own protection, to inspect her sack and mayhap discover her mysterious origins. Was she a threat to his king? But as he'd looked at her, he found it difficult to believe he, or his king, needed protection from her. And then her awakening had forestalled him. He *would* unravel her mystery.

Chapter Twelve

❧

When I arose on the morrow, I found ready saddled a dark-bay palfrey, with nostrils as red as scarlet. And after putting on my armour, and leaving there my blessing, I returned to my own Court. And that horse I still possess, and he is in the stable yonder. And I declare that I would not part with him for the best palfrey in the Island of Britain.
The Mabinogion, an ancient Welsh romance

ROBERT CLEARED HIS THROAT, unused to talking when no need existed. "This is my horse, Perceval. I've had him for nigh on ten years now, ever since I won him at a tournament." He motioned for Kaytee to approach and handed her one of the hides.

She stepped forward, her fresh, clean scent firing his blood. Ignoring temptation, he swung onto the saddle, took the hide and bunched it over the pommel, lifted and settled her atop the hide. Reins in hand, he urged his mount downslope to the river. "We will follow this north to the pass."

As the horse picked his way downward, their bodies, by necessity, swayed and touched, and Robert grit his teeth while his mind sought distraction. "Perceval. My horse. I won him, you know. Oh yes, I've said as much."

"Yes?" though it seemed as if she expressed a wish to tell her more.

"It was my last tournament, the famous Round Table in Nefyn held by our king to celebrate his victory over Wales. Some victory, it seems."

"Round Table?" She repeated the phrase as if trying out the sounds. With a slight intake of breath, she pronounced it in her strange way of speaking the French tongue. She shifted and peeked up at him, her face puzzled. "Round Table? King Arthur?"

"Yes. Smart King Edward was to appropriate a native Welsh hero,

95

who was no Norman." A pang of nostalgia gripped him as he thought of the tales and legends he'd read as a youth, and his former blind faith in its ideals. "You've not heard of this tournament?"

Taking her silence as indication she still didn't fully understand him, he continued, "It was held at Nefyn in Gwynedd, the heart of northern Wales. Quite a statement, and quite audacious." Peculiar it was, to be explaining the obvious. However, even if she understood his speech, he must make allowances, for her origins were still a mystery. Besides, he needed to keep talking, and this was as good a topic as any. By now they'd reached the river, and he turned northward.

"Welsh legends say King Arthur was a Welsh king who fought and expelled the invading Saxons, so for King Edward—a foreigner—to wear the mantle of a Welsh folk hero who fought an invading force..."

Robert trailed off as his own words registered. He'd never thought of the king's actions in such a light. "In any event, I entered the lists against another knight, kept my seat, and broke my three lances and unseated my opponent. Won his armor and this horse. Sold the armor, but kept Perceval."

This was met with silence, and at first he was discomfited, but then he realized he was only talking for talking's sake in hopes she'd learn his tongue. He couldn't expect a reaction. Finding this oddly freeing, he continued as if she'd asked him to elaborate.

"Of course, I wish this hadn't been my last tournament. Whilst Edward has brought them back into favor, the Church still frowns on them. I have no doubt he will resume them once this rebellion ends. A skilled knight may expect to gain much in the way of prize money despite the risks."

Ever since he'd been made a knight in his eighteenth year, he'd participated in any tournament he could afford, legal or not. He'd performed well in each, always trading out his equipment for any better that he'd won.

What he'd earned, along with his shillings as a vassal knight, he kept stored with the Templar bankers in Keele. He anticipated needing the funds to grease the wheels of justice in his suit.

Conversing proved difficult without accompanying responses, without the other taking up the conversation with their own anecdote.

Mayhap he should imagine her responses. For instance, she might inquire as to the nature of the risks.

"There's the expense of the journey and fitting out, which might all be for naught if you lose your armor and horse. Also, it's still not unknown for entrants to lose their life or be severely injured, no matter how much the kings and the Church have worked to civilize it. In my father's day..."

His voice caught on a hitch. How easily he spoke of one whom he'd forsworn. He sat straighter in the saddle and avoided the specifics his mother had told of his father's exploits. "In those times, tournaments were held not in a contained field, but ranged over a countryside and were very much like pitched battles. Sometimes with many left dead on the field."

He halted Perceval and listened sharply. Up ahead was the pass, and another well-worn path joined theirs from the east. With the rocky terrain, it provided a perfect position for an ambush. He silently drew his sword and felt Kaytee take a sharp breath.

"Shhh." He wished he could scout ahead, but he dared not leave her behind. He urged Perceval into an easy walk and watched the path and the curve ahead.

Muscles relaxed and mind clear, ready to react, he passed the bend and witnessed naught but a small coney dart into the scrub, its gray fur but a blur. He sheathed his sword and continued along their trail. At the summit, Kaytee gasped. His muscles tensed, alert, but her foreign words sounded reverent, and her gaze was fixed on the view below. He looked out as well, trying to see the Abergwynant valley through her eyes. But he saw naught but unrelenting hills and valleys they must traverse. He led them down to the zigzagging path into the valley.

By late morning, they'd reached the shores of Afon Mawddach. Their journey had been easier this day as they traversed the valley instead of the mountain paths. They stopped and ate what little food they had. He refilled their flasks of water and resumed their journey northward, crossing the river at a man-made ford near Penmaenpool. He continued talking as he steered them north through a valley toward Diffwys mountain.

When he tired of hearing his own voice, she seemed to sense this, and took up the burden, likely telling stories of her life with awkward pauses and a sense of self-consciousness in the beginning, as it had been for him. She possessed an interesting voice, lower-pitched than most ladies, but oddly comforting.

In the early afternoon, he brought them to a halt. A hafod perched on the eastern slopes of Diffwys, and a nearby stream fed into Lake Llyn Cwm-mynach to the east. They were unlikely to find another ideally placed shelter, and he could use the remaining daylight to set traps for such wildlife that roamed these parts, like the coneys. Besides, he could tell she grew weary of the saddle, and he worried about her weakened condition.

Robert hobbled his horses near some good grazing and shifted their burdens to the hafod's interior.

"We need to set traps as well as hunt tonight, for we ate what little I was able to gather during your illness. In the morning, we will check the traps."

It still felt peculiar speaking of his intentions, but the effort was worth it, for already it appeared she understood more words. He collected the last of the rope and motioned for her to follow.

"Collect sticks like such." He lifted a straight piece and made a show of looking in all directions.

She nodded and fell in beside him, eyes on the ground. He did likewise, remaining alert to their surroundings. After they'd collected a handful each, he inspected the ground until he found a favorable spot, a low-hanging berry bush.

He set to work crafting and bending the sticks and rope in such a way to ensnare any passing coneys. "Collect berries from here and upward only." He directed her with his hand, indicating his wishes by plucking some himself. He sprinkled them on the ground leading to the trap, and the rest he dumped in the hood of her mantle.

She giggled, and he tipped his head. What was so amusing?

She shrugged, made exaggerated marching movements, and motioned to her hood. Still unsure why that was amusing, he nonetheless smiled, glad she could find humor in the situation. Lucky they were that it was still early October, not late winter, or their prospects would indeed be grim.

She stopped her antics and stared, her gaze seeming to penetrate some place deep within. What had he done? She pointed to her mouth and smiled.

Huh. So he'd smiled. What of it? He frowned and left her to collect more berries, whilst he did likewise, their hands, at times, accidentally colliding when dropping berries into her hood.

Hood full of fall berries, they constructed two more traps and worked their way back to the hafod, collecting more berries on their way. He stooped when he saw a longish branch that, if shaped, would have a good weight and length for a spear. They were in the middle of a drought, so he didn't hold out hope for bigger game, but it was worth pursuing. And, in truth, he had no wish to dull his sword when a makeshift spear would do.

At the hafod, he whittled it with his eating knife and, when satisfied, he stood and made several practice throws. He made some adjustments and turned to Kaytee, who was sitting on a rock overlooking the valley below.

"I wish I could leave you here, but it's not safe." He lifted his spear. "We must hunt."

❧

KATY TURNED AT THE SOUND of Robert's voice. She replayed his words, studying the tones and lilts. When he spoke directly to her—as opposed to his monologues—the gist came across more and more. Coupled with what he now held, it wasn't difficult to parse.

He was hunting with that spear? A reply sat ready on her tongue, using the shifted vowels and consonants she thought she'd gotten a handle on, but she pressed her lips flat. As always, she understood a new dialect before she could speak it.

She nodded and rose to her feet. "Oh, man, I'm sore," she said absentmindedly in English.

Her muscles screamed from riding so long in the saddle. The most she'd ever ridden a horse before was in one-hour stretches on horse trails back home. Plus, riding crammed on top of that saddle—yeah, she'd been grateful for the fur Robert had placed. That saddle was the weirdest she'd ever seen—high curved "walls" in both the front and back, and it was the front wall—the pommel—that she rode astride. Ouch.

He frowned and cocked his head.

She switched to French, but her own dialect. "Sore muscles from riding." She pointed to the horse and stretched her arms wide.

He shook his head and hefted the spear again, gesturing behind, down the mountain slope.

She took a deep breath. "Right-o."

They crept through the brush and around trees until they reached a screen of bushes overlooking a clearing. She couldn't get enough of the view. Below lay a lake nestled amongst the dips and crests of wherever the heck they were in Wales. Robert crouched, motioned for her to do the same, and put his fingers to his lips, which only drew her attention to them. They were fine lips—sculpted and full and berry red nestled in the dark hairs of his beard—no mean, skimpy lips for this knight.

And when he smiled? Her breath had caught, for it had reshaped his stark features into a carefree, almost boyish face. His face didn't appear to smile often, which was a shame. Could she make him smile again? It was obvious he needed more levity in his harsh life.

Gah, what was she doing thinking of his damn lips, his damn smile? She settled beside him and nodded her understanding. Barely visible through the branches, the clearing wasn't much bigger than a family swimming pool, strewn with rocks and browning grasses. On the far side, the forest swallowed the light as it marched down the mountain slope. Would they sit here all afternoon? Would an animal really stroll by for the taking?

No matter, she had waiting-quietly in her skill set from all the hours she spent sitting for long stretches at meetings in case she was called in to interpret. She touched the bump under her mantle, where her bandage hid. She'd need to change it again. She shuddered. So far, she'd been damn lucky. But she also felt like a ball ricocheting inside a pinball machine, battered and flung by others. How much more could she take? She wasn't used to not being in control.

Freed from needing to listen to his speech, she analyzed her options. Stay here in medieval Wales—uh, no. Too chaotic, too...too...raw. Follow along with Robert until they reached Harlech—no choice there, really. But then what? Hopefully the villagers remained there, and she could find the lady possessing her case.

She reviewed the moment when the villager stumbled and dropped her small trunk. Katy used the wait to list every detail about the woman and her clothes, repeating it several times to commit it to memory. The details might be her only chance out of here.

Several hours later, still in their hidden area by the clearing, Katy shifted position again to give her left butt cheek a break and clasped the mantle tighter against the late afternoon chill. Robert shifted too and then froze.

She froze as well, attuned to his movements. She followed the direction of his intent stare. There, near a tree on the opposite side, a hare rooted in the grass.

Slowly, silently, Robert rose, deadly purpose etched in his taut features, taut muscles. He braced his feet and aimed. She held her breath.

The hare must've heard the spear whisking through the air, for it glanced up, muscles bunched. It started forward, but the spear thunked into its hindquarters.

It cried out in pain. Robert drew his knife and broke through the brush. She squeezed her eyes shut. *Sorry. Sorry. Sorry.*

Robert returned, holding the hare by its hind legs, blood draining from a slash at its neck.

Good God. She quickly looked away. Nothing like having to hunt for their food to drive her situation home. Death and life were so inextricably bound in this time. But strangely, this primal action arrowed her down into this moment, with life as it happened, a strange feeling. She trailed mutely behind Robert as they descended to their camp.

Back at the hut, she searched for a distraction—anything—while he did what was required. Because watching that? Not an option. "We need water."

He frowned, and she pronounced it slowly, the way he might inflect it. He nodded, and she grabbed the bucket someone had left. He pulled a hide from the shelter and, with the hare, followed.

They worked their way down the slope, every pebble and stick knuckling her feet through her thin leather soles. Feeling the ground's contours, while initially strange, actually gave her better balance, made her more connected to her surroundings. After about twenty minutes, they reached the swift-flowing stream. She filled the bucket and got to her feet, ready to return.

However, he settled near a rock, laid the hare on its side, and drew his knife.

So he was going to do that here? Made sense to keep the mess away from their camp, but still, she couldn't watch.

The berries. She removed her mantle and poured the berries into her lap. Should she wash them?

She spread the mantle out, dumped the berries on top, and searched the bank for large, container-shaped leaves. She selected several and washed them and the berries, collecting them onto the leaves propped nearby on her mantle.

"What are you doing?"

She looked up at Robert's voice. "Washing them."

He frowned and shook his head. Yeah, it probably was silly out here, but she wasn't ready to rough it that much. She perched on another rock still receiving the late afternoon sun, closed her eyes, and soaked in the sun's warmth, desperate to ignore the sounds he made dressing the hare.

"Katy."

She startled awake. He had a hide bundled, presumably with the meat. She scrambled off the rock and followed him back up the slope, her already aching muscles protesting the climb.

She was embarrassingly short of breath when they reached their camp, and she gratefully collapsed against a rock near their hut.

"I'm going to collect wood for a fire. I will not be far."

Her pulse sped up—she'd understood that.

She nodded and shooed him away with a listless hand, grateful for the privacy to regain her breath. She put a hand to her forehead—it had to be beet red from the exertion.

He returned shortly and made a fire, his movements efficient, practiced. She tore a strip from her tunic for a bandage, boiled it, and hung it to dry near the fire.

He stuck several pieces of meat onto sticks propped over the fire. Soon the air filled with the enticing smell of cooking meat. Her stomach rumbled. Yeah, she'd not be turning that away.

‹∂

ROBERT SHOOK HIS HEAD. Kaytee was agreeable enough to do as she was bid and remain admirably quiet while they awaited game, but her habits were odd, and some bespoke of not only coming from a different culture, but also that she was high-born. Her smooth hands testified as much, but her studious avoidance while he butchered and dressed the hare confirmed his suspicions. Here was someone who had servants to do for her, who lived not in close proximity to such happenings.

He turned the meat and studied her. Clearly, she understood more and more of his speech. His regard caught her attention, and their gazes locked, the sizzling pops from the fat dropping into the fire punctuating the charged air around them.

He swallowed, his mouth dry. "Where are you from?"

For it was time for answers. Answers to explain her presence. Answers to explain his attack of chivalry where she was concerned. Answers to explain why he felt as if the gaping hollowness within ached less when in her presence.

Chapter Thirteen

༄

And Owain took the roebuck, and skinned it, and placed collops of
its flesh upon skewers, around the fire. The rest of the buck he gave
to the lion to devour. While he was doing this, he heard a deep sigh
near him, and a second, and a third. And Owain called out to know
whether the sigh he heard proceeded from a mortal; and he received
answer, that it did.

The Mabinogion, an ancient Welsh romance

AYTEE'S HEAD JERKED BACK to stare at Robert, confirming his
suspicions—she understood him better now.

She dropped her gaze. "Far."

"How far?" His pulse raced at the prospect of getting some answers. Mayhap then the curious hold she had on him would lessen.

"Very far."

He grunted and rotated their meat before the fire. "Does this far
away land perchance have a name?"

She nodded, her curiously cut dark hair falling forward. She mumbled something, but he understood it not.

"What is it?"

She raised her face and beheld him for a moment. She took a
deep breath. "Ahmairica."

He knew of no such place. It must indeed be far. "Where is this
land?"

She squinted at the sky. To his surprise, she pointed toward the
setting sun.

"You are from a region in Ireland?"

She shook her head and waved further west. He'd heard tell of
sailors who'd dared cross the great ocean, like Llywelyn the Great's
uncle, Prince Madoc the Shipbuilder, whom Welsh bards said had
settled in plush lands to the west over 120 years ago. Mayhap she

was a descendant returning to her ancestors' shores? Until now, he'd thought the tales prideful boasts, told around campfires, and grown into folk tales. "How did you journey here?"

She opened her mouth and closed it. She looked down. "I don't know."

Had she been captured in a raid? But then how did she know her strange version of French and the peasant tongue, English? And the bits of stilted Latin.

"How do you come to be so educated?"

"How do you...know I am?"

"You speak several tongues, including Latin. Do you know how to read and write as well?"

He was not in the least surprised by her slow nod. Yes, wherever she hailed from, she was high-born. Which made her appearance in the wilds of Wales, alone with no protector, more curious.

"At the castle, why did you dress as a man?" But how she'd believed those lips could fool any warm-blooded male was beyond him.

She shook her head. "Say that again. Slower."

He repeated his question, and she said it several times. She straightened. "Oh. Seemed safer."

He could understand that. It had been smart to do, for certes. "Why are you alone?"

"It...it couldn't be helped."

He pulled the sticks holding their meat from the fire and set them aside to cool.

She was hiding something, but for the life of him, he couldn't find it in himself to believe the intent evil in nature. And he wondered at that, for his easy trust in her.

In truth, she appeared to have no agenda. If she did, she had not one now, for how could she have contrived to be wounded during the retreat and be saddled with him on a treacherous hike to Harlech Castle?

She couldn't have planned their retreat in the first place. No, she seemed a victim of circumstance.

He tested the meat with his fingers and handed over her share. She took it and bit into it tentatively. Then with more relish.

Something primitive stirred within him at seeing her eat what he'd provided. He cooked the rest of the meat and settled beside her, eating his portion in silence.

He passed her the flagon of water, and his fingers brushed hers. The surprise contact pulled his body to attention.

Instinct made him shift away and lean back on his arms, looking out at the darkening forest. Huh. Another surprise. No, not his attraction, for he was fully aware of her charms long ere now, but that he still had a shred of chivalry lurking in his hide of a knight. No longer was she ill, so his forbearance made no sense, but there it was. She was under his protection, and to violate that would dishonor them both. The thought alone made his stomach curdle like spoiled cream. Others in his position would not forbear, he knew, and at the thought, his hands tightened into fists.

A noisy flock of siskins chattered overhead, a muted yellow mist among the autumn leaves, as he explored this odd sensation. He thought himself devoid of personal honor, a luxury expunged in the harsh realities of a landless knight. The only honor that mattered, the only that he pursued, was familial—the honors of his rightful inheritance, the honor of the king's favor—all of which he'd lost. Lost when his treasonous father sacrificed all for his *personal* honor.

Youthful memories stirred of tales of chivalry—of knights who had the luxury to rescue damsels in distress, of knights who had the luxury to pursue personal honor—which only highlighted how calculated and cold he'd become in the pursuit of his goal.

This, he *felt*. It coated the hollow feeling inside and agitated.

Seeking distraction, he motioned to her. "Practice my tongue. You're improving."

She nodded and spoke some basic sentences and greetings. He corrected her pronunciation when she erred. She was a quick study.

"Tell me a story in my language, not yours." From his surcoat, he extracted a chunk of wood he'd scavenged earlier and began whittling. The shape mattered not—it was the action which soothed.

He watched her eyes and saw her draw inward, mentally gathering herself. Another curiosity—he'd become so used to gleaning meaning from her every expression and movement, he could tell her moods, her thoughts.

She launched into a tale about a cow leaping over the moon, of all things, and some of her words he did not understand. At those times, he stopped her and asked their meaning. Once he understood, he either corrected her pronunciation or her word choice. She would nod, start the sentence again, and continue.

By the time she finished her strange story—the cow befriended a mouse and went on many adventures—it had grown dark. She sighed. "That helped. Thank you."

"You're most welcome." He blew off the last bit of shavings from his carving. A cow. He'd carved a cow.

"I need to see to my...wound again. I think this bandage is dry." She fingered it. "Do you have any soap?"

He nodded and retrieved the small pungent ball of ash and goat tallow from his trunk. She washed her hands and rolled up her sleeve. He sat beside her again and leaned forward to watch, telling himself he was this close to lend assistance, not because he craved her nearness, craved catching an enticing whiff of her scent. All day in the saddle, it had filled his senses and...he missed it.

She ripped another strip from her mantle, wet it with water, and lathered on the soap. She untied the bandage and pulled it away, wincing.

"It appears to be healing well," he ventured.

She poked around the pale, reddened edges and breathed a sigh of relief. "Yes, thank God." She wiped the area with the soap mixture, rinsed it, and looked at him for a moment.

"What do you need me to do?"

"Can you wash your hands and then bind this around the wound?" The glow from the fire highlighted the smooth curve of her cheek.

"Why do you wish me to wash my hands first?"

"I notice you wash your hands before you eat dinner. Same reason. Our hands are dirty."

He shrugged. Always, he had washed his hands because it was polite to do so, but he wouldn't argue with a lady.

When he was done, she held her arm toward him. "Is that also why you boiled this?" He plucked the bandage from where she'd left it drying. "Were you washing it?"

"Yes." She offered a quick smile.

He ignored the close proximity of her body, ignored how he was so close all the fine hairs on her arm were visible, ignored the irrational urge to shift even closer and place his lips at the inside of her elbow.

To touch his tongue there and...*taste* the heat she emitted. He ignored all and securely bound her arm.

"Thank you." Her soft, warm whisper near his ear tightened his cods.

"You are most welcome." His voice was rougher than usual.

"No. I meant, for not abandoning me at the castle. And...and when I was sick." The hesitation in her voice caught his attention, for he sensed it was more than mere confusion with the language this time.

He shifted his gaze to hers—her lip, the side of her jaw so close—and beheld an odd vulnerability and a latent fear. He gave a slow nod. It cut him, as surely as a sharp sword, to know she so readily expected such ill treatment to be surprised at its lack. And hadn't he contemplated it? Did he deserve her thanks?

She pulled in a ragged breath, her exhalation soft against his cheek, her gaze still locked with his. "I just... Thank you."

Yes. She was out of her element, for certes. However, for someone left to her own devices in a strange land, she was handling it rather well. She'd maintained her calm throughout. Admiration filled him, for not many men could say the same.

He returned his attention to her wound and laid his hand on her bandage to indicate he had completed the task. From underneath her moisture-tinged lashes, she watched him, and her breathing quickened. He slid his fingers from the cloth and brushed the bare area just above, watching her closely for any sign that this attraction that swirled and pooled between them was not a figment made large in his mind. Her reactions to his closeness could be mere distress.

His senses were not in error—her eyes darkened, and the air between them thickened with carnal possibility.

He yanked his fingers away and jerked to a stand, his agitated movements kicking a spray of dirt into the dying fire. "We need more kindling." He threw his carving into the fire. "It's time for us to retire." He stomped into the forest, eyes intent on finding more kindling.

Christ on a cross, how was he to lie beside her and not touch her?

Even if he were free to indulge, it could be no more than a dalliance. As a landless knight, he could not marry, and his goal for rectifying that circumstance seemed even further away than it had a fortnight ago.

Frustration—at the delay, and at his sexual desires—lanced through him, roiling within, clouding his judgment. Tomorrow, he must push hard on their march. The sooner they reached Harlech—and his situation secured, and her presence removed—the better.

☙

WHAT HAD JUST HAPPENED? Katy shuddered. Heat still pooled in her lower belly, and the air around her held a latent but powerful charge. Despite the man responsible being now fifteen feet away gathering firewood. This was not good.

Preston, Preston. Remember Preston.

But then she froze. Preston? Her image of him was slightly fuzzy, just a general impression of good humor and a friendly smile. Instead, the sculpted features of a dark-haired knight intruded, a knight who looked as if he hadn't laughed in a good while.

She bowed her head and closed her eyes. Not good. She fingered the lighter shade around her ring finger and tried to pull up the feeling she'd had when Preston had proposed over dinner one night. But couldn't.

She eyed her bag. Oh, how she itched to pry it open, pull out her phone, turn it on, and look at their engagement pictures. She'd been happy, right?

Besides, shacking up with some hot guy clad in chainmail—in the *past*, no less—was *not* part of her ten-year plan. Getting married was. Reliable, steady Preston would never abandon her. Unlike her father. The father who'd skipped out on her eighth birthday when Katy had indulged in some stupid tantrum, allowed herself to lose control of her emotions. A father who had never responded to her letters. Letters she stopped sending when she'd turned seventeen.

When Preston had proposed, relief had lightened her limbs, lightened her heart.

Relief. Cripes.

And the fact that it was easier to think about Robert than Preston... Robert's surprise at her gratitude for not abandoning her...

She scrambled to her feet and snatched her mantle. Before he returned, she should be "asleep" inside the hut. It would make the situation easier.

She made her bed along one side of the wall and burrowed under

109

the thick layer of hide and wool blankets. She shivered and concentrated on breathing. She could hear his movements outside as he stoked the fire and performed other unknown activities.

How many more nights would she have to sleep next to him before they reached Harlech?

☙

BRIGHT MORNING SUN FILTERED through the canopy of overarching trees, bathing their trail in dappled light. Birds Katy couldn't name chirped overhead, providing the only sound other than the steady clop of their horses and the creak of the saddle that propped up her aching butt. They'd been in the saddle already for two hours at least.

"Robert!" She pointed at a horizon smudged dark with smoke that had come into view as they rounded a bend. Unease tightened her stomach. He reined in the horse, which danced sideways, head jouncing up and down as it settled.

His hand reached around her waist and gripped his hilt. She moved to the side, giving him room as he drew his sword.

"That much smoke bespeaks of the destruction of something large." He paused, eyes narrowing in concentration, and then widening. "The abbey."

With a decisive kick, he spurred his horse forward, following the curve of the slope westward, and panic seized her. Was he going to race into a dangerous situation with only his sword? And with her death-grip-clinging to the weird pommel? "Robert, wait!"

But along the slope, directly above the smoke, he kicked his legs from the stirrup, swung to the ground, and sprinted forward. She slid down, much less gracefully, and followed as he crouched behind a stand of alder buckthorn. Below them lay a valley of unrelenting tree tops in a palette of early fall golds, oranges, and browns. A river bisected the expanse, and a cleared area hugged the bank, roughly circular in shape. In the center stood a stone church with a longer building running perpendicular to it and a hodge podge of smaller stone buildings huddled close. Black smoke streamed from every building, along with gouts of flames.

Chapter Fourteen

Bendigeid Vran, the son of Llyr was the crowned king of this Island,
and he was exalted from the crown of London. And one afternoon
he was at Harlech in Ardudwy, at his court, and he sat upon the
rock of Harlech, looking over the sea.
The Mabinogion, an ancient Welsh romance

KATY'S HEART BEAT IN TIME with the plumes of flames and
smoke which throbbed and raced through the complex below.

"I see only monks." Robert's voice was flat, perfunctory near her
ear. "Do you see aught else?"

"Nothing, just men in white robes."

He surveyed the valley for a few minutes more. His features were
as flat and impassive as his voice had been, but his eyes tightened
subtly, his jaw and shoulders a bit tenser. He stood and whistled for
Perceval.

She got to her feet and wiped the dirt from her mantle. "You're
angry. What do you suspect?"

"Something I would rather not contemplate. I pray it is from an
accident, a careless monk with an oil lamp, but if not..."

"You think someone did this on purpose?"

"The Marcher lords," he spat. "For that is an old Welsh monastery
that supported the Welsh princes in years past." He removed the lead
to the packhorse from Perceval and swung up onto Perceval. "Let us
see if we can lend assistance." His strong hands gripped her hips and
raised her onto his lap.

"What about your other horse?"

"She knows to follow."

Robert eased the horse down the hill. Little was visible through
the thickness of the trees and scrub, but as they drew near, shouts

111

echoed, and the smell of burning wood assaulted her nose.

They cleared the dense forest, and Robert spurred his horse into a canter on the approach to the monastery.

A weird sense of loss flooded Katy, watching the flames chew through the complex. Before her stood a once proud testament to medieval masonry and faith, a site in her time that would be cordoned off and preserved for its architecture alone. Now it was completely engulfed in flames. What treasures were lost today? Did historians in her own time bemoan this very fire?

Three white-clad monks burst from the nearest building and collapsed onto their knees, hands clasped, tonsured heads bowed, repeating words over and over, inaudible from their distance.

Robert reined in his horse, dirt and pebbles flying. One monk shakily stood, the ring of red hair around his head nearly the same hue as his flushed face. He waved at the burning complex, hands expressive, and then vaguely to the east, all while speaking way too fast. Besides, it sounded vaguely like Welsh.

Robert spoke in reply, voice authoritative but calm. He spoke Welsh?

"It is as I feared," he muttered. "Lord Powys's men raided this place. I convinced them I was not a member of that cursed party, that we mean to help. See to the injured, and I will assist with the last of the fire."

Her breath caught. "The injured? From the flames?"

He cocked his head. "No, from sword thrusts."

Her gut twisted in horror. "What? Those raiders attacked defenseless monks?"

"It grieves me to admit that is so." He leaped to the ground and helped her down. He hobbled his horse and sprinted inside with the lead monk. By then, the packhorse had ambled up and set to grazing near Perceval. Two monks waited patiently, their faces smeared with soot.

She approached. "I am Ka-Kay, how may I help?" she asked in the French dialect she'd learned with Robert, hoping they understood. She made sure to lower her voice and keep her hood up.

They bowed. "I am Brother Owain," spoke the leaner of the two, a scar marring an otherwise soft-featured face, "and this is Brother

Cadfael. Follow us please."

Whew, they spoke Robert's French. They hustled along, their soft steps pattering against the stone walkways of the burning complex. Smoke clogged the air, which thickened with the aggressive heat of the spreading fire to the right, where precious glass tinkled to the ground from a bursting window. Sharp, static orders punctuated the roar and whoosh of the fire as Robert and the monks shouted instructions and concentrated their energy on containing its spread and dousing what they could. Flecks of ash jerked and spun through the air, settling in her hair and clothes. She covered her nose and mouth with her mantle and steeled herself for what she might see. She tried not to gape at seeing an honest-to-God-real medieval monastery. On fire.

In the damage-free great hall, fires blazed in every fireplace and brazier, making the interior stifling in its heat.

She stopped. Two body-shaped sheets stained with blood lay on the stone floor. "Oh."

Brother Cadfael's face was unreadable. "The raiders began stealing the gold and silverplate, and these two brothers confronted the unholy bastards. Brother Morgan fought the one who took our only relic, the knuckle of John the Baptist. The whoreson of a Marcher ran him through with his sword. He was dead before he hit the ground."

"Good God!" She gripped her stomach, horror washing her in chills and a sick churning in her gut. The monks stared, confusion clear on their exhausted faces. Oops, she'd spoken English.

She swallowed. "What can I do?"

"If you could make the injured drink our healing brew, that would be one less burden. We patched them the best we could. Only one suffers from a grievous injury, the rest are minor."

"Of course. Show me."

Brother Cadfael introduced her to a stoop-shouldered monk by one of the hearth fires. They ladled their concoction into a wooden bowl, steam curling into the air, redolent of grassy and fragrant herbs. As soon as the brew cooled, she knelt by the first monk, whose face was sickly pale in the flickering firelight. A blood-soaked bandage was tied around his arm, his face and neck smeared with blood and soot.

Sweat plastered his black hair to his forehead.

She put a supporting arm behind his back and helped him rise. "Here, drink as much as you can."

He took several gulps and turned his head away on a gasp. She eased him down and moved to the next. In all, there were six, and when she finished and returned to the hearth, the first patient was dozing—something must have been in the drink to put them to sleep.

"May I make..." and here she struggled with how to express the word *sterile*. Brother Cadfael seemed curious once she explained her purpose of making sterile bandages, not at all reacting in a fearful or dismissive manner. Instead, as she boiled water and gathered the cloth she'd need, he asked smart, probing questions and pitched in.

Huh. Not how she expected a medieval monk to react to a woman's knowledge. Except...she wasn't a woman in their eyes—they'd accepted her as Robert's squire.

But it might not have mattered. They were Welsh, and during her stay in Caernarfon with her friends, she'd learned that historically, the Welsh hadn't had the same prejudices against women as their Norman counterparts. And the Normans believed the Welsh were uncivilized and needed to be brought into the light and refinement of Norman law and customs?

Another glaring difference—these monks swore like sailors stubbing their toes, even in French.

While their new bandages dried, she prepared two bowls—one with soapy water, another plain—grabbed a clean cloth, and sat cross-legged by the first injured monk. She dipped the cloth in the soapy water, wrung out the excess, and bathed his face and neck. It didn't help the wound, but she hoped her ministrations comforted him. She washed his arms and hands too, and moved to the next monk.

She was on the second to last monk, when footsteps scraped at the door. Robert strode in, the afternoon light behind throwing his features into shadow until he penetrated deeper into the hall.

Soot streaked the hard planes of his face, and his mouth was set in hard lines. His gaze was flat. Emotionless. Like the old Robert.

She shivered, stood, and intercepted him. "Did you put out the fires?"

"Yes, though we failed to save the library and records. All sodden ashes now. What about here?"

God, what a waste. She related how the monks were injured and killed and studied his face for his reaction.

His eyes remained flat. Flat like when they'd first met, with none of the fledgling depths she'd witnessed in the last couple of days. Anger boiled within her, surprising her. When she'd initially heard the horrors, she'd been too overwhelmed to react. Out of necessity, she'd shoved down her emotions and pitched in with what needed to be done. But reciting it now, with no reaction from him, irrationally flipped something inside.

"What? Nothing to say?"

"What is there to say?"

"Doesn't this upset you?"

He shrugged. *Shrugged.* "Death and violence are part of life."

She opened her mouth, but his jaw tightened a fraction, betraying his studied complacency. And really, she *was* in a time and place where such violence existed. She didn't have to like it—God, she couldn't get back to her own time fast enough. Sure, her time had death and violence, but it wasn't like *this.* At least in her sheltered part of the world.

But wasn't she only kidding herself about the realities of her world, a result of her privilege? Brutality existed in war-torn areas, as well as life and death struggles in poor neighborhoods. She wasn't wholly immune there either.

He studied her, eyes dark and penetrating. "But," he said, the word drawn out as realization dawned, "it is not part of yours, is it?"

She took a deep breath, fighting back tears. "No." She spun away. "In fact, I..." *Whoa.* She'd almost said 'I *work* to find diplomatic solutions.' "I don't believe in violence," she finished lamely.

"A strange land you come from to afford such a luxury."

She gaped. It was a luxury, and she'd never thought of it that way. Her anger shifted to the rightful target—the perpetrators. She took his arm, steered him to a bench, and pushed him down. She fetched the bowls and washed his face too, the action taking her mind off what she'd seen and heard.

"Thank you," he murmured, his voice a low rumble in the space between them.

When she finished, she settled beside him, grateful for his strong, familiar presence in the midst of this chaos. "Why did Lord Powys's men do this?"

"Drunk, Brother Gruffudd said, but animosity has long lingered between them."

"Being drunk is no excuse."

"No, it is not." He raked a hand through his hair. "It only allowed them to act out their true nature."

"Does this happen a lot?"

"Not that I am aware of. I have heard tales from earlier Welsh wars, but never knew which were true or mere stories." A minute or two passed in silence. "Enough of this," he growled. He shot to his feet and strode to the nearest monks, speaking to them in a low voice. She followed, and he faced her. "My assistance is needed with their cleanup efforts. They wish the chapel serviceable by vespers."

"Uh, when is that?"

Confusion marred his forehead. "You are unfamiliar with the term? I'm not sure how to say it in your tongue. But it's the bell that's rung at sunset."

She nodded, breath held. She probably should've known that as a medieval-y person. Thank God for the language barrier excuse.

"I will seek you out ere then. The brothers invited us to break our journey here for the evening."

"See you then." She retrieved her bowls and washed the last two patients. By then it was time to change the bandages, and she assisted the monks in cleaning and dressing the wounds.

Would things ever slow down for her enough to catch her breath and make sense of things? Always, she felt like a barely concealed impostor.

☙

"HAVE WE ANY MORE MASLIN BREAD?" Robert's deep gravelly voice asked by her ear, his breath lightly brushing her neck.

Could she please reach a point where that voice didn't spread warmth through her whole body? Earlier that morning, they'd left the abbey behind, the grateful monks stocking them with plenty of food and watered wine. She'd even received a fresh change of both men and women's clothes. They were musty, left behind in a trunk by a visiting lord and his lady, but no way would she complain.

Katy stopped relating yet another story as they wended their way along the mountain trail. By the sun, which—so weird—was their only means of knowing both direction and time, they headed steadily west through the Cwm Nantcol valley. To practice her Norman French, she'd worked through much of the Brothers Grimm, unwilling to share stories of her own past in case she slipped and revealed too much. She fished in the cloth pouch hanging by her side and held up a hunk of bread.

He leaned forward in the saddle, his warm, solid chest brushing her back, his hand outstretched. He tensed, and his strong hand gripped hers, the bread crushing in their clasped hands.

"Quickly. Dismount!"

He'd get no argument from her. She slipped off, and he landed beside her. He eased his sword whisper-quiet from its sheath and guided their horses through a screen of bushes upslope, his hand a solid weight against the small of her back. She heard it now too— voices and the clatter of hooves. But she didn't dare rush faster than he urged, afraid of making too much noise. They broke through the scrub and maneuvered the horses onto the ground. They'd just coaxed the packhorse to settle when the first colorful shape came around the bend below, from the opposite direction. She quickly ducked out of sight alongside Robert.

Katy held still, fear stealing her breath. Welsh, most likely, or Robert would not still be gripping his sword, watching intently.

Two more joined the first, all barelegged and sporting short, bright red tunics. One gripped a spear across his saddle and held a bright blue, round shield. The other two had bows strapped to their backs. Their voices were lilting, dipping and curling along the mountain trail, one teasing another and tossing a wine skin to the third, who caught it deftly from his saddle.

To her amazement, they passed out of sight. She pulled in a deep breath and was horrified to discover her whole body shook. She gripped her arms and looked to Robert. He shook his head. Minutes passed and finally he rumbled, "Good, lass."

"We're safe?"

"Yes, we can resume our journey. These parts are seldom traversed, so it is unlikely we will run across another party today."

"So they weren't Norman?"

"No. Welsh." He rose to his feet and helped her stand. Once back on the trail, he reattached the packhorse, and they remounted Perceval. As Robert urged his horse along the path, Katy eased backward until she settled against his broad chest. She inhaled his now-familiar masculine scent. Not because she was a wilting female and needed some hunk of a man's comfort. Okay, well, a tiny bit. But mainly because they'd shared a tense moment. A moment that pulled her to connect with him physically. Even if it was in such a small way.

He stiffened, and her stomach dipped—would he reject her? Finally, he relaxed, wrapped an arm around her waist, and cinched her tighter against him. Warmth and security flooded her. God, it was nice to be able to reach out...and not explain what she needed.

After a while, she broached a topic she'd wondered about. "Why haven't we come across any towns or villages? Besides the abbey and those Welsh, we've seen not a soul."

"This is a sparsely populated area, and what villages and towns exist are Norman, built next to our new castles. The Welsh typically live in scattered farms, having lost their own castles to Edward."

They continued through the rest of the morning, neither desiring to talk. By noon, after having edged along the western slopes of yet another mountain range and crossing a large river, Robert had them dismount. They trudged upslope a ways more, and he hobbled his horses at the summit of the rise.

"Harlech is near. Before we ride up to its gates, I think it wise we scout the approach, given the circumstances." He patted Perceval's flank. "And given the presence and ease of those Welsh earlier."

"What are you wanting to check?"

"If the Welsh would besiege as obscure a royal outpost as Castell y Bere, they could very well do likewise for such a strategic royal stronghold as Harlech."

Katy's stomach curdled. All of her focus had been on reaching Harlech, so she could find that case and be done with it. Done with friggin' medieval Wales. And now her goal—her carefully organized mental timeline of how this would play out—could be screwed up?

No. The castle *had* to be fine, and the villagers *had* to be there.

At the top of the incline, Robert stuck to the thickly packed trees. Below, the forest spread in rolling dips and bumps until it bled into a cleared green swath surrounding a rocky promontory. Atop, squatted a roughly square gray-stone castle with rounded towers at each corner. Tiny wisps of color flickered all around the top—pennants, she'd guess. A murky green sea painted the backdrop.

"We approached from the southeast to maintain height and cover for as long as possible, instead of taking the shore route." He crouched behind an alder. "And well we did. They are here." He pointed down to the castle's battlements.

She knelt beside him, steadied herself with a hand to the tree, and squinted. She could make out darker shapes, some stationary, some in motion. "The Welsh?"

"Aye. They are besieging Harlech. By the looks of it, they have for some time. Probably at the same time as Bere. This is not a random uprising. This is well-planned."

The tour guide at the church said in 1294... "Madog," she whispered, her hand slipping down the rough bark, biting her palm.

His head whipped around. "How do you know of this?" His dark eyes narrowed.

She swallowed in a suddenly dry throat. Shit. "I heard that name mentioned at the castle. Alfred told me," she lied.

"Hmph." He rubbed a hand over his trim beard. "Madog ap Llywelyn it is." Something flickered across his features.

He knows him.

"Mayhap I do," he grunted.

She hadn't realized she'd spoken aloud. His jaw tightened. "We cannot proceed to Harlech in any case." He pushed against the tree and stood.

Panic threatened to sizzle through her blood, but she forced it down, instead willing a sense of calm over herself, helping her detach. But damn, it was proving harder and harder to maintain control. She got to her feet. She'd find a solution if she remained calm; things only got worse when she got emotional. "But what about the others?

Weren't they headed here?"

"That was the intention. But if this siege indeed began at the same time as ours, our men would not have proceeded. Their party, with more villagers than men-at-arms, would have been too small to lift the siege. Too risky."

She ruthlessly suppressed her panic again. "Are you certain?"

"Aye."

"Robert. It is extremely important to me that you are."

"Why?"

"Because I must reunite with those villagers."

Robert removed his helmet and let it hang from its belt chain. "Why?"

She thumped back against the tree trunk. "It has to do with why I'm here."

He stepped forward so abruptly, she bonked her head against the rough bark. His mailed hand closed around her neck, pinning her to the tree. "Are you a spy?"

Shock coursed through her at his abrupt change in behavior. And then his question registered, and her knees nearly gave way.

Chapter Fifteen

⁓

Then began Manawyddan and Rhiannon to sit and to talk together,
and from their discourse his mind and his thoughts became warmed
towards her, and he thought in his heart he had never beheld any lady
more fulfilled of grace and beauty than she.
The Mabinogion, an ancient Welsh romance

ROBERT STARED INTO KAYTEE'S richly textured eyes, a field of
green flecked with rich brown, like the exotic spice cinnamon. She was exotic too, a spice. A rare spice. He pinned her to the
tree with only the cage of his hand. He did not squeeze—he had no
wish to mar such a beautiful throat. But he did need to scare her. A
little. She was too calm.

His question—*are you a spy?*—echoed in accusation around the
forest.

Her eyes widened. Good.

Jolting her out of her complacency could help him get at the
truth. Her truth. Had she truly heard Madog's name from Alfred?

"No," she whispered.

He tilted his head and studied her features, the openness of her
eyes, the set of those shapely lips. Dealing with men-at-arms under
his command and unruly villeins made him sufficiently competent in
detecting falsehood. None existed in that statement.

Very well. But she was hiding something—the sure knowledge an
itch under his skin. But if her secret wasn't a danger to him, or to his
king, he could afford the time to coax it out of her, cultivate her trust.
For he *would* know her secrets. Secrets were valuable. Especially if
such secrets benefited the English crown, and thus himself.

Then an itch of a different sort tightened his skin and made his
blood pound. She was breathing heavily through her nose, obviously
struggling to regain her calm, but her chest rose and fell in the small

121

space between. If he stepped forward, just an inch, those lovely breasts would be pressing against him.

He stepped forward.

And...Christ, yes.

The pulse visible in the pale column of her neck vibrated faster, her intoxicating scent washed over him, and he was dizzy with lust.

Even through his mail and gambeson, he could feel her womanly curves crushed against his hard chest. He uncurled his fingers from her throat and ran the tough leather of his palm's mitten along her neck and to the enticing curve of her shoulder. He nudged her mantle an inch, exposing skin.

He cursed that his hand was covered in mail. How long had he wanted to taste, to touch her precious skin? Unable to resist, he bent and, with his tongue, touched, tasted the heat of the skin on her collarbone.

Oh, Christ, she was lovely. She shivered, and satisfaction roared through him. He dragged his lips up the soft skin of her neck and gently nipped her ear lobe, sipping on the soft flesh. Her hands splayed against his chest.

Expecting a shove, his senses careened when her fingers fisted his surcoat. Their ragged breath overloud in the forest, he eased his face away, nose rubbing against her jaw on his retreat, and sought her eyes. Hers darkened and—Lord help him—held no censure, only interest.

He stepped back.

Curse his newly recovered scruples. Why did she have to excite him physically *and* dredge up his long-dead chivalry? He dropped his hand, and her fingers loosened from his surcoat. He turned to glower at the approach to Harlech and slowly flexed his fingers.

Behind him, cloth rustled, and she cleared her throat. "So you're, ah, you're certain they're not there."

He smiled—her back was no doubt straight, her chin raised. So strong. The certainty must be of grave importance to her, if she risked his ire to ask again. He studied the encampment. His eyes had always been sharp. The temporary shelters dotting the area could be the work of one night, but not the trampled paths. They bespoke of a longer stay, as did the placement of troops. Absent also was the frenetic pace of a new encampment. No. They'd been here for at least a sennight and were entrenched.

He took a deep breath and faced her. "Yes. I am certain." His gaze lingered on the graceful curve of her neck and shoulders, and so he witnessed when her tension eased. The knowledge that she believed him, trusted him on something obviously important to her, warmed his insides. Only a slight pinkening of her cheeks belied their near... whatever that had been. Temporary madness?

"Where would they go instead?"

He cleared his throat. "To Wrexham, mayhap. Closer to the English border, for certes. We head there, and we can ascertain their whereabouts. I daresay the king's castles along the interior have all been compromised. If Wrexham has no answers, we can head north to Chester or Flint. One of those has to be their destination."

She stood straighter. "Wrexham it is."

ა

BY EVENING, KATY'S MUSCLES ached. And all the tinier muscles attached to them. And her sinews. They were different from muscles, right? Anyway, they were exhausted too, all having called it quits to leave her an aching puddle in Robert's mailed arms. Arms that had caged her so thoroughly and erotically against that tree earlier. Heat speared through her every time she allowed herself to think about it. And every time, she squashed the heat just as quickly.

They had still not come across another hut and so had pushed on, after having retraced their path through the Cwm Nantcol valley and passing the abbey. When she started nodding off in the saddle, a couple of hours after sunset, he directed Perceval behind a clump of trees near a large river.

"What are we doing?"

"We cannot go farther, and our luck has run out, apparently, on coming across hafods. We will make camp here."

He jumped down and held out his hands.

Grateful for the help, she leaned forward and put her weight on him. He eased her down, and she stumbled on numbed legs into his chest.

"Sorry," she mumbled, the green surcoat stretched across his mail filling her vision.

"You are tired." His voice rumbled near her ear, making all her tired, aching muscles grow even mushier.

"Yes," she whispered. *Get a grip on yourself.*

"I regret we had to push on, but I am eager to reach our destination. We have two long days of riding ahead of us."

"I understand." She turned away from that chest and his temptation and began gathering kindling.

"We cannot risk fire. Too dangerous. Presumably we are well past the rebellious region, but I'd rather not risk it in this open terrain."

Crap. She briskly rubbed her upper arms. Of course.

Robert collected long, stout branches and constructed a lean-to, using a low-hanging tree branch as the roof beam. He spread their hides and a blanket over this structure so the opening faced the river. Oh, did it look cozy. Amazing how quickly she'd become accustomed to smelly hides. If only Traci could see her now.

Her breath hitched. Traci.

Her life, her friends.

She'd immersed herself so fully with day-to-day survival it had pushed aside thoughts of her old life. A laugh almost escaped her.

Yeah, if Traci could see her now, her jaw would be permanently affixed to the floor. Days passed without her day planner...without her phone...without planning out the details of her day.

She'd hardly be recognizable.

Together they set up their camp. Working side by side—his efficient movements and their silent, synchronized setup, their easy partnership—struck her as different. Different from her usual method of organizing and focusing on the small details. They silently spread more blankets over a bed of leaves and moss. When they'd first set out after her sickness, she'd fretted at not being able to make lists, nearly tore her hair out trying to stay calm and not lose control. But now, she'd begun to relax into the feeling of partnership.

She probed at her sense of ease, the respect she felt. Attraction, that was easy to explain—hello, hot medieval warrior being all muscley and stuff mere inches away. But the respect?

Realization flooded her. The respect they shared was precisely because Robert didn't *need* her direction. And, wow, she'd never respected Preston. Because he hadn't been involved enough to stand at her side as her equal partner. He'd left all the decisions and details to her. And it had become exhausting.

Shit. What a thing to realize about your possible future husband. Was this what Traci meant about their relationship appearing "uneven"? But she was culpable in that too—her need to make sure everything was perfect had left little room for him to step up and take equal ownership in the relationship. Hence that stupid call from the groomswear place.

Robert stashed their belongings inside their makeshift dwelling and returned with the wine skin and several hunks of leftover cooked rabbit. At least they had food.

He handed her a strip of the meat. She dusted it off and sniffed it. She could feel his curious stare, so she took a bite and chewed. Mouth dry, she signaled for the wine. He passed it over, and she washed down the meat with a gulp.

She managed another bite and pictured a nice blazing fire before her, shifting and popping. This could simply be a camping trip in her own time, where they were roughing it a little more than usual. Yes. A night just like that. With the barely visible river gurgling before them.

Robert ate his last bite, licked his fingers, and drew his sword.

Well, except for the sword. And the fact that he wore a surcoat and chainmail. Yeah, other than that. And the fact that enemy Welsh could be out there in the dark.

She swallowed more wine, marveling at her low panic level. Low, despite the circumstances. She was grubby. She didn't know what the heck to do. She was alone with a gorgeous, muscular knight in the middle of friggin' medieval Wales, and she'd been shot with an arrow.

Yeah, *pffft*. All quite normal for a time-traveling gal. A choked laugh bubbled up, and she covered it with a cough.

Grubby she could take care of. "Could we get some more water?"

"Certainly."

She also felt some kinship—a smidgeon—with Isabelle. Had this been close to what she'd experienced? Constantly amazed at how different, and in some ways how similar, everything was?

Their day's journey had brought them into a valley dominated by a large river, Afon Lliw, Robert said. So they soon had the bucket from the last shelter filled and back at the camp. Too bad she couldn't heat it.

He untied his sword belt, placed it on the ground, and sat, cleaning and sharpening the blade's edge with sand and a stone he had in his trunk.

"That's an unusual..." She didn't know the word in modern French, so she gestured.

He glanced at her and then to where she indicated. "Scabbard? My lady mother crafted it for me."

"May I see it?"

He nodded and placed it in her hands. It was heavier than she imagined, but when had she ever given serious thought about the weight of a scabbard? She angled it to catch the weak glow from the half moon and traced a finger along the stamped leather markings, an intricate pattern of swirls, knots, circles. A green stone graced the top.

"This looks Celtic."

"Celtic?"

"The, er, people who lived here before the Romans."

"Ah, yes, Celticus in Latin. She is Welsh. No doubt it has some meaning to her people."

"*Her* people. But that means you're half-Welsh too, right?"

⁂

AT KAYTEE'S WORDS, ROBERT STIFFENED, waiting for the usual recriminations. Yes, he was half Welsh. But he was also half Norman. But only a genuine curiosity suffused her face, no malice in her expression or intent.

"I don't consider them my people," he confessed.

"Why not?"

"For one, I haven't beheld my lady mother since my tenth year. Have only vague memories of her kin."

"I'm sorry. Losing your mother so young must have been hard."

He ran his sharpening stone carefully down his blade once, twice. "She's not dead."

"So, if she's still alive, why haven't you seen her since then?"

He frowned, but he supposed it was normal for a fosterling to see their parents from time to time. He'd had no such desire. "Too busy, I suppose."

"Since you were *ten?*"

"Indeed, that is the time I was fostered to Sir Hugh."

"She gave you up for adoption?" A trace of horror threaded her melodic voice, which puzzled him.

He set down his tools. "Adoption? No. But ten is the normal age to begin training for knighthood. Some begin at seven. Do your countrymen not send their youth to those who can teach them, whether as warrior, clerk, or priest? Or if of lower birth, to learn their craft or trade?"

"At *ten?*"

No, then. "I served as page to Sir Hugh learning my letters and duties, as well as training in the skills of warfare."

"That young?"

"Of a certainty. One cannot become a knight and fight in a battle with honor if one hasn't become accustomed to the feel of his own bones crunching from a blow, seen his own blood flow."

"Good Lord." She stared at him, then shook her head, her puzzlement clear. She gazed into the gloaming, seemingly lost in thought. He let the silence settle around him, content to rest.

Abruptly, she stood. "I'm sorry. I wouldn't be able to get used to living in a place like this. I'm going to bathe."

Her last sentence was spoken with defiance, as if he might object, but he could see no reason to stop her. Except it shot an erotic image straight into his head, and blood rushed to his groin. He nodded, ignoring his body's reaction.

Hmmm. A bath. Not since the last night at the castle had he availed himself. He lifted his arm and sniffed. Too long in a ripe state would make the metal links of his mail stink worse than Lucifer's sulfurous big toe. He could not wait to reach Wrexham and be able to dunk his mail in a barrel of vinegar and sand, give it a good roll to get it clean.

Seeking a distraction, he collected more vines and concentrated on making rope. He was *not* hearing her soft splashes and imagining what her hands were doing on her body. The curves and soft flesh...

her fingers curling under a luscious breast. He twisted a piece of vine too tightly, and it snapped.

God's blood. *Over, around, under, and tighten*—he concentrated on his task, whipping each vine around, the methodical movement gradually calming.

Some time later, she emerged, face and skin glowing in the half moon, and he found he'd not succeeded in taming his cock. She brought the bucket to the clearing and sat. He scrambled to his feet, snatched the soap and bucket, and retreated to the far side of the lean-to, close enough to ensure her safety, but far enough to satisfy his needs. He could not crawl into their shelter hard as Saint Peter's rock.

He deftly removed his surcoat, hauberk, and chausses and leaned his arm against the tree trunk, his breath ragged, his cock pushing painfully against the rough linen of his braies. He whipped them off, and his hard length jutted into the cool night air. Groaning at the touch of his hand to the sensitive flesh, he fisted it and, with quick, efficient jerks, soon jetted his seed into the darkness.

He stood a moment longer, gulping in air, and then removed the rest of his clothing. Christ. That had barely taken the edge off. He grabbed the soap and scrubbed the grime of several days on the road from his body, glad of the water's bracing cold. Ridding himself of the accumulated dirt felt like a needed purging, as necessary as the purging of his seed.

He donned his braies and linen shirt and stepped back into the clearing. Her blushing face and averted gaze served as further proof she was a sheltered, high-born lass. What other kind was so secluded as to be unused to hearing a man taking care of his needs, either by himself or with another?

Or perhaps she followed the strictures of the church regarding taking pleasure into your own hands. An odd wash of guilt swept over him for his crudeness, but he dismissed it. The responsibility for her situation was hers, not his, and he'd feel no shame for tending to his needs.

As her gaze sought a subject, they eventually alighted on his bare legs. She audibly swallowed and, quick as a sprung arrow, his cock stirred, scraping against the linen of his braies. He willed his body not to react.

She stumbled to her feet and cinched her mantle tight around her neck. "I'm going to bed."

Bed. God's blood, an unfortunate word to use within hearing of his cock, but he wrestled for control and nodded. "I'll..." He cleared the sudden gruffness from his throat. "I'll see to the horses."

He combed down his horses and brought them to a better spot for the evening. "I'm a warrior, a knight, Perceval, and yet I fear to enter that lean-to," he whispered as he scratched his warhorse behind the ears.

He retrieved his grooming pouch—a gift from Sir Hugh when he was made a squire—and settled again in the clearing, wooden and metal grooming tools in hand. Quick strokes with his tweezers cleaned his nails. Then, by feeling along the shape of his jaw, he plucked stray hairs and used his scissors to trim. With a toothpick and clean cloth, he cleaned his teeth and finished by chewing a few fennel seeds.

Judging she'd had sufficient time to become situated and was, if not actually asleep, at least pretending, he ducked around his shield, which he'd propped against the opening to act as a partial screen.

He let his eyes adjust. Soon, the faint moon illuminated her form against the wall. A pallet of furs and his wool blankets lay waiting empty beside her, the makeshift shelter too small for any decent amount of space between them.

"Christ on the cross," he whispered. He laid his weapons and armor down in the remaining space and, against his usual preference for sleeping nude, removed his braies but kept on the shirt. He slipped in between the covers.

Chapter Sixteen

❦

And truly he never saw a maiden more full of comeliness, and grace,
and beauty, than she.
The Mabinogion, an ancient Welsh romance

KATY LAY UNDER THE WOOL BLANKET, afraid to move. He had
entered the lean-to.

Calm down, heart. Jeez.

A soft rustle, a muted exhalation, and his body, radiating heat,
settled beside her.

And the libido she'd finally leashed moments before? Unleashed.

Sweet Jesus on a cracker, she'd heard him jacking off. Shock still
coursed alongside desire. Never before would she have thought the
sound—and the accompanying images that flashed into her head—
would've been at all erotic. But it had. Oh God, it had.

And then he'd returned to the clearing, and—this was the craziest
thing—the moonlight highlighted his bare legs, and she was inexplicably transfixed. She saw guys' bare legs all the time. So why did *his* push
all sorts of buttons inside that she didn't even know were pushable?

Now his presence, their presence, swelled to fill their teeny-tiny,
no-bigger-than-a-gnat's-butt lean-to.

His heat, his erotic pull—she could *feel* it. A weird, pulsing, virtual
pull tugging at her skin, her nerve endings. Made her want to...touch.
Made her *want.*

The more she resisted the urge, the stronger it became. It would
be a relief, really. To just...touch. One little touch. Just one.

She adjusted her limbs—*just getting comfortable*—and let her
hand plop...there, butting up next to his warm skin, and her heart
sped up. Which body part she touched, she had no clue. Didn't matter. All perfectly natural. Yep.

Oh God. That only made it worse. The heated contact surged through her, fueling the pull, fueling the urgency. She lay still, her heart doing the *pound-pound-pound* thing so loud that surely he heard. If he even noticed the tiny contact, she was still in the it-could-be-an-accidental-touch zone. Did she dare more? No.

Her pinkie took matters into its own, er, pinkie, and moved oh-so-slightly, grazing his skin. *His* pinkie, judging by the shape and texture.

Blood rushed and pounded through her veins, flushing her skin. This could not, in *any* way, be explained as an accidental touch. But he could feign sleep if he wasn't interested. Did she want him to do that?

What was she *doing*?

She commanded her pinkie to drop, and thankfully, it obeyed.

A jolt shot through her as his finger made a query, and the need clarified. The need represented her desire for some measure of control. Control over her general situation. Control over her attraction. She answered with a gentle finger stroke along his calloused, warm skin.

A sharp breath pierced the dark air. The need simmered along her skin, pooling heat below.

His strong fingers threaded through hers and squeezed.

Disappointment suffused her—this was a clear "thanks, but no thanks."

Then he wrenched his large body toward her and yanked their joined hands above her head. His scent washed over her: spicy, male, metallic.

The slow flush flared hot. Oh. Oh God. His darker shape, barely visible, was poised just above and to the side. Did those flat eyes now stir with desire?

Exposing her side with her raised arm felt erotic, electrifying, as if this marked a moment she couldn't reverse. A moment that would plunge her into that spontaneous, chaotic life she'd both envied and feared. Envied for the promise of fun and freedom. Feared for the possibility of becoming lost.

His warm breath, smelling of clean spice, stroked her cheek and ear. A thrilling shiver coursed over her, the wound on her arm only a minor sting. Then his lips—those full, sensuous lips—grazed her jaw and the soft spot behind her ear, the hairs of his beard brushing her sensitive skin. Her shivers locked her muscles tight. A bolt of tantalizing heat shot down her center.

He leveraged closer, all that warrior brawn pressing hard against her side, linen rasping over skin, an exquisite feeling.

Yes. This.

She arched up, and his powerful hand clasped her thigh. Slowly, oh so slowly, he skimmed up and over her hip, her linen shirt riding along, whisking across skin. At the curve of her waist, a pause, and a glide upward until his fingers bumped the underside of her breast. All the while, he nibbled across her neck, jawline, ear.

Oh God. She trembled and arched again. *Yes. Please.*

Then, his mouth open and paused in a soft bite below her ear, he shifted and palmed her breast in one sure, possessive grip. He growled, the sound vibrating against her neck, chasing the searing heat coiling through her. She clutched the fur beside her.

"Robert," she blurted.

On a sharp inhale, his beard brushed her cheek and his mouth captured hers in a hungry kiss. Caught in the same urgency, she parted her lips. Oh, he tasted dark, dangerous, with a hint of spice, and their wine. *More.*

With her free hand, she groped for his chest in the dark and gripped a handful of his soft linen shirt.

Closer. He needed to be closer. She swung up a leg and captured his, his leg hairs whispering against her skin.

He moaned and trailed molten kisses down her neck, his hand doing wonderful, tweaky, massage-y things to her breast, driving her insane. She squirmed and gripped his shirt tighter.

Forehead pressed against her breastbone, he paused, breath hot. His whole body stiffened, his muscles rippling with tension. On a torturous groan, he pulled away. "I cannot lay with an innocent," he choked out, his voice rough, strained.

Frustration warred with admiration for his scruples and control. But the need to taste that spontaneity, that chaos, still thrummed through her. She'd fought against chaos for so long, perhaps she should dive right in.

No way was she stepping back from this moment.

She trailed a hand down his muscled chest. In the dark, she

found his fierce arousal, wrapped her fingers around, and squeezed. "I'm not a virgin," she whispered.

He gasped, shoved her hand away, and pinned it to the furs, and her heart—oh, how it beat at that.

"I cannot marry you." His voice, hoarse and rough in the close confines, echoed and teased along her skin.

"I cannot—" she panted, and he released one of her hands and pinched her nipple, "—either." Tension and promise tightened her muscles.

His rough finger circled her breast, and she shivered. Any other thought in French fled. "A one-off thing it is," she whispered in English. She dragged up his shirt and brushed her hand along the bumps, knots, and ridges of his muscled chest and back, the heat of his skin burning into her palm.

He trembled and trailed his fingers down her side and across her belly. Her stomach muscles clenched, and she sucked in a breath.

She gripped his muscled butt and struggled to free her other hand, which he still kept above her head.

He mumbled something and captured her mouth in a punishing kiss. His tongue stroked hers, demanding she match his passion, his need. Oh. She'd comply. His hand, hot and heavy on her belly, skimmed downward, and she shivered in anticipation. One of his blunt, strong fingers slid into the short curls of her landing strip and found her already wet for him. He groaned into her mouth, and his kisses turned greedy. He circled a finger on her nub and dipped inside. Oh God. Oh God.

She squeezed his butt—a very firm, muscular butt it was too, a warrior's butt. She skimmed across his skin, over his hip bone, until his thick, hard length nudged her hand. She traced a delicate path up the underside to the tip, velvety soft against the pad of her finger. The power and passion he barely restrained sent a thrill through her, adding another sizzle of tension in the space between them. If this marked a moment to dive into chaos, she'd not hold back. Just this once.

Their tongue-jockeying intensified—teeth bumping, breaths sharp—and she pinched the head. It jerked in her hand.

"Christ, woman," he choked out against her swollen lips, breathing labored. He pulled away and released her hand. Finally. She reached for his shoulder, desperate to have both hands in play, but his own were on her shirt, blocking her. He raised the cloth, the rough fabric skating past her now-sensitized skin, arms, and face.

"Oh, I wish I could see you," he whispered hoarsely.

He gripped her hands in one of his, held them tight above her head, and rose over her. She squirmed as her sex began to ache for him—delicious, simply delicious, his hovering strength, her helplessness beneath him. His free hand brushed her face and trailed a pulsing heat down her neck, across her collarbone, as if tracing her shape in the darkness, as if layering into her skin more need, more of that *pull*, with each stroke of his powerful fingers. He feathered the tips around her breast, to her nipple. A pinch and, oh, and then his mouth, hungry and heated, sucked hard.

Desire seared downward. She bucked against him, her other breast rubbing against the arm that pinned her. He scraped his teeth across her nipple, soothed it with his cool tongue. Another hot bolt shot down her center and pulsed her lady parts. She bucked, wanting her hands on him, wanting him inside her. *Now.*

"Robert, please," she whimpered. Oh, she was in chaos now. And she wanted *all* of it.

She cinched her legs around his lean hips, arched up, and shuddered at the exquisite feeling of her aching center slicking against his thick, fierce arousal.

He hissed in a breath, released her hands, and ground his hips into hers, his hard length hitting right where she burned for him, sliding against her wet, swollen folds.

Yes. All her focus narrowed down to the absence that throbbed, needing him to erase it. Control still showed in the tautness of his muscles. If she was going to go all in and experience wildness for the first time, she needed him fully unleashed.

Unleashed. God, just the thought of seeing him lose control—over *her*—filled her with such longing it scared her. She shoved that need aside. Before she could figure out how best to break his control, he shoved a hand between their bodies, gripped his length—the blunt tip exploring—and then, elbows planted on either side of her shoulders, he rammed into her in one sure, hot stroke.

"Holy crap." He filled her so completely, almost painfully, a wonderfully achey feeling of invasion. His broad chest above her, she scrambled for a hold on his back, savoring the throbbing fullness. On a groan, he pulled slowly out, the heat searing her again, his tip almost fully withdrawn—*miss you already*—and then he thrust hard, her back rasping against the furs with the force of his possession.

Oh, yes. She wanted it hard. Hard and rough. And when had she *ever* wished that. She gripped the nape of his neck and met each pounding thrust, desperate. Chaos swirled in her blood, fueled her frantic movements, and wound a coil of desire tighter and tighter where their bodies joined. She bit into his biceps, tasted the masculine, salty heat on his skin.

The scent and sounds of their greedy joining filled the space, and oh God, his pubic bone hit just the right spot and, oh shit, *wham*, she broke apart so suddenly, it took her breath and stuck in her throat. Wave upon wave gripped and shattered her. She cried out, clamping down hard. The chaotic energy snapped and fizzled along her nerve endings, jerking her limbs in small aftershocks.

His motions grew more urgent, fingers tightening in her hair, until he pulled out, captured her mouth on a shout, and shot his hot load onto her belly.

He collapsed beside her, and they both fought to catch their breaths.

Wow. Just...oh my, wow.

Her heart pounded with her first taste of abandon. Why had she ever denied herself *this*? This was raw. This was primal. This was *real*.

The chilly air caught her attention first, which made her realize she was coated in a thin sheen of sweat, another first. He stirred, grabbed one of the furs, and wiped her stomach clean.

"You will be the death of me, woman."

He pulled another fur over them and nestled her up against him, his shirt a barrier, though, to his hot skin. She snuggled up, grateful he still had his wits, because she sure didn't, and let her mind thump back into a drowsy blissfulness.

Chapter Seventeen

❦

"My soul," said she, "who art thou?" "I am Peredur the son of
Evrawc from the North; and if ever thou art in trouble or in danger,
acquaint me therewith, and if I can, I will protect thee."
The Mabinogion, an ancient Welsh romance

A BIRD TRILLED, BREAKING through Katy's sleep. She drifted into
consciousness to find a muscled Norman warrior spooned
hot against her back, hand possessively splayed across her stomach.
Awareness prickled along her skin. His soft, even breathing said he
still slept. She waited—any minute now, her inner self should be
chastising. But...nothing. But...she should be shredded with guilt.

Was it the bizarre situation? Even so, that didn't excuse cheating
on Preston. For she *had* cheated. She lay there, Robert's warmth a
solid presence along her back. Waiting. Waiting for her inner compass
to spin, adjust, and make her feel *wrong*.

But. It didn't happen.

She gripped the blankets and started to shove the whys into a corner of her consciousness with the other half-formed questions about
her relationship with Preston, but stopped. Because—hell—this was
the crux.

Robert challenged. Robert made her want to step outside of her
comfort zone. She quivered at the thought of being so exposed to
the world without her artificial shelter of control. But, she'd dared
spontaneity last night. She'd slipped into the chaotic stream and...the
world hadn't imploded. *She* hadn't imploded. Well, okay, she *had* in a
delicious way—hee. But...with Preston? No—their relationship
hadn't been satisfying. And not just in the sex department. He'd never
made her question her *need* for that shelter.

Sex. The hot, heavy coupling with her medieval knight flooded heat through her senses. Because that's what it had been—a coupling. And she had loved it.

And pulling out? Sweet and thoughtful, but unnecessary. She had a month left before she needed another birth control shot.

Her hand lay inches from his under the covers. She could move, clasp his... No—Crap. Damn bladder. Instead, she eased his hand away and scooted out from under the covers. The morning air hit her bare skin, and she shivered.

Over her shoulder, she lingered on Robert's sleeping face, marred by a slight frown. The visual clashed with her body's memory; having sex in the dark made it feel like it could have been someone else, not him. But she latched onto his starkly handsome face, at his bulky frame under the covers, and blended it with last night's charged memories. It was *those* lips that... It was *that* strong hand that... Oh man. Arousal arrowed through her, flushing her skin.

She snatched her mantle and one of the clean strips of cloth she'd gotten from the monks, shifted into a crouch, and shuffled outside and around a nearby bush. She relieved herself and used the strip for a makeshift tissue. She, who'd never been camping in her life. Squatting naked in the woods. Peeing. Who'd have guessed?

Rustling sounds came from inside the lean-to. She threw her mantle around her and stepped into the clearing. He uncoiled from the doorway, and she gasped. The man was buck-naked and oh mercy, never had she seen anyone so built. Real muscles—earned from hard living and fighting, not from a gym or steroids—bunched and flexed over his formidable frame. A jagged pale scar ran down one bicep, and another white, puckered slash ranged along his rib cage, just below his nipple.

Thick muscles corded his thighs and calves from years of steering a horse with his legs.

And—her breath caught—he was hard, and it was large, jutting proud from a thatch of dark hair.

Holy crap. *This* was the body she'd been with last night? Her gaze clashed with his. The heat and desire reflected in his hooded eyes shot through and clenched her lady parts. She tripped a couple of steps toward him. Then he was before her, his warm, strong hands clutching her shoulders. She swayed as everything around her slowed and narrowed down to this spot, this moment—the birds' song muted and elongated, the *swish* and *thumple* as her mantle hit the ground, Robert's slow, indrawn breath. She slow-blinked, slow-blinked. With an eerie inevitability, the dream of the warrior-saint, that feeling of connectedness, snicked into place as she fixed on the honey-brown eyes of the warrior, who was no saint.

"Beautiful," he whispered.

His voice, thick and rumbly from sleep, threaded inside, tweaking nerve endings, which remembered its vibrating tones from last night's sexcapades. His large hands, fingers strong and well-formed, smoothed down her arms, and his heated gaze darted from her breasts to her stomach, to a shoulder, to her neck.

She took in the sights too. Fingers slightly shaky, she traced one of the scars on his side, then up across his abs to one of his pecs, his muscles twitching under her fingers' path.

Her nipples tightened in the chilly morning air, and she grew lightheaded at her body's quick response, ready to again dive into the dizzying chaos of his passion.

"This is crazy," she sighed in English.

Crazy and scary, and God, fast. This was *so* not her. A feeble voice wondered if she could step away, go back to the calm, ordered life she cultivated. She cast a glance downward. Robert's hand crossed the short gap from her arm to her breast and reverently, gently, touched its peak. Oh, yeah, it firmed up at such a touch from that calloused finger. She shivered and pinched his nipple, unable to resist, unable to pull away, unable to deny herself.

He groaned and, holy crap, fell to his knees. His strong hands grasped her hips and yanked her forward. He was so tall that, even kneeling, his mouth was level with her chest. He sat back and licked her belly button, and her stomach clenched, heat coiling and pooling below. She reached tentative fingers to grip his silky black hair, to feel it against her skin. She was mere inches from her goal, when he freaking lifted her, as if she weighed nothing, and brought her sex down onto his mouth.

Oh God. She dug her fingers into his hair, wrapped her legs around his neck, and held on. His hands, tendons stark with strain, slid up until he gripped her just below her breasts, the muscles and blood vessels cording on his powerful forearms. His wet, warm tongue and mouth sucked and flicked and twirled and did all sorts of tingly things that really just made it hard for her to think.

His tongue slipped inside her, and she cried out, her whole body shuddering under his onslaught. Overhead arched a stout, low-hanging tree branch. She slapped her hands to the rough bark and gripped tight, palms abrading. Finding some of her weight taken from him, Robert dragged a hand up and massaged her breast. He worked his wickedly talented mouth on her, his tongue rasping, sucking, flicking, adjusting as he read her reactions. Her legs shivered against his neck, his trim beard teasing her soft inner thighs. A delicious, insistent pressure built, tightening and spiraling and swirling until she panted and quivered like a needy thing.

Dear God. Increasing his pace, he worked his lips and tongue, sucked hard on her aching nub. She clamped her legs against his face and screamed, a mind-blowing orgasm rocketing through her, coursing hot and wild through her veins.

Fingers stiff, she let go of the branch, mind, body, heart reeling. He eased her to the ground, her knees still over his shoulders. Relentless, on a strangled shout, he thrust into her in one smooth motion, her crumbled defenses barely mustering a protest. She convulsed again with another orgasm as he pounded into her, thick and full, his movements jerky, out of control, his beautiful warrior's body on display, muscles working in a synchronized pursuit of pleasure. She quivered, powerless, as another release built, on the edge.

His whole body stiffened as if about to come, but he flew off her so fast she barely registered what happened. Her body trembling, dazed, she sat up, swayed, and caught a glimpse of his firm backside as he knelt into their lean-to. He sprang up and sprinted back to her, removing his sword from its scabbard with a rasping scrape.

A rasping scrape that swept her heart in a tight swoop down into her stomach and then up to her throat. Where it frantically beat.

Holy crap, what the—

Then she heard it. Hoofbeats and voices. She grabbed her mantle and jumped up, swinging it around her, legs shaking. He seized her arm and shoved her behind him, backing up until she reached the entrance of the lean-to.

Chapter Eighteen

And thence they journeyed forward; and that night they came as far
as that Commot in Powys, which also upon account thereof is called
Mochnant, and there tarried they that night. And they journeyed
thence to the Cantrev of Rhos, and the place where they were that
night is still called Mochdrev.

The Mabinogion, an ancient Welsh romance

"ESUS AND ALL THE SAINTS," Robert spat. What an unforgivable lapse in vigilance. He pushed Kaytee down, hoping she understood he wanted her out of sight.

The small band of Welsh trotted into view and reined in at the clearing, their mounts prancing from side to side.

On the surety of his soul, he'd venture 'twas the same party they'd espied yester morn. One deftly slid from his horse and hefted his spear. The other two notched arrows and pulled, the creak of stretching sinew stark in the morning air, the shafts swooping down to aim straight for his chest. One of them grinned, mischief in his eyes, and dropped his aim still lower. At his giblets. Bastard.

"*Beth sydd ydym yma? A ydym yn torri ar draws rhywbeth?*" the spear-wielder asked.

"Speak French," he growled to the speaker.

Robert understood the query but thought it prudent to keep that a secret—he might glean information from their unguarded conversations. Plus, there was no chance in passing himself off as Welsh, since his allegiance and liege lord was plain for all to see in the arms displayed on his shield. Nor did he have a chance against the reach of the man's spear and the two Welsh bowmen. Alone, mayhap he'd have attempted, but not with Kaytee to protect.

He also entertained a thread of hope as to the outcome. The Welsh bred strong, swift horses, but the terrain favored infantry. The horses' mere presence meant these men were wealthy or were in the retinue of someone of wealth. If so, Robert and Kaytee had a chance to escape with their lives.

"I was merely speculating what we must have interrupted between you and..." the spearman leaned sideways and looked down, "...your lady."

"None of your damn business." Robert took up a defensive stance— By God's holy teeth, he'd protect her if their minds took an evil turn.

"No doubt you are correct. Now, there is no need for bloodshed." The man eyed Perceval, Robert's shield with his lord's heraldic markings, and nodded, saying, "You ought to fetch a decent price. We shall work out the terms of your ransom back at Rhuthun castle. As for your wench, well..."

"She's not my wench. She's my lady wife," he heard himself saying.

Kaytee gasped behind him, and he prayed she'd contradict him not. No other remedy existed if she wished to be decently treated. In truth, the Welsh treated their women better than his own people, but he'd rather not consign her to their tender mercies. If she possessed value as a hostage, though...

Besides, he'd been the one to endanger her with his carelessness. He'd erred. Greatly. By not venturing farther off the path for their camp. By forgoing basic defensive measures due to his lust. By not hearing them sooner...due to this lust. If he had, he could have collapsed their structure and burrowed into the nearby forest's depths until the danger passed. But he hadn't.

His captor grinned. "Even better. So I have your word as a knight in the king's service that you and your lady wife are my hostages, the price of your freedom to be determined once we reach our castle?"

"How can you have a castle? All were forfeit to the crown a dozen years ago."

His captor's grin spread wider. "A little matter of re-appropriating what was ours." He motioned with his spear. "So, your word as a knight?"

"Yes," he ground out.

"Very well, then. I'm Rhys ap Owen. Make haste and dress yourselves. A long day we have ahead of us."

KATY MIGHT ONLY HAVE THE BAREST GRASP of what was happening, but one thing was certain—she'd been saddle-bound for five-plus hours as their captors headed northeastward.

Anger and confusion frazzled her nerves, though the anger had settled into a slow burn. What could happen next? Anything. Not a comfortable feeling.

She clutched her mantle closer—damn Robert. Yeah, she understood why he claimed her as a spouse—to protect her—but it rankled. She'd wanted to turn around and conk him on the head. Another event happening *to* her without her say. Another event she could not control as if the whirlwind she'd dared step into with Robert last night had careened off with a life of its own. *This* was why she avoided spontaneity.

Thank the self-preservation gods the Welsh had interrupted whatever had happened between her and Robert. It scared her, made her heart trip along faster than the horse's hoofbeats, at how fully and how quickly she'd thrown herself into that. She doubted she'd have had the strength to stop on her own.

A small, still rational, part of her knew she was blaming Robert for everything she couldn't control, but...

Now she was just freaking exhausted, with no idea when these cheerful Welsh warriors would stop for the night. Though she supposed she should be grateful for the simple lady's tunic he'd procured at the abbey. Saved questions. She touched the piece of bark tucked into her waistband. Earlier, at their first break along a beautiful lake which they traveled alongside for a good while, she'd found the smooth clear bark, and with a piece of flint, she'd made a rough map of their path.

Crude, and probably useless, but it helped. Somewhat. At each stop, updating the map helped her feel as if she had some control. And in between each stop, memorizing the features, their path's twists and turns, occupied her mind.

She leaned back and let herself rest against Robert, something she'd resisted.

He wrapped an arm around her, pulled her tight against him. Warmth and security spread over her. That felt good. *Dammit.*

A shout came from ahead, and the leader answered. In the lowering afternoon light, columns of smoke spiraled skyward, and darker shapes moved among the trees, accompanied by the sound of barking dogs, wood being chopped, and the low hum of voices.

As they neared the camp, the shapes resolved into men erecting small shelters, others building fires and cooking food. How many were there? Too many for her to count.

Their captors led them into the center, and the leader—Rhys?—talked to another, who studied Robert and Katy and nodded. Rhys directed them to a clearing that fetched up against a rock outcropping. He jumped off his horse and grabbed Perceval's reins.

"We camp here. Unload your burdens, and assist us," he said in French.

They slid to their feet, Katy unable to suppress a groan at her protesting muscles. Probably not the best time to quip about being ridden hard in more ways than one. Robert put an arm around her and walked her to a rock. "Sit. I will assist them."

She nodded, slumped onto the rock, and sighed. The movement and new position returned feeling to certain portions of her anatomy.

Robert unharnessed Perceval and unstrapped their few possessions from his packhorse. She watched, quiet, as they collected branches and constructed a crude lean-to against the rock outcropping. When they were done, two short hide and stick walls jutted out from the rock, with a roof of the same stretching across. All in all, quite large and roomy for the two of them, and her spirits lifted. Until they filled the space with four pallets of hide, side by side, with a fifth stretching across the feet at the entrance.

So all of their party were going to be crammed in there. Oh joy.

∽

ROBERT ASSISTED THEIR CAPTORS in making camp, praying he had enough money saved to effect their release.

During their journey, Kaytee's cooperation—not only with his lie, but also protesting not their capture, nor giving any trouble—was admirable. But as the day progressed and his few attempts at conversation had been met with short replies, he noted her body's posture. He'd grown accustomed to watching it for meaningful clues these past days and, combined with their new intimacy, he easily read the subtle signs. She was *not* composed. She was *seething*.

For some reason, the realization heartened him, admiration for her fortitude swelling. Despite the chance of another part swelling, he'd ached to wrap his arms around her delectable form and pull her close. But he'd refrained, sensing that part of her anger was with him. So when she finally relaxed and sought his comfort, just before they approached the camp, his relief had been acute.

He was not forgiven, but she'd called a truce.

Now they were heading back to the lean-to after spending a considerable time around the fire eating with their captors as they passed wine skins and shared ribald jokes. They spoke in Welsh, but either dared not risk that he'd lied about understanding their language, or genuinely had no important information to discuss, for they talked only of their successful raid against one of King Edward's convoys and other previous feats. He noted the number of men, however, and their weapons and supplies. Most wielded spears typical of the northern Welsh, but the presence of archers attested to perhaps a southern Welsh alliance.

The Welsh wit was the hardest to endure, for it took great effort to pretend he understood it not. For as long as he dared, he'd remained at the fire side, hoping some morsel of information would slip, but when Kaytee's eyes drooped, he'd bade them good night and tossed into the fire that night's whittling.

"Wait," he said when she moved to drop to her pallet. "Sit here first." He drew back her cover and pointed to the middle of her pallet. She slumped bonelessly down. He grabbed his pallet's hides and spread the fur against the sloping rock behind her.

He settled himself against the upright perch and parted his legs. "Here, sleep with your back against me. I shall protect you better this way."

She nodded, shuffled closer, and leaned back against him. Her unique womanly scent washed over him, and he fortified his resolve, though having her so close on a bed of furs fired his blood. She dragged her fur up, and he draped his extra across, tucking it in around her shoulders and arms.

"I do not fancy having one of them lying next to you. Besides, I wish not for your pinkie to wander." He wrapped his arms around her, cinching her against him.

She lurched up. "I would not—"

"Shh." He held her fast so she'd not disturb the blankets. "I tease." He kissed the top of her head, the fine hairs silky against his lips. He inhaled and placed another kiss at the crown. "Go to sleep, my sweeting."

She was quiet for a moment. "What about you?"

"Worry not for me."

"Will you be able to sleep like this?"

"I'll not be sleeping."

"But—"

"Relax. I know you're tired." He nestled her closer. "I also know you're wroth with me and wish to vent your spleen. I promise I'll give you a chance to yell at me anon."

"I don't want to yell at you." She struggled again in her cocoon.

"Yes, you do. And I blame you not. You shall have your chance."

She huffed. "Now, I want to yell at you."

He chuckled and stroked the ends of her glossy, black hair where it lay against her neck. Her breaths slowly evened out. She'd fallen into slumber.

The Welsh continued to carouse, trading jokes and stories, and the fires slowly bled out. How his cock could be at full attention while in the middle of an enemy encampment, Robert could not fathom, but he did have Kaytee nestled temptingly and trustingly against him, so he forgave his pintel for being so ignorant of their situation. For she was unlike any other woman. Who would have known such passion lay under that calm exterior. To be the one to bring out that side of her again, how he ached for it. Curse these Welsh.

He grinned. But then his smile froze. He'd meant what he said. He couldn't marry her. Even if his suit were granted, he must ally with an heiress who brought her own property in her marriage portion, to bolster and solidify his gains and position in the court of King Edward.

He gazed down on her short hair, a dark splash across his chest. He knew not what to do, but giving her up? That, he was not yet willing to do. He lifted a hand to smooth her hair away from her soft cheek, but let it drop.

So beautiful... Who was she? He studied what little of her face he could behold from this angle and the flickering light from the surrounding fires. Her pert nose, lush lips and...he suppressed a chuckle... those lips now emitted quiet little puffs of air as she softly snored.

He leaned his head against the rock. Christ, when was the last time he'd seen the humor in life? And now, of all places, in an enemy camp, with a strange woman who made him burn. Burn with desire. Burn with need. A desire and need not only for her and her body, but for something he couldn't quite name.

Her reply to his bout of honesty last night came back to him, when he said he couldn't marry her—*I cannot, either.*

He frowned at her sleeping form.

"Why not?" he whispered.

೪೦

"IF I NEVER SIT ON ANOTHER HORSE again, it'll be too soon," Katy whispered.

Yet again, she'd listed to the side, and she gripped Robert's arm banded around her waist. Robert and Katy rode in the midst of their escort, now increased to five since breaking camp that morning. Each step of their horse took her farther and farther from her goal, and as they ambled through the flatter terrain, what little chance she had of rendezvousing with the villagers dwindled.

The more they traveled, the more her ability to cope stretched thinner and thinner. How would she find her way? The sweeping mountain vistas of northern Wales were breathtaking, sure. But the vastness...the vastness seemed to overtake all and left her feeling...lost.

And her pitiful map? Ha.

Panic and a touch of hysteria threatened to crawl up her throat and emerge as either a scream or a crazy laugh. She swallowed hard. Plus, she was dirty, tired, and convinced she had an insect or two in her hair.

As the deep shadows of dusk settled over the valley, their party halted at a clearing. Finally. Robert slid off the saddle and clasped her around the waist. Too exhausted to protest, she accepted his help off Perceval. But in the shifting movements, she stumbled upon landing, her bark map slipping loose. Perceval sidestepped out of her way and stepped on it with a *crunch*.

"Oh, shit." No, no, no.

She fell to her knees and picked up the small pieces of bark. Her one link to some semblance of control, gone. She opened her mouth, and what came out was not a scream or a hysterical laugh, but a howl of frustration that echoed around the forest. She pounded her fists on the ground, and tears choked her throat.

And then she stopped her howl-snivel fest mid-choke. Horror and shame flushed her skin. She *never* acted out like this. Well...not since her eighth birthday. What the hell was happening to her? Had she finally lost her mind?

A warm arm draped over her shoulders, and she recognized Robert's scent. "What troubles you?"

"My map. It's destroyed." God, that sounded stupid out loud, because, really, what kind of map had it been? Probably not something she could've used. But dammit, so much of her need was wrapped up within the stupid thing—her need to find some way to organize and make sense of her surroundings and her situation—and it was gone.

Whether he sensed this somehow, or to humor the crazy lady, he kept quiet, gathered her up, and held her tightly as she fought and then gave in to the wracking sobs.

After a moment, she angled away and wiped her nose. Not very lady-like, but at this point, who cared? She pulled in a deep breath and risked a peek at Robert. What would he think of such a loss of composure?

Under his eyes, dark circles bruised the skin, his mouth rigid with strain. He hadn't made up his sleep while in the saddle, and knowing him, he'd insist on staying up all night again to protect her. *This* she could fix. *This* she could control.

She opened her mouth to tell him not to stay up, when he asked, "It's not just the map, is it?"

She looked away, unnerved by how well he understood her. "No," she whispered. "I feel so out of control. Where are we, Robert? What will happen?"

"Ease your mind on the former. I know these lands. As to what will happen, I know not. But we *will* get out of this, I promise you."

She flapped her hands, anxious energy coursing through her. "How can you be so calm?"

He got to his feet, unfolding with an easy grace. He held out a hand, his dark eyes focused solemnly on hers. "Come with me."

"For what?"

"That's part of the lesson." Was it her imagination, or did a twinkle of humor stir in those eyes? "Center yourself, and grab onto the here and now."

That made no sense—what was he now, Sir Medieval Zen Master? But she slipped her hand into his strong, calloused one. He hauled her up until she bumped into his chest. With a finger under her chin, he tilted her face until she looked in his eyes.

"Listen to the world around you. Hear the birds? Hear the small animals scurrying? You are in this moment, this moment only, and sometimes that's all you can do, all you can be." His finger pulled away, brushing against her skin, and he tapped her nose, stepping away.

He scanned their surroundings, picked up a good size rock, and held it out to her.

Stupefied, she accepted it. "What is this for?"

"Sometimes, I find movement, movement of any kind, can ease the frustration when I feel overwhelmed. Movement also helps ground me in the moment." He nodded to the rock. "Throw it as hard as you can."

"At you?" she asked with a slight teasing note in her voice.

"To be honest, I rather hoped you would toss it in the other direction. Put your arm into it, and give a good shout."

She eyed the rock, and then him, and his eyes grew wary. The rock's rough contours bit into her palm's soft flesh, and she imagined doing something so friggin' out of character.

A strange clarity punctured the surface of her frustration and sense of helplessness—she was done. Done with being poised. Done with trying to be perfect. Done with behaving exactly as she should. All her life, she'd constricted herself to this...this *role*...this *need* out of...out of...

What?

What exactly drove her?

Fear.

Ha. Yes. Fear that if she lost control—didn't show her best self—

her world would fall apart. Fall apart as someone she loved left her. Like her father.

But where had that fear gotten her? In the middle of a scary-ass war zone in medieval Wales. Where *nothing* could be controlled.

A crazy, burbling need to laugh choked up her throat, and some of that need must have shown, because Robert's eyes widened further.

She spun around, pictured her fear stuffed into the rock, and— "*Gah!*"—flung it, her shout echoing and blending into the sounds of the forest, into the here and now. It smacked with a satisfying *thunk* into a nearby tree.

"Feel better?" Robert's voice was laced with understanding.

She folded her arms as her adrenaline fizzled, leaving her shaky and shivery. "No." But she did, slightly, and he knew it, judging by the tilt of his mouth. Not only had she felt as if she'd thrown away her fear, but also her need to always control.

And now his tired, drawn features made her close the distance between them and place her hand on his arm, not out of a need to control, but because she *did* feel more connected to the moment, to her surroundings, and to him. And right now, he was tired.

And they'd have more moments to get through tomorrow.

"You don't need to stay up this evening."

He looked down at her arm, then at her, his eyes dark and curious. He opened his mouth.

She squeezed his arm. "How can you protect me tomorrow, if you don't sleep tonight?"

He grunted.

"Are you afraid they'll attack us in our sleep?"

"No, we hold more value alive as hostages than dead."

She led them to their pallets, again encircled by other pallets. She sat down, sighing at her aching muscles, and caught his gaze. "You may, er, wrap your arms around me if that will make you feel I am safer."

He chuckled—a hoarse chuckle, rusty, but a chuckle nonetheless. She'd take it.

"May I indeed?" He lay beside her and pulled her back against him, settling her head on his arm, bunching the other hide up to use as a pillow. "If I must." His warm sigh tickled across her neck. "After all, I must ensure that pinkie does not wander."

Would Robert never let her forget that? Katy elbowed him, and he snickered in her ear.

"Robert," she whispered.

"Hmm?" The low hum of his voice rumbled against her back.

"Why do you throw away your wood carvings? I've seen them. They're beautiful."

No answer. Around her, rustlings and calls from night animals increased as the camp settled. Had Robert fallen asleep? But he tightened his grip. " 'Tis my way to ground myself, to be in the moment. Consigning them to the fire reinforces that they're only a product of that moment."

As his breathing slowed and grew even, she let his words settle in and marveled at what had happened earlier. Never had she felt so emotionally raw, so out of sorts, and instead of her behavior driving Robert away, he'd understood. Understood and now held her, safe in his strong arms.

And God help her, she couldn't help comparing him to Preston. Which wasn't fair. Preston had never seen her like that because she'd carefully managed her life and their relationship. Which should be ideal—the perfect relationship—but she suspected only proved it shallow, hollow. He'd never seen her true self.

Chapter Nineteen

And hereupon, behold there came the Queen and her handmaidens, and Peredur saluted them. And they were rejoiced to see him, and bade him welcome. And Arthur did him great honour and respect, and they returned towards Caerlleon.
The Mabinogion, an ancient Welsh romance

*M*ID-AFTERNOON THE NEXT DAY, their party crossed a draw-bridge into a gate between two towers, and into the bailey of Rhuthun Castle.

"What a journey," Katy groaned, massaging the muscles in her thighs.

"One that is almost over. Fear not, we shall be treated well within."

God, she hoped so. First thing on her list—rustling up a hot bath.

They rode Perceval through the gathering crowd, who cheered a hero's welcome to their five escorts and stared with open curiosity at her and Robert. She swallowed hard and straightened as much as her abused muscles allowed.

Robert's soft gasp rasped near her ear, and his whole body went rigid.

"What, Robert?" She angled her head to see his face, a face set in tense lines as he stared into the crowd. Confusion and pain crossed his face, and he looked sharply away.

She whipped around and scanned in the direction of his gaze. Then she saw her. An older woman, proud and tall, hungrily drinking him in with her eyes. The way she stood... The proud angle of her chin... Katy's heart thumped harder. His mother?

A stable boy scampered forward and held Perceval's reins. Ugh. Could she even lift a leg and slide out of the saddle?

Robert dismounted, his ramrod stiff back to the lady, and his warm hands clasped too tightly to Katy's waist. "I have you." His voice and actions, while solicitous, seemed too forced into this moment, as if in avoidance of something larger.

She slid down, steadied by his sure, strong grip. She untied her bag and joined Robert. The boy led their horses into the stable, and Robert draped an arm around her waist and faced their captors. While his nearness and warmth made her aware of his determined poise, she was grateful for the support and inclusion. She was *not* alone.

"What now?" he said evenly to Rhys.

"Now we go within and present you and your lady to Madog ap Llywelyn. His men will see to your comfort."

"Madog is here?" Robert stepped forward, his grip tightening around her, his voice tinged with equal parts curiosity and unease.

"Aye, he is. Arrived yesterday with his *tuelo* to consolidate our hold on this castle and the region."

Twela-what? Not a French-sounding word, so must be Welsh. Later, she'd ask Robert what it meant.

"Very well." Robert placed a comforting hand on the small of her back as Rhys forged a path through the bustling crowd. Katy glanced over her shoulder. The older woman kept pace with them on a parallel path.

Soon they stepped into a large building set against the far wall, flanked by two towers. Like at the great hall at Castell y Bere, her feet crunched over rushes strewn across the floor, but this time, the action stirred up a pleasant scent of lavender. Rushlights flickered around the perimeter.

A group of men congregated near one of the huge-ass fireplaces, and Rhys made introductions. But dang if any of the names registered—they were so different from what she was used to hearing. One man—the largest, and whose whole demeanor screamed I-lead-warriors-and-I-kick-ass—had a name she *did* catch: Madog ap Llywelyn. Like the other Welsh, his hair was cut to shape around his forehead and ears, and he was clean-shaven except for sporting a Fu Manchu-style mustache, each end drooping to a point.

Madog stepped forward. "Welcome, Robert of Beucol. And welcome Lady Beucol. I look forward to your stay with us and discussing the terms of your release. My seneschal—" Madog indicated a lean, stern man in his fifties. "—will see to your comfort. Surely, your lady must wish a respite." He motioned to a boy of about fourteen.

"My son Maredudd ap Madog will show you to your room, and I will send for you when I am ready."

Maredudd looked rather proud to be given such a task, and they followed him a few feet until Robert halted. "One moment."

He hurried to their host, exchanged words, and rejoined her. "Carry on," he said to the boy and replaced his hand at the small of her back.

In the corner, a dark opening revealed stone steps circling upward, and Maredudd stepped inside. Katy glanced at Robert with concern, but when he nodded, she pressed a hand against the cool stone wall and shuffled up the unevenly spaced steps not yet worn with age, her palm rubbing against the bumps and dips of the stone as she ascended. Her muscles complained with each step, but she'd have gone slower than the kid anyway for fear of tripping in the sparsely lit, confined space. Robert said nothing and finally—as her thighs contemplated a work stoppage in protest—they arrived at a landing.

Maredudd opened a stout wooden door and ushered them through. Katy caught her breath as she stepped into a large, round room straight out of every fairy tale she'd read. A fireplace crackled and sparked in one wall, with an intricately carved marble facing and mantle. Several Oriental rugs overlapped on the ground, no rushes. Two rectangular-shaped windows punctuated the far end of the wall.

A carved, rather large, four poster sat near, but not against, one wall, its posts painted red and what she could only describe as a white picket fence encircling the frame—gaps on each side allowed easy access to the mattress. Red cloth draped from the canopy. A decorative screen and a trestle table with a bench before the fireplace comprised the rest of the furnishings.

But the most charming feature was the wall—it was covered in a white, plaster-like layer and dotted all over with red rosettes, except for the portion between the windows. A larger than life depiction of St. George overlooked the room, with a dragon writhing along the edge near the floor.

The boy said something in Welsh, startling her, lit the rushlights inset in the wall, and ran out of the room. The door heaved shut.

Katy plopped onto the narrow wooden bench and stuck her hands before the fire. "All in all, better than I expected." She studiously avoided looking at the bed. Oh God. Did it have to be so alluringly unusual?

"The Welsh are known for their hospitality. What did you expect?"

"Honestly, I pictured a dungeon."

An are-you-serious frown sharpened his features. "We are not prisoners. We are hostages, which is another matter altogether. We shall be treated as guests until I meet their terms."

"Really? This is so strange."

"You have never been a hostage before?"

"Uh, no. What will—" She stopped at the rattle and thump against the door, which swung out, and two boys trotted inside hefting a wooden half-barrel the size of a one-person hot tub, which they placed behind the screen. They filed out and closed the door.

She gasped. "A hot bath. Oh, I'm in heaven."

"I thought you would wish for one." He joined her on the bench, the wood creaking with his added weight.

"You arranged this?"

He gave a curt nod. "No doubt the seneschal would have arranged for one eventually, but I did not wish for you to wait."

She scooted across the bench and hugged him. While she waited for the water, she focused on what else had caught her eye. "Food."

"I imagine there is a drop of wine as well."

"Fresh bread. Heavenly." Her stomach perked to attention and growled. "And cheese." She bit off a huge chunk of warm, crusty bread, flakes and crumbs cascading onto the trestle table.

Robert laughed, the sound bounding around the room, filling it, and her heart kick-started. She stopped chewing and stared, bread in one hand, cheese in another.

"What?" he asked, frowning.

She swallowed her bite. "I've never heard you laugh. You have a great laugh."

"Hmpf. I laugh."

"Maybe, but I've never heard you. You should do it more often."

"Well, times have been rather trying since we met." His mouth twitched.

"True."

"Here, have some wine." He grabbed a flagon and poured, the red liquid glinting in the firelight and emitting that thick gurgle common across time as it filled her cup.

She took a grateful sip—while it was watered down like the other wine, this had been somehow sweetened. She tore off another bite of bread and cheese. "So who was that woman?"

"What woman?" His tone and posture was casual, but she wasn't fooled. There was a studied quality to his voice and a slight tension in his jaw and neck—cues she'd never have noticed if she hadn't become so attuned to him.

"The one in the bailey. The one who—" A scrape interrupted her, and the door opened again. "Saved by the bell."

A line of boys tromped into their tower room, each carrying two steaming buckets of water, the scent of lavender permeating the space. They dumped the water into the wooden tub.

A woman entered next, loaded with lots of cloth.

Robert talked with her a moment and brought her over to Katy. "This is Elen. She will assist you."

"Assist me?"

The lady clasped a stool in her chapped hands, her florid face a stoic mask.

He frowned. "Yes, with your clothes and your bath."

Katy fought the urge to raise her eyebrows, sensing this was something quite normal in his world. She only nodded.

"I shall leave you to your bath then." He switched benches so his back was to the screen.

The woman spoke no French, but Katy muddled through getting undressed and into the blessed tub, though Elen made her sit on the stool she'd placed inside. Then, to Katy's complete amazement, the woman took a sponge and soap and began *washing* her.

Wow, okay, this was weird. Katy wasn't helpless or sick, and having this woman wash her underscored the cultural differences. But as she sat there, the hot steam relaxing her sore muscles to mush, the careful, indifferent strokes of the sponge and the tinkling of the water dripping back into the tub, her token protest died on her tongue. She should feel guilty but couldn't muster up the energy for that either.

ROBERT SAT AT THE TRESTLE, head in hands, hearing her splashing, picturing it, and remembering the other time he'd heard her bathe. The night of her wandering pinkie... Christ, nightfall could not come soon enough.

The door scraped open, and a woman entered.

She raised her head, and Robert stiffened.

She stepped into the room and said in Welsh, "Did you think I would not recognize my own son full grown?"

Chapter Twenty

❦

And they partook of meat, and drink, with songs, and with feasting;
and of all the Courts upon the earth, behold this was the best
supplied with food and drink, and vessels of gold and royal jewels.
The Mabinogion, an ancient Welsh romance

ROBERT SHOT TO HIS FEET and waved his lady mother inside. His face he kept impassive, but inside his feelings churned. For he was at a loss on how to react. How to greet her. He settled for, "Mam, how do you fare?"

"So it's to be like that, is it?" She stepped into the room and stood by the window.

"I haven't seen you since I was ten." Seeing her before him though, it was hard to fathom twenty-three years had passed. For this was his mother, and some mysterious mechanism of the mind cast him back, caused him to feel he was that same lad who'd begged not to leave her, not to leave his sister and all he knew. What a sniveling reed he'd been.

"Whose fault would that be? And your Welsh is unpracticed."

He took a deep breath to disguise a sudden urge to laugh. In truth, she'd not changed in biting tongue or looks. Her back was still proudly straight, her black hair still lustrous, hanging loose about her shoulders, her features still well made. Still his mother of memory, though slightly...softer around the edges.

"You know the demands of a landless knight. Whilst a page and a squire, I wasn't at leisure to leave." *And you could have visited.*

She studied him for some moments, no doubt debating whether to point out that once he'd earned his spurs as a knight, he could have found the time.

"You are married, I hear."

He switched to French, not wishing for Elen to be privy to their conversation. "Not in truth." Estrangement or no, he found that with his mother, he could not lie.

"What do you mean?"

How much to reveal? Could he trust her with their true situation? Though even he was ignorant of Kaytee's full circumstances. However, he wished not to raise any suspicion.

"She's a refugee from the village of Bere at the foot of the castle where I was garrisoned. We were besieged by the Welsh, and during our retreat she was wounded, and we were separated from the others. You know she would have been ill-treated if they believed her to be of common English stock."

"So you felt the need to lie? Doesn't that go against your Norman knightly honor?"

"I believe it not against my knightly honor to aid the defenseless."

"Not all in your class agree with you."

He gritted his teeth. "I know." He knew all too well after being taught that lesson when still a squire. It had taken several years for the events of that day to cease haunting his dreams.

"What are your plans?"

He began to pace. "I know not. All depends on Madog. He'll set our ransom, and if it's not too dear, I'll pay, and we'll depart."

"What of the woman?"

"She wishes to find the other villagers from her town, so we'll proceed to Wrexham in search."

She narrowed her eyes at him. "And...?"

"No doubt I'll earn a rebuke for my delay and subsequent capture, but I'm in hopes I shall be able to redeem myself in the fighting to come."

"Fighting. You mean the war against the Welsh? Your people?"

"They are *not*..." He filled a cup with wine and took a sip. "This war is necessary, Mam. Sooner or later, the Welsh must accept that recognition of the suzerainty of the English crown is for the best."

"It is, is it?" His mother bristled, and the atmosphere grew more charged.

Kaytee bathed still, but the sounds had quieted. Mayhap his mother's presence caused her unease, and she'd stay in the tub until she turned cold with shivers leading to a fever. His concern for Kaytee, as well as his own mixed emotions surrounding his mother, clawed at him, made him itchy to move. "Can we finish this discussion at another time? I am begrimed and wish to bathe before the water cools further."

His mother gifted him with a baleful stare. "Another time, then."

Her clear disappointment knifed through him. He looked upon the once familiar, though older, features of his mother and felt a pang of deeply suppressed longing. Longing for acceptance. Longing for the unconditional love she'd always given him. Longing for that carefree time when he was but a child, and his mother and father were everything.

At the door, she turned. "Your cousin Dafydd is here."

He remembered the youthful visits with his cousin Dafydd and his siblings. "Only Dafydd?"

"His bothers Cynan and Gruffydd are with Maelgwn ap Rhys. And his sister Aelwen is married to a Welshman in the service of Madog and is besieging Harlech."

"Why is Dafydd not fighting?"

"He was made lame from an accident that befell him in his youth."

Robert could well imagine that had not pleased the high-spirited youth of his memory. Always eager he'd been for adventure and battle. "I'd love to see Dafydd, of course."

His lady mother nodded and left, closing the door behind. He heard Kaytee emerge from her tub, and he returned to the bench to ruminate on Dafydd, his mother, and this entire infernal mess.

එ

WHEN THE DOOR CLUNKED SHUT, Katy stepped out of the bath, and Elen vigorously rubbed her down with a linen cloth. Katy's fingers flexed, wanting to yank the cloths from Elen and do it herself, but she resisted giving away that this was *so* not normal for her.

Her skin buffed pink, she breathed in relief when Elen shook out a white linen gown, revealing colorful garments beneath. She'd been dreading donning her grimy and worn clothes after getting so clean.

Elen first helped her into the thin gown, like a slip. Over that, a robin's egg blue velvet tunic, followed by a buttercup yellow brocade surcoat with an apple-green lining. Unlike the men's surcoats, or even the one women's surcoat from the monks, this one laced up the front from her belly button to her low scoop neck, and was open on the sides all the way to her hips.

Oh, wow. It definitely, and flatteringly, emphasized her figure. Lastly, Elen placed a sheer white cloth on her head with a cloth band, but without a mirror, she had no clue what it looked like. She felt her hair being tucked up in it, though.

Delicious, so delicious to be in fresh, clean clothes, even if a strange design. She stood there and closed her eyes, cherishing the feeling of clean, natural fibers against her skin.

Elen helped her step into matching buttercup yellow slippers embroidered with blue vines.

Katy edged around the screen, and Robert turned to face her, his eyes widening as he took in her new look.

She couldn't help it. She twirled in a circle, feeling like a princess in the tower.

"You are lovely," he said in a low voice as Elen slipped out of the room.

"Thank you." She smiled and sat down to help herself to more food. "More wine?" She held up the flagon.

"No. I shall use the water before it cools. You're not the only one wishing to be clean."

"After me? In the same water?"

He stopped, surprise evident on his face. "Yes. I have no time to wait for its disposal and for them to heat another batch."

She stopped herself from saying, "eww," aware her feelings were a cultural bias, ingrained since birth, but she must not have shielded her feelings completely.

He tilted his head. "You find this an odd practice, I see. However, we are due downstairs for supper soon, I was told—for unlike our people, the Welsh have their main meal in the evening."

He stepped around the screen, and soon she heard his quick, efficient splashes as he also scrubbed off the dust and sweat from the road.

Oh, she did *not* need the visual of him naked, muscles bunching as he bathed. She needed a distraction. "Was that your mother?"

The splashing stopped. "Are you going to converse while I bathe?"

"Why not?"

"Feels rather unseemly."

She laughed, picturing him sitting there, shocked and indignant. "We're supposed to be married, right?"

"You have a point, however I would rather not discuss her right now."

"I think you're evading me."

"Mayhap. Is it working?"

"For now. So we're to have supper before talking terms with Madog?"

A large splash and the splat of wet feet on stone was her reply. Then, "Yes. Most likely he'll not find time to meet with me until tomorrow." He emerged, completely naked, as if that was quite normal. And it was, judging by the unconscious way he moved. Her gaze darted around the room, a nervousness prickling her skin, making her jumpy. The supposed intimacy it symbolized, as if they truly were married and at ease with each other, clashed with their true situation. Highlighted how fake their relationship was, like her relationship with Preston.

She shifted on the bench and cleared her throat. "So what's a twel...a twello?"

"A *tuelo*? A Welsh prince's personal guard. Usually around 160 men." He pulled out a tunic and the funny Jesus underwear from his trunk, as well as a surcoat he hadn't worn on the trip. "So the man has high aspirations." He dressed with efficient movements.

"How come you don't have a servant to dress you?" Didn't knights and nobles generally have personal servants?

He paused, surcoat covering his head, and then pulled it down with a sharp tug. "I have not yet attained the means for one. For now, it is me." His voice had gone flat, like how he sounded when she first met him.

ひ

LATER THAT NIGHT, ROBERT SHARED a bread trencher with Kaytee. It seemed his host had decided to make supper a festive occasion. Word had spread he was Gwendolyn varch Llywelyn's son, and the evening became an odd mixture of welcome to the family hearth, common Welsh hospitality, and celebration for capturing a Norman knight and his lady to ransom. Which mood predominated, he couldn't tell, but they sat at the main table, a mark of honor.

Since no one nearby spoke French, he made sure to include Kaytee with a smile or look and, if he had the chance, a quick translation. He savored, as well, tasting remembered dishes of his childhood, taking extra portions of salt duck for their trencher and more familiar fare like numbles of a hart.

His cousin Dafydd sat to his left, and they amiably swapped stories about their lives since last they'd seen each other. Robert was careful to avoid all talk of his cousin's accident and subsequent lameness.

"Your sister married Owain ap Owain," Dafydd related, breaking off a piece of barley bread. His black hair shone in the rushlight, his features an adult version of the boy of Robert's memory. Despite Dafydd's misfortune, he was fit. He had a hitch in his step, but Robert wouldn't wager on arm wrestling with his cousin.

"That wily bastard, huh?" Robert joked, but his throat tightened with a long-forgotten emotion.

When last he'd seen Marged, she'd been a wee lass of six, all dark hair and fierce eyes. From the moment he'd seen her swaddled in her cradle, so tiny, so trusting, he'd been swamped with a strange desperation and fear. Fear that such a tiny creature was vulnerable to the world, desperation that she might ever lack a protector. And so with that sense of desperation and fear, he swore he'd protect her with every fiber of his four-year-old being.

He was her champion against all taunts and teases from their many cousins and children inhabiting their family's castle. And she repaid him by following him everywhere, looking up to him with big, intelligent eyes, his partner in their scrambles around the castle grounds, pretending they were Arthurian knights.

And then he'd left her and never returned. Did she remember him even?

Dafydd chuckled, no doubt also remembering their childhood pranks and fights. "Aye. He's made her a good husband, in truth. They've settled near Flint." He took a swig of wine and wiped his mouth. "Remember when the three of us were allowed to rub down Prince Llywelyn ap Gruffud's favorite stallion?"

"And Marged braided his mane?"

"Ah, yes, I'd forgotten that. Wasn't the prince unhappy at that? I remember now. Made her take them out, he did."

"Indeed." Robert smiled.

"A great man, the prince. But not half as great as his uncle. If only he'd not been tricked. His murder was a sad day for all true Welsh, for his brother Dafydd was a fool."

"Though Edward is no fool," Robert countered. "The outcome was inevitable."

Dafydd stabbed his knife into the table and faced him, his features now serious. "How can you do it? How can you fight for them?" His host had avoided all talk of the war, but Dafydd obviously had no such qualms.

Robert's shoulders tightened, and he gripped his tankard until his knuckles turned white. "I am half Norman. Have you forgotten?"

"No. Your attitude is beyond my ken. Even your father knew on which side to fight when it counted."

As ever, when Robert thought of his father, a sense of shame heated his blood. "My father was a fool." He wished to avoid the topic, as he always did, but also because Kaytee's quiet presence beside him made him fully conscious of how isolated she must feel the longer the conversation could not include her. Her stiff posture indicated her awareness of their increased tension.

"Was he?"

Robert glanced around the great hall, but the revelers were too focused on their own food and their own cheer to pay them any mind. Nevertheless, he lowered his voice. "My father rebelled against his king, for whom he'd sworn an oath."

"But he'd sworn an oath to uphold the Oxford Provisions, had he not?"

"A fool's dream. The world is what it is." He'd once thought elsewise, when a boy and reading of the quests of knights errant, but life had cured him of such twaddle. Again, that long suppressed memory of the day he'd witnessed that truth came to mind. That day when he learned ideals of a knight were just stories. The screams of that English milkmaid...

"Think you de Montfort was a fool?"

Yes. Simon de Montfort was the biggest fool of them all. "Reality allows naught for scruples. His cause was just, I grant you, but it's unrealistic to expect a consecrated king to relinquish an iota of royal power."

"So tell me then, you believe we should obligingly roll over and present our bellies? Roll over and accept that England wishes to subjugate our people and force their laws, which are inferior to ours, onto our people?"

Robert gritted his teeth. "Yes. Edward is relentless. You've witnessed this. He's cunning and calculating. Already, he has built stout castles across Wales to shore up the gains he made in the last wars. Settled English and foreign merchants in his new towns and boroughs. Even now, he coordinates supply trains to bring in skilled workers and materials to build more and to clear roads—"

"And we attack every convoy he sends." Whether Dafydd realized it or no, his hand had gone to his knife embedded in the table, and alternately gripped and flexed his fingers as Robert argued his point.

"He's determined, Dafydd, to subdue your land. Better to make peace now than suffer his tender ministrations."

"You do not understand, do you, Robert?"

"From your perspective, I suppose I do not."

Dafydd grasped Robert's sleeve. "We can regain our sovereignty. There's talk of an alliance with Scotland. Balliol has been crowned king, but the Scottish are not happy the cost is homage to King Edward. If we join our strength to theirs?"

Now Madog's bard caught the attention of all as he approached the main table with his harp, and Robert was thankful for the interruption.

He'd enjoy catching up with Dafydd, enjoy the Welsh hospitality, but he'd be damned if he'd let himself be pulled into another such conversation again. His talk with Madog, and discovering the terms of their release, couldn't come soon enough.

And neither could finding his pleasure in Kaytee's warm thighs.

℃

KATY WOUND UP THE STONE STEPS, her rushlight casting sputtering, smoky shadows along the curving wall. Robert's sure tread echoed behind her, and Katy grew increasingly nervous.

His looming presence weighted the space between them, the pos-sibilities, the inevitabilities, thickening the air. God. Soon, in maybe ten more measly steps, she'd be in their room. Alone. With him. With the sensuality he oozed so strongly she could almost taste it.

And to taste that again? No way.

Her resolve had firmed since their capture. Her desire to indulge before had been lust, pure and simple, and she'd mistakenly believed she could do so without ramifications. But she had lost control, and that had scared her. The forced break had given her time to reflect and re-erect her emotional barriers. Take back control.

Now that they'd gotten to know each other better, lowering those walls would be too risky, would invest any intimacies with more meaning. No good could come of falling for this guy, so it needed to stop. Now. Besides, it wasn't as if he were the stick-around kind of guy, even if she could stay. Sure, he'd helped her, but he was a friggin' knight in the middle of a war, and he'd been upfront about his inabil-ity to marry. No picking out copper kettles for their wattle and daub any time soon.

But marrying Preston was out of the question. Her betrayal was un-forgivable, though Preston probably *would* forgive her...but she couldn't.

Katy stumbled, and Robert put a warm, steadying hand on her back. She shivered as his warmth spread through her to places she was increasingly trying to get to stand the eff down.

Hell. Sleeping with Robert wasn't the issue, only a symptom of her already-failing relationship with her fiancé. Without love and respect, their relationship would eventually have failed in its comfortable bland-ness, Robert or no Robert.

And while she was being honest...just the thought of experienc-ing Robert's raw sensuality again left her feeling...discombobulated, as if she were skidding across a scary-long patch of ice in the dark.

The sound of the door closing, shutting them in for the night, jolted her into awareness. And there he stood. By the bed. The gor-geous, red-draped, white-picketed bed. She gulped, shuffled to the table, and picked up some cheese. And put it down. She readjusted the wine flagon and cups. Moved the bowl ever-so-slightly to the left. There. Centered.

She took a deep breath to summon her nerve, and that stupid, spineless nerve stuck in her lungs, cravenly hiding in all the little air sacs. He was undressing. She could hear the rustle of clothes. Over by the—*gulp*—bed. Heat flushed over her whole body.

She whipped around. He was sitting on the bed, taking off his soft leather half-boots.

She straightened and crossed her arms. "I can't sleep with you," she blurted.

Chapter Twenty-One

❧

"Owain," said Arthur, "wilt thou play chess?" "I will, Lord," said
Owain. And the red youth brought the chess for Arthur and Owain;
golden pieces and a board of silver. And they began to play.
The Mabinogion, an ancient Welsh romance

OBERT'S BOOT-CLAD FOOT thunked to the floor, the weight of his searching gaze on her. What did he see? She was too far away to read his expression well. Her heart pounded-pounded-pounded.

"As you please."

"As you please?" She stepped back, the rough wood of the bench bumping her upper calf. She'd braced herself for a battle and now felt oddly deflated. "You aren't going to try to talk me into it?"

"I need not talk women into lying with me. If you do not wish it, I will not seek to change your mind."

"Oh." She sat down hard.

He cocked his head. "Are you wanting me to talk you into it?"

"No! I just..." *What?*

"What?" he echoed her own question.

"I expected a different reaction. I didn't think you'd understand."

"I am not sure I do. I shan't deny I still wish to lie with you. I know women's lustful appetites are stronger than men's, however, so if you no longer desire the same..." He shrugged, but it didn't quite achieve the nonchalance he strived for—his eyes failed to completely revert to his standard flat. Confusion and, yes, desire coiled within.

And what was he blathering about women's sexual desires being stronger? She got to her feet and stepped forward. "No, it isn't that. I...I still find you attractive," as *hell,* "but now that I've gotten to know you..."

A frown crossed his face, and his eyes made the final switch to flat indifference.

"This isn't coming out right. I'm sorry." She spun around and paced to the window and back. "Now that I'm getting to know you, the risks...the risks seem greater. Does that make sense? And I'm not sure I'm ready."

He tilted his head and continued studying her, which thrilled *and* scared her. He was so good at listening, paying attention. And knowing that one word from her could unleash his passion...?

"Things are very complicated right now," she rushed onward, heart pounding. "I have to get a certain item from those villagers and return home. I don't think—no, I *know* I can't risk getting emotionally involved. Not that I think *you* would become emotionally involved too. I'm not saying that..." Good Lord, was she babbling! "But on my part...and I can't risk that." Logical reasons all, but a part of her feared the element of chaos unleashed when they had sex—his raw strength, his raw sensuality. Feared her inability to control that chaotic feeling, and thereby inability to protect herself from the inevitable hurt at his loss.

"So you are afraid that if we resume physical intimacies, you might form an attachment, and you do not wish to do so?"

"Yes." She breathed a sigh of relief.

"I appreciate your honesty. However, I cannot ask for another room as Madog and his lady likely occupy the only other. Removing to a bench in the great hall would seem suspicious. I shall make a pallet on the floor, for I have slept in much worse conditions, believe me."

Her relief, tinged with a thread of guilt, left her even more exhausted. "Thank you."

He stood and nodded. "Get some sleep." He grabbed a woolen blanket from the bed and, with an economy of movements, chose a spot near the fire and settled in. While she stood there.

"Robert?"

He lifted his head. "Yes?" his voice wary.

"Why *did* you tell our captors we were married?"

"You do not understand?"

"You did it for my safety, I think, but I can't figure out why that guaranteed it?"

"Surely you are aware the chivalric code, whatever is truly practiced, only applies to those of noble birth?"

"Um..."

"Katy, if I had not given you the status as my lady wife...well, let us say I do not want to contemplate your fate at their hands."

His words chilled her as she stepped behind the screen. So much of this world she didn't know or understand. She undressed to her shift and, wincing at the sound it made, used the chamber pot. She washed her hands with the pitcher of water, blew out the rushlights, and settled into bed.

She had more than enough blankets, so she clambered back out and brought one to him, shuffling across the floor in the scant light from the window.

"Here is another," she whispered and dropped it on his dark form. She made her way back to her bed and crawled in. "How long do you think he'll keep us here?"

"Not too long, I should think," his voice already lower with approaching sleep. "He will want the funds he can extract from me to spend for their rebellion. It is not to his advantage to keep us o'er long."

"That's good."

But as she stared at his bulky frame, at the strong arms that could hold her and make her feel safe in this strange land, she wondered if she'd made the right choice in turning him away.

∽

"THREE HUNDRED MARCS!" Robert spluttered as he sat with Madog in a corner of the great hall. At most he had five marcs on him, and combined with the hundred the Templars held, he had hoped that would be enough to secure their release. "I'm not such a prize as all that, I assure you. I'm no earl, only a landless knight in service to a minor baron. Such funds are out of my sphere."

"Your mother avers otherwise."

Betrayal sliced through him. He tightened his fists. "My mother? What could she know? Not since my tenth year have I seen her. My fortunes, or paucity thereof, are beyond her ken."

"Nevertheless, those are my terms."

"Ones I cannot meet." It galled him to say it, but now was not the time to quibble with pride.

"Then we're at an impasse, I'm afraid." Madog poured Robert another cup of wine, his movements measured, as if all time belonged to him.

Robert took a sip, noting its quality. So they traded with France; a Welsh-French alliance would be unwelcome news in England. "What is your game?"

"There is no game, I assure you. We need the funds. You have them, and it's always been my experience that you English understate matters."

Robert clenched his fist around the cup of wine. "I do not lie."

"I did not call you a liar. I'm only relating my experiences with your kind."

"I'm Norman, not English."

Madog shrugged. "Same difference to us."

Robert set his cup down with a *thunk*, rattling the pewter ware on the table. "Where's my lady mother? I wish to speak with her." For speak with her he must, though—by all the saints' beleaguered knee caps—he only seized on it as an excuse. His head was not in this negotiation. Though he'd feigned indifference to Kaytee's request to refrain from further intimacies, the reality was far different. He'd barely slept for thinking of her mere feet from his pallet, and his nerves and temper were on edge. Not ideal for negotiating. He must fix his mind on their situation and how to get out of it and not on the bed sport he fantasized with Kaytee.

"She's in the kitchen garden, I believe, tending to some herbs she has planted." Madog stood, setting down his wine cup. "I'll send for her. Remain here."

Robert had no choice but to comply, considering the hall was crowded with Madog's household knights and retainers. He had not long to wait—his mother appeared shortly, and Madog left them alone.

"Mam." He crossed his arms and looked upward. "Why have you given Madog the impression I have the means to pay three hundred marcs for our ransom?"

"Three hundred? I told him only a hundred and fifty."

He whipped his hands into the air. Confounded woman. "Still too high. Why?"

Her face settled into stubborn lines, and she lifted her chin, smoothing out the folds of her dark green bliaut.

"Why, Mam?" he said with a little grit, frustrated with her machinations.

"All right. I wished not to lose you again."

"So you intend to keep me here by making it impossible for me to set myself free?"

She crossed her arms and leveled her gaze on him, her bearing proud. "If that ensures it, yes."

"There is a war, and I mean to take part in it. No. I *need* to take part in it."

"More reason for you to remain here."

"Do not coddle me."

"It's not coddling. You'll be fighting your own people."

"You do not understand what's at stake."

She leaned forward, a determined gleam in her eye. *This,* he realized, was what she truly wished to know. "Then tell me."

He strode to the nearby hearth. Spinning back around to make another circuit, he saw his lady mother had settled on a cushion. He couldn't very well converse with her in a reasonable tone if he remained pacing, so he sat nearby. "You realize, do you not, how hard it has been to achieve what I have?"

"How could I? You barely wrote, and it was never to share your good or ill fortunes."

"Thanks to my father and the shame he brought on our family, I was entirely beholden to my liege lord for whatever scraps he could spare."

She flinched. "I had no idea you harbored such animosity toward your father."

He pounded his thigh. "This campaign against the Welsh will be my first true opportunity to distinguish myself since I was made a knight. I saw little action in the final battles against Llywelyn ap Gruffudd. Tournaments have been few and costly. So you see, if I acquit myself well, Edward will doubt not my loyalty and will surely grant me my father's lands and title. De Buche has had it too long, and the villeins suffer for it."

"Your father's lands?" she whispered.

"Aye, I've petitioned the king."

"And then what?"

He studied her, puzzled. "What else? I shall oversee the tenants, repair any damage, collect my rents, and serve my king with my sword arm when need arises. Mayhap negotiate an advantageous marriage."

Why did the latter statement feel like a betrayal?

"And this will make you happy?"

He gave a short bark of a laugh. "Happy? What comparison does my happiness have with the restoration of our family's honor? If I am blessed with children, they'll not have the stain of my father's treason to shadow them as I did."

She plucked and shifted the fabric over her knee. "It grieves me to hear you deny happiness and to denounce your father thusly. But more so that you feel this to be an honorable undertaking."

"How could it not?"

"It would be honorable to follow your own heart and not that of a treacherous king who oppresses your kin."

Acquiring the status and respect of a landed knight was the only honor left in these modern, tumultuous times. His mother was wrong. And he would prove it to her. Prove it to everyone.

❧

ROBERT FOUND KAYTEE PLAYING CHESS with one of the guards, who held decidedly more pieces on the board than she.

"There you are," she said, her voice carrying a trace of relief, which shouldn't have gratified, but did. "I'm in a muddle. You people play by different rules, and I was never that good at chess anyway. But there's little else for me to do."

"Why not join the ladies with their needlework?" His voice sounded neutral enough, though every inch of him ached to lean forward and caress the cheek awash in the sunlight from the window, to assure himself it was indeed as soft as he remembered.

With a glance around the great hall, she muttered, "Maybe later." She straightened. "So, how did it go? Will we be able to leave soon?"

He nodded for her to step outside of others' hearing. Once alone, he said, "I'm afraid that will not be possible."

"What happened?" She gripped his wrist, and warmth spread up his arm and heated his blood.

Christ, grant me patience.

He told her of the exorbitant ransom being asked of him.

"What will you do?"

"I hope to convince Madog that the amount is preposterous. Even so, I daresay the price will still be too dear. This will delay my suit with the king."

"What suit?"

"I need to right a wrong of my father's. I have hopes I can distinguish myself to win the king's favor, and this money would have helped."

She bit her lip, something he'd not observed her doing ere now, and erotic images shot straight to his groin. "I might have something you could use. Would a gold ring set with a diamond fetch enough to help?"

Her hand was still on his arm. God help him. "The gold, mayhap, but the diamond holds little value." He inwardly winced for 'twas plain she thought it a valuable stone. "But I could not ask you to sacrifice your own property."

"Why not? I'm being held hostage too."

"But only due to my negligence."

She pushed his arm away and stepped back. "Well, if I hadn't been shot by an arrow, we wouldn't be here either."

He cast a glance to the side. No longer did her quiet strength surprise, and that she might have personal property of value shouldn't have. But he couldn't do it. "I'll figure out a way. My guess is you shall need that gold for the money it will fetch once we're free."

She opened her mouth and closed it with a snap.

"What is on your mind? I'm familiar enough with your moods and expressions. You're frustrated with me."

An impatient breath escaped her. "I'm torn. That's all. It's true I might need the ring later, but will there be a later if we can't get free?"

He straightened his shoulders. "I will find a way." He was surprised to hear his voice held more confidence than he felt.

Chapter Twenty-Two

*"Ah! maiden, thou art she whom I have loved; come away with me
lest they speak evil of thee and of me. Many a day have I
loved thee."*
The Mabinogion, an ancient Welsh romance

"TOO BAD IT IS THAT YOU ARE MARRIED," stated Madog. Robert was seated with his host in the main hall, badgering again over their terms.

Curiosity made him ask, "Why?"

"Otherwise, it would have pleased me greatly to give you my daughter Goewyn, lately turned fifteen and needing a husband. I would give this castle as her bride-gift to someone strong enough to hold it. Your reputation as one of the best Norman fighters in the region is something I would welcome into my tuelo and my family. We need your strength here. It would also mean you'd no longer be my hostage."

"And swear fealty to you."

"Of course."

"I could not have done such in any case." Nor would he disavow Kaytee.

"Come, Robert. You know allegiances on the Marches are always, shall we say, fluid. You wouldn't be the first Norman to marry Welsh and switch sides."

His father having been such a one, Robert gritted his teeth at Madog's bald statement. "That might have been so for others, but I cannot. My honor will not allow it. I swore an oath to King Edward." In a way, Robert had less freedom than a full-blooded Norman. He couldn't afford a whiff of collusion.

As he worked to impress on Madog his loyalty to the English crown, he also steered their discussion to a more sober assessment of his worth as a hostage.

At last, Robert was venting his frustration by wearing a path around the inner bailey as the Welsh warriors regarded him with a wary eye. He'd talked Madog down to one hundred and fifty marcs, but that was still too high.

Even if a letter was dispatched to the Knights Templar, requesting his full deposit be honored, 'twould not be enough. Not even with the addition of Kaytee's ring. It would also deplete the funds he'd planned to use to win his suit.

He stopped and looked skyward. No matter. Regardless of the final terms, he'd need those funds. Funds he'd painstakingly collected from his tournament winnings. He turned to one of his guards. "I'm returning within. Can you see to it I'm brought parchment, wax, and quill and ink? I must write to Keele. Will you be able to dispatch a courier?"

"I'll confer with my lord. He may know how to get a courier across the border."

Robert nodded and stalked back inside. One thing at a time.

℃

"GAH!" SHE THREW HER STUPID EXCUSE for embroidery across their tower bedroom, the only thing she could do solo to pass the time while they were stuck at this castle. Without meaning to, her haphazard aim made it sail right through the window.

She snorted a laugh. A soldier would have a puzzling find later.

On a sigh, she plopped onto the bed, the feather mattress giving slightly. "What am I going to do?"

None of her normal coping mechanisms were available—like making a task list in her smart phone or creating spreadsheets.

Ha. Not like she could've anyway, regardless of the technical impossibility, what with fighting for her life at the castle, fleeing, what-have-you. Reacting—that's all she'd been able to do. Now, sitting idle at this Welsh castle, an uncomfortable truth percolated up—the chaos was strangely and frighteningly freeing. So many things *completely* out of her control, so no responsibility on her part. But she couldn't let herself get too complacent. She needed to do something.

"But what can I do?" she whispered into the room, shoulders slumping.

Even if she could sneak out of this castle, she had no idea where she was or where the villagers went. No getting around it, she was a foreigner to this culture and could run afoul of some nasty folks. So far, she'd been damn lucky.

She slapped her thighs and stood. No option but to put her trust in Robert. Robert, who'd sacrificed more than she'd understood at first by not abandoning her during their escape from the castle. Robert, whose sacrifice shouldn't be repaid by abusing his trust. But why had he sacrificed?

A rush of confused emotions she'd been trying to bury roared to the surface. And what of Robert?

Calling a halt to doing the nasty with him again had been the right decision, but Good God she still wanted him, ached for him. And the intimacy of sharing the same room chipped away at her hastily erected defenses. She couldn't resist much longer.

Especially, whenever her eyes sought his, and she caught him staring at her with a heated look that took her breath away. And set her lady parts tingling.

For two nights now, they'd been at this castle, and he was always doing some small thing for her, some courtesy that showed she was on his mind, like bringing a pressed flower from the garden, or upon learning she liked hot beverages, bringing her a mug of hot apple cider every evening.

How was she supposed to resist that? But resist it she must. She couldn't stay here. And he'd made it clear he couldn't marry her. She had no life here.

Her life, her family and friends, were all about seven hundred years in the future.

"Focus on *that*, you idiot," she whispered fiercely.

Then why did the thought of leaving send her pulse to beat hard in panic—a panic that threatened to choke her with the feeling that to leave was somehow *wrong*.

♋

"I HAVE SOMETHING FOR YOU."

Robert's voice behind her sent her skin to tingling. She set aside another pathetic attempt to embroider after the first hapless monstrosity sailed through the window yesterday afternoon. Each day that passed made it harder to hide her "otherness" from the ladies. She squirmed out of most things by feigning shyness, plus none knew French or English, so that simplified things.

"Close your eyes."

She smiled, anticipation fluttering in her chest, and dutifully held out her hand. What did he bring her this time? Something hard and cool touched her palm.

"You may look."

She opened her eyes and looked down. And her heart nearly stopped.

It couldn't be.

Blood roared *it-can't-be-it-can't-be* in her ears, and she swayed, dizziness assailing her. *Breathe.* Fingers trembling, she brought it closer, inspecting it from every angle. No mistake.

Except for being freshly carved, the object she held, growing warmer in her hands, was the exact same artifact Isabelle had sent. Good God, it had been *the* reason—drawn to it as she was—that she'd even booked the trip to Wales.

"Do you not find it pleasing?" Robert's voice sounded nonchalant, but a faint whiff of doubt rode in its undertones.

"I love it." She met his eyes, blinking rapidly against the blossoming tears. "Thank you."

" 'Tis a sparrow. I saw one the other day, and it reminded me of you."

"How so?"

He shrugged, his large warrior's body otherwise rigid with tension. "Sparrows are usually the harbingers of spring, and well..." Strangely, crimson darkened his neck and face. "You..." He cleared his throat. "You are like that for me."

His sweet, stumbling confession seared right through her. She lurched to her feet and crushed him in a hug. His body stiffened but soon relaxed, his arms encircling her and holding her tight. His heart pounded against her upper breastbone, and all of her pent up desire for this man flushed her skin hot.

He broke away, his reaction to her evident in his heightened breath, his flaring nostrils, and dilated pupils. "I have some other news, sure to gladden your heart." He waved to the bench behind her.

She sat down, and he joined her, the tension between their bodies still crackling. "We shall leave on the morrow. My lady mother and I convinced Madog that what I have on hand and the funds arriving from the Templars are the extent of my funds."

Her heart picked up. "So what's our plan? Where are we going? I need to go wherever the villagers went."

"Unfortunately, I'm uncertain of the villagers. My mother learned that my commander is in Flint, not Wrexham. He will know where they are if they are not in Flint. Madog has provisioned us with food for our journey as well as a horse for you. Our passage will be much easier and swifter than before, what with the extra horse and the relatively flatter terrain."

"How long will it take?"

"It is not but fifteen miles from here. At a nice walk, we can be there before sunset."

"And then you will be sent to fight the Welsh, and I..." She swallowed a serving of panic that threatened to come up her throat.

"Yes," he said after a weighted pause. "What are your plans?" He crossed his arms and looked to the side as if her answer didn't matter.

She took a deep breath. "I lost something of mine before the siege. Outside the castle walls. You brought me inside while I was searching, and I was never able to return."

"I'm sorry to say, the chances of it remaining are nigh on impossible. Besides, it's too dangerous to return. I've heard the region is firmly in the control of the rebel forces."

She scooted forward on her bench, a tad closer to Robert. "But I don't have to go back. Just as we were retreating, I saw it with one of the villagers. I plan to find her and get it back."

"How do you know she still has what you seek?"

Yeah, she'd been worried about that too. "I don't. But it's unique and valuable, made of silver. I expect she'll hold onto it until she can get a good price. If I'm too late, and she's sold it, I'm hoping it's distinctive enough to be remembered, and I can trace who has it now."

Robert stretched his hand forward, as if to clasp her clenched fingers, then made a fist and thumped it against his thigh. "Why is this object so important?"

"It's the only way I can return to my...land."

His eyebrows rose. "The money you could fetch from that ring will not be sufficient?"

"It's not the monetary value, but the object itself. It is the, uh, token, by which I will be recognized and allowed to return."

"And it's important for you to return to your land?" His voice was low, thready, and his piercing gaze held hers, questions and some kind of suppressed emotion lurking in their depths.

She straightened, swallowing her doubt. "Yes," she choked out. "It is."

"Then I wish I could lend you my assistance when we reach Flint, but I know not what will be asked of me. I may be sent directly on some errand for my lord or put in service to fight the rebels. Once we reach Flint, I'm afraid we will have to go our separate ways."

"I know," she whispered.

Damn her moratorium on sleeping with him. Yes, she had to go home, but she knew she couldn't marry Preston. Well, she'd wanted to know if they should marry—had even wished on the stupid calling card case—and she had her answer. Calling it off and facing her mother would be a bitch, since her mother had never understood her.

The shadows and light in the room played across Robert's handsome features. Yes, this felt right to say. "Do you still wish to lie with me?"

His eyes widened, and he took her hand in his firm grip, his callouses deliciously rasping against her skin. He raised her hand, turned it over, and brushed his mouth against her palm, his lips whisper soft. Shivers coursed all over her at that simple gesture.

"Very much so." His voice was dark with sensual promise.

"I think...I think I was wrong before. Since we'll be parting at Flint, and tonight is our last night together..." Truth was, she couldn't deny herself one more taste of him before she left. Consequences be damned.

ↄ

SUPPER TOOK FOR-FRIGGIN-EVER. Since it was their last night, their host had turned it into a celebratory feast. But finally Katy was slipping up the tower stairs, Robert's strong form one step below. Knowing he was right there, knowing he was intent on the same goal once they reached their room, was getting her just a little hot.

And then he touched her hand and stroked up under her sleeve, the contrast between his calloused fingers and the supple velvet of her sleeve brushing against her skin sending a flash of chills over her body. She faltered on the step, the sole of her slipper scraping across the stone. One strong hand gripped her wrist, and another clutched her hip.

A jolt of desire went through her, and she stopped to get her balance. She grasped his hand at her waist, but didn't dare increase her pace on the steep spiraling stairs. He kissed her hand, and his warm lips brushed her wrist through the cloth of her sleeve. His nose nudged the cloth aside, his sharp breaths bathing the inside of her wrist, and his lips softly skimmed the sensitized flesh. A light touch by his tongue, and desire pooled in her sex.

He climbed another step, closing the space between them until his chest dragged up against her back, his heat pouring over her. Their soft, strained breaths bounced off the stone walls, loud in the narrow confines. Warm air on her neck narrowed her perception to his puffs of breath on her skin. Warm lips nibbled, brushed, kissed.

The hand holding her wrist circled around and pressed into her belly, pushing her bottom flush against his hips, against the hard evidence of his arousal. Oh. God. A shudder rocked through her.

Must. Get. Up. Stairs.

She drifted up to the next step, and the next, his heat, his presence, following until she reached the top. Robert leaned over, a breath near her ear, and helped open the door. Which was a good thing, for her fingers had been fumbling, shaking, eager to get inside. With a sure hand at the small of her back, he guided her into their space.

Alone now, she whirled around and faced him.

"Katy—"

"Robert—" she said at the same time, both of their voices breathless, on edge.

Their gazes locked. The heat and desire and naked longing in those fascinating eyes made her knees soften. Just a little. She leaned back and steadied herself with a hand to the trestle table. Eyes never leaving hers, he reached for his tunic. No. She wanted to do that. She took a couple of steps and then stumbled forward in her eagerness and bumped into him. Seriously. It was as if she had no control over her suddenly awkward limbs.

His strong arms banded around her waist, steadying her. "I need you," he grunted in her ear, his voice laced with dark intent and stark need—and slightly distorted as if wrenched from deep within.

Longing, urgency, and something else she wasn't ready to analyze, coursed through her at his words.

On sharp inhales, their mouths collided in a hungry kiss, one that punished the other for their absence, but also expressed how much they'd missed the other. With his hands, he carved paths into her hair, his nails a pleasant sting along her scalp. He angled her head, deepening the kiss, tongue stroking tongue, while she skimmed her hands up his back and gripped a handful of his tunic in each fist.

Oh God, she'd missed this. Missed his taste, his heat. Missed *him*.

His hard length pressed insistently against her stomach, and she ground her hips against him, rising to her tiptoes to get a better angle.

He moaned into her mouth, spun them around, and crushed her against the wall, trapping her deliciously between two hard, unyield-ing surfaces—one cold, one hot. Frantic, she fumbled with his tunic while he attacked the lacings of her surcoat, his hips pinning her in place, their arms tangling, brushing, and bumping into each other in their haste. She giggled, her frantic desire a heady rush, and whipped off his tunic in triumph. And his linen shirt.

"Ha. Beat you." Then her breath caught in her throat as she al-lowed herself the luxury of drinking in the splendor of his chest. He took advantage of her stillness and pulled her arms free of her tunic and yanked it down, freeing her swollen breasts. Cool air kissed the stiffened peaks, replaced in an instant by his warm hand, cupping one, the battle-hardened skin rasping along her soft curves. His thumb flicked her nipple.

"Robert. Robert. Robert." Need roughened her voice.

Eyes hidden by his thick lashes, he gazed downward. He hiked her up the wall to bring her breasts level with his mouth, and then he slowed, urgency bleeding from the moment. Reverently, he kissed the underside of her breast.

No way, buster. Don't you slow this down. She was in this for the kiss with chaos being with him gave her. No way could she let him change the dynamic, infuse it with meaning beyond that. She was hightailing it out of the Middle Ages as soon as she could.

She arched into him, gyrating her hips against him. Dark, intense eyes snapped to hers on an oath, and he captured her breast in his mouth, his hand holding it firmly in place. He sucked hard and she bucked, her body humming. Eyes now locked with hers, he flicked his wet tongue over the hardening peak. The erotic sight had her quivering in his arms. She shoved her hand between them and, ah, yes...she stroked hard down his length through his braies.

"Oh, Christ, woman," he gasped, his eyes closing tight.

She grazed his erection again, gently this time, and at the bottom of the stroke, reached around and delicately squeezed his balls.

The next instant, she was flattened against the wall with his upper body, his hand yanking on the string holding up his braies. He fisted the hem of her tunic in great handfuls, and she caught the fabric, bunching it around her waist. Their breaths stuttered in their throats, her sensitive breasts crushed against the hot skin of his muscled chest. He grasped her waist and lifted her, breaths heightening in anticipation. She whipped her legs around his lean hips. On a shout, he plunged inside her, pushing her back up against the stone wall.

"Oh. Oh holy shit!" she cried out at his exquisite invasion.

Chapter Twenty-Three

And the usual bond made between two persons was made between
Geraint and the maiden, and the choicest of all Gwenhwyvar's apparel
was given to the maiden; and thus arrayed, she appeared comely and
graceful to all who beheld her.
The Mabinogion, an ancient Welsh romance

ROBERT'S VOICE, ROUGH WITH DESIRE, whispered unintelligible words in Katy's ear, sending a fresh wave of chills and heat over her skin.

Breathless, she dropped her hem and gripped his shoulders, digging her fingers into his flesh. Robert's hands on her waist kept her pinned against the wall as he pounded into her without mercy, his breaths sharp and fevered. It was glorious. His hot need, hers spiraling tighter and tighter.

The sight. Oh God.

She spread her arms against the wall, the stone cool against her bare arms, and drank in every detail, like a woman starved: his powerful arms corded and straining as he pinned her in place, the firelight glistening across the smooth planes of his chest, the angle of his jaw tight with strain, the dark smattering of hair that circled each nipple and speared downward to disappear beneath her tunic, unable to see him working in her but oh, was she feeling the hot, hard, relentless glide. So close.

His gaze lifted to hers—hungry. The angle of his hips shifted, filling her impossibly fuller. The pulsing ache within built in successive waves, coiling, coiling, coiling, making her frantic for release, as if it would never, ever happen. Until it did. She tightened around him, her release exploding through her, her whole body shaking from the force of her orgasm. She clasped her arms around him and rode out the potent waves.

His speed increased, and it almost became too much, bordering on pain, but a delicious, fevered pain. He gave a roaring shout, head thrown back, neck taut. His hot warmth shot inside her, triggering another orgasm for her as she milked his pleasure.

She squeezed him, her body quivering—his too. Their sweat mingled and cooled as they fought to catch their breath, to calm the pounding beats of their hearts. His forehead bumped into hers.

She clung to him, hands in his hair, unwilling to let go, but her legs had turned to mush and slid down his. He slipped out of her, and she ached already at the loss. He cinched his arms around her, holding her up, and kissed the crook of her neck, his lips warm and lingering.

"Ah, *cariad,* finally I have you to myself, with a bed behind me, and what do I do? I had not planned to take you in such a fashion." His words came out in a ragged line as he struggled to get his breathing under control. "Please forgive me. Did I hurt you?" His eyes locked with hers, worry lurking within. He brushed a blunt finger across her cheek.

She touched his jaw. "No, I...it was exactly what I craved."

"I wished to take it slower though."

"Well, we do have the whole night..." She smiled against his shoulder and planted a nibbling kiss there, savoring the heat and strength radiating from his sumptuous skin. The moisture against her lips, the salty tang of his skin, his spicy, musky, warrior scent mixed with the essence of their love-making, a heady perfume.

"Indeed," he said, his voice a tad huskier. His manly bits jerked against her belly. A radiant smile transformed his handsome face, and her breath caught. So beautiful.

He scooped her up, and she squealed with delight. He marched to their bed and set her gently on her feet, which freed her tunic, shift, and surcoat, still bunched at her waist. The fabric dropped with a soft *whoosh.* His smile still playing at the corners, he turned her around.

"Beautiful," he whispered, his breath on her shoulder. He traced along her body, one curve after another. His calloused hands, so gentle, had her vibrating again with need.

She sighed, arched, reached back, and dug her fingers into his silky dark locks, gripping his scalp. Breath ragged, he yanked her against him and cupped her breasts, pinching, kneading, teasing, his body hot against her back. Oh God. She wanted him all *over* her. She gripped his butt—his very muscular butt—and ground against him. He groaned, his deep voice rumbling along her back. Shivers of delight coursed through her at the feel of him stirring and hardening against the small of her back.

He edged her forward, and she stepped out of the fabric at her feet. Her shins bumped against the bed, and he skimmed his hands from her breasts to her shoulders. Gently, he bent her forward between the gap in the picket-fence bed frame, his hands stroking down her back. A thrill of anticipation tightened her skin, tightened her sex. She braced herself against the feather tick mattress, the worshipful tracing of her body's curves making her feel more beautiful, more sensual, more special than she'd ever felt. Why had she denied herself this whole time? She shoved down the burgeoning regret—*enjoy the moment, this time with Robert. My last time with Robert.*

His erection rubbed against her now-slick sex, and she squeezed her eyes shut. Her awareness shrank to his firm, roving hands, to her sharpening arousal, to his velvety hard length stroking against her wet folds, her clit. Without warning, she cried out and shuddered with a small orgasm.

He gasped, bent over, covering her with his body. "So responsive," he choked out.

With a blunt fingertip, he stroked her as her shudders faded. Growling softly in her ear, he pushed slowly into her, filling her, stretching her, driving deeper than ever in this position. She dropped to her elbows and clutched the soft linen covering the mattress, her body quivering at his delicious and achingly slow invasion.

Normally, she hated this position, as if she were a mere object for her lover's pleasure, but, God, this was different. She trembled again as he pulled back out, inch by greedy hot inch and...

Fuck!

She wanted him to slam into her.

Take her. Possess her.

What the eff was wrong with her? This was *so* not her. But her body screamed otherwise as she pushed back against him, protesting his withdrawal, urging him to pound into her.

With one hand firmly gripping her hip, he stroked his other up the small of her back.

"Robert." She shuddered in frustration and need. "Take-me-take-me-take-me," she urged, though part of her realized she babbled in English.

"Shh, shh," he whispered. His wandering hand braced against the mattress, and he drove into her on a grunt. He cursed, set his teeth into the soft part where her neck met her shoulder, and drew slowly out again, obviously determined to take it slow.

On his next languorous thrust, she growled and pushed back, crying out. "Please, Robert." Already, a worry thumped alongside her heartbeat that this was starting to mean more than it could ever be allowed to.

His pace increased. His heat left her back as he lifted upward, gripped her hips and pounded into her.

"Yes, Robert. Yes." Her worry vanished at the force of his primal onslaught.

But on the next thrust, he stopped, his hands flexing and clamping on her waist. "No," he ground out.

He withdrew completely.

No. No. No.

He pushed his knee against the back of hers. Legs already weak, she fell easily onto the soft mattress, his large body tumbling with her, covering her. He flipped her onto her back and settled himself against her side, his dark eyes roaming the length of her body, while her sex throbbed at his loss. His nostrils flared. Now she could look at him again, and touch him, so she skimmed her hands along the hard planes of his chest, the tight, wispy curls tickling against her palms. She pinched his nipple, and he jerked.

He wanted to take it slow? She'd play along. She wanted to know *all* of his sensitive spots, since she'd not yet had that luxury, and if she was in control... She raked her nails over a nipple and trailed swirly strokes down his abs to his stomach, alert for the smallest reaction. He went completely still, which told her volumes—he feared doing anything that would stop what she did.

Did his past lovers not caress him, explore him, pleasure him?

His smoky, heavy-lidded gaze locked with hers, desire and a touch of vulnerability lurking there. Knowing she caused this shot both heat and a touch of trepidation through her. Smiling, shifting sideways to hide what she intended from his view, she lifted her hand away and grasped his erection.

His body jackknifed. "Christ." He clasped her hand with a groan. "Much as I burn for your touch there..." He swallowed and took a deep breath. "...I fear it will hasten the event, and I wish..." He kissed her neck. "...to take my time with you."

He placed a kiss below her ear, his breath a delicate puff that sent shivers racing along her nerve endings. His fingers flitted down her stomach to her sex—oh, yes—and... He paused. His head, poised to possess a hardened nipple, pulled away. He frowned, scooted down her body, and stared.

What—? She pushed onto her elbows. Was there something wrong with her girly parts?

He leaned over her, picked up the candle from the bedpost, and held it over her.

Uh... *Killing the mood here, buddy.*

He skimmed his hand along her upper thigh to her small landing strip of pubes. "You are mostly clean shaven here. I have never seen the like, though I heard tell of some ladies at court adopting the customs brought back by the knights from the Holy Land."

Oh. Whew. The bikini wax from several weeks ago. She plopped back onto the mattress.

"Is this a custom in your land?"

"Er, yes." *Let's get back to the sexing.*

"What a remarkably close shave..." His head tilted up, confusion clouding his eyes. "But I've seen you with no razor. How are you able to maintain its smoothness?" He fingered the sensitive, bared area, sending tingles of delight through her.

"Um, my culture has a way of pulling it out by the roots."

He winced, his head jerking back. "That sounds painful."

She smiled. "It is." She grazed a finger along the scar bisecting his chest. "But I imagine not as painful as this."

His eyes glinted with humor. "I don't know..."

She squirmed. "Can we, um, get back to...?" She wanted her one more chance at giving into his erotic chaos. Before she had to leave. Leave him.

He broke out one of his rare smiles, and it pierced right through her. "Yes." He leaned up, replaced the candle in its holder, and kissed her pubic bone. "Is this how you achieved your smooth legs as well?"

"Yes."

"An interesting custom. I noticed the legs whilst you were ill, but later when we first joined, I must have been lust-addled and missed the rest." Guilt slipped over his features. "Forgive me, I should have taken more care earlier to ensure you don't become implanted with my babe. I'm usually more careful. I will not be so careless again, I promise."

"You don't have to worry. I...I'm taking herbs that prevent pregnancy."

He frowned, trailed a finger down, and parted her already-wet folds.

The stone-chilled air caressed her inner skin, and she gasped. His warm lips touched her, and he flicked his tongue on her swelling sex. She nearly arched off the bed, would have too, if his strong arm hadn't held her hips firmly in place.

He worked his tongue around her aching nub, sucking, stroking, teasing, adjusting to the subtle signs he must've read in her reaction. A finger, and then two, slid inside, languidly thrusting as his talented tongue and mouth went wild on her. Delicious heat coiled tighter and tighter. She couldn't take much more. How many orgasms would this make? Was this an undocumented medieval torture tactic—Death by Orgasm?

Desire raced and fired along her nerves. She fisted his silky hair in her hands, and he chuckled, the vibration along her sex all that was needed to trigger another intense release.

Another orgasm, another blast through her rapidly crumbling defenses. She clamped her thighs against his face and rode out the pulsing waves as he milked her.

When her quivers subsided, he pried apart her legs, shot forward so his warrior's body covered hers, and captured her mouth. She moaned at the taste of herself on his lips, and he drove into her in one smooth, hard thrust.

Oh God. She stilled, glorying at the feel of him inside her, his hot length stretching her. He remained motionless below, propped up on his elbows, taking some of his weight, and continued to plunder her mouth with hot, demanding kisses. She smoothed her hands up his muscled arms, across his back, and gripped his butt, pulling him deeper, and grinding him harder against her.

Oh, that was so delicious—*move*. His kisses grew more fevered, but stopped, his breath fanning against her cheek. He resumed his languid kisses, still not moving in her. She cinched her legs around his lean waist, locking her legs behind him, as his tongue swirled a slow rhythm.

On a sigh, she surrendered completely to his pace. Surrendered and dropped deeper into the moment, into each movement of his, of theirs, with his hot length inside her like an anchor around which all else moved. She trembled in his arms.

When their kisses became all she knew, he drew out, his velvety thick column sliding exquisitely against her feminine walls, and she gasped, the loss more acute and, because she was so attuned to every small move, more intense. He eased inside again, and she arched up at the same pace, shivering when her hips met his, and they were completely joined again. His handsome face set in determination, tawny eyes locked on hers, he maintained the slow rhythm, languidly kissing her jaw, her earlobe, her nose, her chin. She met his gentle thrusts each time, not rushing him. Oh, her serious knight had some serious moves.

The slow build gripped her, and she fought against the cresting desire, fought the urge to speed him up. But the need grew too acute, almost painful and, because held at bay for so long, more powerful in its urgency. She raked her nails up his straining back, and he arched his head back on the next thrust, mouth slightly open, his breath hitching, his eyes clasped shut. He opened them and locked his hooded gaze with hers. His thrusts became faster, his powerful body surging inside her over and over.

"Yes, oh, yes!" she breathed. He hit her in just the right spot on the next plunge, and she convulsed. Heat flushed her skin, and she cried out, slammed with an orgasm so intense, gripping her so tightly, she wondered if it would ever end.

"Christ and all the saints," his breath was ragged as he rammed into her faster. Her mind and body pulsed and shuddered with wave after wave of searing pleasure. He shoved a hand under her hips, and drove into her once more. His face contorted, his body stiffened, and, on a rough shout, his hot seed bloomed inside her, flushing her again with an intense thrill.

He collapsed on top of her, still inside her, and she wrapped her arms and legs around him, holding him as tight as her languid, satisfied body could. Far from making her feel as if she were spinning out of control with the force of their passion, she felt as if they'd forged something new together, something unique to them, that grounded her in the moment.

He rolled onto his back, his arms around her, and she snuggled against him, already half asleep. But then she remembered the candle and reluctantly eased away and snuffed it out. His hands followed her and pulled her back to nestle against him, placing a gentle, sweet kiss on her forehead.

Oh God, how could she ever let him go?

❧

DAWN SENT A REFRACTED GLOW through the small tower windows, and Robert lay there in the semidarkness, reluctance weighting his limbs. As eager as he was to reconnect with his commander, another undefinable emotion held him back. He contemplated Kaytee's sleeping form, her short, dark locks a splash against his chest. He kissed the top of her head, inhaling her now familiar scent, and was seized by an unfamiliar pinch of protectiveness and longing. If he started their day, 'twould put in motion the events that would divide them.

Careful to not awaken her, he slipped a finger behind a lock of her hair and twined it around, reveling in the silky feel of her tresses against his rough skin. But he was not careful enough, for she stirred, and her head moved against him, her sleepy gaze seeking his.

"Morning," he murmured.

She smiled. "Morning." She kissed his chest, her warm lips lingering for a moment on his skin. Then she sighed and propped her chin upon him. "So, we leave today."

"Yes."

Her eyes, still on his, deepened with curiosity and a trace of hesitation. "Robert. What happened with your father? Why are you so driven to be honored by your king?"

He broke her gaze. Christ, was she ruthless in the morning. "Same as any landless knight, I suspect. For security. A steady income. A holding to pass on to my descendants."

Her fingers were on his chin, turning his head to face her again. "No. There's something more. Something to do with your father, but you've never said."

Of a sudden, her slight weight as she lay draped across him seemed to intensify, his chest tightening as if she'd pinned him there with her body, her stare, her questions. He pulled in a shaky breath and searched her lovely hazel eyes for...for...what? Would she think less of him if she knew? The thought chilled his blood. But so did the thought of their parting, and that was already a surety. What harm could it do? Mayhap it would make their farewell easier. For her, at least.

"My father committed treason when I was but a small lad."

Chapter Twenty-Four

If thou hear an outcry, proceed towards it,
especially if it be the outcry of a woman.
The Mabinogion, an ancient Welsh romance

ROBERT DREW IN A SHARP BREATH. Having the worst of it out of the way lent him freedom. He'd need only supply the details. "My father was a staunch Montfortian, killed at Evesham, his lands and honors forfeited to the crown. To redeem them, like most others, we needed only pay an exorbitant fee and swear fealty to King Henry, but I was too young to do so, and my mother was too Welsh. We lost our demesne."

Then, he waited. For disgust to enter those lovely eyes. For her body to stiffen and pull away, gaze averted.

She frowned. His heart stuttered a beat. "I think I understood most of that, and I feel horrible for your pain and loss, but...what is a...a Montfortian?"

Not what he'd expected to hear, for certes. Ah, yes, French was a foreign tongue to her. "A follower of Simon de Montfort." He braced himself again, muscles tightening.

"Who is Simon de Montfort?"

He leaned slightly away and looked at her in amazement. "You have not heard the name Simon de Montfort?"

She shook her head.

"Christ on the cross," he breathed out. "I thought every blessed soul in Christendom was familiar with him. You truly know not?"

Inexplicably, her cheeks pinkened. "No," she mumbled.

He let his head fall back on the pillow and closed his eyes. Could he discuss this? Never before had he needed to elaborate, everyone only too aware of the man, and the name. Depending on the person,

Montfort was either a saint or the devil's own.

A soft hand brushed his shoulder. "Will you tell me?" Her chin made a jouncing movement against his chest as she posed her question.

He nodded. "Montfort was the Earl of Leicester, and from the tales of those who knew him, he was intelligent, arrogant, charming, and lit by moral certitude. He surprised all by marrying King Henry's sister, Eleanor, and enjoyed, for a while, the king's favor. But after a time, he and many other barons grew frustrated with the king's abuse of power and sought to limit him, to make him abide by the Runnymede Charter—"

"The Runnymede Charter?" She shifted higher on his chest.

"Your land must indeed be far. It was the document drawn up by the barons in King Henry's father's day, the devil's own King John—"

She gasped and pulled back, hands on his chest. "You mean the Magna Carta?"

He cocked his head. "The Great Charter? I haven't heard it called thusly, but an apt description for its supporters."

Her lips rolled together, virtually disappearing.

"But back to hapless King Henry. Montfort and his supporters made him sign the Oxford Provisions, but Henry—"

"Wait. The Oxford Provisions?" She settled against his chest, hands linked, chin resting atop, not at all perturbed by her ignorance.

"An additional document designed to curtail the king's power and holding him to the provisions in the...Magna Carta. However, once King Henry was able to ignore it, he did so. Montfort and the others had sworn to uphold the provisions, and when diplomacy and compromise failed, it led to a trial by combat."

"What do you mean?"

Yes. Of a surety, she hailed from a faraway land. "Each side came together in a clash of arms at Lewes to see which side God supported, to see who was right. Montfort won. With Henry and his son Edward captured, he ruled England through Henry for the better part of a year. Shocked all by his notions that chivalry and justice extended to the lower classes. Called a council together not only of the earls and barons, but knights from every shire and even town burghers."

"Parliament. You're talking about parliament," she whispered, eyes round.

193

"I've never heard that term, but I take your meaning. It fits."

"But how does your father figure in?" She shifted so she leaned an elbow on the mattress and absently rubbed his chest. Ah, God, that felt divine.

"He supported the Oxford provisions and Montfort from the start. And though many other Marcher lords defected to the royalist side after Lewes, my father remained steadfast, loath to cast aside a sworn oath. Besides, my mother's kin supported Prince Llywelyn, a staunch ally of Montfort."

"What happened at Evesham?"

For the first time since Robert had begun his confession, he dared touch her. He smoothed his palm along her upper arm, to the curve of her shoulder, and back. "Montfort and many of his supporters were cornered there by Prince Edward and his army of loyalists. I've heard tell, it was more of a slaughter than a battle true, such was the vengeance the royalists sought with their swords. In total disregard of the chivalric code, knights were hacked, not held for ransom."

Her arms tightened around him. "And your father was one of them."

"Yes." He swallowed down the long ago hurt, the long ago pain. "And denounced a traitor. Even today, twenty-seven years later, rancor still runs high, especially here on the Marches. And with none more so than the Earl of Gloucester, erstwhile ally of Montfort. Gloucester loathes him still."

"So you lost not only your inheritance, but also your father. And it sounds like, your pride as well."

He sucked in a breath. "Pride is a mortal sin."

She looked startled at that for some reason. "I didn't mean it as an insult, only in the sense of a healthy family pride. It must've been hard growing up."

It had been. Of his father he remembered little, nor did he remember much about that time, only that they were living in Wales with his mother's kin, ignorant of everything but that his beloved father was gone. It wasn't until he'd fostered with Sir Hugh that he learned of his father's treason. Once de Buche and the other pages and squires, Marcher lads all, learned of his father's deeds and declared it treason, the taunts became his new reality, the crucible which forged his dream to regain his land and his family's honor. "I managed. Sir Hugh was good to me."

"If your father committed treason, why did Sir Hugh agree to foster you?"

"He was an old friend of my father and was himself a Montfortian. But unlike my father, he'd survived the conflict and was able to pay the forfeit for his land and position. Allegiances here switch. It's not so unusual."

She searched his face. "So how did you become a knight?"

"I served Sir Hugh faithfully as his page and squire." He pulled her around to snuggle against him. "As his squire, I participated in Edward's push against Llywelyn ap Gruffudd that led to the Treaty of Aberconwy. Several years after, he knighted me, gifting me with armor and horses as his hearth knight. He gave me leave to enroll in tournaments, and it was at Nefyn that I not only gained Perceval, but also the attention of my lord Chirkland, whom I've served since as one of his household knights."

"So this is what drives you." She shifted her head to rest her chin on his chest, her eyes searching his, digging deeper into his soul.

Lord, even he knew not what lay there. Would she see there was naught?

"Indeed." He risked studying her for signs of a change but beheld only acceptance. Strange it was, to reveal an all-too-familiar history to one who had no prior knowledge, no prejudice. Unlike the first time he'd naively entrusted his father's story to another whilst still a page. The bitter sense of betrayal, the loss of newfound friendship when he'd been so achingly alone, had embedded a soreness on his soul, coloring everything thereafter.

He had no wish for her to see that stain on his soul with her probing gaze. "But enough of this, we must make ready for our journey."

She lifted away slightly with a frown. "What of the Welsh?"

"What do you mean?"

"What if we run across another band of them?"

"Madog has issued me a document ensuring us safe conduct to Flint, affixed with his seal."

"Will you see your mother before we leave?"

"Yes." He gave her a light spank. "Arise, my fair lady, we must be off." At her mock effrontery, he grinned.

"But first..." He stood and strode to his mostly depleted chest. "I took the liberty of acquiring a new set of squire clothing, but we will stop after we depart, when you can change. I believe it safer to continue your ruse once again."

"I think so too, thank you."

"Unfortunately, the mantle is white, hence why it came so cheaply. It had a flaw in its cut and was not worth dying. And take this." He tossed a leather pouch at her, which she deftly nabbed.

"What is it?"

"I held back some silver from Madog. I wish you to have it. I know not what situation we shall find upon arrival. I will shield you as much as I can, but just the same, you might have need of coin."

"I have my ring." She gripped the pouch.

"You might not find the time or means to sell it. Please..." He pushed her outreached hand with the pouch back to her side. "It will put my mind at ease." He pulled her close and kissed her forehead. "As much as I wish it otherwise, I cannot keep you at my side."

Was that hurt he saw flash through her eyes? Mayhap she'd been right before to refuse him her bed, for the thought of letting her go clawed at everything inside him.

Ω

ROBERT SAT ON THE CUSHION beside his mother in the great hall. "We are to leave today for Flint."

She clasped her hands together. "So it is rumored. When will I see you again?"

Guilt and a sense of inadequacy hit him. He glanced away. "I know not. Mayhap after this rebellion is settled."

Her features tightened into grim lines, but she nodded. "I wish for you to have something of your father's." She reached inside the pouch at her waist.

He stiffened. "I do not—"

She held up her hand. "Your father was a brave and honorable man."

"He committed treason."

She *tsked.* "So says King Edward, but that was not what was in his heart, my son. His aim was not to depose the king, but rather to have him honor his own sworn oaths, oaths he forsook at the earliest convenience. Your father was a man of honor. He could no more have forsworn his solemn oath to uphold the Oxford provisions than cut off his own hand."

Robert remained still, his emotions and thoughts warring with each other. He kept his counsel though.

She laid a hand on his arm. "There's no shame in honoring a vow, honoring in your heart that which you know is right."

He fidgeted. Personal honor such as that was feasible only in the Arthurian romances of his youth. No matter how much King Edward styled himself as the embodiment of King Arthur, the reality was much different. But he wished not to take away his mother's illusions.

She opened his hand. "Here. A memento from his pilgrimage to the Holy Land." She placed a smooth, multicolored stone in his palm and closed his hand over it.

"He took the Cross?"

"I told you so as a child."

"I did not remember," he murmured, embarrassment burning in his gut.

She nodded, her face solemn. "He found this stone in Palestine. He didn't rank high enough to acquire such relics as a nail from the Crucifixion or a piece of the True Cross, but your father valued it just the same. He espied it the morning after a fierce battle against the Saracens and was thankful he still drew breath, though he believed fervently enough in his cause to die for the faith. The stone spoke to him, and he treasured it."

Hearing this about his father, about something unrelated to his treason, was a tight fist around Robert's throat. It made his father more complicated, more concrete, so he no longer fit into the tight role Robert had made for him.

A sense of loss swamped him. Reciting his history to Kaytee this morn had acted as a strange sort of purging, as if the act of revealing had allowed him to see it through another's eyes, allowed him to examine it anew and form new opinions. Robert placed the stone in his own pouch at his belt. It gave him the time he needed to control his emotions.

Only to have them stutter when his mother asked, "Will you visit Marged and Owen? You will be near their land. She would love to see you."

Chest tight, he responded. "Will she even remember her faithless brother?"

"She worshiped you. You know that. No, she will not have forgotten you. She crafted stories of your imagined adventures. She was proud of you. Hurt you never visited, but proud nonetheless."

Could he see his sister? *No.* His prolonged absence in her life deserved more than a harried visit. And harried 'twould have to be during this time of war. He swallowed past a knot in his throat. "I'm not sure I'll be able."

Sadness lurked in his mother's eyes. "If you change your mind," and she gave him instructions on how to find their demesne from Flint.

He stood. "Will you see us off?"

"Of course." She took his hands and squeezed, offering him a watery smile. "You know I had to foster you to Sir Hugh."

"I am aware of the path to knighthood." A long-buried hurt surfaced. "But why Sir Hugh? Why not with Pedr, or one of your other brothers?" He'd not realized how much he'd resented being pulled from her bosom and his Welsh kin.

"I kept you for as long as I was able. But Sir Hugh had been named in your father's will as your legal guardian. I had thought him ignorant, and when your seventh year passed, my heart began to ease. But he sought you out, and I had no legal standing in their Norman courts, mother or no. Believe me. I did not relish putting you in such a man's hands."

"Sir Hugh is a good man."

"Let me tell you how I feel about Sir Hugh and those other barons. If your father had lived, I have no doubt he would not have broken that oath." Her voice turned bitter. "Unlike Sir Hugh and those faithless barons. Your father honored his oaths. Unlike this King Edward you follow. How can you serve a king, and call yourself honorable, when that king doesn't honor his own oaths? And be ashamed of a father who did?"

He stared at her hands, still lean and strong, and felt long-held beliefs begin to crumble. He shored them up until he had the time for reflection. And as his father had become a more complicated figure with this new knowledge, so had his mother and his feelings for her. He had much to contemplate, but under all rode a thread of affection that had survived from his childhood despite himself. It swelled for a moment within, competing with his long-held feelings of resentment, to form a hot ball in his throat. He squeezed her hands and kissed her on the cheek, unable to articulate further.

"I hope you find that which you seek, my son." She held his cheek, brushed it with a mother's kiss, and stepped away.

"Thank you, Mam." But his quick bow was not quite so smooth, for instead of envisioning his suit being granted—earning back his lands and family honor—her words had conjured Kaytee, always by his side.

⁂

LATE AFTERNOON SUNLIGHT SPILLED through the trees crowding close along their final approach to Flint. The extra horse from Madog had indeed made their trip faster. An hour ago, the path across the forested, rolling flatlands had widened to something resembling a thoroughfare. The trees on either side had grown unnaturally quiet, and the first refugees stumbled across their path. The numbers increased, Welsh and English villagers alike, wary of Robert but causing no trouble. The reports were the same—the region was in chaos and completely lawless. Katy now held scant hope the villagers would have stayed in Flint, if they'd gone there at all.

The lawlessness left her feeling raw and exposed. She latched onto the sight of Robert's formidable form, bobbing and swaying with an unconscious grace in his saddle ahead. What would have happened to her without him? He'd chosen to stay with her, even when it hurt his cause. Even when she was a burden. Even through all this chaos, even through her mood swings, one thing had been a constant—he'd never abandoned her.

Unlike her father.

But as she nudged her docile mount along the road, a new understanding flooded her. It wasn't anything *she* did that had caused the people in her past to leave. *She* hadn't driven away her father with her temper tantrums. *He'd* made that choice. *He'd* lacked the maturity to meet the demands of fatherhood. *He'd* been the weak one.

Desperate to avoid abandonment again, she'd circumscribed her life to play it safe, to guarantee she'd never feel that pain again. The pain of being unwanted.

And this had botched her relationship with Preston and prevented her from truly opening up to the possibilities Robert presented. Too scared to risk herself or her heart.

Shit.

They passed a burnt-out farm house, the grim-faced family huddled beneath a tree. Plumes of smoke smudged the horizon ahead. The air thickened with the smell of burning wood, straw, and other unknowns, adding up to aw-shit-not-good. Shouts and screams echoed in the near distance, and a cold wash of fear flooded her spine.

Katy spurred her horse. Robert slowed, and they drew alongside. Since she was again posing as his squire, she held his shield and lance, the latter purchased from the Welsh before leaving that morning. He'd also given her a short-handled mace, which she kept belted at her side.

Robert twisted his upper body toward her, his brows furrowed. He motioned with his hand, and she silently passed him his shield, proud her grip held steady despite the blood pounding through her veins. He urged his mount into a trot, and she did the same. She sure as heck didn't want to stay behind. The packhorse behind her kept pace.

They passed a bend in the road, and Robert drew his sword with a steely hiss.

What—?

And then she saw it. A Norman knight struggled with a woman and ripped her dress. She screamed, twisting in his grip as he ran his tongue up her neck.

Oh. God. No.

Robert galloped toward the attacker, his horse's strides eating up the short distance. The other knight was so focused, he didn't notice Robert's approach until the last moment.

No. Robert was not the cynical, hardened warrior he pretended to be. Or believed himself to be. Her heart stuttered as he heroically dashed to the lady's rescue.

The attacker swung his head around at the same moment Robert raised his sword. The man looked familiar, which seemed odd. *Wait.* He was one of the knights at Castell y Bere, the surly one. His blond hair was matted to his forehead, his helm missing. Mud and blood streaked his craggy, harsh features.

Oh God. It was that Nasty Knight, Ralph de Buche. The one who relished cruelly toying with his enemies. The one who snapped when his victim fought back, however feebly. The one who seemed to hate Robert.

Chapter Twenty-Five

And Blodeuwedd looked upon him, and from the moment that she looked on him she became filled with his love. And he gazed on her, and the same thought came unto him as unto her, so that he could not conceal from her that he loved her, but he declared unto her that he did so. Thereupon she was very joyful. And all their discourse that night was concerning the affection and love which they felt one for the other, and which in no longer space than one evening had arisen. And that evening passed they in each other's company.
The Mabinogion, an ancient Welsh romance

OU GOING TO RUN ME THROUGH, Robert? 'Tis only a Welsh wench. Or did you want her for yourself?"

Anger, sharp and hot, flashed along Robert's muscles. And that long ago day when he'd attempted, and failed, to save another defenseless woman superimposed in his field of vision. But *this* time, the outcome would be different.

"What's happening here?" And then fear chased the anger. Not for himself, but for his sister and her family. If the environs were in such chaos, how did they fare? He should have listened to his mother and visited. Made sure she was safe.

"Teaching a lesson to the locals. They got out of hand, thought they could rise up and overthrow their local lord."

"A lesson to their local warriors, you mean. This lass is no warrior." He lowered his sword so it pointed at de Buche's heart.

"No matter. These are merely Welsh. They'll get what's coming to them." Genuine confusion battled with disgust across de Buche's face. "Ah, I see. Protecting your own, are you?" He whipped out a dagger from his sword belt and yanked the frightened woman around by her hair.

Enough of this.

Robert angled his sword back and whacked de Buche across his temple with the flat of the blade. The cur of a knight slumped to the ground, the woman falling with him. She lurched back, crab-style, her eyes round with fear.

Speaking in Welsh, Robert encouraged her to seek protection elsewhere in the forest. She bolted up and ran into the surrounding woods. Robert slapped the rump of de Buche's horse and watched until it galloped out of sight. He wheeled his horse around and rode back to Kaytee's side.

"Come," he said, straining to grab her reins. "We must ride for Flint as hard as the packhorse can manage. De Buche will not be out for long. Of a surety he is not alone."

Frankly, that he'd not run de Buche through with his sword was a bit of a surprise. Leaving him alive only complicated matters, but as he'd ridden toward his nemesis, the weight of Kaytee's eyes on his back stayed his hand. He wanted to be what she'd hinted she saw in him—honorable. And he'd not forgotten his mother's words from this morn.

᠙

KATY ANGLED FOR A BETTER VIEW of Flint. Folks on foot and carts pulled by stout ponies shared the road as they wended toward town. Ahead trudged two white-robed monks.

At the town's edge, a threadbare and grimy man was leaving town, pushing a small wooden handcart overflowing with a large, dark, fly-covered mound. As they neared, she gagged and turned her head away. It was poop he was carting out!

The town didn't have a wall but instead was surrounded by a deep, wide ditch and a wooden palisade. Soon they were through the palisade gate, and a grid-like town spread before them, but more than half of the buildings were burnt to the ground.

She looked to Robert. "What happened?"

"We'll find out soon enough." They turned right down a lane with charred, smoking ruins and reached an area that had been spared. They fetched up in front of a two-story building, which had no windows but had a large double door open wide at the moment. As they passed through, she discovered it wasn't the side of a building but a gate in a wall connecting the ends of a U-shaped wooden structure. Now they were in an open courtyard. Was this an old wooden fort?

"I will see about a room."

"This is an inn?"

"Indeed. Did you not see the emblem out front?"

The ground floor of one side held a well-kept stable, and plain doors on the other sides indicated it might house storage. A wooden porch ran along the second floor on all three sides, overlooking the courtyard. They collected their belongings, and a boy emerged from the stables and led their horses away.

"Let's see about that room," Robert said with a wink.

A room they'd share as knight and squire to the outside world, while inside...

A thrill shot through her. Oh man, was she in trouble. Having sex again had mucked up her emotions exactly as she'd originally feared. Now, she craved more of him, more of his touch, his strength, his gentleness. His roughness. But there was more to it than that.

Even when she'd altered it yesterday, her plan had been clear. The Original Plan—avoid sleeping with Robert to protect her heart and return to her time. The Altered Plan—sleep with him to experience his raw passion once more before returning to her time.

Now? Her Plan had a big, fat wrinkle in it—learning and experiencing a sense of connectedness, not only with him, but also with the world. With Robert, everything felt right. Everything made sense.

But she had to leave... Didn't she? Yes. Because despite her feelings, or even what he might be feeling for her now, he'd said he couldn't marry.

Her throat thickened, and she blinked back tears as she followed Robert up the wooden steps at the base of the U-shaped inn into the main public room. It was kind of how she'd have pictured the interior of a medieval inn, but not quite, for her imagination couldn't have filled in all the details, or the myriad smells. A fire blazed in a stone hearth in the center of a large room, the ceiling exposing the roof beams. Trestle tables and benches filled the floor space. Stale body odor mixed with the scent of rushes and herbs spread on the floor, with an over note of horse poop. Travelers and locals filled the benches, drinking and gossiping, while a harassed serving girl did her best to navigate the customers' shouted instructions.

Several scruffy-looking dogs lay curled up before the fire, and a cat sat on the counter, very much looking like a lord surveying his domain. The walls were white-washed, but dark smoke stains marred them near where rushlights burned.

Robert conversed with the innkeeper, a short man with a leather apron and thinning blond hair. Robert returned shortly. "We are in luck. They still have one of the better rooms off the hall. Otherwise we'd have to share a room off the outside gallery with others."

"Did you find out what happened to the town?"

"Aye. Burned by order of the constable to protect the castle against the Welsh. The townsfolk are quartered within the outer bailey, preferring to make do there for free than pay for accommodation here. The innkeeper was glad for our fare."

She dared not stand there any longer, peering around like a nosy busybody. She picked her way across the rush-strewn floor. Their room was toward the back of a short hall and, while small, was rather cozy, with a fire already blazing.

"I daresay we should have something to tide us over ere long if the innkeeper is quick with my request." He unbuckled his sword belt and sat in the settle by the fire.

"What's your plan? Do you see your commander?"

"Yes. But not tonight. It is too late, and I will do myself no favors seeing him weary from travel. After we break our fast on the morrow, I will seek him out. The innkeeper confirmed Staundon's whereabouts."

"Will you ask where the villagers went?"

"Aye, that I will do, for certes. I'll return as soon as I can. If unable to get away, I'll send a messenger here with what I learn, so I'll not delay you."

Emotion choked her throat to hear him speak so casually of their separating, at how easily he'd let her go. But she knew this was coming. Very well, then.

She approached the trestle table and ran a finger along the rough wood. "Robert, I thanked you earlier for not abandoning me when I was sick, but I..." From the corner of her eye, she could see his large frame engulf most of the bench.

Robert. Robert whose presence, whose pull, was stronger than ever. Again, unable to resist, she swung around the table and settled beside him, placing her hand on his arm. She swallowed a lump in her throat. "Now knowing what you sacrificed, I want to say, again, thank you. You have no idea what it means to me. I hope it won't permanently affect your plans."

What a completely lame thank you. The full depth of her fear and her gratitude swelled up within and almost—*almost*—burst from her tongue. Thank God, some sense of let's-not-look-pathetic stayed her. It was *her* hang-up, one she'd finally recognized. They needed to part ways tomorrow. He needed to be able to leave her, free of any fear she might feel abandoned.

Robert's warm hand covered hers, then rose and tipped up her face, rubbing back and forth under her chin. His touch sizzled across her skin, and she worked on keeping her breaths even. Her heart's lurch she couldn't help. His gaze held hers, stirring with a cautious emotion.

"Of course, *cariad.*" He gently brushed a strand of hair behind her ear. "All will be well tomorrow. A setback only."

His eyes seemed to question, and her mind raced for a change of subject. If she didn't, she'd make a pathetic spectacle of herself. "The man earlier today, I saw him at Castell y Bere..."

"Yes, Sir Ralph de Buche." The bitterness was clear in his voice. "I didn't endear myself by disabling him in such a manner."

"He doesn't seem to be a very nice man."

He cocked his head and searched her eyes. Then, he stared at the wall. "Who is?" he muttered.

"What will he do now?"

"No doubt he will continue his aborted activities of teaching the locals a lesson."

She opened her mouth, thinking he was being too flippant, but noticed the death grip he had on the trestle table and the hard set of his jaw.

"Robert. You aren't the cold-hearted warrior you pretend to be. This bothers you."

His eyes bored into hers, seething with rage and pain and...disillusionment. But he said nothing and returned to glaring the poor wall to death. His pain squeezed at her heart. He kept every-one at a distance with that attitude, preventing him from opening up. It was as if he didn't expect love, so he preempted it from happen-ing with his behavior.

She placed her hand on his. "It does. And I don't know why you're afraid to admit it. You're a loyal and caring man, but you hide behind this...this cynicism as a shield to deal with the world—to prove to others you don't really care."

"Enough, woman." He threw off her hand and stood, causing the bench beneath them to rock back and forth.

His harsh reaction didn't bother her—she'd hit too close to the truth. Something lay at the root of his cynicism, or someone, and perhaps she could get at it from that angle. "Do you know this Ralph well?"

A hollow laugh escaped his throat. "Aye. Would you believe we used to be bosom lads?"

Two boys came into the room then, carrying platters of food and a flagon of ale.

Robert filled two tankards with the ale and handed one to her.

"What happened?"

ↄ

ROBERT SWIRLED THE ALE in his tankard. "De Buche and I joined Sir Hugh's household at the same time."

So lonely he had been as a lad, torn from his mother and sister and his kin. His most vivid memory was of a throat choked up with hot tears and how he'd had to suppress them, behave manfully, show no emotion or weakness. That journey to Sir Hugh's as a lad had been an exercise in taming the hot lump in his throat, in blinking fast, and resisting throwing his arms around his mother and not let-ting go. A mewling infant he'd been. So ashamed he'd been of himself.

He'd forgotten, until now, that he'd questioned her sending him to Sir Hugh, a Norman stranger. Begged to be fostered with his uncle Pedr. And she'd met his pleas with silence or a sharp word.

"I, uh, needed a friend, and I suppose de Buche did as well, and we were soon inseparable. Those first months getting into scrapes with

207

him, sneaking treats from the kitchen, playing merrills, and catching fish helped dispel my homesickness. I'd begun to think I could adjust with de Buche as my companion, adjust being in a strange Norman household. The Two R's, Sir Hugh used to jest, saying the nickname mimicked his steward's constant refrain when complaining about us—'Arrgh.'"

"What came between you?" She took a sip of ale, her gaze holding his over the rim.

What indeed. "My father."

"I thought—" She set her tankard down distractedly, causing it to tip. She righted it quickly. "—I thought your father had already been killed?"

"True. Mayhap I should say, his ghost. You see, I hadn't fully grasped the implications of my father's treason. One day we got to boasting about our forebears, and I innocently piped in with my father's deeds."

Christ on a cross, never would he forget the look on de Buche's face as he realized who Robert's father was. Disgust, mainly. "His uncle had been killed at Lewes, and de Buche had been raised to despise Montfortians. It was also to his father that my father's lands and titles were awarded, though he'd not made the connection until then. Thereafter, de Buche shunned any association with me. He even complained to Sir Hugh that he did not wish to foster in a household that harbored traitors."

And Sir Hugh had promptly dismissed his concerns as not being relevant anymore—allegiances were always shifting on the Marches. Which only hardened de Buche's sense of outrage into an impotent bitterness. A bitterness that manifested into him becoming the instigator of all the subsequent taunts and pranks from the other lads. Until Robert learned to defend himself with his fists. It had driven him to practice with sword and on the quintain during his leisure time.

Robert sipped from the tankard, the memories still a sour taste on his tongue. "So you see, our enmity is long and this another notch in the tally. In truth, I should have ridden onward. His behavior is normal in war. I cannot change these things as much as I wish otherwise."

That was another bitter lesson. Not only had he relentlessly pushed himself to train at arms, he'd also read as many of the Arthurian romances as he could find and truly believed the ideals expressed within were the standard state of affairs awaiting him when he be-came knighted. But it was as Sir Hugh's squire he'd learned this was not true.

He flexed his free hand, the faint scars on his knuckles visible still, as was the one along his jaw under his beard, earned when he'd been beaten to a pulp by a knight when Robert was naught but a squire. An English milkmaid, alone and defenseless as their party swept through the Marches subduing Llywelyn ap Gruffudd, had incited Robert to her defense against that knight and his pleasure.

But what purpose did all this resentment serve? Instead of fol-lowing his own dictates to keep himself in the moment, he'd been blind to this side of himself—for too long he'd allowed de Buche and others to dictate how he lived his life, Christ, even to dictate the goals he pursued. And he'd no longer allow himself to believe pro-tecting that woman had been foolish.

"No. You did the right thing," Kaytee said, her clear voice bring-ing him back to the present. "And you know it. I can see it in your stance and in your eyes. What you did was instinctual to you. This hardened, cynical attitude you project to others is a shield to hide what a compassionate man you are on the inside."

"Compassionate? Woman, I am not soft." But he was not in earnest. He loved that she could so provoke him. But as he stared at the only person who made any goal worthwhile, a new bitterness surfaced. "And I'm not the only one who hides behind a shield."

"What do you mean?"

"You erect walls around yourself. Any whiff of strong emotions heading your way, and up goes your drawbridge with you huddled inside."

⁊

KATY REELED BACK FROM HIS WORDS.

Close. Oh, he was close. Not strong emotions necessarily, but... She took in his raw sensuality, his fierce gaze. Okay, yes, she'd erected a barrier. But a barrier against the chaos generated when they were together, not against strong emotion. She felt spontaneous and free when they made love, tempting her to live like that in general. Live as if she didn't have to organize every corner of her world to feel safe. And, boy did that make her scared. Scared because it meant giving up her protective shield.

Vulnerable.

But, damn it. She didn't want to live in fear. Live jealously guarding her veneer of control. And he'd helped her see this.

Hell, who was she kidding? She...she... "Robert," she croaked, tears thick in her throat. "Make love to me."

His breath quickened, and, if possible, his eyes grew darker. "No," he growled.

The air punched from her lungs, and pain lanced her heart.

His large hands clasped her face, caging her in a warm cocoon. He made her meet his gaze. "No," he said, his voice gentler. "You are not escaping this way."

His thumbs rubbed her cheeks, brushing aside an escaped tear, a warm dot smearing across her cheekbone.

What was he saying?

"Katy. Listen. I wish to make love with you now more than anything I have ever desired. Actually, no."

Jeez, her heart couldn't take this ping-ponging.

He cleared his throat. "I'm making a hash of this. What I desire more than anything, is you. But only if you are with me, wholly and completely."

"What are you saying?" she whispered, as a hope in her heart shyly unfurled, a hope she didn't realize had taken root.

He touched his forehead to hers and closed his eyes, his soft sigh brushing across her lips. "Please tell me you might come to have feelings for me. That you might be willing to stay here in this land. With me."

Her breath caught in her throat, and her heart pounded with a cadence that spelled, *This is Right*. "But. I thought...I thought you couldn't marry." She hoped she hadn't misinterpreted him.

"No more do I care for regaining my family's demesne. Katy—" his thumbs rubbed circles on her cheeks, "—if I could live in a villein's hut and be with you, I would. But you deserve more." His Adam's apple bobbed. "If you will have me as your husband, I will withdraw the suit. The king would surely reward me enough for my current service." He took a deep breath, and his fingers flexed behind her ears. "If not, I will earn prize money in the lists after this cursed war is over. Either way, I *will* provide for you."

With his hands warm against her cheeks, his forehead leaning sweetly on hers, she grounded herself in the moment, with him, and listened to herself. And what her self told her was, yes, this was the person she'd ached to find. The distant lure of her life in the future just wasn't tugging on her any more. *This* is what she'd sought. *He* was who she'd sought. *She* could—she took a ragged breath—she could *do* this. Step into this moment and *be* with him.

"Yes," she whispered, the one word carrying all the hope and anticipation and gravity of her decision.

And, at last, she also finally understood her friend Isabelle. Understood why she'd decided to remain with the man she loved, regardless of the surroundings.

His hands gently tightened on her face. "Yes, what?"

"Yes. I'll stay. I'll stay for you. For us."

His breath brushed across her lips. "Oh, *cariad*."

જી

THE ATMOSPHERE IN THEIR ROOM fair crackled with the gravity of their commitment. He knew not what she left behind, but he judged it to be a great sacrifice nonetheless, and it humbled him. Humbled him that she'd chosen him despite his lacking title, lands. Humbled him that she'd chosen *him*.

All day, he'd thought about his father and mother, his fixation on righting a perceived wrong. Each time he held that goal in his hand, envisioned attaining the honor he'd been denied and triumphing at last, he felt hollow. However, when he looked upon Kaytee, a feeling of completeness and purpose suffused him. The contrast had become so apparent, even an idiot knight such as himself could come to no other conclusion: only being with her mattered.

Robert cradled Kaytee's face in his hands. She wished to stay. *With him.*

He traced his thumb across her lips.

He would do anything for her. Anything to prove that she'd made the right decision.

A raging, primal need to possess her gripped him. His mind wished to be gentle, to prove her decision was the right one. His body, however... His body wished to claim her. Mark her as his.

Hands shaking, he leaned in and swept his lips against hers. Her soft breath feathered across his face, and a shiver chased down his spine, pooling as heat in his lower back.

Be gentle.

He sipped on her lips, tasting her—her desire, her love, her anticipation. So different it was, tasting her now, knowing this was only the start of their commitment, their sharing of each other. Her tongue darted against his, and she gripped the nape of his neck, her nails softly scraping against his skin. He shivered.

"*Cariad*, I want you."

"I want you too," she whispered against his lips. "I've been meaning to ask. What does 'cariad' mean?"

He swallowed hard. This would reveal much. "It is Welsh for beloved."

Her eyes softened, her mouth parted slightly against his, and she kissed him with more urgency. "Cariad," she murmured.

He skimmed his hands across her shoulders, pushing the fabric down one delicate slope, then the other.

The soft glow from the rushlights flickered across her skin, tempting him to explore further. He traced a finger down her neck, to the curve of her breast. He teased the tip, delighting in watching it stiffen into a hard, pert peak. For him.

He brushed his mouth down her neck, tasting, nibbling, breathing in her unique scent. He plumped up one of her firm breasts and touched the peak with his tongue. This was *his* woman.

"Robert," she breathed, her body squirming. She leaned back, arching toward him, and he wrapped his arms around her waist, supporting her, while he worshiped her perfect breasts.

Never would he get enough. And thank Christ he'd have the rest of his life to explore her every curve, teasing and testing to find what drove her wild.

Wild. Oh, that thought alone—her wild beneath him—coursed through him, fighting against his desire to take things slow. He nudged her backward, his mouth sucking and kissing more frantically.

Wild. No. Not wild tonight. He'd delightfully discovered that this calm, collected woman would light up like a torch with but the merest touch from him, which felt...oh, hell, it felt exhilarating that he alone knew that side. But tonight, he wished to blend and meld with her calm, collected self, to experience that she was his in all ways.

She fell against the bed, and he landed next to her. He covered her, holding his weight on his elbows. He skimmed his hand over her smooth stomach, caressed the generous curve of her hip, something primal curling through him at the sight of his darker, rougher hands against her creamy smooth skin. When his fingers brushed against her feminine curls, he gently explored, parting her flesh and finding her wet.

He groaned, his body tightening, and the perfume of her growing pleasure filled his senses, making his cods ache. He caught her gaze in the dim light, her hazel eyes burning bright with love, acceptance, with everything he'd ever hoped to find in this life or the next.

I'm loving you, now, my sweet.

Her breath caught on a tiny hitch, flashing heat through him again. He teased with his fingers, circling her tight bud and felt it plumping under his attention. He dipped a finger into her tight channel, then moved slowly down her body.

He knelt between her legs and took in the sight of her body arching and trembling. Her face flushed a luminous pink. He let up slightly with his touch, careful to stoke her fire slowly.

He eased down onto his stomach between her legs, threaded his arms under her luscious thighs, then reached around to part her feminine lips. He groaned at the sight of her pink, wet flesh, and then, unable to resist any longer, he moved in, tasting her sweet flesh.

She bucked and trembled, and he moved a hand forward and held her down at her hips.

"I have you."

She clutched his hair and tried to arch again. "Robert. I don't think I can—"

"Don't think..."

Oh, how he ached to smooth his hand another inch upward to squeeze a perfect breast, but he knew, by the shudders and flushes of her body that she was close, and he wished to draw it out. Wished to find their initial completion tonight together, to mark their new beginning.

In this way, he teased her flesh with breaths and lips and tongue, applying more and less pressure as needed to bring her to her peak by slow degrees instead of a sudden flash. Never had he been so hard in his life, but he pressed his hips against the mattress, welcoming the ache, and concentrated on *her*.

Her fingers flexed harder across his scalp, and her voice became only a repeated whisper of *Robert-Robert-Robert-Robert.*

He timed his next move when her body needed him to relent somewhat, and when she'd built to another edge, he pulled away, surged upward, and—at the same moment he captured her mouth—he slid inch by inch into her, her body shaking the whole duration of his slow, deliberate invasion.

When he was fully seated, with her hot feminine flesh clutched so tightly, so sweetly around him, he broke their kiss and cupped her face with a free hand. He looked into her eyes, and this time he had no fear of her probing gaze, of her burrowing inward to see what was there. He was no longer hollow. Indeed, he'd only believed himself to be.

His chest swelled with emotion, and he pulled slowly out and, oh it was so difficult not to close his eyes and relish the sweet slide of her flesh against his, but he held her gaze, feeling their joining. The air around them pulsed and snapped with meaning. How soon before her herbs would wear off, and he'd be making love to her and implanting her with their babe?

Nearly fully withdrawn now, he again eased into her, tilting his hips, and she met his, her fingers touching his face, her eyes brimming with emotion. In unison, they established a rhythm, slow, but exquisite, never breaking eye contact, and again their passion leisurely built until it filled the whole room with its possibility, its potential.

And the peak arrived, not of a sudden, but as a natural inevitability to their building passion, and he could see it there in her eyes too. On the next slow thrust, he gave an extra twist to his hips, to stroke her bud of pleasure with his hard body, and she gasped, bucked, shuddered in his arms as he pulled out and drove in one final time, giving up his body to the most exquisite release, the longest he'd ever experienced.

No. He was not hollow. She'd made him see this. He pulled her against him and rolled over, a bone deep contentment...and happiness...suffusing him.

She smiled languidly, her hand trailing across his stomach. And he became even happier when her temptress eyes shone brightly, and she moved slowly down his body and took him in hand. Licked his tip. He didn't think he could be ready again so soon, but she proved him wrong.

Ah, God. And when her delectable mouth closed over him, he was in heaven.

Yes, this was right. Yes, this was his woman. He was whole.

☙

ROBERT STRODE TO THE CHAMBER in one of the castle's towers where Staundon was headquartered. His steps were light, for still it seemed unbelievable Kaytee had accepted him, but he would question not his good fortune.

All too soon, he found Staundon deep in conversation with several knights at a scarred table, surrounded by several flagons of ale.

Robert waited until the others departed and approached. He bowed. "I've finally arrived. I apologize for the delay. It could not be helped."

His commander regarded him with tired eyes, dark circles bruising the skin underneath. He scratched the head of his rangy greyhound. "Thought you'd met with the sharp edge of a Welsh blade. Care to explain your absence?"

Robert opened his mouth, but his commander held up a hand. "Hold on. Sir Reginald de Grey will wish to hear your report as well." He motioned to a knight in deep conversation with another in a far corner.

The knight nodded, a stout man in his sixties, lord of Rhuthun Castle and the cantref of Dyffryn Clwyd. He could not be pleased with the taking of his castle by Madog.

While they waited, Robert sought to satisfy his curiosity. "What's transpiring in these parts? Utter chaos reigns without."

"Welsh rebels are active. We arrived at the same time as Grey's

215

forces and razed most of the town and enlisted the villagers to aid in preparing the castle. We expect the Welsh to besiege us any day now."

"Speaking of, do you know where the Bere villagers were sent?" True, Kaytee no longer needed the information, but he sought to know, nonetheless.

"They stayed behind in Wrexham."

So he'd guessed right in their initial destination. Grey arrived, and Robert was introduced. "Your report?"

Robert began detailing his activities upon leaving Bere, omitting only Kaytee's true sex, casting her solely as his squire.

But when he reached the part of his tale concerning his capture, he hesitated. Why? He'd watched and listened for this very purpose. "When I was taken to their camp about a day's ride east of Harlech, a sennight ago now, their party numbered fifty-four, forty being spear, and fourteen longbowmen. They were well-provisioned for food, but talked only of past exploits. They were careful in what they said, even in Welsh."

He described the garrison at Rhuthun castle, and any tidbits he'd gleaned, which naturally interested Grey. He forebore relating de Buche's activities, for that was unfortunately common behavior for warring knights.

But the abbey? He hesitated. "There's something else, my lords. On my journey, I came across the smoking remains of Rhinog Abbey. Two monks were killed in cold blood, the sacristy looted, and the buildings put to the torch. They claim it was perpetrated by Lord Powys's men."

A shout came from the sidelines. "That is a lie."

Chapter Twenty-Six

❧

Madawc the son of Maredudd possessed Powys within its
boundaries, from Porfoed to Gwauan in the uplands of Arwystli.
And at that time he had a brother, Iorwerth the son of Maredudd,
in rank not equal to himself. And Iorwerth had great sorrow and
heaviness because of the honour and power that his brother enjoyed,
which he shared not.

The Mabinogion, an ancient Welsh romance

ROBERT FACED HIS ACCUSER, a man ten years his junior if not
more. Christ, he looked to be no more than seventeen.
"And you are?"

Grey narrowed his eyes and waved his hand. "Sir Robert Beucol,
meet Griffith de la Pole, the new Lord of Powys."

"Why would monks lie?" Robert kept his voice flat.

The lords of Powys were one of the few Welsh families to emerge
from the Welsh wars with their fortunes intact. Siding more often
than not with the kings of England, they were rewarded with the
lordship of Powys after their principality and those of the other
Welsh princes, were abolished by the king.

The other spat. "Those are not real monks. They are Welsh!"

Robert gripped the hilt of his sword. "I swear on the surety of my soul,
I report the words of the abbot. These were defenseless men of God."

The other man's hand flew to his sword as well.

His commander said, "Some doubt they are true followers of
Christ."

"I have no doubts," Robert bit out.

"Enough. Other matters demand our attention," said Lord Grey.
"Once we've routed the Welsh, if you feel it necessary you can en-
gage in a trial by combat. Let God settle it." He drained the remains
of his flagon and held it out to Lord Powys. "Fetch me more ale."

Lord Powys took the flagon roughly from his hands and stomped away.

Grey turned his attention back to Robert. "King Edward still gathers his men and supplies in Chester. We expect them not for another month or so. Meanwhile, our lands are suffering from the deprivations caused by Welsh raids. On the morrow, lead a party Wrexham way, and recruit locals able to wield a spear or bow. Promise two pence a day and exemption from service in Gascony. Report to me first thing in the morning, and I'll have men and supplies assembled."

"Very good, my lord. I'll not disappoint you. How many recruits can you afford?"

Grey laughed. "If you manage as much as one hundred, I'll be surprised, but pleased."

Robert bowed. "A hundred it is."

"On the morrow, then, after first light. Meanwhile, take your squire and join the others in aiding and protecting the villagers." He beckoned to someone behind Robert, ending their discussion.

Robert spun about and marched away, lest he say anything more revealing. Outside, he gazed up at the patchy clouds, squinting at the sun. A squeal to his right had his hand on his hilt, but it was naught but a laughing lad chasing a mongrel dog down the lane, the dog looking just as excited.

He inhaled a deep breath, the autumn air still tinged with the scent of burning wood. To his duties, then.

༄

ROBERT AND KATY HAD BEEN TASKED with helping the villagers create temporary shelters in the outer bailey. Robert and the rest of the knights and squires took turns patrolling the walls surrounding them.

But a more gruesome sight for a refugee camp she'd never seen. A gallows loomed against the wall near the gate to town, with two unfortunates suspended, barely moving in the still air, crows and flies swooping and swarming, attesting that the victims were very much dead.

Bile rose up her throat, and she swallowed hard, grimacing. She stretched out a leg, adjusting her position on the ground as she held an armful of straw while a village woman secured it into a bundle to use as thatching. The stuff itched and made her sneeze, but she gamely continued on. It kept her occupied, in the moment, instead of dwelling on the aspects of her new life still outside of her control. Aspects like how soon this rebellion would be over so she and Robert could start their new life.

A boy on horseback galloped through the main gate into the bailey and reined in sharply before Robert. The layout of the castle was unusual—it could only be reached by first going through the palisaded town and through a gate across a drawbridge stretched over a ditch and through another gate into the outer bailey where she now worked.

The boy handed something over to Robert, wheeled around, and trotted toward the castle.

When the woman she was helping had tied off the bundle, Katy excused herself and hustled over to Robert, enjoying the stretching of her muscles. She was a little sore from their lovemaking last night, but she also savored the new strength she could feel from the past week and a half's near constant exercise. Robert had removed his helm, and judging by the scowl on his face, the news wasn't good.

Without a word, he handed her the note and whistled for Perceval. The non-standard spelling of their French was difficult to quickly decipher. "What does it say?"

"Fetch your mount. We leave at once. I should have known I would hear more from de Buche. He mocks me for my weakness yesterday and declares he will enjoy teaching my sister a lesson."

"Your sister?" They crossed the lane to where her mare grazed.

"Aye. She is nearby with her Welsh husband and family. We must ride there at once."

"Should we get others?"

He helped her mount, handing her his shield. "No. This is between us. He is drawing me out—no doubt he wishes for a personal trial by combat. His strength against mine. The chaos of this rebellion, especially in these parts, makes him bold."

"You there," he shouted to a crossbowman. "Inform Staundon we leave to investigate reports of a disturbance outside of town."

He swung onto Perceval, who'd dutifully appeared. To her, he said, "We will stop at the inn to retrieve my lance and your mace and be off." He donned his helm and urged his horse into a canter through the gate.

She had no choice but to follow—he knew his own culture and would know how to proceed.

❧

THE CONFRONTATION WITH DE BUCHE had been inevitable, Robert supposed, since their estrangement as lads. But bringing his innocent sister and her family into the mix scoured his insides. He worked on suppressing the rage and guilt roiling within as they cantered several miles west to the small farm his sister called home. If de Buche had done aught to cause harm, he would pay.

They dashed around a bend in the road, and the dark plume of smoke they'd seen in the distance now had a source—it curled up from the remains of his sister's home. He dug his spurs into Perceval's sides and charged forward, his gaze focused on the milling shapes, heart in throat as it became only too apparent that several forms were laid out upon the ground. And unmoving.

He recognized de Buche's stance and armor, horse nearby, and changed the angle of his approach. Robert spared a glance behind, gratified to see Kaytee keeping pace. He signaled for her to halt. Christ on a cross, but he didn't need to embroil her. What had he been thinking bringing her along?

Robert's instincts screamed to run de Buche through now, explanations be damned, but he resisted. Now that his future with Kaytee was set, he ought to be more circumspect. He hoped still to win some kind of honor from the king to make her life with him more comfortable.

Robert reined in near de Buche, careful to do so at a nearby puddle and splashing it onto the bastard. He sprang from his mount and crowded de Buche's space, refusing to look rightward, where lay the bodies. If they were... No. He refused to believe de Buche would kill them.

De Buche held his ground. "Good of you to come, my friend. I thought you should bear witness to what transpires, being so interested in my affairs yesterday."

"If you've harmed my sister or her family, you will pay."

"Let go of me," a feminine voice shrieked from his left.

A knight pushed a young woman forward, her simple gown's bodice torn. A cold, mighty fist squeezed Robert's heart, and his vision swam red, for despite her height and womanly curves, the slope of her nose and the spark and shape of her eyes told him true—this was Marged.

"Ah," de Buche sneered, "your sister deigns to join us."

She pulled up short and locked gazes with him. "Robert?" she whispered, and the blood drained from her face.

Robert yanked his sword free. "Leave her be. Your fight is with me, de Buche." Robert stepped back to give himself more room and swept his gaze behind. Kaytee's horse stood off to the side—she mounted still. Closing in from the opposite side were two more knights on foot, and he recognized the colors of Lord Powys. He returned his attention to the knight holding his sister.

"Let us settle this with a trial by combat. This is what you wish, is it not? Let us see whom God favors in this contest." Robert swirled his sword in front of him in a practiced move. How he'd longed to face de Buche thusly.

De Buche sauntered over to Marged and squeezed a breast. She spat in his face and struggled against the knight's hold. Face twisted, de Buche looked over his shoulder at Robert. "No. I'd rather make you watch as I fuck her and make her scream my name."

Chapter Twenty-Seven

❧

And the knight thrust at him, but he was not thereby moved from
where he stood. And Peredur spurred his horse, and ran at him
wrathfully, furiously, fiercely, desperately, and with mighty rage, and
he gave him a thrust, deadly-wounding, severe, furious, adroit and
strong, under his jaw, and raised him out of his saddle, and cast him
a long way from him.
The Mabinogion, an ancient Welsh romance

ROBERT GROUND HIS TEETH, his control naught but parchment
armor against a blazing need to wreak vengeance. "I said,
your fight is with me," he bit out. "Step away from my sister and face
me. We settle this now."

"I think not." De Buche leaned closer to Marged. "I think I'll
find more amusement beneath her skirts." At that, the whoreson
yanked on the fragile cloth of her bliaut, the shredding tear loud in
the tense atmosphere. "Hold him," he said to his knights. "Hold him,
and make him watch." He reached under his surcoat and shoved
Marged to the ground.

With a roar, that parchment barrier holding back his rage burst,
and Robert sprang forward. The two knights were behind him, but
de Buche was closer. Robert would run the bastard through before
the others could interfere.

An arrow thunked into the ground before him. He leaped to the
side and spun. An archer crouched in the darkened space under the
eaves of the stables. Reassessing the odds, Robert squared off with
the approaching knights and deflected a forceful swing from the
closest, their blades ringing with the impact. He planted his foot
against his opponent's chest and shoved, then countered the second
knight's attack with his shield. Both blows gained him precious time,
and he bolted for his sister who was being held down by a knight as

de Buche fumbled with his chausses and her skirts. She kicked, spat, and landed a powerful blow with her knee into the bastard's cods. De Buche howled and backhanded her across the jaw, knocking her cold.

Rage seared through Robert, his breaths harsh as his pounding steps closed the distance, shield protecting him from the archer, sword at the ready.

"Take that, motherfucker," a feminine voice behind him yelled.

No. He glanced behind, and ice slushed through his veins— Kaytee was swinging his lance at the head of one of the knights. The sound of tempered wood hitting metal reverberated, and the knight crumpled at her feet, his lance breaking in half. The other knight stopped his chase and faced this new threat.

Pauper's piss, what possessed her to interfere? The rage searing through him urged him to rescue and avenge his sister, whilst the chilling horror witnessing Kaytee's actions urged him to come to her aid. The rage and horror swirled and settled into cold clarity. Kaytee was on her horse, she still had her mace, and she could flee. His sister could not. But God, it killed him.

He plowed forward and shouldered de Buche to the ground, the latter's attention distracted still because of the blow to his jewels. Robert planted his feet on either side of his nemesis' shoulders and burrowed his sword tip under the flap of mail protecting de Buche's neck.

"I'd submit if I were you," squeaked a nearby voice.

Robert spared a glance to his left. Lord Powys had pinned his sister by her shoulders with his knees and held his own sword at her neck. Her face drained of color.

"I'll run him through if you so much as draw her blood," Robert growled.

"And I'll slit her throat if you touch him."

A hard body slammed into Robert from the side. He threw out a foot to regain his balance, spun around, and blocked a thrust from the attacking knight with his sword. He followed it with a stunning blow to the head with the flat of his shield. The knight staggered back and fell to his knees, his upper body swaying. Pain lanced Robert's forearm, and he spun about, shield raised, as de Buche danced backward, triumph at drawing first blood clear in his eyes. Robert advanced, and de Buche retreated until he reached Lord Powys. Blows from both men came fast, and with labored breaths heating the inside of his helm, Robert fought back both of their determined attacks.

As he moved, his muscles humming with determination and purpose, he was gratified to see his sister scoot away and rouse her family, who'd only been knocked out—not dead—thank the heavens. They slipped into the woods.

The recently stunned knight gained his feet and marched toward him.

Two, Robert could safely battle against. He knew de Buche's strengths and weaknesses, and he was learning Lord Powys's with each parry and thrust. But three. Three would be tricky. And too much was at stake. He needed to end this. Quickly.

ↄ

KATY, HER HEART A BIG, PUMPING LUMP in her throat, watched as Robert battled three—three!—friggin' knights. No way could she let him face this alone. Her thwack to the one knight had knocked him to the ground, but it drew the attention of another, who now advanced on her.

Oh shit. Oh shit. Oh shit. She had no time to reach for her mace.

The knight swung for her horse's reins, but Katy dug in her heels and her horse thankfully reared, knocking the knight backward. When her mare's hooves smacked back into the ground, Katy rode by the attacking knight, like she was one of those fancy English toffs playing polo, and whacked him across the head with the thickest part of her broken lance.

She glanced back, and her first knight was starting to stand. She raced toward him and knocked him flat the same way. Both were unconscious, but she had no clue how long that would last. Or why the archers stationed around didn't join in. The rules of this encounter were inscrutable, but one thing was clear—Robert needed her help.

She swung off her horse and rushed toward him, not trusting her horsemanship to the situation—too many were around, with one she had no wish to accidentally harm. But then Robert's sword flew from his hand and clattered to the ground.

"Well, my Lord Powys, look at this," de Buche sneered. He pulled a thin blade from his belt. "The mighty Beucol at our mercy.

Not so mighty now, are you? What? Can't fight three at once?" de Buche *tsked*.

Robert's arms were yanked behind him. "Get his squire," the nasty knight said to the other. "I say murder them all. Teach this half-breed a lesson. But first we make him watch as I take his sister."

Bile rose in Katy's throat—she'd witnessed how he liked to torture his opponents. No thank you.

Nasty knight glanced around, then let loose a roaring shout. "Where are you, you bitch of a Welsh whore?"

Katy darted her gaze around too and was relieved to see Robert's sister and her family were gone. Then her blood chilled as de Buche lowered his head. She didn't need to see his face behind that helmet to know Robert was now the focus of all his rage. And she'd seen how he reacted when thwarted, however little, by his victims. Now Robert would be his focus.

She hunched her shoulders, attempting to impersonate an American football linebacker, and rushed the man holding Robert captive.

ఴ

BLOOD POUNDED IN ROBERT'S EARS as his arms twisted higher against his back. His sword lay so close, only a mere lunge away. But too far now. Mayhap he could use the knight holding him as leverage and plant his feet against de Buche's chest.

Before he could determine the most effective, but most likely futile, move, Kaytee was rushing to his side, and his body was knocked off balance, his arms blessedly free. He gained control of his stagger and lurched for his sword. One chance, he had one chance only to turn this situation around.

Time slowed as his hands reached for the sword. No time. No time to grasp the hilt, which faced away. He wrapped his mailed hands around the blade, spun around, the weight of his sword gaining a satisfying momentum as it whipped around.

At the end of the sword's arc, the crossguard crunched into de Buche's neck. His nemesis fell to the ground, neck broken, still in death.

But he had no time to ponder the impact of his nemesis's death. He swung about, ready to combat Powys and the others, but found

Kaytee with her arms secured behind her back, struggling in a knight's grasp. Fierce pride rose in his chest at her warrior's spirit while dread choked his throat. For five more knights emerged from behind the house and advanced upon him.

"You've done it now, Beucol," Powys grimly announced.

Kaytee was captured, but alive. His sister and her family were safe. Robert had better odds with the king's justice, than with six knights and an archer. He dropped his sword to the ground with a clatter.

Again, Robert's arms were yanked behind him. Powys glanced to the advancing knights. "You bore witness to his treachery. He denied Sir Ralph de Buche the right to personal combat for their grievance."

The cur! Robert yanked against the restraining hands. So the new Lord of Powys was as dishonorable as de Buche to utter such an untruth.

Powys sauntered forward. "We're taking him in for murder of a fellow Norman in our fight against the Welsh. His true nature and allegiance is clear. He is his father's son, for certes."

Heat flooded Robert's veins. "The sins of the father should not be visited upon his sons."

"Perhaps. Perhaps not. But when laid against your recent actions, it makes your *abduction* sound rather interesting. Perhaps a way to exchange information without suspicion? And you were one of the most vocal in your wish to abandon Castell y Bere to the Welsh, I have heard. And this nonsensical accusation against my person for the destruction of that worthless Welsh abbey..."

Yet another lie to add to the others. Robert had been the most vocal for *staying*.

The knight pushed Kaytee toward her mare—the only horse left, he noticed with satisfaction. His sister had shown foresight in the face of fear. But at another shove from Powys, that satisfaction and Robert's triumph over de Buche turned sour as his insides turned to liquid and then chilled. He'd known fear on the battlefield and in tourney lists, but that was fear he could control, for his actions were his own. This was different. He was powerless.

❧

ROBERT'S CAPTORS SHOVED HIM into the stinking hole they called a cell.

"Enjoy your new accommodations, for they will be your last ere you're strung up for murder," jeered one.

Robert's gut clenched, and he stumbled upright, his movements awkward with his hands bound behind him. "I demand the king's justice!"

"The king's justice?" sneered Powys. "Have you forgotten where you are? You're on the Marches, and here we dispense our own justice. And do you truly wish to risk the king's justice? For murder is one matter, treason another, and I can make a case for such and thereby see you endure the new punishment King Edward meted out so slowly but efficiently to Dafydd ap Gruffydd nigh on eleven years ago."

Cold fear flashed through Robert's blood. Though he'd been no witness, he remembered well the tales of Dafydd's death. Hung, revived, his insides pulled out and burned before his eyes, and then his body cut into four parts.

The scab on a whoreson's ass laughed as they shoved Robert to the far wall, restrained him, and stripped him to his braies. Amidst random punches, they clapped him into chains, securing his hands and ankles to the slimy wall. They slammed shut his door, leaving him in his prison—dank, filthy, and dark.

But how could that matter for aught, when Kaytee was without? The only satisfaction he had was that de Buche was dead. He'd not be able to harm her, or his sister, or any other woman again. Sir Hugh's advice came back to him—clearly he'd foreseen this ambush by de Buche, since he'd practically told him that his nemesis *never* faced him head-on—de Buche had known only too well how he'd fare if he did.

Eventually, Robert dozed and woke in fits and starts. A rat ran laps around their small space more times than he could count. As the early morning sun's rays pierced through the piglet-sized window high above, steps echoed outside his cell door. He stilled.

The door to his cell banged open, and a slight figure was shoved inside. In the weak light of dawn, he could tell not who it was.

"Robert?"

Sweet Jesus. His knees buckled with panic and relief. "Kaytee?"

They'd been separated when they'd been brought within the castle's walls. He jerked on his chains, his body thrumming with the need to yank her to him, feel her heart thump against his, confirm she was fine and whole and *his.* "Are you well? Have you news of my sister?"

"Yes, I am, and your sister is safe now with her husband." She shuffled forward, no doubt unable to see well in the dim light. "I don't know how long they'll let me have, so we need to focus on the important things first. Plus, they're debating your case right now, and I want to get back to hear their decision."

That was his Kaytee. Calm and focused. Organized.

"They have not harmed you?"

She closed the distance, finally, between them, and she bisected the ray of light from the window. His whole body lurched, and he was able to see her fully. She was unharmed. He'd worried so.

"Oddly, no. They still think I'm your squire. It seems all of that Powys asshole's energy is directed at bringing you down, and I'm seen as inconsequential. Perhaps he thinks it makes his case seem stronger against you if he treats me nicely."

Never had he been more thankful for another man's manipulations. "What is Powys saying?"

"Nothing good. He, of course, has a different take on what happened at your sister's, says your allegiance is with the Welsh and that *you* denied *de Buche* the right to personal combat. Leaving the retreating party was so you could rendezvous with the Welsh and pass on troop movements and the like, that you were never a hostage. That you argued for abandoning one of the king's holdings to your kinsmen. He's saying you're a traitor."

Robert could plainly see how it would all unfold. Of a sudden, his limbs felt the weight of inevitability. "You need to leave, forget me and get back to your land."

"I can't—"

He steeled himself. "Associating with me now is poisonous. Today, I proved I cannot keep faith with my king, and even if I escape this alive, I have forfeited any chance of his favor."

"How did you fail to keep faith—" and here she bent her two fingers on each hand as if emphasizing those last two words, "—with the king?"

He frowned. "By killing a fellow knight sworn into his service."

"They would have killed *you!*"

"It's their word against a knight of suspicious motives. I cannot prove I challenged and was denied trial by combat by *him*. No. In their eyes, I am the scoundrel of this affair."

"So, I should abandon you to your fate? You're not worth the effort to save?"

"Yes," he ground out. "Even if I get out of this, I'll be less than nothing."

Her face turned mulish. "I'm sorry, Robert, but that's bullshit. You did the right thing. The honorable thing. Who cares about the king if you can't stay true to yourself in the process?

"Careful what you say about the king."

"Why? He's not *my* king." She stepped closer and put her hand on his face, her touch warm—*Christ*—comforting. His arms spasmed with the need to hold her.

"Robert, you aren't nothing. Everything you do is with honor. Don't you see that?"

"How is defying my king honorable? I killed one of his vassals." He would *not* lean his head into her touch. He would *not* move his head just so and kiss her sweet palm.

"How can it be honorable to follow him at the expense of your own personal honor? To me, that's more important. Those men were about to *rape* your sister. From the moment I met you, your actions were always about serving others, about acting from your own sense of honor and values.

"Your behavior was above reproach with me when I was most vulnerable. How many knights in your position would have just taken their pleasure with me? How many would have taken a stranger under their care and not abandoned her even when it was most inconvenient?"

But that was because it had been *her*.

She continued. "How many would have saved that woman from de Buche when we first came into Flint? Or delayed his rendezvous with his commander to help those monks? It's one of the things I...I admire about you. You didn't abandon me, and I will not abandon you now. You don't need the trappings of land and title to have honor. Not to me."

He shook his head in vehement denial. She was wrong. Staying here with him when he still had honor and the prospects of royal favor was one thing, but...

She took the last step needed to bring her body flush to his, and they both trembled at the contact. She gripped his face and held his gaze. "Not to me, Robert. Not to me." Her voice was strong with conviction, and it rang through him, vibrating in the scant space between them.

God, the way she portrayed him made him ache in a strange way. And the touch of her hand on his face was torture, the feel of her body pressed against his was torture, her sweet breath brushing his face...torture. Torture to be unable to touch her, hold her, be with her. He wasn't sure if she was right. She was probably mad, but her words, her conviction, touched the hardened kernel within him, the kernel that had read and loved the Arthurian romances and the ideals of knighthood. The kernel that had become starved and desiccated from the realities of knightly life. She fed that kernel, indeed had been feeding it all along, and it expanded and bloomed within, suffusing him with peace and rightness.

"Here. I brought you something to give you strength." She opened her palm and revealed his father's pebble from the Holy Land, which he'd told her about only the night before.

His heart clenched. His mother's words came back to him and blended with Kaytee's. With a clarity that shook him to his damned soul, he saw that he'd denied his own personal honor, believing it had no value, no place in the world. That he'd believed the only honor he could achieve was what could be bestowed by others. By a dishonorable king.

"Roll it up at my back," he said hoarsely. "Less likely to be found there."

As she tucked his keepsake away, his sole regret was that he'd most likely die now as a traitor, unable to be with her, this woman who beheld his inner self and embraced it, nurtured it.

His Kaytee, his woman, reached up and placed the sweetest kiss on his lips. She pulled away, her lush lips lingering, just before the door scraped open.

❧

KATY TRAILED BEHIND THE JAILER ALONG the dank stone hallway in one of the castle's towers. Forty minutes ago, she'd left Robert in his cell.

Forty minutes ago now seemed like forever. The new knowledge she held colored every stone she crossed, amplified the stink, distorted every cry and whisper and groan. Chaos gripped her lungs, her throat, and weighted her steps.

God, Robert.

Finally, she reached the stout wooden door, and the jailer unlocked it with a metal key. She steeled her shoulders. *Don't show Robert any fear.*

As the door groaned shut behind her, and the keys rattled and clicked in the lock, she let her eyes adjust to the gloom.

God, Robert.

Her heart stretched toward him, aching to comfort, he looked so haggard. Even more than last time.

And then her heart lurched when he straightened for her. My God, so proud.

"Tell me," he rasped.

"How do you know I have news?" Was that her voice? It sounded so small.

"You were here a short time ago, so your quick return can mean only one thing. They have decided. And your face is grim."

God, Robert.

She couldn't voice it. She couldn't. Her throat constricted, swelling with a painful, choking heat. "Couldn't I just be coming to see you? To comfort you?"

"Katy. Tell me," he commanded.

She stumbled forward and wrapped her arms around his torso, pressing her body to his warm skin. "They..." She pulled in a choking sob. "They mean to hang you for a traitor."

Chapter Twenty-Eight

❧

So he set strong men upon Peredur, who seized him, and cast him
into prison. And the maiden went before her father, and asked him,
wherefore he had caused the youth from Arthur's Court
to be imprisoned.
The Mabinogion, an ancient Welsh romance

ROBERT'S CHAINS RATTLED at her news, and Katy ached to feel his arms around her once more. "When?" his voice cracked through the dank surroundings.

She counted each beat of his heart against her ear, each beat proof he still lived. She squeezed her eyes shut, and hot tears slipped between her cheek and his chest. "I don't know. We have a few days maybe. Powys is pushing this hard, and with the chaos surrounding Flint, the officials can't seem to give a damn—are even denying you a right to defense. 'Let God sort it out,' one of them said. I don't understand why they aren't allowing you a fair trial."

Robert's laugh was bitter. "I've been denied the king's justice."

"But why?"

"Here on the Marches, the lords are allowed to dispense their own justice. They are using the chaos of the revolt to be rid of someone they find troublesome. You heard how they justify it—if I'm innocent, God will reward me in heaven. But what of you?"

"Honestly, they've forgotten about me."

At that, his muscles relaxed, and his head came to rest on the top of hers. "Katy, please. Listen to me. I am marked for death. Get away while you can."

"I told you, I'm not abandoning you," she said with a conviction pulled from every cell in her body.

"There is nothing you can do." He took a deep breath. "Know that I...what you said, about me, it has given me solace, peace." His laugh was bitter. "It matters not now, but you are right. My personal honor *is* more important."

"Robert..." she squeezed him tighter. "This is all my fault." If she hadn't come back in time, he wouldn't have had to save her...

"No. What is done is done. The confrontation with de Buche was inevitable. If not this opportunity, he would have pounced on another. He lured me to my sister's knowing how I would react, and I obligingly played into his hands. I should have known he would not have faced me honorably. He did not wish to leave anything to chance when it came to his inheritance."

"But there's got to be someone who will advocate for you."

"There is no one."

"What about Sir Hugh?"

He tensed in her arms. "No. Absolutely not. I will not have his honor and allegiance stained by association. Besides, he has been sent to Chester to report to the king. Katy, I am in God's hands now."

She pulled away and gripped his shoulders, gazing with determination into his shuttered eyes. "I'm not resigned to leaving it up to God, thank you very much. Please. I can't let you die. There must be something I can do. Maybe I can drug the guard and help you escape?"

He jerked on his chains again, his head dipping close to hers, his eyes blazing. "No. Promise me you will not do something so foolhardy. I will not have you put at risk. Forget me, and return to your land."

She couldn't abandon him. No.

"Katy, please. Promise me," his voice laced, for the first time, with true fear. "Go to Wrexham. The villagers are there. Find your token, and return to your land.

Her heart lifted at the command he'd just given her, the idea he'd planted in her head. "I promise I will go to Wrexham and find my token." She felt his muscles relax.

Let him believe what he would, she'd not abandon him. She'd not let him die. This was *not* over.

❦

KATY TRUDGED DOWN WREXHAM village's main street, following the directions to The Thirsty Boar where the villagers were staying. Immediately upon leaving Robert, she'd hired a guide. By leaving her non-essential belongings at the inn, and cantering and walking the horses by turns, they'd made the eighteen-mile journey in two hours instead of six and a half. To keep her load light, all she'd taken along was a pouch of coins and the burlap bag containing her purse from her time.

She'd exhausted at least an hour finding out the villagers' location. Turned out there were only two inns in the village anyway. As a well-dressed squire, she garnered more respect than she'd seen others given, so at least there was that.

She pushed open the heavy oak door of the inn and approached the woman behind the bar, whose strong jaw rivaled her large, but all-wise eyes.

"I'm looking for the villagers who came from Castell y Bere. I understand they are here?"

The woman frowned and said something that sounded like, "I don't speak French."

Ah, yes. Katy closed her eyes and mentally recalled her conversations with Alfred, got her mind grinding along in Middle English again.

She repeated her question, this time her English inflected the way she'd spoken with Alfred. But that still wasn't clear enough, apparently. Frustration and panic threatened to overtake her, but she pushed it down and spoke slower. Robert needed her. Needed her calm.

"Yes, there are some of them at that table by the window, near the corner." She flicked a linen towel in that direction.

"Thank you."

At the table, Katy introduced herself and described the woman she looked for. As she spoke, more and more of her lessons learned while speaking with Alfred rose to the surface, and her Middle English conformed better.

"Aye, I remember you," said an older woman with graying blonde hair and flushed red cheeks.

The guy in the bunch, young but stoop-shouldered, crossed his bony arms. "What do you want with her, anyway?"

"She has something..." she stopped from saying 'of mine.' Not the time to quibble about ownership and easier to avoid antagonizing them. "...I'd like to buy."

"Aye, she was here," the older lady replied, "but she and her family are hitching up a wagon they bought and moving to Shrewsbury. They might still be in the stable yard."

Katy hurried outside and around back to the stables. A short man in his early thirties was hitching a wagon to a horse, three kids were climbing in and jumping down, while several adults were loading their belongings and tying them down.

There she is. Katy ran up to the lady she remembered, out of breath, startling everyone. "Hello. I was at Castell y Bere also, and you had an object I...I fancied, and I wondered if I could purchase it? A little silver case, about so big." She held out her hands. "With a chain loop?"

The woman smiled. "That was a pretty thing, wasn't it?"

Dread settled like a dead weight in Katy's stomach. She didn't like the use of past tense.

"I would so like to have kept it," the woman continued, "but with the loss of our home and business, and no surety that the town will be rebuilt, we needed the money."

"You sold it?"

"Aye, for the silver. Fetched a fair price. Enough to buy this horse and wagon and still set us up nice and proper in Shrewsbury. No more of this colonizing business. The king can find some other fools."

"Who did you sell it to?"

"Gilbert the Goldsmith."

"Where is he?"

The lady gave directions. "You'll see his sign once you're there."

"What does his sign say?"

The lady shot her a quizzical look. "Say? No signs that talk around here. Look for the gold coin. You're a daft one, aren't ye?"

Katy raced back through the yard, palms sweating, heart pretty much stuck on the fast tempo now. Across the way, a blacksmith worked a bellows, and Katy clutched her money sack. The coins Robert had given her might not be enough, and she needed more to pay the guide. A blacksmith could melt down her engagement ring, which would be simpler to pay with. She fetched the ring from her sack and fingered it. Any regrets?

No.

Well, then.

She couldn't believe she was about to do this, but she didn't have a choice.

The blacksmith, a burly guy with a huge upper torso glistening with sweat and sporting a leather apron, stood over an anvil and banged on a long piece of steel. She waited until he paused.

"Excuse me."

He straightened, his brows lifting. "How can I help you, young sir?"

She handed over her ring. "Can you melt this into a nugget, with the diamond separate?"

He frowned. "Why would you wish this done? Appears to be a finely crafted ring."

"It, uh, has too many memories." More like she didn't want to confuse the heck out of future archaeologists with its dated inscription.

"Stole it, huh?"

"What? No!"

"Only jesting, noble sir. Allow me a few minutes, and I'll have it ready." He stoked the fire in his forge higher, snipped off her diamond, pulled out a glowing, ruby red beaker, and dropped her ring inside. With tongs held in gloved hands, he gripped the container and held it over the hottest part of the fire.

"Kay, you're alive."

Katy didn't register that the voice was addressing her until she felt a tug on her tunic. "Alfred! You made it. How are you?"

Alfred puffed up his chest. "We had a merry time of it, for certes. Where is Sir Robert?"

Katy swallowed a hard lump. "He's momentarily in Flint, and I'll be returning there shortly."

"Alfred, come here, you rascal," called a young woman who could either be an older sister or his mother.

Alfred bowed quickly. "See you anon!"

Ten agonizing minutes later, the blacksmith poured the molten gold into a small mold. Seconds later, he removed the gold and dropped it into a bucket of water. Steam flashed high, *tshhhhh*, obscuring his hand momentarily.

Shortly, he handed Katy a piece of wool with a lump of gold no bigger than a green pea on steroids and her diamond on top. "I've never seen such a curiously cut stone. Where did you acquire it?"

"Er. In France." She tied the cloth into a knot and put the bundle into her money pouch. "How much do I owe you?"

"Worry not. It was but the work of a moment."

She smiled at him. "I thank you. If you don't mind me asking, how much is the gold worth?"

He scratched his ample beard. "A pound of gold should fetch you ten pounds silver, though that doesn't weigh a pound. Three or four grams would be my guess. I don't know about the gem."

"How many grams in a pound?"

"It doesn't divide evenly, but 453 grams to a pound should get you close."

"That helps though, gives me an idea. Thank ye." She hustled through the nearby lanes, her nerves on edge, her stomach in knots. If her lump of gold weighed four grams...and there were 453 grams in a pound... Dammit. There was a reason she sucked at math. She edged to the side of the lane, pulled the knife from her belt, and hashed out the calculations in the dirt.

Okay. Her lump was worth roughly seventeen shillings, or 211 silver pennies. Robert had given her a shilling's worth in pennies.

She turned onto the street the woman said held the goldsmith, and sure enough, a hundred yards ahead the wooden sign with the golden coin creaked lazily in the stilted air. A well-maintained wooden structure, it kind of looked like an outdoor bar, with its wooden countertop running the length of the front, revealing the interior. Was only missing the bar stools and beer taps. She approached and knocked on the counter. There was no door.

A well-dressed man in his late fifties sat up where he'd been reclining on a bench. "Good afternoon. How may I assist you?" His Middle English accent was pretty similar to Alfred's, thank God.

What a weird shop. She didn't see a lot of merchandise, but the space had a variety of tools, weights, and scales, all neatly arranged.

"Yes. A friend sold her silver trinket here today? Do you still have it?"

"Aye, I do." He swung his legs around and stood.

"How much do you want for it?"

"An unusual item, to be sure." He rubbed his stomach.

Great. He was going to up the price. She kept her stare cool and tried to look like she didn't care. She didn't, except if he hiked the price higher than she could afford. "May I see it?"

"Of course." He disappeared behind a partition and returned with a trunk, whistling a soft tune. With a key, he opened the immense iron lock and pulled out a fist-sized bundle of rough cloth. He untied it and laid it out on the counter.

Her heart thumped double-time. It was her case. "May I look inside?"

He opened it, his big thumbs fumbling with the catch. "Clever little thing it is. Took me a king's age to realize it opened, but it was lighter than it should be if 'twere solid." He got it open but didn't hand it to her, just held it up. Inside were nestled Podbury's cards. "Unusual bits of parchment too, but I've ceased attempting to figure the ways of the fancy." He studied her, his eyes narrowed. "I could part with it for ten shillings."

"Ten shillings?" She had no idea if that was overpriced, but relief swept through her—she could afford it.

"For the silver alone, melted down, I could get five. Calculate the craftsmanship, its uniqueness. Did you see that it opens? A bargain at ten shillings."

"Deal."

"Eight shillings, six pence and that's... Wait. What? You will not haggle?"

"No time." She dug out her tightly wrapped little bundle. She'd have laughed at his stunned-plus-disappointed expression if the situation were different. "Can you weigh this and take my payment out of it, and give me the change in coin?"

His eyebrows shot upwards. "No." Now he looked at her like she'd offered to pay with Monopoly money.

"No? But this is real gold. You're a goldsmith."

"Oh, you'll be able to pay for this, fear not, but I cannot exchange this for coin. Even if I had that much, how would you carry over a hundred and forty silver pennies? No. Here is what we will do." He brought the gold lump to a scale and weighed it. He then cut off a little less than half, and weighed that. He shaved it down and handed her back the larger lump and smaller pieces.

"Oh, thank you." She looked at the pieces in her hand. "Do you have enough to convert these tiny pieces into coin?"

"That I can do, lad."

He weighed them and counted silver coins into a bag. Seemed like a lot. "Sorry I do not have any groats. All I have are pennies, but this will do you." He handed her the bag.

"No, this is wonderful, thank you." She tied it by the strings to the belt at her waist.

"Where are you from? We're seeing all sorts now that the king is pushing settlers to move here. Your speech is unusual."

"From far away," she muttered.

He tapped his chin and narrowed an eye. "Yorkshire?"

"Er, yes, from York."

He beamed. "Never met anyone from York. Wait until I tell m' woman. She loves to hear me tell of the folks who travel through here." He shook his head, smiling. "From York. Isn't that something. Here, you'll be wanting this, I expect." He folded her case up in the cloth and handed it over the counter.

He pointed a finger at her. "You be careful out there. Wouldn't want an urchin to cut those strings on your purse."

Her hand flew to her waist. "No. I wouldn't." She stuffed her case in her larger money pouch and arranged them on her belt so her mantle hid them in its folds.

He nodded. "That's better. Best of luck to you, lad."

"You too. Thank you." She waved and stepped away, trying not to run. She scooted around the corner, bumping into a man who headed for the goldsmith. She mumbled a quick apology and pressed herself flat against the shop wall, the timber framing pressing into her back. She'd done it. She could rescue Robert and go home!

Robert.

Please be still alive.

She pushed away from the wall to start back for Flint, when she heard the goldsmith's new customer say, "I understand you have a silver case here? It used to belong to me. My name's inside."

Katy's breath hitched.

Mr. Podbury.

Again, she pressed herself flat against the wall and edged to the end of the alley. Once on the next lane, she sprinted for the stables, glancing once behind her.

Gasping for breath, Katy skidded in the straw outside the stables and wrenched open the main door.

"Saddle my horse, good sir," she shouted to a stable hand, kinda amazed with how she took on this role so well. Her guide from Flint lay snoozing in a pile of hay, and she shook him awake. "We're leaving. Get ready."

"Aye, sir." The kid jerked awake, alert.

They lost a few minutes getting onto their horses, but soon they were cantering down the main road for Flint.

☙

LATER THAT AFTERNOON, Katy jumped off her horse as soon as she reached the gate leading from the town of Flint into the castle's outer bailey. She couldn't ride straight through to Robert like she'd wanted, for a thick crowd blocked the gate and drawbridge. She didn't dare trust her minimal equestrian skills navigating that mess. Getting thrown by a spooked horse was not a risk she could take.

"Return my mount to the stables, thank you," she said to her guide, giving him his payment in coin.

She jostled through the milling crowd across the drawbridge and through the second gate. Finally the crowd thinned. To the left, the gallows cast a pall shadow over her steps, spurring her on in her determination. A knot twisted her insides. She had to look. Please God that she wasn't too late. Quick glance.

No one on the gallows at all.

Relief animated her steps. Okay. Through the next gate into the castle's inner bailey, then left, then five minutes later, she'd be in his cell, and this nightmare would be over. Now her only worry was whether her case could transport them both. Or that he wouldn't agree. In the privacy of his cell, she planned to confess her origins and convince him to return with her to her own time.

He'd be shocked, but he simply *had* to agree. Then she'd wrap her arms around him and make her wish.

And poof, they'd be gone.

Leaving a puzzle for the jailers. Hee.

She wormed through the thicker crowd at the inner gate, unease trickling in as she noted the avid looks in the passersby leaving through the gate. Avid looks that felt…off. Twisted. Then, the pattern of the milling crowd sank in. They weren't milling at all, they were heading for the gallows.

Shit.

She broke into a run, not caring whom she elbowed, and turned onto the lane that would bring her to the tower housing Robert. And all of her insides turned into a solid chunk of ice and then flash-heated, dropping right through her, rooting her to a stop, arms windmilling for balance.

"Robert!"

Her voice came out in a squeak, all the horror and helplessness choking it in her throat.

He marched down the lane, still stripped down to his braies, his arms tied behind his back, accentuating the muscles of his chest and biceps. Proud, he walked. Determined.

The crowd lining the lane pelted him with rotten garbage. He never flinched. Others shoved her to the side to get closer. For a moment, all she could hear was her breath wheezing in and out of her lungs as her panic and terror narrowed her focus to the two of them.

Then, as if the mute button was switched off, the jeers and taunts filled the air, deafening. She shrieked his name into the din, just one voice of many, despite her fear finally giving her voice volume. She shoved and pushed her way forward, screaming his name, but he didn't see her as he passed.

Oh God. She was too late.

Chapter Twenty-Nine

∾

...*"and wheresoever thou wilt, there will I meet with thee."*
The Mabinogion, an ancient Welsh romance

*A*S THEY PRODDED ROBERT THROUGH the raucous crowd, he fixed his gaze before him but held the memory of Kaytee's face. He shrugged off the jeers and the rotten cabbages and eggs that pelted him.

By every damn saint in all of Christendom, he prayed she'd done as he'd bade—fled to Wrexham, her token, and to her own land. Naught was here for her now.

He sucked in a fortifying breath. A traitorous hope snaked through him that she'd disobeyed, and he'd catch one final glimpse. A glimpse for his selfish soul, yes, but also for assurance that she was safe. He scanned the crowd of eager spectators, but was denied her lovely visage.

They swept through the gate, and soon the worn wooden steps of the gallows were before him. He stumbled on purpose to slip his father's memento into his palm and clasped it tight. He would not give them the satisfaction of showing fear, but blood pounded in his ears as he took each step. Black crows scattered as their small party gained the platform. High above the crowd he was now, and watching him with a grim face was a priest, hands folded before him.

At least he'd be shriven.

Breaths even, Robert pivoted, and Lord Powys approached. "Any last words before you confess to the priest? Will you confess to the crowd?"

Confess? What? Why bother? Robert gazed out at the men, women, and children jostling in front of the gallows, easily a hundred. Then he saw her.

His sweet angel.

Fear and anguish twisted her face, and he cursed his selfish wish to see her once more. The mere sight of her strengthened him, yes, but at what cost to her? Too much.

He nodded to Lord Powys, kept his gaze on his beloved, and his grip on his father's memento, and took a deep breath. With a loud voice he said, "I have committed no crime but that of compassion and honor. I stand accused of being a Welsh spy." Several rotten eggs hit him, but he continued. "On the surety of my everlasting soul, I avow I am not. Honor and compassion dictated my actions, for how can we face Our Lord God on Judgment Day if we have treated fellow Christians in a reprehensible manner? How high a price will we pay to subjugate the Welsh? Will we pay it with our honor? How can we feel honor in our achievements if earned through broken oaths, hurting innocent women and children, and running men of God through with a sword?"

At first, the crowd stared, their expressions stunned—not from the power of his speech, but because he'd dared make it at all. That he'd not begged forgiveness and absolved the executioner instead. Then murmurs arose, and someone yelled, "*Cefnogwr Cymru!*"

Yes, he was a Welsh sympathizer. Perhaps the English cur thought himself a wit by taunting him in Welsh. Who knew.

The crowd picked up the words, and began to chant, "Cefnogwr."

Lord Powys yanked him to the priest. "Enough of this."

Robert caught Powys's gaze and held it, unflinching, until the callous youth glanced away. Only then did Robert bow his head before the priest and confess his sins. The ointment smeared onto his forehead and palms was cool as the priest performed the last rites.

❧

KATY GASPED FOR AIR, HER BODY SHAKING so uncontrollably she almost felt separate from this body of jerking limbs. Even if she could barrel through the crowd, what could she do? Risking having him disappear from a cell to save him from a fate she'd caused to begin with was one thing, but in front of all these witnesses? Did she even care how that would get recorded in history?

Finally, as if he felt the weight of her stare, her terror, he locked his gaze with hers. Bursting from his eyes was all the love and determination which filled him. He began his speech, and her throat closed up tight. She dared not turn away, for him. She could feel it in his gaze, his taking strength from her, and she'd not fail him in this. All her horror and helplessness lashed at her, drained her strength, her will, as if it truly was passing to him via their connection.

Oh God, how could she possibly watch this?

Everyone around her remained oddly hushed as he spoke, his voice ringing with conviction, but when he finished, the jeers and shouts erupted again, buffeting her with their animosity.

One shout nearby jolted her. "Hang him. Hang Robert de Beucol, Robert the Cefnogwr Cymru."

The cry of "Cefnogwr" was taken up by others until it became a chant, rolling through the crowd. A chill sliced up her spine and jumpstarted a tiny flicker of hope in her heart. A way to save him flashed in her mind, sharp with inevitability. As the chant spread, Katy reeled, remembering the tour at the little Welsh Church of St. Cefnogwr and the warrior-saint rescued by an angel.

Her heart lurched, taking that new flicker of hope and igniting it into a newfound strength. After all, it had already happened.

But how? The crowd was too thick between her and the gallows. She raked her gaze desperately over the grim platform. Both sides were packed as well.

Then her gaze fell on the gatehouse and the battlements above. And the exact words of the tour guide rang through her. She muscled her way through the crowd toward its side. Her idea was so crazy, she could scarce process it. But she didn't let it stop her.

She stumbled through the last of the spectators, which gave her a clear path to the gatehouse. She broke into a run and slipped through gate tower door. The three pouches strapped to her waist bounced against her hips as she pounded up the stairs. At the top, she pushed onto the battlements where more spectators had gathered for a better view. She sprinted along the rough stone and peeked over the side—the gallows were closer than she dared hope.

But—Oh God—his head was already in the noose. The executioner's hand pulled on the knot until it was tight around his neck.

And all the while, he stood there, calmly.

She drew even with him and braced her hands on the parapet. There he was. A leap away.

The executioner stooped, picked up a rope—a rope attached to the stool Robert stood on—and yanked.

And Robert dropped.

And Katy's whole body seized in horror.

Oh God, Robert!

Fear and remorse gripped her but...his feet kicked! It hadn't been a sharp drop to snap his neck like the Old West.

She still had time for her plan. She climbed onto the parapet. *Don't miss.*

"Stop him!"

Oh shit. Guards.

She gripped her case in her hand, its cool metal and sharp edges biting into her palm, and jumped, arms outstretched.

The rushing air caught the folds of her white mantle, snapping them into the wind. Timing was everything—she had to wish with all of her heart the instant she touched him or she'd snap his neck with her weight.

Conviction sang through her. She was the angel. This would work. It had already happened.

A second later, her body slammed into his, and she made her wish.

Chapter Thirty

And after the first meal, Pwyll arose to walk, and he went to the top
of a mound that was above the palace, and was called Gorsedd Arberth.
"Lord," said one of the Court, "it is peculiar to the mound that
whosoever sits upon it cannot go thence, without either receiving
wounds or blows, or else seeing a wonder." "I fear not to receive
wounds and blows in the midst of such a host as this, but as to the
wonder, gladly would I see it. I will go therefore
and sit upon the mound."
The Mabinogion, an ancient Welsh romance

KATY'S BUTT THUDDED against a hard surface, and she rocked
onto her back with a pained gasp. Robert's warm body was
firmly in her grip, and under her palm, his heart beat—thank God—
but too fast. He gagged and sucked in several labored breaths.

Oh shit, oh shit, oh shit. Did she do it? Or did she merely break the
rope?

She pulled air into burning lungs and fought a wave of dizziness
and nausea. Her heart fluttered alarmingly, as if it would zoom right
out of her body.

Okay. Okay. Okay. Open an eye.

Face scrunched against his back, she popped one open to a near
darkness, only to have a car horn blare, and a bright light blind her,
approaching rapidly.

"Crap!"

Her heart nearly exploding out of her now, she rolled until they
thumped against a curb, and the car swerved in the other direction.
Yeah, it appeared her heart beats had no intention of slowing down
now. But...that close call meant... She craned her head, her chin
brushing against Robert. Lights from streetlamps glinted off a paved
street, a sidewalk, and a neatly printed tourist map on a green sign.

Loud music blared from the headphones of a passing teen, a laughing couple strolled by, their clothes from her time.

Now her heart was *really* pounding.

Holy crap, she'd done it.

Holy crap, what now?

His noose!

She swept frantic hands around his neck, but the rope was gone; only she and Robert, and their clothes and possessions, had made the trip. The wrist bindings were gone as well. She had to get him isolated. Isolated so she could explain. Everything. And he could freak out in private.

Please understand, Robert. Please understand.

"What's the deal with the Jesus dude?" an American-accented voice said, piercing her thoughts.

Huh?

Katy stared at the gathering crowd. Jesus? She stumbled upright and helped Robert to stand. He gasped for breath and swayed. Oh. The onlooker referred to Robert, with his trim beard, semi-longish hair—seriously it was only just past his ears, not Jesus-length—and the fact that he wore nothing but that funny underwear, which, yeah...

Hotel. Where was a hotel? The curious crowd was making her skin itch in nervousness—she so didn't need to expose Robert to all this. She tucked her case behind her belt.

"I'm telling you, they just appeared out of thin air," another on-looker said, his words slurred.

"Ah, lay off the drink, why don't ya, Owen?"

Where the hell was she?

She helped Robert to the tourist display, their feet crunching over pebbles. The sign read, "Castle Park Flint." Okay, wow, the same spot as the hanging, only hundreds and hundreds of years later. Good. That was good.

Another couple, in their early thirties, walked by, and she asked for directions to the closest hotel. She would *not* ask the growing crowd of drunk youths.

"Katy." Robert's thick, strained voice cut through the night's air. "What has transpired?"

"Hold on. I'll explain. Please." She pulled Robert's arm around her shoulder, ignored the crowd, and aimed him down the road the couple had indicated. *Please be too polite to bother us*, she silently pleaded to the crowd behind.

Thankfully, they were, and she hustled a stumbling Robert into the lobby of the old hotel where she asked for a room.

The proprietor only raised an eyebrow. "Identification and method of payment."

"Oh, um, hang on." It was weird speaking and thinking again in her normal English.

She settled Robert in a chair, his gorgeous eyes open, but glazed. "I can explain," she whispered. "Please stay quiet until we're alone."

He jerked his gaze to hers but didn't respond, his face blank.

Please don't freak out. Not yet. She grabbed his hand and squeezed it, hoping her touch helped ground him. "Trust me. I can explain. You with me?"

His eyes held hers and gradually focused. He gave one short nod and straightened in the chair.

Katy squeezed his hand again and untied the burlap bag from her belt. She spread it open, revealing her purse. Fumbling through the contents with shaking fingers, she grabbed her identification and her money. As she handed them to the attendant, a strange feeling of disconnect stole over her. Earlier today, she'd paid for something with gold measured from her melted ring. Now she used an intrinsically worthless piece of plastic. Somehow *this* felt less real.

The attendant, his light brown hair slicked back and parted on the side, was too polite to ask, but curiosity obviously animated his movements, his quick, searching glances as he completed her registration.

"We were, uh, in a reenactment, for the tourists, and my friend here got a little sick, so we skipped out."

He seemed to accept this. "Ah, sure. I hope he feels better. Not contagious, is he?"

"No. Just, uh, overheated. Thank you."

What day was it? She pulled her phone from her purse, turned it on, and peeked. It picked up a signal from the nearest tower, and the date and time glowed at the top. 8:43 p.m. October 23rd. Sixteen days since she'd left.

Good God, her friends and family must be worried sick.

"Come on, Robert. Let's get you up these stairs."

She didn't dare subject him to the elevator and, besides, their room was only on the next floor. But how to explain all this to Robert? How to help him adjust? Would he be mad at her for taking him from his time without asking?

She rehearsed what she'd tell him. Sweat beaded her skin—yeah, from the effort of getting a hunky but disoriented medieval warrior up a flight of stairs, but also from the worry.

ତ୍ର

ROBERT MOVED ONTO ANOTHER STEP, touched the abraded skin on his neck, and winced. But the pain and soreness was as nothing compared to the panic surging through him. Where the hell was he? Was he...in the afterlife?

When he'd dangled from the rope, he'd found a measure of peace and acceptance for his fate. A good death.

But as his vision had grown spotted, his body had fought his mind, desperate to live despite the circumstances. And his body had shouted, "No!"

Kaytee. He hadn't wanted to leave Kaytee.

But what could he do? Naught. Naught but pray to his Maker for leniency for his sins. Leniency that would allow a reunion with Kaytee in the afterlife.

Then his breaths had become harder to pull into his lungs. White spots had filled his vision. Then blackness.

Blackness...until the warmth of his woman's body had embraced him, her sweet scent surrounding him.

Ah, this was peace. He could die now.

Blackness...peace...pierced of a sudden by an unholy noise and bright light. All was confusion.

But then he'd smelled her.

As he'd gasped for air, he'd pulled her tighter to him. A dream? How else could his beloved be with him?

When his eyes had adjusted to the new surrounding blackness, he'd realized he was...well, he knew not where.

Now, he took another painful step and rubbed his neck.

Kaytee.

Kaytee was the only common element in all this madness. A madness that threatened to choke his pounding heart. Kaytee was familiar. Kaytee would aid him. Kaytee would explain.

He repeated this belief, over and over, as she assisted him up a flight of stairs. A flight of stairs whose angles were so precise, it stunned him.

Kaytee would explain. Explain these hellish surroundings. She'd said she would.

Yes. As blood and feeling animated his limbs once more, strength returned with each step. They were together, were they not?

⁊

KATY LED ROBERT TO A RECLINER, eased him down, and closed their hotel room door. She leaned back and sighed.

"Okay. I can do this," she whispered.

She spun away and paced from one wall to the next several times, marshaling her thoughts. "I'm going to tell you what's happened. It's going to sound completely crazy, and you most likely will think I'm insane, but, well, the proof is all around us."

She stepped to the foot of his chair and knelt, placing her hands on his knees. "Keep your eyes on me for right now, and listen to what I'm about to tell you."

"How did you spirit me away from the gallows?" His hand rubbed his neck, confusion clouding his gaze.

"Um, yeah, that's tied into what I'm about to tell you. You see, I'm from the future."

He shook his head. "The future? What do you mean?"

"Well, you know how events happen and end up as history—they make up our past?"

"Yes..."

"And you know how people will live past you, have their own lives—children and their children's children. Well, picture that that history keeps happening, events keep going. With me?"

"Yes..." he said, as if she were explaining the obvious. Okay, so she'd backed up the explanation too far.

"Okay, so... Well, I come from one of those future times. Somehow I got pulled from my time, back through all my history, to your time."

His eyes grew rounder, his eyebrows drawing downward. Yeah, parsing time travel concepts gave her a headache too.

"How is that possible? Do people from your time do this often?"

"Er, no. I don't know how it happened. Wow. You're taking this better than I thought."

"Well, there is much magic in this world, who's to say what's possible?"

Funny, but the farther back one went, the chances were better that they'd accept what happened. It had been a lot harder for Isabelle to convince Phineas in their more scientific-based world. "I guess you're right."

"So it was magic?"

"Why not? I certainly can't explain it. That token I told you I needed to get from the villager, it was the device that brought me to your time." She took a deep breath. Now for the biggie. "And it's what brought me back to my time, brought *us* here."

He jerked in the chair, the thigh muscles under her palms tensing. "What are you saying?" He braced his hands on the armchair and looked around the room, eyes dazed and frantic.

"I found that token, Robert. I couldn't let you die. I hope you understand. After I left you in the cell, I went to Wrexham and found the token." She quickly filled him in on her frantic mission and how she'd jumped from the battlements to save him.

He swallowed hard and held her gaze. "How far have you sped me ahead in time?"

She winced and squeezed his thighs. "About seven hundred years."

He reeled back and then folded forward, arms around his middle as if he'd been punched in the stomach. His breaths came harsh and fast. After a long moment, he slowly unfolded and braced himself again on the armrests. His gaze held hers, bleak. "So, everyone I know is dead?"

"Yes," she whispered and rubbed his thighs. "I'm so sorry, Robert. I meant to ask your permission. Find you in your cell and take you with me if you agreed. But when I got back to Flint, I was too late. Please tell me I did the right thing."

His eyes were roiling with anguish and confusion. "There is much

251

for me to absorb. Please, allow me some time to adjust to what you have revealed."

Certainly understandable. But—oh God—she just wanted to wrap him up in a big hug. "Of course. I need to contact my friends and family. Take all the time you need."

Please understand, Robert. Please understand.

ↄ

"You're *WHERE?*" shrieked Traci.

Katy held the phone away from her ear. "I'm in a hotel in Flint." She gave her the name of the hotel on Chester Road.

"Where the hell have you been? I know you were having second thoughts, but you didn't have to just up and leave. You know how worried we've been? We were starting to believe the worst. Not cool, Katy. Not cool."

"I didn't do it on purpose. And I couldn't contact you until now. I...I had amnesia."

Amnesia? Wow, that was lame. Was she suddenly channeling a cheesy soap opera? Who the hell gets amnesia in real life? Embarrassment heated her face.

Traci's tone was still strident but now all bent on getting the story and making sure she was okay.

Katy cleared her throat. "Um, yeah. I was...wandering around that ravine where you left me? And I slipped and fell. The ground gave way under me, and I fell into this crevice. I woke up in the middle of the night, and didn't know who I was. I only just regained my memories."

"Good Lord, Katy. I'm glad you're okay. We're still all in Wales, except for Catherine. She had to go back to work and also to console Preston. We hadn't given up looking. We're in Aberystwyth. We'll settle up here, pack, and be there in three hours. Book us a room?"

"Will do."

Katy ended the call and then looked down. Crap. Clothes. These would be hard to explain away. And it was too late to go to a store.

ↄ

OVER THREE HOURS LATER, she sat with her friends and Robert, drinking coffee around the small table in their room. After the phone call, she'd talked a couple at the hotel into selling their spare clothes, looked up amnesia symptoms, and answered Robert's questions once he'd gotten over the initial shock.

"So you two met after your accident?" Traci asked.

She'd had time to come up with her cover story too. "Yes. He'd been camping nearby, and I wandered into his camp."

"And he doesn't speak English?"

"No. He's from a remote village in eastern Brittany." Her friends wouldn't know the difference between Gallo French and regular French to know he wasn't speaking Gallo at all. But they'd heard enough regular French in their lives to know his sounded off.

Lizbeth had pretty much been drooling over him since they'd arrived, and for the first time *ever*, Katy had gone all primal with the he's-mine feelings. "So he can't understand us?"

"Nope."

"Then I'll just say it. He's bloody hot. If I wasn't with Lawrence... Just sayin'..." At Katy's stare, she tacked on, "What? He can't understand us."

"Well, I'm single," Traci said. She gave Robert an appreciative appraisal.

"What are they saying?" Robert asked in Norman French.

Her face flushed with heat. "They're, uh, asking about where you're from. I told them a region in eastern Brittany."

He cocked his head and looked like he was about to protest, but she could just see how this could go, each one asking what the other was saying. "I'll explain why later. Trust me."

"I do, *cariad*." His gaze softened.

She'd been trying to keep her feelings from showing, to give her friends time, but nothing got past Traci. "You guys are...together," she whispered. "What about Preston?"

"I...I called him earlier, to let him know I was okay, but also to call off the wedding." Everyone went still. "Given everything that happened, I couldn't. I have my memories now..." She cringed at having to use that as an excuse. "But it doesn't change how I feel and what I learned about myself in the last couple of weeks."

Her friends looked between the two of them and were silent long enough that Katy had to resist the urge to squirm in her chair.

Finally, Traci spoke. "Are you happy?"

"Yes." And unlike that day outside the ruins of Castell y Bere, her voice rang with conviction. She'd never been more sure of anything in her life.

Traci smiled and nodded. "Well, then."

"How did Preston take it?" Lizbeth asked.

"Pretty well, actually. My mother, however, was in hysterics." Preston's easy acceptance pretty much summed up their relationship, and that said a lot. "I'm sorry, guys. We're exhausted, and I'm still trying to adjust to...having my memories back. I'll see you tomorrow, okay?"

They totally understood and, after promises to meet up in the afternoon for lunch, they finally left them alone.

God, Robert had been so patient.

✺

ROBERT SAT IN THE MOST COMFORTABLE chair he'd ever had grace his hind parts. Outside the window of the inn Kaytee had procured for them, evenly spaced patches of lights—which did not flicker and shone as bright as day—pierced the early evening gloom.

He was unsure if he yet grasped this *future* land she'd transported him to, but it was wondrous indeed. He smiled, hitting the lever that popped out a cleverly hidden footrest, and sat back with a sigh.

From what he could observe in their private chamber, and through the window, this future differed vastly from his. Much cleaner. More people crowded the streets without than he'd ever seen gathered, except at the largest tournament.

How could he make a life here? Without burdening Kaytee? Would she still have him?

God's piss, he felt as helpless as a swaddled babe. He collapsed the chair with a *thunk* and stood. He had not even the means to provide for her, for at this moment she was out—alone—procuring their evening meal, while he waited in the room for *his safety*. He, a knight.

Aye, he'd agreed after much debate, for he needed more time to adjust to the changes without, but it rankled.

Anything could happen to her out there. Alone. Undefended. She had no weapon with her...

He ran his hand down the...*blue jeans* which she'd procured and now clad his legs. He liked them not. Too constricting. Armor was constricting, for certes, but it served a purpose. When not armed for battle, he preferred the looser garments of his period.

The door opened, and Robert swung around, braced for anything.

"I got us some roast beef from the pub down the street, along with some carrots and potatoes. I hope you like it."

Kaytee's bright face coming through the door, her soothing voice lilting across the room, eased Robert's shoulders, and he smiled. Roast beef, he knew, and surely these *potatoes* she spoke of must be appetizing as well. But carrots? Who would eat such a tiny, purple root?

But then he frowned at her attire. Everyone out there, the men of this time—all of them—could see her every luscious curve in those *blue jeans* and snug *sweater*. He closed his eyes and willed himself to relax. This was *her* culture, *her* time. Through the window, he'd observed that most women dressed thusly, or in even more form-revealing attire.

She set the food on their small table, and Robert pulled her into his arms and kissed her forehead. Her whole body must have been tense, for she relaxed. When he held her thusly—body to body, breath to breath—he felt centered, grounded, the frightening and noisome and bewildering world of hers disappearing. He wished, upon the surety of his soul, he could hold her and never again let go.

But then, as if remembering herself, her muscles tightened. Uncertainty lingered in the depths of her eyes.

"What is it, *cariad*?" He brushed her hair from her forehead and tucked it behind an ear.

Her gaze dropped, and she stepped back. No. He would not allow her to retreat. He sensed she needed his touch, his assurance. He brushed his hands over her shoulders.

"I just..." She locked her gaze with his and stepped into his arms, her hands sliding around him and gripping him tight. She laid her head against his chest. "I'm worried about you. About us. Did I do the right thing? Everything's been so hectic since we got here last night. I haven't really had a chance to slow down and find out."

He cupped her jaw, holding her against him. In truth, it *had* been rather trying. Most of their time together, especially when her friends arrived, had been bewildering, especially since he couldn't follow the conversation. But he used the time to soak in his surroundings. Some items in their chamber were familiar enough, like the plain but amazingly comfortable bed, whose frame was made of white metal. But the chamber's decorations were odd. The wall was covered in a bright floral design. At first he'd thought it was painted, like walls in his own time, but these were covered in paper. There was a version of a trestle table shoved against the wall, and it was the area in the chamber that had the strangest of all the objects. A large flat, black shield, which she called a television, though he didn't know what that meant.

An array of white vessels stood to its side in the smoothest of material, along with one vessel made entirely of precious glass. It was from this that she crafted a bitter drink she called *coffee*. After a meal shared with her friends in their room earlier, they'd left.

He held her tighter and nuzzled her ear. "I am well. I am here. I am alive. And I am with you. That is all that matters."

Kaytee shuddered. "I was worried you were upset with me. You've been rather quiet, and I know all of this is overwhelming. I've, well, I've just been worried. About you."

"Let's take everything a moment at a time for now. I will adjust. I have faith that I will."

She squeezed him, arms wrapped firmly around his waist. "I know you will. Okay, let's eat while the food's still hot."

Reluctantly, Robert let her go.

Kaytee sighed and distributed the food. "I wish I could know if everyone bought our story. I really hope there *is* a crevice somewhere around Castell y Bere big enough for me to have fallen into."

"I'm positive there is."

"If anyone pokes at our story too much, they'll find holes. And amnesia? Why couldn't I have been more creative? I panicked." She licked gravy from her fingers and settled across from him at their table.

"I think they're so relieved to have you returned to them that they will not worry about the details."

"I hope you're right." She set her knife and fork beside her plate.

"Robert, there's something else I need to tell you. One of the people I called last night, well, it was my fiancé."

A cold fear gripped his innards. "You are betrothed?"

"Not anymore. I couldn't go through with the wedding, which was to be three weeks from now, and I told him so last night."

The tightness in his gut relaxed. He gripped her hand. "I am sorry." Not truly. "So. That was why you said you couldn't marry when we first joined. Come here." He pulled on her hand and coaxed her into his lap. "He's a fool to let you go so easily. Though it relieves me to hear so."

He stroked her face and tucked some stray hairs behind her ear. He looked down at her hands, clasped in her lap, inches from his, held loose on her knee. Slowly, he eased his hand across and, with just his pinkie, brushed the tip of her little finger.

A short chuckle escaped her. Then her pinkie lightly stroked his. And shortly he discovered the wonders of having carnal relations while bathing in a *shower*. There was much to recommend her time, for certes.

౸

Three weeks later

KATY STRETCHED OUT BESIDE ROBERT on the picnic blanket. They'd finished eating lunch in the green expanse by the moss-covered remains of Flint Castle, a habit they'd started since arriving back in her time. He'd soon insisted on going outside and interacting, and being near something from his past, no matter how crumbled, helped anchor him as he soaked in the changes and happenings around him. Though it took him aback at first that there was no branch of the Dee running between the town and the castle.

"I have something to show you." Katy sat up and pulled out a tissue-wrapped package from her backpack. Carefully, she peeled back the delicate paper to reveal the antique bird carving Robert had carved her and Isabelle had sent her hundreds of years later. Traci had returned it, along with all of her other things, but for some reason, she hadn't shown him yet.

His fingers touched it with care. "Your bird. You brought it with you? Why does it look so old?"

"Actually, no. I left it in our room at the inn when I traveled to Wrexham. I didn't want to damage it on my harried dash."

"So then how...?"

"I received it as a present from one of my best friends *before* I traveled back to you. It's..." her throat closed up with an emotion she couldn't articulate. "It's... In no small way, it's responsible for me finding you. It's why I went to Wales for my trip. My friend said it reminded her of me, and it held some pull for me too. And then when you presented it to me, that's when I knew..."

Robert sat up and cupped her face, his fingers cradling her jaw, and kissed her gently. She lost herself in that kiss. Which he broke too soon.

"When do you need to return to work?" Robert shifted his head so it rested in her lap.

She brushed a lock of hair from his forehead and twined her fingers into his hair. "One more week." She'd worked out a medical leave from her job. All in all, her boss had been very understanding.

She sighed. "Too soon."

"You wish not to work?"

Katy had explained her job, and Robert had adjusted to her working surprisingly well. His only worry had been what *his* job could be.

"I do. It's just that this time with you here has been almost magical—like stolen time. But I'm...I'm also a little afraid."

His head lifted at that. "Afraid? Of what?"

"Of myself. I'm worried I'll fall back into old habits and not value what's happening around me, that I'll get caught back up in over-planning everything instead of facing—enjoying—life."

"I'll help you." His eyes held hers, serious, full of love, and her breath caught. It was the first time he'd mentioned anything about the future, about what would happen next. She knew he loved her. He said so every night they made love in their inn. Boy did he love those showers. But she knew how hard his transition had been, and she wanted to give him the space and time he needed to adjust without any pressure from her.

She smiled and squeezed his hand. "I'd like that."

They'd need to talk in more detail about her work and figure out where they went from here—she hoped like hell he still felt the same commitment to her he had in the past. He hadn't indicated otherwise. She had to make time for that discussion before the week was up, if he didn't bring it up himself. This was his time to adjust, to learn.

He'd been an eager student. At night, they watched TV, and sometimes she read while he watched the Welsh language channel. But he'd taken to watching the English channel more and more. He also grew irate at times when he came across movies set in his time that got the history wrong. He'd talk to the TV, saying things like, "We bathed. Why do you think we were all filthy?" or "We had tweezers and scissors. Do they think we were barbarians?" or a muttered, "We drank water if it was clear in color and smell."

His English was still minimal, with a charming accent that wasn't quite French, but he was determined to learn. His eagerness and delight in learning her ways and customs had only made her love him more. They'd taped English words written on strips of paper to all the objects in their room, and every day, he memorized a new sentence to use in daily life. Today it was, "I'll have another pint."

A fresh breeze ruffled the edge of the picnic blanket, and she smoothed back her hair. Robert raised his head and said in English, "I'll have another..." and he pursed his lips together.

She laughed. "Kiss?" She traced a finger along his lower lip.

"Yes. I'll have another kiss." He palmed the back of her head and brushed his lips against hers. Nibbled on her lower lip. Having come from a lustier era, Robert had no qualms about PDA, and she loved it. Though he'd been quite pleased with how much more *private* everything was in her time.

He pulled away with a last lingering tug on her lower lip. His face grew serious, and he sat up and took her hand.

She straightened, alert still to his body language. "What is it?"

"I have something to ask you," he said in his Norman French. "I don't have the words in your English."

"You can ask me anything," she whispered, her heart giving a little lurch at his shift in mood.

He cleared his throat. "We haven't talked about the future, and I want you to know I appreciate this time you've given me to adjust to your world. I also know I don't have much to offer you. My skills are of another era." He pulled an object from his pocket, his hands shaking.

"Katy, I love you. I wish to spend my life with you. Will you do me the honor of becoming my wife?"

She blinked through tears as he opened his palm, revealing a small, hammered silver ring.

She swallowed hard. "Yes. Yes, I will. I love you, you beast. And I can't imagine spending my life with anyone else. How...how did you know to get an engagement ring?"

He lifted a brow. "From that reality television—is that the right word?—show."

She nodded and touched the ring, drawn by its beautiful Celtic knotwork twined around a beautiful, hand-cut diamond. Last week, she'd sold some of his coins and put it on a card for him, explaining how to use it.

But the band looked too small.

Funny, she'd always had it in her head what her ideal engagement ring would look like. In fact, she'd worn it until recently, since she'd picked it out for Preston. But now, looking at this gorgeous sparkling silver ring whose loops and swirls came from an ancient heritage, it felt *right*. Heart full, she smiled up at him. She could get it refitted.

He gently took her left hand and slid the ring onto her pinkie. "Ah, it fits perfectly, as I knew it would."

Katy's throat closed up as tears welled, her heart swelling. She laughed, surprising even herself with how carefree it sounded.

"Oh, yes, Robert." She put her lips to his and murmured against them, "It's perfect."

Epilogue

...she passed her time pleasant, enjoying honour and friendship. And
in the meanwhile, it chanced that she became pregnant, and in due
time a son was born unto her, and the name that they gave him was
Gwern the son of Matholwch...
The Mabinogion, an ancient Welsh romance

Two years later

SO THIS IS ME?" ROBERT'S amused tones carried through the
hushed interior of the little stone church in St. Cefnogwr.
"Looks nothing like me."

Katy rubbed her finger down the stone nose of his effigy, remembering the last time she'd traced the outline. Awe suffused her.
"Doesn't matter, I was drawn to you regardless. Some part of my soul
knew you."

She'd tried to explain when she'd first brought him to her time.
She'd told him about her dream and how he'd burrowed into her
soul before she'd even met him in the flesh. He always smiled and
pinched the end of her nose.

One thing he'd not left to the vagaries of fate, and she'd agreed—
the case had brought her the love of her life, but she didn't want it to
interfere again. That was one bit of chaos she was *not* okay with intro-
ducing into her life again. She'd given it to Traci not long after her
return, explaining its workings, but so far, Traci hadn't used it. Though
she'd been shocked as hell to hear what had really happened. Along
with a triumphant, *I knew that amnesia story was bullshit!*

His phone chirruped. "A moment." He pulled it out. "It's Greg. A
membership question at the institute, but it can wait."

He put it back into his jeans pocket. Modern technology fascinated Robert, but he'd somehow found a way of making it work for

him, instead of being a slave to it, like she'd been. Her detox period in his time, as she called it, had cured her of her obsession, and, with him as a guide, she'd managed to have the same outlook as well. Robert's sharp mind was still medieval in the best sense, able to keep them both rooted in the moment. Though he'd been fascinated as hell about being able to measure time to the minute, much less the second.

"Have you hit five hundred members yet?"

"Maybe." He fingered his father's crusade stone, which was now mounted on a small silver chain around his neck. "I'll find out later."

Greg was his business partner in a medieval combat school he'd opened last year in Cardiff, where they'd made their home. It had immediately become popular, serving those in reenactment groups, as well as those looking for the newest way to get in shape. Lately, though, their services had piqued the interest of Hollywood movie types. They'd just landed a consulting gig for a new period drama set in the thirteenth century. She'd given up her job and opened an adjunct business next to his, offering consulting services for academics—and now movie producers—on the history, culture, and language of medieval Welsh, Middle English, and Norman French.

His new goal was to get a degree in medieval history so that he would have accepted credentials for his knowledge. He was constantly combing old documents and maps as well as museums for surviving objects. Studying what he found, he then published short papers in journals where he presented his own "interpretation" of their use or meaning. While his theories were based on his knowledge, he found creative ways to explain them from what was visible in the objects or documents. Already academics were fascinated by his "refreshing and unique outlook."

Standing before his effigy now, something inexpressible stole over her again. But this time, instead of feeling lost and adrift, she felt whole and complete. Part of life.

No better time than the present to let him know her news. "Robert?"

"Yes?" He took her hand and kissed the tips of her fingers.

She pulled his hand down to her belly and pressed it flat, her hand covering his.

His hand jerked under hers, and then he spread his fingers and looked into her eyes, questioning.

Through a sheen of tears, she smiled and nodded, her heart bursting with love for her hunky medieval warrior.

He caught his breath and raised her hand to his lips, kissing the ring on her pinkie finger. His eyes glinted with joy and love, not needing to say a word, each of them grounded in the moment and its marking of their next adventure together.

Historical Note

Wow, where to start! I had a lot of fun (and some frustrations) researching this novel. The main rebellion on which the events in this story hang, Madog's Rebellion of 1294, is an often overlooked, and short-lived, uprising against King Edward. If anyone is only glancingly familiar with the Welsh attempts to maintain or regain their sovereignty, it's usually those centered on Llywelyn the Great and Llywelyn the Last prior to the events of this novel, or that of Owain Glyndŵr from 1400-1415. Focusing on this rebellion was a little frustrating due to the paucity of the information, but this was also a blessing, as it gave me more narrative freedom.

Castell y Bere was one of the first castles to be besieged by the Welsh, but the records are unclear as to what exactly happened. Some scholars take at face value that since King Edward ordered a relief party to be sent (twice) to this castle meant that the party arrived and relieved the besieged. But the total silence of any mention of the royal town of Bere and its castle after this could argue otherwise (as some scholars have). Combined with the discovery of a layer of ash over the remains, I seized on this as a plot point—having the besiegers succeed via fire. The low numbers of defenders is on record, however. Originally, I'd meant for the castle to be fictitious, but when I stumbled upon Castell y Bere in my research, I'm pretty sure I got the goose bumps as I realized how perfect it would be for my story.

The Welsh did besiege Harlech, Caernarfon, and Rhuthun (Ruthin) castles, but whether or not Madog occupied Rhuthun, much less made it his base like I portray, is unknown as far as I could find—according to one history, they were successful in besieging it, but beyond that, I don't know. Historical figures included Simon de Montfort, King Edward, Sir Robert Staundon (commander of Castell y Bere), Sir Robert Fitzwalter, Madog ap Llywelyn, Sir Reginald de

Grey, Sir Griffith de la Pole (Lord of Powys), and Maelgwn ap Rhys. Apparently de Grey was in Flint, even though his castle had been besieged, and the chaos around Flint, and the burnt town is true. However, I only made it partially burned, so Robert and Katy could have an inn to stay in. I also took liberties with ascribing the destruction of a monastery to Lord Powys, which is completely fictional, as was the event itself and the monastery; apologies to his descendants! For a good history of this rebellion, see *The Revolt of Madog ap Llywelyn* by Craig Owen Jones.

While Robert and his father are fictional, the events Robert describes surrounding his father and the Oxford Provisions were pulled from history. His description in Chapter Twenty-Four of that conflict were accurate as far as I could make it, except for his own father being a part of it, of course. Simon de Montfort was a fascinating historical figure, and if you're wanting to read a great historical fiction surrounding him, as well as the early Welsh wars with Llywelyn the Great and Llywelyn the Last, Sharon Kay Penman's *Welsh Princes* trilogy makes for an absorbing read.

The legend Katy mentions, about anyone who spends the night on Cadair Idris Mountain will wake up either a madman or a poet is a real legend.

When Robert is asking Katy where she's from and hears that she's from the West, past Ireland, he mentions Madoc the Shipbuilder. This Welshman does exist in the legends and historians and enthusiasts have come up with various possible places where he settled. One of which, of interest to me since I live in Mobile, Alabama, is that his party settled here and his descendants intermarried with the native population.

On their last night at Rhuthun castle, as Robert follows Katy up the stairs, I drew inspiration from the wonderfully sensuous painting *Hellelil and Hildebrand, The Meeting on the Turret Stairs* by Frederic William Burton, which hangs in the National Gallery of Ireland.

Finally, a note on language. I had to take liberties with writing Robert's point of view, since the actual language he'd have spoken wouldn't be possible for me to write. So I wrote it in modern English, using modern words that I'm going to assume he'd have the equivalent word for in his. For instance, the concept of the word "fuck" would've been around, if not the word itself (though some debate how old that word truly is). Anyway, I had de Buche use it, as the power of that word worked in that scene and I'm sure he'd have used the equivalent in his language. "Machinations" is another example—the etymology for *English* is late 1400s, but it's derived from Old French, so I took the liberty of making it a part of Robert's French. I tried to avoid using words for concepts or technology Robert wouldn't have been aware of, but some might have slipped by me. With that said, I took the literary license to cast his speech and syntax so that it sounds "older." Hopefully, I struck the right balance with getting you immersed in his time period without it being overloaded with thees and thous to where you gritted your teeth and wanted to smack me upside the head.

About the Author

Photo by Keyhole Photography

Her debut novel, *Must Love Breeches*, swept many unpublished romance contests, including the Grand Prize winner of Windy City's Four Seasons contest in 2012. Angela loves history, folklore, and family history, and has been a hobby historian for twenty+ years. She decided to take her love of history and her active imagination and write stories of love and adventure for others to enjoy. When writing, she's either at her desk in the finished attic of an historic home in beautiful and quirky Mobile, Alabama, or at her fave spot at the local Starbucks. When she isn't writing, she's either working at the local indie bookstore or enjoying the usual stuff like gardening, reading, hanging out, eating, drinking, chasing squirrels out of the walls, and creating the occasional knitted scarf.

Angela has had a varied career, including website programming and directing a small local history museum. She's an admitted geek and is proud to be among the few but mighty Browncoats who watched *Firefly* the first night it aired. She was introduced to the wonderful world of science fiction by her father, by way of watching reruns of the original *Star Trek* in her tweens and later giving her a copy of Walter M. Miller Jr's *A Canticle for Leibowitz* as a teenager. She hasn't looked back since.

She has a B.A. in Anthropology and International Studies with a minor in German from Emory University, and a Masters in Heritage Preservation from Georgia State University. She was an exchange student to Finland in high school and studied abroad in Vienna one summer in college.

Find Angela Quarles Online:
www.angelaquarles.com
@angelaquarles
Facebook.com/authorangelaquarles
Mailing list: www.angelaquarles.com/join-my-mailing-list

Acknowledgments

Writing a historical novel cannot be done solo, at least for me! I'm hugely indebted to a number of people who helped me out with the historical aspects of the plot, description, and characters. I'd like to specifically thank the following for helping me; any mistakes or inaccuracies, however, are my own.

Randall, Eric R. Allen, and the other knowledgeable members of the myarmoury.com forum for answering questions about mail, Welsh Wars, and providing great sources for my research. Randall was also kind enough to review my outline back during the first draft phase in 2013 and gave me wonderful guidance. He also took a look at the first half of the book and pointed out some inaccuracies, which I fixed. Eric and his wife, Erin, also read the early outline and gave me invaluable feedback. It really helped to nail down the historical plot points before I delved too far into revising. Eric also Beta read the completed novel and not only pointed out historical inaccuracies, but also provided great reader feedback on plot and characterization. Thank you!

Huge gratitude to Mike "Lochko" Slone, a member of the Society of Creative Anachronisms (SCA) through Mobile's local chapter, the Barony of the Osprey. Two years ago, I showed up announced at one of their meetings, and he was immediately a willing fount of knowledge. He was always willing to chat with me via Facebook about any historical point, and was always supportive. I'd also like to thank other members of the barony who volunteered to Beta read and give me feedback, including Beau, Sonja, and Amy.

Thank you to the members of goldrefiningforum.com who helped me with the specifics of melting gold.

I'd also like to thank my best Beta buddy Jami Gold and Tess Gingrich for taking a look at the initial outline and helping me nail that down.

Alpha readers of the full manuscript who gave me helpful feedback include Jami and Kate Warren—you helped me see where I was on track, or wasn't.

I had two Beta rounds, and I'd like to thank Shaila Patel for reading it both times, as well as Alice Keyes, Buffy Armstrong, and Celia Breslin for the early round, and Jami (again!), A.F. Dery, Merry Farmer, Megan Finnegan Grimes, Meggan Haller, Karen Kirby, Alex McLeod, Joseph Quarles, Marlene Relja, Angie Stanton, E.W. Trigg, and Julie Trigg for reading the second round. Every one of you gave me invaluable feedback that made this book better than it would have been on its own. Special thanks goes to Jami, Buffy, and Shaila for always being available for me via Facebook chat when I needed encouragement or yanking me back from some fruitless rabbit hole of research detail. Shout out also to the Divas on RomanceDivas forum for their help and encouragement.

I'd also like to thank various instructors I had who helped me with elements of this book, including Margie Lawson, Suzanne Johnson, Greta Gunselman, and Carol Hughes.

To my editors who helped me get this into final shape! Jessa Slade for reading a pretty rough draft and helping me firm up the plot and characterization; Jody Allen with Rings True Research (not the same as the wife of Eric) for the medieval history fact checking; Erynn Newman for the word-smithing—you understood my voice and helped me make it shine; and finally to my proofreaders Dana Waganer and Elizabeth (Elizabeth Edits)—you caught what slipped by me, thank you!

I also want to thank the few but awesome members of my street team for helping me spread the word!

To Pam, Diane, and the rest of the crew at the Government Street Starbucks who keep me supplied in food and decaf when I camp out there to write/revise; I get so much work done there and it helps me stay off the social media. I revised this book there numerous times.

I'd also like to thank my facebook and twitter friends who are always willing to answer questions I pose, whether it's about writing, or character ideas, or an opinion sought.

And finally to my family, who have always believed in me and make it possible for me to pursue writing.

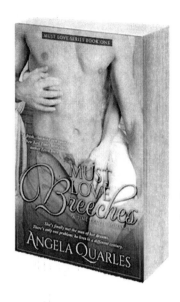